UNLEASHED

Also by Jami Alden

CAUGHT

KEPT

Published by Kensington Publishing Corp.

UNLEASHED

JAMI
ALDEN

KENSINGTON PUBLISHING CORP.
www.kensingtonbooks.com

BRAVA BOOKS are published by

Kensington Publishing Corp.
119 West 40th Street
New York, NY 10018

All Kensington titles, imprints, and distributed lines are available at special quantity discounts for bulk purchases for sales promotion, premiums, fund-raising, educational, or institutional use.

Special book excerpts or customized printings can also be created to fit specific needs. For details, write or phone the office of the Kensington Special Sales Manager: Kensington Publishing Corp., 119 West 40th Street, New York, NY 10018, Attn.: Special Sales Department. Phone: 1-800-221-2647.

Brava and the B logo Reg. U.S. Pat. & TM Off.

ISBN-13: 978-0-7582-2548-1
ISBN-10: 0-7582-2548-2

First Trade Paperback Printing: October 2009

10 9 8 7 6 5 4 3

Printed in the United States of America

*To Hilary, my great friend,
who made me strive to be
a better writer with every book.*

*And to Gajus, who makes me strive
to be a better person every day.*

ACKNOWLEDGMENTS

As always I have to thank my usual cast of characters: Monica McCarty, for coming up with "the big creepy," and Bella Andre, for quickly and enthusiastically reading when she was on a deadline of her own. Seriously, I don't think I could make it through a book without you two. To Barbara Freethy, Tracy Grant, Anne Mallory, Penny Williamson, and Veronica Wolff for all the lunchtime brainstorming that helped me get my story straight. And to Kim Whalen for her endless enthusiasm and support.

CHAPTER 1

Danny Taggart sprinted the last quarter mile of his run. His feet flew over the ground, kicking up mud, his lungs sucking in fog-moist air as he pounded along the red-wood lined trail that led to his backyard. His thigh muscles burned as he pushed it hard for the last fifty meters, summoning up one last surge of juice after a two hour run through the densely wooded hills surrounding his property.

His brothers thought he was psycho the way he ran, far and fast as though the hounds of hell were chasing him. But Danny ran because it was one of the three things that managed to keep the all the shit in his brain semistraight, the other two being booze and sex. Booze was out—if he drank enough to take the edge off, he was left with a wicked hangover. And sex—well it worked occasionally, but even a Grey Goose headache was nothing compared to a woman who refused to believe that all you wanted from her was a lusty fuck and a hassle-free good-bye.

In an ideal world he'd have sex every day, probably twice, and maybe cut his runs down to five or six miles. As it stood, the runs got longer, and the sex was depressingly less frequent as Danny lost all taste for the idle chitchat and stupid human games that went into getting laid.

Sweat dripped from his face and steam rose off his Capilene clad shoulders to mingle with the mist laden air of a typical January morning in the coastal mountains of the San Francisco Bay area. As he tracked mud up the wooden stairs to his front door, rain began to fall in fat, cold drops. The sky was silty gray with clouds that had settled in for the long haul. The rain would continue all day, maybe all week.

It suited Danny just fine, as he stripped off his muddy clothes on his front porch, the rain running in icy rivulets down his exertion-heated skin. Winter, such as it was in Northern California fit his world just fine right now. Rainy, dark, and cold.

As he walked through his front door and made for the laundry closet, he noticed the message light blinking on his phone. A chill coursed through him, chasing away any residual warmth from his run. His running clothes landed on the floor with a plop, forgotten as he headed straight for the phone.

Goosebumps coated his naked body as he punched in the access number to retrieve his voice mail. *"Danny, it's Derek. You need to come to Dad's as soon as you get this."*

His mother was dead. Derek's message was characteristically curt, but Danny knew that was why he was calling. An icy band wrapped around his chest and his breath caught as the full weight of reality hit him. Danny headed for the bathroom and set the shower to scalding before getting in the stall. He didn't bother to try to look on the bright side, didn't try to convince himself that Derek's call had a different, more positive purpose.

If it was anything else, Derek would have told him over the phone or waited till he got to the Gemini Security offices in a little over an hour. Even though Derek tried to keep his tone as flat and emotionless as possible, Danny knew the sound of someone bracing himself to deliver a blow.

Danny met the blow head on. There was no other way than to bite the bullet, face the truth no matter how ugly.

Just like that, the almost quiet, semirestful state his brain had managed to achieve on his daily fifteen mile run was obliterated. A level of calm that took nearly two hours to achieve, gone in the five seconds it took for Danny to listen to the message. His mind roiled with a thousand images and impulses, but one truth superseded them all.

She was dead.

After all the years, waiting, wondering, searching, they finally knew the truth. Thanks to a week long rainstorm and a mudslide that uncovered two sets of bones that had been lost for nearly two decades, Danny finally knew what happened to his mother.

He felt something rip in his chest as he turned his face directly into the shower spray. In the eighteen years since she'd disappeared, Danny's father Joe had never given up. He'd chased down every lead, no matter how thin, entertained every possible theory of how she was spending her time, no matter how ridiculous. But now everyone, including Joe, had to face the hard fist of reality. She wasn't living in some exotic country with a lover. She hadn't changed her name and started a new family in Montana. She wasn't tooling around the island paradise of Bali.

Anne Taggart was dead.

Whatever infinitesimal shred of optimism that might still have existed in Danny's mind disappeared the moment he walked into his father's living room thirty minutes later. One look at his brother Ethan's grim face as he sat, tight lipped on the couch next to his father said it all. Still, he needed to hear it, loud and clear, on the record.

"So the DNA was a match?" he asked.

Ethan met his gaze, his blue eyes flashing in irritation at Danny's usual bull in the china shop approach. But Danny didn't have it in him to soften his style or ease into it. Blunt, hard, truth was the only way he was going to make it through this. "Yeah. DeLuca called a little while ago with results from the lab."

Danny's vision fractured for a second as he took it in. He'd been certain of the truth as soon as Derek had called him, but bracing himself for this news was like trying to brace himself for a knife blow. It hit him just the same. Cold and sharp and slicing him to the quick.

"I'm so sorry, Danny," a female voice, husky with tears, penetrated the high pitched buzz in his head.

He turned and looked at Toni Crawford who was sitting to Ethan's left on the couch. Toni was Ethan's girlfriend and Gemini's resident tech head. Danny liked Toni for her sharp mind and cool, logical approach—not to mention it was fun to see Ethan panting after a woman instead of the other way around for a change. But this morning her eyes were bloodshot behind her glasses as she dabbed her eyes and nose with a Kleenex with one hand and clutched Ethan's fingers with the other.

But that was nothing compared to Joe. Danny's stomach twisted as he saw his strong, robust father, slumped on the couch on the other side of Ethan, tired, weak, and wasted. He'd aged a decade in the nearly six weeks since the bodies had first been found and they all faced the possibility that one of them might be Anne.

Guilt racked him as he sat down in a leather club chair across from the sofa. All the horrible things he'd said to his father, telling him he should forget about their mother and move the fuck on, stop chasing a woman who thought so little of all of them that she could take off without a backward look. Because that's what it had looked like, that Anne Taggart, unhappy and unfulfilled in her marriage, had packed a bag, left her family behind, and covered her tracks so well they'd never found a trace.

"The bitch is still haunting us," he'd said when Detective DeLuca from the San Mateo County Sheriff's office had tipped them off that one of the bodies was a possible match for Anne Taggart. Shortly after she'd disappeared she'd been spotted in the small town of La Honda, located in the surrounding coastal mountains. Danny had taken dark satisfaction from the news. Finally, he thought, a chance for closure. If they could confirm, once and for all what Danny had long believed—that Anne was dead—they could stop wasting their time and money chasing half baked leads that never led to anything but trouble. Danny had a recently healed broken nose and dislocated shoulder to prove it.

But when he'd imagined finally learning the truth, finally getting closure, he hadn't taken pain into account—his own, his brothers' and especially his father's. He hadn't anticipated the toll the past several weeks would take on his father, draining him of strength and purpose.

Joe didn't say anything, just stared at some point past Danny's shoulder, the gray eyes that matched Danny's dull and flat behind the lenses of his glasses.

Danny bowed his head, fighting back the sting of tears, pushing away the guilt as he realized that while he was blaming his mother, cursing her for walking out on them, she'd been buried in a hillside less than fifty miles away.

Don't forget, she took off with a suitcase full of clothes and over five thousand in cash. She still ran, she just didn't get all that far.

Danny seized at the thought, using it to chase away the guilt, to chase away the grief. Still, another voice nagged at him, reminding him that whether she left them or not, Anne was still his mother. And even if she left, she didn't deserve to end up in a cold unmarked grave.

Danny silenced the voice. He couldn't give in to emotion now. Nothing would be accomplished by crying like a fucking girl. The best thing he could do was to find out the truth of how she and another woman ended up buried together in a densely forested hillside. Maybe that would make up in some small way for all of the shitty things he'd said and thought about his mother over the years.

"Any closer to IDing the other body?"

Ethan shook his head. "All they know is that she was young and had given birth at some point in her life."

Danny leaned against the chair's padded back and closed his eyes. None of this made any sense. What the hell was their mother doing in a shallow grave with a teenage mother? Danny's memories of his mother were of an unhappy, borderline alcoholic, frustrated with her marriage, a housewife who may or may not have been cheating on Joe at the time of her disappearance. But the police, and later they themselves, had pursued every lead and had never come up with anything. If she'd been cheating, no one knew with who. And if she did anything with her time other than have long lunches and playing the occasional tennis game, none of her friends knew anything about it.

Derek walked into the room with a carafe of coffee, followed by his girlfriend, Alyssa who had six coffee mugs hooked on her fingers. Derek set the coffee on the table in front of Joe, and Danny stood to accept his brother's swift, brutal hug. Before he could sit back down his breath whooshed from his chest as a small, warm body hit him head on. "I'm so sorry, Danny," Alyssa said as she wrapped her arms around his waist. She radiated warmth like a tiny sun, and Danny found himself hugging her back, absorbing her heat, though it didn't make a dent in the icy chill frosting his blood.

Danny never would have pegged Alyssa Miles, one of America's most famous for nothing celebutantes, as the woman for a hard-hearted bastard like Derek, but she'd surprised the hell out of them all. She was about a hundred times smarter and kinder than the press ever gave her credit for, and Derek would walk through the gates of hell to keep her safe. She pulled away from Danny and went to sit next to Derek on the love seat. As Derek curved his arm around her, his whole body seemed to sigh with relief. As though, regardless of all the shit flying around them, Alyssa's presence provided some measure of peace.

Something tasting faintly of jealousy rose in his throat as he looked at his brothers, taking comfort in their women, knowing no matter how much shittier things got, they'd go home and fall into bed with the beautiful women who loved them.

He shoved the thought aside, not about to let grief turn him all sentimental. He focused instead on his father, his weathered, wasted countenance. This was the face of love Danny knew. Bitter. Disillusioned. Danny learned that lesson early and hard, and unlike his father, kept himself from succumbing to the hell that came from needing a woman to make his life worth living.

"Dead," Joe whispered, the first words he'd spoken since Danny arrived. "All this time, she's been dead. And we'll probably never know what happened."

Danny had never heard his father sound like that, so defeated, so exhausted. It sent a shot of panic down his spine.

In eighteen years, Joe had never wavered from his cause. He'd taken the steely determination and resourcefulness that defined his military career and later his career in investment banking and focused it on his search for his wife. Even in her absence, Anne had given Joe Taggart's life purpose. Through everything, through all the years, Joe loved her. All he wanted was to bring her back so he could prove that to her once and for all. Danny didn't understand it, and Anne's death didn't change the fact that she left them.

But he needed to wipe that look off his father's face, needed to obliterate the defeated slope in his shoulders. "We're going to find out what happened, Dad, I swear. I know I can't bring her back to you, but I promise you I'll find out the truth about what happened to Mom."

Too bad he didn't have a fucking clue where to start.

"This is the last of it."

Caroline Medford stepped forward and took the box from her stepdaughter, staggering a bit as she absorbed its weight.

"Sorry, I should have warned you," Kate laughed and blew a thick red curl out of her face.

"What's in here, anyway?" Caroline braced the box against her hips and skirted her car to get to the door of the storage area under the house.

"Books," Kate answered. "Actually, I think that one might have been Dad's and somehow got mixed in with my stuff when Mikey and I moved."

Caroline immediately went on high alert. "Are you sure it's just books?"

Kate had ducked out of the storage space and back into the garage. "Michael, what are you doing? Come out where I can see you."

Kate's four-year-old son, Michael, popped his head around Caroline's silver Mercedes which took up most of the garage. His big blue eyes stood out in stark contrast to his dark auburn hair and pale skin, made even paler by the grayish light of the overcast day. "I'm just looking at this shovel Mommy," he replied and waved a gardening trowel danger-ously close to the side of Caroline's car.

Kate leaped over and stayed his hand. "Let's watch how close we get to Aunt Caro's car. We don't want to scratch it."

"I'm not scratching Aunt Caro's car," he said, "I just want to dig with this cool shovel."

Caroline felt a smile stretch her lips at Mikey's pronunci-ation. He still hadn't quite mastered his "r" so her name came out "Aunt Cawo." They'd come up with the nickname right after Kate had him, deciding that at only ten years Kate's senior, Caroline wasn't exactly grandmother material.

Although these days, Caroline felt about a hundred years older than her thirty-four years.

The smile vanished as quickly as it appeared, as though her cheek muscles, so unfamiliar with the motion over the past several months, couldn't hold it for more than a few seconds.

"Mikey, honey," Caroline called, "why don't you go use the shovel in the planter right outside. Maybe you'll find some buried treasure." Another stiff smile broke free at Mikey's exclamation of how cool that sounded.

So what if he dug up all her daffodil bulbs? It was worth it to experience that kind of pure, simple joy, even vicariously. And besides, one way or another, Caroline doubted she'd be in this house next year to appreciate them.

Satisfied that Mikey was occupied for the time being, Kate ducked back into the storage space. The single bare bulb cast shadows over the custom-made shelving unit that held boxes of clothing, books, and unused suitcases. An old metal file cabinet that contained decades of Caroline's late husband's financial documents was tucked into a corner. Caroline knew the contents of every single box, bag and drawer, because she'd been through every shred of paper and clothing in the past six months, looking for something, anything, that would help her find the truth about what had happened to James.

"Sorry, you asked me something before," Kate finished with a wave and an eyeroll in Michael's general direction.

"Oh, I just asked if there was anything interesting in the box," Caroline said, trying to keep her tone casual, trying to quell the shred of hope that never failed to raise its ignorant head whenever she came across something, anything, that might help her case.

The grim set to Kate's full mouth said it all. "It's just books, Caroline, I checked. You can look yourself, but I don't think you'll find anything."

Caroline nodded, but kept the box near the front of Kate's growing pile so she could look through it, just in case.

"So how is everything going?" Kate asked. "You look a lot better than the last time I saw you."

Caroline huffed out a laugh as she heaved a box of sweaters onto one of the shelves that lined the space. "I should hope so, considering the last time you saw me I just got out of jail." As soon as she'd been released two months ago, she'd made a beeline for her favorite salon and gotten a cut, color, eyebrow wax, bikini wax, a manicure, and a pedicure.

It would have been heaven had she not had to endure the suspicious looks of the other women as they whispered about her behind their impeccably manicured hands. Caroline had provided enough speculation and gossip when she'd married James ten years ago and moved to his beautiful house in the wealthy enclave of Piedmont, California.

Perched in the hills east of the San Francisco Bay, Piedmont was an oasis of wealth and privilege. James, his first wife Susan, and their daughter Kate had fit in perfectly. Then James had courted scandal by marrying a trophy wife over twenty years his junior and moving her into his dead wife's house less than two years after poor Susan was cold in her grave.

Aside from James's closest friends, Caroline had been tolerated, but never truly accepted by his circle. The wives, especially, treated her with a veneer of courtesy that barely disguised their disdain. And fear. Fear that one day their husbands might find themselves charmed by a young, beautiful bartender who served drinks at their spouse's favorite after work spot.

But the scandal that erupted when James appeared at the tony Oakland Hills Country Club with his twenty-four-year-old trophy wife at his side was nothing compared to the hell that broke loose when James was murdered a little over six months ago. And Caroline was named the prime suspect.

Kate huffed and heaved another box on the shelf. "I can't believe they wouldn't set bail. I mean, rapists and gang-bangers get out on bail all the time. It's a travesty." Kate's cloud of red curls shook with indignation.

"They thought I was a flight risk," Caroline said. "So no bail." She hoped Kate would pick up on her tone and consider the conversation over. Kate was always trying to get her to talk and share about what it had been like those two months she spent in jail, convinced that if Caroline would just talk about it, she'd get over her insomnia and get a full night's sleep.

Caroline had no desire to go there. No desire to think about the loss of freedom, the complete loss of dignity and comfort. All she wanted was to cherish every single day of freedom she'd been granted, and do everything in her power to make sure she never ended up back in a cell.

Besides, she knew, and she supposed Kate did too, that talking about her time behind bars wasn't going to cure her insomnia. The only thing that would accomplish that was finding the real killer before the DA had a chance to rebuild his case and take Caroline back into custody.

"At least the judge didn't have her head up her ass, unlike everyone else involved," Kate said as she whipped out a Sharpie marker and scrawled the word "shoes" across the top of a box before pushing it onto a low shelf.

Caroline stopped her. "Shoes go on the second shelf," she said, indicating the other neatly labeled boxes. Kate rolled her eyes but moved the box to the second shelf. Caroline knew her need for organization bordered on OCD, but she liked having everything in its properly designated space. Besides, her penchant for organizing everything—even a garage storage space no one would ever see—had turned into a surprisingly lucrative side business organizing household spaces for Caroline's friends and acquaintances. Not that she'd seen much business since she'd first been arrested for James's murder.

"The judge didn't have much choice other than to dismiss the charges. The police didn't have a warrant to seize my computer. Without those e-mails, they didn't have a strong enough case." Not that they had a particularly strong case even with the e-mails Caroline had written to her oldest, closest friend, Diana Vasquez, the only person Caroline had really kept in touch with after she married James.

Sure, Caroline had bitched about the state of her marriage, and her desire to somehow get out of it without dealing with divorce and the financial messiness that would ensue. She might have even expressed a moment's regret that she would have to figure out how to support herself, her parents, and her brother once he got out of jail on the amount stipulated in their prenup. Sure, five million was generous, but it wasn't infinite.

But somehow the DA had twisted Caroline's cabernet fueled ramblings into a motive for murder. When combined with an accusation from a former cell mate of her brother's it had been enough for the DA to bring her up on charges.

The sad truth was, and as Caroline had tried to explain to the police and later the DA, Caroline had known her marriage was in trouble long before James had actually filed for divorce.

It wasn't just James's late nights and long absences for business travel. Even if James had continued to be the most attentive husband on the planet, Caroline knew they weren't going to last. Caroline had loved him, but she wasn't in love with him. She'd loved his friendship and the security he gave her, but after ten years she was starting to chafe under the confines of being married to James. She was starting to resent the compromises she'd made, the dreams she'd chosen to give up. But as their relationship faltered, Caroline had to face the brutal truth that she had a lot of years left, a lot of time to still have the things she was missing in her life. Things she wasn't ever going to get if she stayed married to James.

When she'd found James with another woman one Saturday afternoon, Caroline had been almost relieved. She'd come home after her weekend at Disneyland with Kate and Michael was cut short when Kate came down with the flu. It didn't take a genius to see what was going on between her husband and the beautiful, oh so young woman who was sobbing in James's study. Caroline had frozen in shock, and heard several seconds of muffled conversation before James noticed her.

"I'm sorry, I can't give you what you want," James said, frustration in every line of his body as he stood next to the leather club chair where the woman sat.

"You must," she sobbed, her voice accented and thick with tears. "You are the only one, the only one."

James started to pace as he raked his fingers through thick hair only recently gone completely silver. He was still strong and fit as he approached his fifty-sixth birthday, his shoulders firm under his broadcloth shirt, his belly barely bulging over the waistband of pressed khakis. He lifted his gaze, staring at nothing until it caught on Caroline, standing in the doorway.

"I guess I don't have to ask why you haven't returned my calls," Caroline said in response to his horrified gaze.

After the shock wore off, Caroline thought that, along with relief, she was miffed that James would bring another woman into their house. But as she listened to James order the woman to get out she realized she wasn't very hurt. As she'd confessed to Diana in her long, rambling, e-mails, Caroline had been fooling herself for a long time, hanging on by a thread to a marriage that wasn't making her happy and never would.

Then again, she hadn't exactly been in the best frame of mind when she'd accepted James's proposal. When she'd met and married James, she'd been reeling, coming off the tail end of the worst time in her life. She'd gotten it into her usually resilient and levelheaded brain that James was exactly what she needed. Capable. Responsible. Reliable.

Rich.

Call her a shallow greedy gold digger, but at the time the security of James's wealth had felt as warm and reassuring as the world's coziest fleece blanket.

When they first got together and for the first five or so years of their marriage, he'd seemed to be everything she needed. And for the next four years Caroline had shoved aside her doubts, refused to acknowledge that maybe she'd given up too much in the name of security. That maybe she shouldn't waste too many more years on a childless and increasingly passionless marriage. James was good and generous—not only to her, but to her family. And, as always, there was Kate and Mikey, whose pure little boy love Caroline soaked up like a sponge, hoping it would plug up the gaping hole left in her soul so many years ago.

But the justification wore thin, especially after Kate and Mikey moved out when Mikey was almost two. Mikey's absence reignited Caroline's desire for a baby with a vengeance. But no matter how hard she pleaded, James wouldn't budge. He was finished having children and had the vasectomy to prove it. He wouldn't consider adoption or artificial insemination as an option. Caroline's resentment grew and James grew increasingly distant. She soon found herself bouncing off the walls of her perfect home, bored out of her skull in their perfect enclave of suburbia.

So when James had filed for divorce three days after the Disneyland Debacle, Caroline had taken it with a little bit of sadness and a lot of relief.

Until three days later, when James turned up with a bullet in his head, and a former cell mate of Caroline's brother, Ricky, claimed Caroline Medford had approached him and offered him five thousand dollars to do the hit. Caroline's protest that she'd met Hector Ramirez once, at a barbecue for her brother during one of his brief stints on the outside, fell on deaf ears.

"Well if you ask me, the DA is a total fucktard," Kate continued, jarring Caroline out of her unpleasant memories.

"Mommy, what's a fucktard?"

Kate jumped at Mikey's high pitched inquiry. "Uhh—"

"It's a not nice word for somebody who does something silly," Caroline jumped in to explain. "Don't use it."

"Yeah, that'll work," Kate said as Mikey marched around Caroline's car, chanting "fucktard," in time with the stomping of his rubber booted feet. "They can't still think you did it," Kate said, wincing as Mikey repeated the profanity for the dozenth time. "The whole life insurance thing is a crock of shit. I told the DA myself. I mean, you'd think of all people, I would be gunning to get my wicked stepmother behind bars, right? So if I'm in your corner, it should say something, shouldn't it?"

Caroline grabbed Kate in an impulsive hug. "It means a lot to me that you're on my side," Caroline said. Especially when that number could be easily counted on one hand. There was Kate, and James's friend Patrick Easterbrook, who was in his class at Stanford way back before Caroline was even born, Patrick's wife Melody, and Caroline's defense attorney, Rachael Weller. And Rachael probably didn't count because she took Caroline's case mostly for the publicity, not to mention a hefty thousand dollar per hour attorney fee.

Even her own mother asked her why she had to get her brother's name mixed up in it.

Right. Ricky was the one in prison for manufacturing and selling meth, but Caroline was the fuckup.

"Hey, you had my back even when I treated you like crap." The tiny emerald stud in Kate's right nostril caught the light as she shot Caroline a wry smile. "The least I can do is return your loyalty." Kate paused in labeling the boxes and took a deep swallow. "Seriously Caroline, what's going to happen to us if you go to jail?" She flicked a glance at the door to make sure Mikey was still occupied outside. "And yeah, I know exactly how self-centered that sounds. But Mom's gone, Dad's dead, and you're the only one who really stuck by me through everything."

Caroline swallowed back her own tears and wiped her nose on the sleeve of her fleece pullover. Now was not the time for yet another sobfest. "Everything will be fine. I've got Rachael Weller, for Christ's sake. She was able to get Bryan Roberts off and I'm pretty sure that guy was guilty." Her bravado was thin even to her own ears. She'd gotten a reprieve when the judge dismissed her case, but she knew it was only a matter of weeks at best before the DA fortified his case against her and tried to put her back in jail.

"And worst case scenario," Caroline said as she stacked the boxes along the shelves so their edges perfectly aligned, "you and Michael will be fine. I already signed over your trust, and as soon as everything settles out one way or another, I'll sign the house over to you, too." The only reason she hadn't yet was because she didn't want it to look like she had something to hide. She also didn't want Kate to have to deal with the reporters that would no doubt swarm the house as soon as the case went to trial.

"I don't want the house," Kate said with a shudder. "I

don't understand why you're still living here after what happened."

"It would look weird for me to sell it right now," Caroline said. She hated living in the house where her husband was murdered. Yet with its new state of the art alarm system, it was one of the few places she still felt safe. "As soon as everything settles down, you can sell it."

"But it's the house I grew up in."

"Then don't sell it. I don't care. One way or another, I'm not going to be living here much longer."

Caroline sat back on her heels, speared with guilt as she took in Kate's tight mouth and damp eyes. She knew Kate was scared of having no one to fall back on. Caroline didn't bother reminding her that she had the financial security to go to school and hire top notch childcare, and would always have a more than adequate roof over her head. Having someone die or go to prison wasn't the end of the world, even though it might feel like it at the time.

"And look on the bright side," she said, flipping open a box to check its contents before she stacked it. "If you and Mikey decide to move in, half your stuff will already be here." She poked around a pile of clothes and shook her head. "Why do you keep all of this? You're as bad as your father." She yanked on a sleeve and held the purple sweater up to the yellowish light. "I think you had this when I met you!"

Kate shrugged. "It has sentimental value." She pushed off the floor and slid open a drawer to the metal filing cabinet. "But no one has anything on Dad. He probably has my vaccination records from elementary school in here. He saved every piece of paper from—"

Caroline looked up as Kate choked off mid-sentence.

"Why do you have this?" Kate was staring, white lipped, at the contents of a binder.

"What?" Like she didn't know exactly what was in there.

Kate hurled the binder in Caroline's direction. It clipped her knee before hitting the ground and splaying open to display a news article, clipped and covered by a three hole punch plastic page protector.

Grieving Wife or Black Widow?

She flipped the binder closed. It was thick with clippings, each in its own individual protective cover. All with similar headlines. All having to do with the murder of James Medford and the probability that his wife did it.

"Why the hell would you keep all of those?" Kate shook her head. "It's like inviting bad karma into your house, you know? You're creating negativity in your space and right now you need to fill your life with positive things. It's like that book *The Secret*."

Caroline shoved the binder back into a drawer and let Kate ramble. She didn't have the heart to tell her that a wish on a bulletin board wasn't going to bring James's real killer to justice. Besides, she didn't have an answer for why she saved the clippings. Morbid curiosity? A pathological need to know exactly what the press was saying about her so she'd know what she was up against?

She had no idea. But from the second she'd come across that first article, she'd been compelled to save it, slicing it out of the paper with her Exacto knife in a clean, straight cut before sliding it into the plastic.

It wasn't the first time she'd found herself morbidly, obsessively collecting and saving news clippings. She had another similar binder, in her old bedroom in her mother's house across the bay in Redwood City. An even thicker binder full of clippings that essentially said the same thing in fifty different ways. Anne Taggart was missing, and no one had any idea where to find her.

She'd left the binder behind when she'd moved in with James, as she'd left all of her past behind.

But in the past few days Caroline had found new articles

to add to that old binder. A now familiar stab of pain lanced through her chest. It hit her hard, stopped her in her tracks as it had several times a day for the last three days since it was front page news on *The San Francisco Tribune*. The body of Anne Taggart, along with another as yet unidentified woman was found after a landslide exposed their remains.

"Look, I'm sorry I got all over your ass about it," Kate said, mistaking the cause of Caroline's distress. She bit her bottom lip uncertainly. "I'm going to go fix Mikey a snack, and then we'll get out of your hair."

"No," Caroline squeezed the word past her throat. "Stay. I Tivo'd some movies for Mikey and got us some stuff to make for dinner." Not that she expected to have any more of an appetite than she'd had for the past six months. "Let me finish organizing this and I'll be right up."

Kate nodded and went out to collect Mikey. Caroline sat back on the floor, clutching the fabric that covered her chest, as though that could stop the deep ache that stole her breath.

Danny. How was it possible to hurt so much for him, after all this time, after everything that happened? It had been over ten years since she'd so much as laid eyes on him or heard his voice, and yet as soon as she saw the news it all came roaring back. The anger. The hurt. The love. The bone deep ache of knowing how much he must be hurting right now, and her irrational desire to find him, comfort him.

As though he'd ever take comfort from her. As though she could keep her own anger under control if she ever saw him face to face.

She swallowed back tears and stood up to turn off the light. As she did so her gaze landed on one of the boxes Kate had brought from her old apartment.

DAD'S BOOKS, Kate had scrawled across the top in a sloppy hand.

She'd been through every single paper, document, book, file, there and at James's office, looking for the smallest hint of who would want James dead. There was nothing to be found here, she told herself even as she pulled the top off the box. Yet her curiosity had to be satisfied.

She heard laughter outside, Mikey's followed by Kate's as she chased him into the house. Caroline pulled one book after another out of the box, not really disappointed when she saw it was exactly as Kate had described. The box was full of leather bound legal text books, with an occasional hardback mystery thrown in.

Still, she didn't stop until the box was empty and the books were piled high on the concrete floor. She pulled out the last book. The spine was cracked because another book had gotten wedged inside. It was too small to be another textbook or hardback novel. Probably one of Kate's paperback romances had gotten mixed in the bunch.

But when Caroline opened the heavy text book to shake the novel free, she wasn't greeted by a colorful clinch cover.

This book was covered in caramel-colored leather, embossed with a gold monogram on the cover. Heart in her throat, Caroline flipped through the pages and saw that it was a daily planning calendar, the kind that was popular over a decade ago before the advent of the PDA.

She blinked hard and stared at the cover, the stylized letters intertwining.

She knew that monogram.

A.T.

Anne Taggart.

Caroline didn't remember the planner, but she remembered the purse and the wallet that came with the set. Remembered that Danny's father, Joe, had given it to Anne for her birthday. And she'd smiled absently and said the custom made set, which must have cost hundreds, if not thousands of dollars, was "cute," before setting it aside.

Despite her apathy, she'd apparently used the planner. As Caroline skimmed through it, she saw notes about her schedule, medical appointments, sports practices for her sons.

But nothing in there explained how James Medford had come to possess the daily planner of a woman who'd died eighteen years ago.

CHAPTER 2

"I'm so sorry."

Danny was grateful his sunglasses hid his eye roll as he braced himself for another hug. His hand was stiff from endless handshakes, his brain numb from the meaningless condolences.

I'm so sorry. That's what everyone said. But what were they sorry for? That she was dead? That they'd wasted years searching the globe for her when she was dead and buried practically in their own backyard? That Anne Taggart was in such a state when she disappeared that it was plausible—even probable—to most of the people who knew her that she'd walked out on her family?

Danny was really fucking sick of all those "I'm sorries."

"At least now you have closure."

Danny bit back a retort and returned his Aunt Cheryl's embrace after she uttered the only words more annoying and offensive than "I'm sorry."

He wasn't sure what kind of closure he was supposed to appreciate when the discovery of his mother's body raised about a thousand more questions than it answered, starting with how did she end up dead in the first place and who the fuck decided an unmarked grave in a redwood forest was an appropriate resting place?

But he didn't figure his Aunt Cheryl, whom they hadn't seen in over a decade, was up to discussing any of those hard questions.

Cheryl, his mother's younger sister by two years, pulled back and clasped his right hand in both of hers. A niggling ache clutched his chest as he took in her carefully styled, chin length hair, its sunny blond color no doubt aided by a hairdresser, her lightly lined skin and watery blue eyes. Cheryl looked a lot like her older sister, and Danny knew this was the closest he'd ever get to seeing his own mother age.

He fought the urge to yank his hand away, slam himself into his Jeep and haul ass back to his house so he could run for the hills and get good and gone for a few hours, maybe a few days.

He stood firm, returning Cheryl's affectionate squeeze while he fought the blackness threatening to swallow him whole.

"If you need anything, anything at all, let me know, okay? You have our number, right?"

Danny nodded, humoring her, bending his head so she could place one last, teary kiss on his cheek. He had no doubt she was sincere. In that moment, right that second, she meant he could call her for anything if he or his brothers were so inclined. But Aunt Cheryl and her husband lived outside Minneapolis, near her own children. Other than birthday cards and Christmas cards, they hadn't had any contact once the initial stir caused by Anne's disappearance died down. He didn't blame her—she needed to get on with her life half a continent away. Still, her offer to "be there"— whatever the fuck that meant—rang just as hollow as the endless "I'm sorries."

Cheryl was followed by an endless stream of mourners, people he'd never met or barely remembered who'd shown

up at Menlo Presbyterian, supposedly to mourn Anne Taggart.

Or to rubberneck and rehash one of the biggest local
scandals of the last decade was more like it.

He shook infinite hands, endured endless maternal pats
as he watched Cheryl walk over to his father. The grim knot
in Danny's gut tightened as he watched his father woodenly
return her hug. God, he hoped Cheryl didn't say anything
about closure horseshit to Joe. It was the last kind of closure Joe needed. The kind of closure that was going to drive
his father into an early grave if they didn't find something,
anything, to point them in the right direction.

But the case was so cold it bordered on permafrost, and
the police seemed content to leave it that way. Danny, Derek,
and Ethan had worked nonstop to find something—anything to go on, retracing her last days, going back through
every pocket and purse and leftover scrap of paper she left
behind.

And Joe had sat by through all of it, saying little, doing
less, as he worked his way through a bottle of Ketel One
vodka.

Danny was very afraid Joe was going to lose himself in
the bottom of a bottle if they didn't find something soon.

Finally the last of the mourners trailed out, and Danny
made his way over to where his father stood with his brothers, along with Toni and Alyssa. Alyssa was doing her best
to take one for the team, posing for the cameras and grant-
ing interviews to everyone as she tried to deflect the press's
attention away from the family. Danny uttered a curt no
comment as he plowed his way through the throng and
went to stand at his father's side.

Like a bunch of good lemmings, the herd of reporters
trailed Alyssa out to the parking lot. She threw them a wave
over her shoulder, motioning to Derek that she'd call him.

As the crowd moved, Danny could see one last mourner exit the dark interior of the church.

He did a double; then a triple take.

No fucking way.

His breath caught and his nostrils flared as he took her in. He knew the thick black waves spilling to her waist, the mouthwatering curves elegantly draped in black wool. Her dress went from neck to wrist to knee and should have been modest, but only served to highlight the lush swell of her breasts, the deep curve of her waist, the sexy flare of her hips. The heels of her black pumps tap tapped their way down the concrete steps and headed in his direction.

He dragged his gaze up to her face. Her luscious mouth was painted red and set in determined lines. Even though the sun was hidden behind a thick layer of clouds, like him she wore sunglasses, her oversize frames hiding half her face. As though, like him, she didn't want to chance anyone getting a peek into her soul.

Caroline fucking Palomares.

No, he reminded himself. Caroline fucking Medford.

Raw emotion spun up inside him, threatening to take him down. Lust. Anger. And a bunch of other crap he wouldn't touch with a ten foot pole.

As she strode toward him, shoulders back, hips swinging like she had every right to be walking back into his life, today of all days, he struggled to put the lid back on the swirl of emotion struggling to break free. He reminded himself savagely of who she was. Caroline *Medford.*

Wife of James Medford, rich attorney twenty years her senior. The same James Medford who could give her the affluent lifestyle he hadn't realized she coveted until it was too late.

The same James Medford she may very well have killed to keep herself in fast cars and high fashion.

She was not the seventeen-year-old who'd promised she'd never leave him when she gave him her virginity. She was not the twenty-year-old who'd sobbed when he'd announced his plans to join the Special Forces after he graduated from West Point. She wasn't even the twenty-two-year-old who'd told him to fuck off one final time before walking out on him without another word.

As she drew closer he focused on those differences. She was thinner, for one, he noticed as she got closer. And older, her mouth bracketed by fine lines that came from stress and age. Not to mention the wardrobe. He bet her outfit topped out at over a grand, even more if you counted the purse. A far cry from the wardrobe of a girl from a working class neighborhood who shopped at discount stores and went to private school on scholarship.

She was nothing like the girl he'd known, and he was nothing like the dumb kid who'd entertained romantic illusions like true love and happily ever after.

He took off his glasses, feeling a smile curl his lips for the first time in several days as she stumbled a little.

She was off center. Just the way he liked it. And he was in perfect control. Because Caroline Medford meant nothing to him.

Danny's gray stare hit Caroline like a blast chiller, freezing the marrow in her bones as she tried to cover up her little stumble. His face was carefully neutral, and it was only because she knew him well that she could read the icy disdain in his eyes.

No, scratch that. She didn't know him, not anymore. She hadn't known him for over a decade. He was a completely different person now, as was she. She needed to approach this as a purely business decision. Two adults helping each other get the information they needed, without letting their past relationship interfere.

But as she closed the distance between them that cool gray gaze slid down, then up over her black wool-clad form. Heat unfurled low in her belly as her libido chose that inconvenient moment to wake after a long hibernation. God he looked good. Her Jackie O glasses hid her eyes, allowing her to hungrily drink in every inch of him, all the ways he was the same, all the ways he'd changed.

Danny had always been tall and muscular, even when she'd first met him in high school, but his six-foot-four frame had filled out in the ten years since she'd seen him. He'd packed on a good twenty, twenty-five pounds, and though she couldn't say for sure with the suit coat hiding his chest, she bet it was all pure, hard muscle. His face was still all planes and angles, his tanned jaw already hinting at a five o'clock shadow. His thick, nearly black hair was cropped short, but not as short as the military buzz cut he'd worn the last time she'd seen him. His blade of a nose was no longer perfectly straight. It now sported a bump on the bridge and pointed ever so slightly to the left, evidence that he'd broken it at least once. It gave an almost menacing cast to a face that didn't betray an inch of softness.

Except for his eyelashes, which were still so ridiculously long they brushed his eyebrows as he regarded her with his level stare. And his full, sensual lips, which pulled down at the corners as she stopped about a foot in front of him.

"Hi Danny," she said after he stared at her for what felt like a century without saying anything. Then, because she had no idea what else to say to him, "I wish this had turned out differently for you."

He flinched a little, and for a split second, almost so fast she missed it, there was flash of pain in his eyes, a peek into the abyss he tried so hard to hide. Tears stung her eyes and she struggled with the crazy urge to throw her arms around him, offer up her body and soul just to make him feel better.

And hadn't she learned the hard way that was a losing proposition any way you sliced it?

"What are you doing here, Caroline?" he asked, any hint of pain wiped from his face.

"When I heard what happened, I wanted to offer my condolences," she said, sounding lame even to herself.

He quirked a thick, dark eyebrow at her, and pinned her with another variation of his laser sharp stare. "Really? After dropping off the face of the earth, you decide to show up unannounced at my mother's memorial service?"

Right. He chose to join an elite branch of the military and participate in some of the most dangerous missions on the planet, but she was the one who had dropped off the face of the earth. In his mind, it was her fault, and always would be.

She squared her shoulders and shoved back the urge to argue and set him straight about what had really sent her marching out his door all those years ago. She had more important things to do than rehash all the ways he'd chased her away.

"Believe it or not, I cared about you and your family. And I felt I wanted to pay my respects. But you're right. There's another reason—"

She was cut off as a pair of strong arms wrapped around her from the side, lifting her off her feet and enfolding her in a rib crushing embrace.

"Holy shit, Caroline Palomares."

On firm ground again, Caroline looked up into the face of Ethan Taggart, the face that dropped a thousand panties, if the whispers in the girl's bathroom at Peninsula Priory were to be believed. Caroline hadn't doubted it for a second, then. And she bet it was even worse now. Almost as big and built as his brother, Ethan had a dangerous charm and a look in his blue eyes that said he knew things to do to a woman that she didn't even know existed.

"Hey Ethan," she returned his hug, shocked at how good it was to see him again. When she'd been with Danny, she'd always had a semi-big-sister thing going with Ethan, who liked to crash their dates and pick Caroline's brain for advice on girls. Not that he needed the help.

"How are you doing?" he asked, his blue eyes dark with concern.

No need to ask if he'd kept up on the local news. "I'm coping," she said, and pushed her sunglasses up onto her head. "But you shouldn't worry about me, with everything else you have to deal with."

He nodded grimly and she followed his gaze to his father, who stood several yards away, staring off into space while a woman—she guessed Anne Taggart's sister from the resemblance—spoke in a low voice as she blotted her eyes with a tissue.

A woman approached on Ethan's left and curled her hand around Ethan's arm as her hazel eyes cast a curious look between Ethan and Caroline.

"Hi. I'm Caroline," she offered her hand to the tall, black-haired woman who had the kind of creamily perfect complexion most women would kill for. "I'm an old friend of the family," she said, sensing the woman's curiosity about Caroline's connection to Ethan.

"I'm Toni," the woman replied. "New friend of the family."

"Caroline and Danny used to be engaged," Ethan said with an evil half smile, and Caroline felt Danny stiffen next to her.

"About a hundred years ago," Danny interjected.

Toni's eyes widened with surprise. "You were *engaged?*"

"What's that supposed to mean?" Caroline could feel Danny bristling behind her.

Ethan slipped his arm around Toni's waist and pulled her against him in a move as natural as breath. Caroline had to give her credit—she didn't look at all fazed by Danny's Cro-Magnon routine.

"Nothing," the woman replied. "I'm just wondering in what universe any woman would find you marriageable."

"Obviously none," Danny said, his voice dangerously quiet. "Because Caroline here dumped me and married someone else."

Toni turned her attention back to Caroline, did a double take, and quirked her head to the side. "Why do you look so familiar to me?" Then her eyes widened and she swallowed hard. "You're Caroline Medford, aren't you?"

"You probably didn't recognize her without the orange jumpsuit and shackles," Danny bit out.

And just like that Caroline was ruthlessly reminded of her true purpose there. As nice as it was to reconnect with old friends, it was time to get down to business.

"That's actually why I came to talk to you," she said, hating how far she had to tilt her chin to meet his eyes. She used to love how big he was, how feminine and protected he always made her feel. Now his size highlighted her lack of control over her fate.

"To talk about prison fashion?"

Dickhead. Still loved to play the deliberately obtuse card when he didn't want to hear what she had to say. "My husband."

Eyes that were icy before went downright glacial. The nostrils of his crooked nose flared as though he'd smelled something rotten, and his lips flattened against his teeth. "Why the fuck would you want to talk to me about your husband?"

Ethan sucked a breath through his teeth his eyebrows shooting straight to his hairline. "Toni and I are going to take Dad home," he said, with a look at Danny that meant he expected to hear all the gory details. He dropped a quick kiss on Caroline's cheek and told her to take care as he steered Toni away.

"I want you to help me find out who killed James," she said.

His eyes narrowed as he took his time answering. "I thought the police already did that."

Pain stabbed her, stealing her breath, so fierce she took a step back. Did he really believe she was guilty? Or was he taking a jab at her by making her think he did?

"You know I'm not capable of murdering anyone."

"I don't know you at all. I haven't for a long time." That he didn't want to renew their acquaintance rang loud and clear.

"Fine. Then you'll treat me like you would any other client who hires you for your services. I know you run a security and investigation firm with Derek and Ethan. I want to hire you to investigate my husband's murder since the police aren't inclined to entertain the possibility that I didn't do it."

"I'm sure that barracuda you hired will be able to get you off."

Caroline didn't disagree. With her shrewd legal mind and sheer ruthlessness, Rachael Weller had kept dozens of clients out of jail, even the guilty ones. "That's not enough. Even if I go to trial and a jury finds me innocent, there will always be that stain. People will always wonder."

"Let them think what they want. You'll be laughing all the way to the bank."

She winced at his brutal assessment. He really thought she was that shallow. "It's one thing for people to think I'm a gold digger, and another for them to think I killed my husband. Besides, it's not just about me. My mom already has one child who's an admitted criminal. She doesn't need her neighbors giving her the stink eye when I come to visit, too." Not to mention, once the DA built his case, she'd have to go to jail to await trial, and no way in hell was she doing that again. Danny made fun of her orange jumpsuit, but he had no idea what it was like to be confined, with only meetings with her attorney and court appearances to break up the monotony. She swallowed back a wave of nausea at the thought of having to spend a single hour back in confinement.

But even more frightening than the threat of confinement was the deep-seated fear that whoever had killed James was coming after Caroline next.

He feigned a look of regret. "I wish I could help you, I really do. But our client list is pretty full. I can recommend some other firms—"

"I think they're after me too, Danny."

For a second hope flared as she thought she saw something like concern flicker in his eyes. "Right. The notes you received. The ones the cops think you wrote yourself."

The hope disappeared like a wisp of smoke, leaving behind an ache like she'd been kicked in the gut. Did he really believe she would lie about something like that? She willed herself not to care, intent on getting him to agree to help her. "I'll make it worth your while."

"You can't pay me enough to take your case."

"I'm not talking about money."

He did another head to toe scan, this time letting his eyes linger at the tops of her thighs and on her breasts. To her horror she could feel heat collecting between her legs and her nipples harden against the front of her chest.

He finally moved his gaze to her face and gave her another shake of his head. "No offense, Carrie, but been there, done that, and it doesn't look like it's improved much with age."

"That wasn't what I was talking about, but trust you to

go straight for the gutter. I have information you might be able to use."

"Oh yeah, what's that?"

"Information that connects your mother to my husband."

He froze, every cell on alert like a predator ready to pounce. "What, exactly, did you find?"

"Oh no," she shook her head, faking bravado. "Not until we have a deal."

He grabbed her arm, moving so fast his hand was little more than a blur as it reached out. "Don't fuck with me, Caroline. What did you find?"

"Help me clear my name."

His grip tightened, hovering on the edge of pain. "So you've become a blackmailer as well as a gold digger? Nice."

She swallowed hard, not about to let him see how much that hurt. "I'm bargaining. There's a big difference. You help me, I help you."

"If you have evidence you should turn it over to the police."

"I don't know if you've been following the news, but the police and I aren't exactly on speaking terms these days. I'd rather we handle this ourselves."

His fingers flexed, then loosened one by one. He took a step back and slipped his hands in his trouser pockets. His suit jacket flipped back, revealing a mile-wide chest tapering down to a lean waist and hips. "Thanks, but no thanks. If my mom had a connection to your husband, I'm sure I'll find it on my own."

Panic set in, along with desperation as she realized how badly she'd tipped her hand. "You really think you can find it, when for eighteen years you never found anything that linked her to James?"

"That's because we didn't know where to look. Now thanks to you, we do. Nice seeing you again, Caroline."

This time he was the one who strode away without a backward glance, his casual dismissal his final fuck you.

"I thought you said we were going to get something to eat," Kaylee Edwards said. Hunger scraped at her belly. She hadn't had anything to eat since the afternoon before, when she'd managed to scrape together enough change to buy a taco.

"I told you I had to run an errand first," Ericka, who was in the driver's seat, had to almost yell to be heard over the ancient Ford's rumbling exhaust system.

Kaylee tried to calm the sense of dread that rose up, mixing with the hunger as she watched miles go by with nothing but grass covered hills spotted with oak trees. They were more than two hours out of Sacramento, had left interstate 80 forty-five minutes ago, and Ericka's errand was out in the middle of fucking nowhere.

Kaylee rubbed at her temples, trying to ease the throb that came from going too long without food and kept her mouth shut. Ericka had offered her a safe place to stay and an introduction to her manager, and Kaylee wasn't about to mess this up.

It was the break Kaylee had been hoping for when she spent the last of her money on a bus ticket to get her away from Wichita nearly two weeks ago. The night before she left, she'd woken up with her twenty-four-year-old loser of a stepbrother on top of her, one hand over her mouth, his dick out as he tried to shove her boxers down her legs. The scream he'd let out when Kaylee sank her teeth into his palm brought her stepfather running.

But instead of beating the crap out of Jimmy, Don had gone on a drunken tirade about what a slutty cock tease Kaylee was, and how she'd only gotten exactly what she'd been asking for.

Her mother said nothing, as usual.

Kaylee knew better than to go to the police for help. Until she was eighteen in a year and a half, she'd be put in foster care, or worse, a group home, and no way in hell was she going through that again.

Everyone was always telling her how pretty she was, with her waist length blond hair and blue eyes. She'd figured if she could just get to Los Angeles she'd be set. Once she got there, she figured, even if no one wanted to offer her an acting or a modeling job, at least she could find work as a waitress. Then maybe a producer or director would discover her, just like Natalie Portman had been discovered by a modeling scout at a pizza parlor.

But it hadn't exactly worked out that way. Kaylee only had enough money to get herself as far as Sacramento, and she had spent the last several days begging change, trying to avoid cops, and other panhandlers who thought she was trying to move in on their turf.

She was ready to admit defeat and call her mom to beg for bus fare back home when she met Ericka. Kaylee was sitting on a park bench next to her beat up duffel bag when Ericka plopped herself down next to her. Unshowered and in the same clothes she'd worn for three days straight, Kaylee squirmed self-consciously next to the woman who was skinny and beautiful enough to be on the cover of a magazine.

She'd introduced herself as Ericka and struck up a conversation. In the course of about ten minutes, Kaylee knew that Ericka had moved there two years ago from Portland, was half Korean, and worked as a model. "You know, you're really pretty," Ericka said, studying Kaylee with dark eyes that tilted exotically at the corners. "I don't know if you'd be interested, but I can introduce you to my manager. He's always on the lookout for new talent."

Kaylee's jaw nearly hit the concrete. Could she seriously see through the days of street grime enough to think Kaylee had any kind of potential? She couldn't do anything more than nod and mutter, "That would be great," as her heart pounded and her mind raced with the thought that this could be it!

Kaylee had heard stories about people posing as photographers to take dirty pictures of girls, but Ericka looked legit, and she was a woman, and she seemed really nice. She'd even offered Kaylee a place to sleep and shower once she learned how Kaylee had spent the last several nights.

When Kaylee woke up that morning, Ericka had barely given her time to pee before she said they had to go. They were going out for breakfast, she said as soon as she did an errand.

Now it was almost noon, and there wasn't so much as another car around, much less a place to grab breakfast. Ericka slowed down a little and did a quick sweep behind her, almost like she was worried about being followed. A battered mailbox listed to the right of a cracked asphalt driveway that was lined with trees. Ericka followed the long drive and pulled up in front of a wood frame house.

Kaylee would have been impressed by the sheer size, but the white paint was peeling in sheets and the front porch was propped up on one end by cinder blocks. The drive continued past the house and seemed to get swallowed up by the brush and trees.

Ericka got out of the car and motioned Kaylee to do the same. The dread Kaylee had tried to quash as the miles passed returned in full force. Ericka hadn't said much on the drive, and Kaylee worried that she regretted offering to help Kaylee out. Now she looked back at Kaylee with an expression so cold it reminded Kaylee of the snakes that sometimes slithered out of her mother's garden.

Telling herself she was imagining things she followed Ericka up the crumbling front steps. Instead of knocking Ericka whipped out her phone.

"I'm here," she said to whoever answered.

Kaylee heard the sound of several bolts sliding free and a slither of unease traveled down her spine. Why did they need that many locks out here in the middle of nowhere, where there was no one around to steal your stuff?

The door opened and she followed Ericka inside. A man opened the door, his stocky frame back lit by the light spilling from the hallway behind him. He had a gun tucked into the front of his pants and three teardrops tattooed under his left eye.

Kaylee remembered reading somewhere that the tear tattoos were worn by gangbangers to show how many people they'd killed. Her throat went dry as the man looked her over with dark, hooded eyes. Ericka better finish up her errand fast, because this place was creeping her out.

The guy motioned for Ericka to follow him inside, and Ericka grabbed Kaylee's arm to make sure she followed. The inside of the house wasn't much better than the outside. The wood floor of the entryway was scarred with deep gouges and scratches. Faded wallpaper flaked from the plaster. Kaylee half expected a bat to come flapping down the staircase.

The muffled sobbing coming from somewhere upstairs didn't do anything to reassure her.

The guy walked halfway down a hallway and knocked on a closed door. A muffled voice said something in Spanish.

The door opened and Kaylee saw two other gangster looking types sitting on chairs across from a battered wooden desk. A man sat behind the desk. Unlike the other guys, he wore a slick looking suit and didn't have any visible ink. His dark hair was slicked back from a dark, angular face, and he regarded Kaylee with a cold yellow stare that made her skin crawl.

"Very nice," the man said in faintly accented English. "We can always use more blonds."

"How old is she?"

"Tell him how old you are," Ericka snapped.

"Sixteen and a half," she stuttered, panic rising as she felt the mens' eyes crawling over her skin. What had Ericka gotten her into?

The man shot Ericka a look. "The older ones do better."

Better? Better at what? Kaylee's stomach started to sink. The creepy vibe was getting out of control.

"I want my bonus this time," Ericka snapped.

The man's lips tightened, his eyes narrowing behind hooded lids. "We need to check her out first."

"Why do you need to check me out?" Kaylee asked, though she was pretty sure she knew why.

Ericka shook her head and flashed her a look and in that instant Kaylee knew she'd been duped. She started for the door, but only got two steps before two of the guys grabbed Kaylee by the arms. Her heart tried to beat through her ribcage as she thrashed to get away, but in a few minutes Ericka had stripped her to her bra and panties.

She stood frozen, as the man walked a slow circle around her, coldly assessing her like she was a car he was thinking of buying.

"Good," was all the man said. Then he called out in rapid Spanish. A woman appeared dressed in nurse's scrubs, and before Kaylee could react she felt a sharp stab and burn in the muscle of her upper arm. The men released her, and though deep down she knew it was futile, she made a staggering run for the door. She grabbed the doorknob as her legs noodled under her and she slid to the floor in a heap.

"We'll check her out, make sure everything's okay to go, and you'll get the rest in a week," she heard the man say.

Her vision tunneled but she held on to consciousness long enough to see her "friend" accept a fat wad of bills.

Kaylee didn't know how long she'd been out when the sound of crying finally woke her. Her eyelids felt like anvils as she dragged them open. The room was nearly dark. The only source of light was a strip of daylight shining weakly through the gap where the curtains didn't quite meet over a window. It was several seconds before she could fully focus on the huddled form quietly sobbing on the bed across from her.

Her stomach soured and her heart thudded as the details of the day slowly slipped into place. Ericka, offering her a shower and a place to stay. Ericka, offering to set Kaylee up with her manager. Ericka, driving her out to the middle of bumfuck nowhere and selling her to some creep.

"Where am I?"

The only answer was more sobs, and Kaylee pried her head off the pillow to look around. Her head throbbed, making her squint as she took in the small, sparsely furnished room. She was on the bottom of a set of bunk beds, lying on top of a scratchy blanket. The room had two more sets of bunk beds, but only one other bed was occupied. A small form huddled on the top bunk across the room. The source of the sobbing.

The girl was curled up into a ball, her face hidden, and Kaylee could see nothing but a dark, scraggly ponytail hanging down her back.

"Hey, you," she yelled and threw her pillow at the girl in case there was any mistaking who she was talking to. "Where are we?"

The girl started and lifted her tear-stained face. She was Asian, her narrow eyes nearly swollen shut, her round face blotchy and wet.

"What the hell is going on here?" Kaylee snapped.

The girl started bawling all over again, babbling in some language Kaylee couldn't understand.

"English?" Kaylee tried. "You speak English?"

"No good," the girl said. "Me Thailand." She moved her hand in an up and down motion that Kaylee finally got was supposed to be a boat. "I come here, work. Tell me, good job, much money to have." Then her mouth trembled and she said, "Me here. Many men. Many men." She wrapped her arms around her waist and started to sob again.

Kaylee had a pretty good idea what they had planned for her, and she swallowed back a surge of nausea as panic swelled in her chest. She wasn't a virgin, not by a long shot, but that didn't mean she wanted to give it up for sweaty old men so desperate they needed to pay for it.

"Where are we?" she asked the girl, not really surprised when her only answer was more sobbing.

She needed to think. There had to be a way out of there, even if her Thai roommate hadn't found it yet. She sat up, pausing when it felt like her brain smacked into the side of her skull, and took stock of herself.

Oh, God, had the creepy guy raped her while she was out?

Tears stung her eyes as she took careful stock of all of her sexual parts. When she and her best friend Kristin were freshmen in high school, they'd gone to a senior party. Kristin had gotten so drunk she'd passed out, and when she'd woken up her pants were gone and she hurt between her legs.

Kaylee hadn't understood why she was so upset. If she couldn't remember it, it was like it never even happened. Nothing to freak out about.

Now as she tugged her shirt and bra aside and tried to focus to see if she was sore between her legs, Kaylee wished she'd been a little nicer to Kristin. No wonder she took her off as a faceplace friend.

There was nothing. No marks. No come stains. And it had been awhile so she was pretty sure she would be sore if she'd had sex.

Kaylee shuffled to the door and tried the knob. The door didn't budge. There was a shiny round knob with a flat surface, almost like where a deadbolt would be but there was no keyhole.

Right. Because if there was a keyhole someone might be able to pick a lock.

The Thai girl's sobs raked down Kaylee's spine, pulling at the skin of her neck and shoulders until Kaylee wanted to scream. She moved across the room to the single small window and pulled back the curtains. It didn't matter that the window was locked and painted shut. There was no way she or anyone would be able to squeeze past the bars covering the glass from the outside.

Fear clutched her chest, choking her, making her thoughts swim as she tried to shake off the effects of the drug. She dropped to the floor and looked under the beds, scoured every corner for something, anything that might be used for a weapon.

The creepy guy might not have raped her while she was drugged, but Kaylee knew it was only a matter of time. If she didn't get out of there, she would be sold, used up, as good as dead.

CHAPTER 3

"So are you going to help her?" Derek asked as they waited for the paper targets to make their way back on the line. He snapped another ammo clip into his Sig Sauer 45.

"Did someone from Alyssa's Hollywood crowd slip you some dope? No fucking way." Danny yanked the target off the line and held it to the light, slipping his glasses down under his chin for a better look, then moved around to Derek's side of the particle board partition to look over Derek's shoulder. Derek's target showed only two big holes. One in the center of the outline's forehead, one in the center of its chest. He'd neatly divided his shots between the two kill zones and hadn't missed a single one by so much as a millimeter.

Showoff. There was a good reason Derek had become a sniper for the Seventy-fifth Regiment of Army Rangers.

Danny's shots, in contrast, were all over the fucking place, as scattered as his brain had been ever since Caroline Palomares—no *Medford*—had dropped in on his mother's memorial service and dropped a great big nuke all over his day.

"And that's why you've spent the past two days digging

up everything you can find about James Medford's murder?"

Danny didn't answer right away. As far as his brothers knew, Caroline had made a surprise appearance to pay her respects to the dead and try to hire him to help her find the "real" killer. He hadn't told anyone—not even his brothers—what Caroline had said about finding evidence linking her dead husband to his dead mom. He told himself it was because he didn't want to give anyone false hope or waste their time chasing false leads—Christ knew they'd done enough of that for the past eighteen years. He didn't want to get anyone else involved until he had something solid.

Yeah, that was what he told himself, but as much as he hated to admit it, that wasn't even close to the truth.

The truth lay in the middle of a convoluted mess of emotions he didn't even want to try to unravel. Starting with the one-two punch of ball tightening, knee weakening lust he'd experienced at the first sight of her, immediately followed by an upsurge of anger he would have sworn was dead and buried.

"Seeing her again sparked my curiosity."

He didn't have to look at Derek to know he didn't believe him for a second. To avoid any more prying questions, Danny pushed the button to set another target and slipped his safety glasses and ear protectors back into place.

Curiosity. Yeah, Danny was pretty fucking curious about a lot of things having to do with Caroline Medford. Starting with how she'd ended up married to the old fart in the first place. Never mind that Medford was good looking—for an old raisin anyway—a successful attorney, prominent on the San Francisco social scene and rich enough to have a mansion in one of the East Bay's wealthiest communities.

But he'd never pegged Caroline for a gold digger or a status seeker, even when she'd questioned his choice of West

Point for college and his determination to join the Army like his father before him.

Guys like you don't join the army. Guys from my neighborhood join the army so they can go to school. Your dad has money. You can do whatever you want.

She hadn't understood, at first, his desire to fulfill the family legacy. Four generations of Taggarts, including his father, had served in the military. To him, joining the military wasn't a last resort, something a man did because his choices were limited. It was the choice of a man who knew exactly what he was getting into and chose to face the challenge to be all he could be.

Yeah, he'd quoted the Army recruiting poster back to her. So what?

Caroline still hadn't understood that—not completely—but she had understood his need to feel like he was doing something useful, worthwhile, on behalf of a cause greater than him, instead of being stuck at home spinning his wheels as his father fell apart in the wake of his mother's disappearance. She also knew, even though Danny had never voiced it out loud, Danny's hope that if he went to West Point, followed in Joe Taggart's footsteps, his Dad might notice something else in his life other than his single-minded drive to find his missing wife.

But even if Caroline claimed to understand Danny's decision, she'd never accepted the reality of what it would be like to be an army spouse, especially the wife of someone in the Special Forces. The long absences where she didn't have any idea where he was or when he'd be back. His need for periods of quiet and decompression when he came back so he could deal with the blood, the violence, and the death on both sides he faced every time he was sent on a mission.

In the end, no matter what she said about love and loyalty and their plans for the future, Caroline couldn't hack it.

And just like his mother, when the going got tough, Caroline had turned her back on him and walked away for good.

Good thing she'd done it before they did something really stupid, like actually marry each other.

Danny leveled his Glock at the target, took aim and squeezed the trigger. The target shuddered on impact and he squeezed again.

Derek fired off three rounds, paused, and emptied the rest of his clip.

"Did you find anything good?" Derek asked after they both removed their ear protectors and Danny punched the buttons to retrieve the targets.

"You know, if I wanted to chitchat, I would have suggested coffee instead of the firing range," Danny snapped.

So much for keeping his cool. But Derek's question picked at a raw spot. Despite all of his research into James Medford's murder and a careful dissection of his own mother's life before she disappeared, he couldn't find a single shred of information or evidence that indicated they'd ever been in the same room together, much less crossed paths in any meaningful way.

Then again, there was a lot they didn't know about the last weeks and months in his mother's life. Gaps of time when they didn't know what she was doing while they were at school and their father was at work. Mundane details they'd pieced together from bits of information provided by friends and acquaintances, because none of them paid much attention at all to how Anne Taggart was living her life.

Danny shoved aside the surge of guilt that came with that reminder. He wasn't going to waste time wallowing, not when there was a chance to redeem himself for every cruel word and thought he'd had for his mother since she'd disappeared.

"I still think you should help her." Derek unloaded his

gun and packed it in a locking gun case while Danny did the same. Though they both had conceal and carry permits, neither wore their sidearms unless the job called for it.

"What the fuck. Just because you and Ethan jacked off to visions of Carrie in a bikini before you could get pussy of your own, you have a soft spot for her."

"Ethan and I did just fine on our own without having to spank it to images of your girlfriend," Derek replied in his annoyingly calm voice. "But I think we should help her out. For old time's sake. Shit, she was going to be part of our family. That should count for something."

Danny slammed his guncase on the ground and threw his ear protectors so hard a piece of plastic casing went pinging through the air. He was sick of his brothers pushing, sorry he'd told them even half of what she wanted. "Yeah, and the only reason she didn't marry in was because she found out I wasn't the trust fund kid she thought I was. As soon as she realized she'd have to live on my military pay, she said fuck you to the six years we were together, turned around and found herself a sugar daddy to shack up with. So I don't owe her shit for old time's sake, and neither do you."

Derek opened his mouth to protest but Danny cut him off. "And another thing. She didn't show up at Mom's memorial service out of some long lost affection for Mom or for us. She was there because she's a user, and she wants to use us to help her beat a murder rap."

"You don't really think she did it."

"Even if she did, it's not like she won't get off, not with Rachael Weller covering her ass. That woman could get Pontius Pilot acquitted."

"Which brings me back to my earlier question. If you really don't give a shit about all this, why have you pulled up every piece of information you can find on James Medford?"

The truth surged, clamoring to break free. He and his

brothers were tight; they never kept things from each other, especially something as big as this. But something held his tongue. He didn't want to get anyone's hopes up, not even his own, until he knew whether Caroline was really on to something.

He refused to think that it had anything to do with protecting Caroline. Or protecting himself. Because he knew the second he let them in on it, they wouldn't let up on him until he gave in, or they'd go behind his back to help her themselves. Either way Danny would be smack back where he didn't want to be: way too close to Caroline. "Morbid curiosity," he said.

Derek finished packing his Sig away and leveled Danny with a stare that made him want to squirm. Instead Danny turned away and headed for his Jeep.

Danny slid into the driver's seat and turned on the ignition.

"For someone so dead set against helping her, you're sure doing a lot of due diligence."

Danny didn't say anything, and it stuck in his craw not to tell Derek the truth. Maybe he should just call the cops, tip them off that Caroline might have some information. But he knew what would happen. Whatever the cops found would disappear into a black hole of an evidence closet, and Danny wanted to know exactly what Caroline had before it got mired in the legal system.

That was the real reason he wasn't going to the cops, and why he wasn't letting anyone else in on the information. It had nothing to do with the fact that something inside him physically recoiled at the thought of siccing the cops on Caroline again. At the thought of cops showing up at her house, questioning her, maybe even getting a search warrant to tear her place apart. Her face would be all over the news, the new sensational angle putting her right back on the front page.

But he didn't care about protecting her from that, not at all. The only reason he was keeping Caroline's revelation to himself was because it was best for everyone involved.

Derek was silent the rest of the way back to the office. They entered the building and Derek started down the hall to his office, then paused as though reminded of something. "Don't forget dinner at our place tonight."

Danny feigned a look of regret. "Can't. I have some stuff I need to take care of. Moreno's helping me with the post-mortem on the GeneCor case."

Derek glared at him.

"I wouldn't miss Alyssa's lasagne if it weren't important. They need the report by tomorrow." Total lie. Danny planned to be working on a case all right, but it had nothing to do with the biotech company that had been a Gemini client for the past two years. He planned to recruit Moreno—the one man in their organization guaranteed to keep his mouth shut and ask no questions—and they were going to start some heavy surveillance and figure out exactly what Caroline Medford had to hide.

"Garage light just came on." Ben Moreno's low voice whispered through Danny's earpiece. At five-thirty in the morning, the moon was still peeking through wisps of clouds as the sun struggled up over the bay. For the last several days Danny and Moreno had staked out Caroline's house, familiarizing themselves with her routine. While Danny slouched low in the Lexus he'd borrowed from his dad, Moreno had posed as a member of the gardening crew. He'd managed to get into her garage and put a tracking device on her car.

Not that they needed it. If the last few days were any indication, Caroline didn't get out much. She left briefly one afternoon when a cleaning crew arrived. They'd tailed her to a coffee shop where she'd sipped a cappuccino and pretended not to notice the speculative stares and whispers as the other patrons recognized her. She didn't lead the trophy wife life he'd imagined. No long lunches with friends. No leisurely afternoons at the spa.

The Caroline he'd known had been outgoing, social, the kind of woman who made a new friend everywhere she went.

Now it seemed she was a virtual shut-in.

Danny shoved aside the involuntary tug of sympathy. Caroline had made her choice when she married a much older, wealthy man. If that left her with few friends to rally around her while the DA built his case against her, that was her own damn problem.

Other than the cleaning crew, her only visitor was a young, pretty redhead who showed up with a little boy in tow and stayed for several hours. Danny knew the young woman was Caroline's stepdaughter, Kate, and the little boy her son, Michael. Evidently Kate had had no issue with her father marrying a woman who was closer to her own age than to her father's. Not only did Kate visit two of the four days Danny and Moreno watched the house, she'd been all over the press voicing her support for Caroline. In one of her more memorable quotes she'd said, "Only a complete retard would believe Caroline was capable of killing my father."

Despite her homebody ways that made it difficult for Danny to get a good look around and bug her house, she had one regularly scheduled outing they could count on. One they would have missed had Danny not idly checked the tracking device a few days ago before his morning run. Everyday for the past three days Caroline left the house at five-thirty a.m. and went to the Piedmont Hills Fitness Club, where she worked out with a private trainer for at least an hour. She didn't arrive back home until at least seven-thirty or eight, leaving Danny plenty of time to get inside and look around.

He stood on the side of the house that faced the neighbor who didn't have any motion detector lights on his house—he'd already disabled Caroline's switch yesterday. It was the kind of neighborhood where the houses were big but the lots were small, leaving a narrow gap that provided plenty of shadows for concealment.

He caught a glimpse of Caroline as she backed the silver Mercedes out of the garage. Her dark hair was pulled back into a ponytail, her face pale and strained in the glow of the streetlamps. Nothing like the siren in black who'd shown up at the church nearly a week ago.

But still pretty enough to make him feel like he'd been kicked in the chest.

Danny shoved the thought aside. He needed to stay focused. The last thing he needed was to fuck up because he was distracted and end up with the cops all over the place. Caroline pulled into the street and paused a second as she reached up to press the garage door control. Like most people, she drove off without bothering to see if it closed.

Or to make sure no one used the opportunity to sneak into her garage.

Crouching down, Danny ran the few steps to the garage and slid under the door before it fully closed. In the back right corner was the door that led to the house. He held a flashlight between his teeth as he quickly overrode the alarm. Next he picked the deadbolt, going smooth and slow. If anyone ever cared to look, they'd never find evidence the lock had been tampered with.

"I'm in," he whispered into his collar where his mouthpiece was clipped.

"I'll let you know if anyone approaches, sir."

Danny rolled his eyes at the formality. Back at the office or out at the bars, Moreno called him Danny or dickhead or whatever the hell he wanted. But when they were on the job, Moreno reverted back to their days in the Special

Forces, when Danny had recruited Moreno straight out of Ranger school at the tender age of nineteen. Even though Moreno had been nearly a decade younger than everyone else on the team, he'd turned into one of the best small arms and hand to hand combat specialists Danny had ever worked with. As annoying as Danny sometimes found Moreno's acknowledgment of rank, it worked to his advantage at times like these. When Danny said their surveillance of Caroline was confidential and off the clock, Moreno hadn't so much as blinked in curiosity.

Danny found himself in the kitchen, predawn light washing the room in gray. Lots of granite and stainless steel, including a professional grade cooktop that didn't look like it had been used in a decade.

Danny shook his head. What a waste.

He moved through the kitchen, pausing at a built-in alcove that held a phone and a small desk. Mail was neatly stacked and separated, organized into piles of bills, magazines, and catalogs.

His lips pulled in a half smile as he had a sudden flashback of Caroline, in his old room in his parents' house in Atherton, trying to put all of his papers and books and other random crap into some semblance of order. He'd lured her over under the guise of helping him with his math homework. Even though she was a year behind, she kicked his ass all over the place in honor's calculus.

Caroline had arrived at seven p.m. sharp, just like they'd planned, her calc book tucked under her arm and a mechanical pencil clutched in her fist like a weapon. She was different from any girl he'd ever dated, cute creampuff cheerleader types who brandished Daddy's credit cards at the mall like it was a competitive sport.

Caroline was quiet, headdown, a scholarship kid who pulled straight As and didn't do any extracurriculars because she worked as a waitress five nights a week. Danny hadn't even noticed her until she'd ended up in front of him in honor's calc. The first day of class he asked to borrow a pencil since all he could come up with were pens.

She'd turned around at his shoulder tap. One look at her face, olive skinned and faintly exotic, and Danny had felt something twist deep in his gut. One look at the full curve of her breasts pushing against the front of her white uniform shirt, and he totally forgot what he'd wanted from her in the first place.

"Did you want something?"

Her dark eyes were narrowed in a glare, but a flush darkened her cheeks. She'd caught him staring at her rack.

He searched his suddenly blank brain, trying to remember what he wanted when all he wanted was to kiss her full pink mouth right there in the middle of second period.

She started to turn away.

"Pencil," he'd managed, pointing at the one in her hand like he was a caveman. "You have one I can borrow?"

She'd rolled her eyes and muttered something about dumb jocks. Danny tried not to take it personally. Just because he was a fullback and captain of the football team didn't make him a brainless meathead.

Then again, he had been caught staring and drooling over her chest.

She held out a red number two, but snapped her hand back before he could take it.

"You better give it back to me after class," she warned with a hard look in her dark chocolate eyes. "It really pisses me off when people borrow," she made little airquotes around the word, "stuff when they have no intention of giving it back."

"I swear," he said, smiling stupidly in response to her glare. Like a stupid cliché, his fingers brushed hers as he took the pencil. Heat shot straight between his legs, generating a boner so fierce and persistent he'd had to walk out of class holding his backpack in front as he pretended to rummage around looking for something.

Caroline didn't seem to notice. Which made her all the more intriguing.

Danny didn't consider himself particularly sensitive or intuitive when it came to girls, but somehow he knew if he was obvious enough to ask her out on a date he'd get shot down. His brother Ethan, already a stud in the making as a sophomore, advised Danny to appeal to her brainpower.

"Chicks love it when they think they're helping you."

"She will be helping me," Danny reminded him. Going into finals he had a C–, unacceptable in his, and more importantly, his father's view.

"Good. Get her over to help you with a problem set, and once you get done with the math, ask her to help you solve an even bigger problem." Ethan's lewd grin and rude hand gesture made them both laugh.

Ethan was right. Two weeks before their calc final for the semester, after a lot of coaxing and pleading, Caroline had relented and agreed to help him prep for the test. He'd nearly blown it when he'd offered to pay her.

For that he'd gotten a stony stare and a curt, "Just because I'm on scholarship doesn't mean I'm a charity case."

Back then she hadn't wanted anything from anybody.

Funny how Danny couldn't remember what he had for lunch two days ago but he could remember exactly what Caroline had worn the first time she came over to his house. Jeans, slim fitting but not too tight, tapering down to converse high-tops with a close fitting navy T-shirt tucked into the waistband. Her waist length dark hair was pulled back in a ponytail, and her dark eyes had filled with suspicion when he told her they'd be studying in his room.

He ignored it, playing it off as no big deal as he led her up the stairs to his bedroom.

"God, you're a slob," was her only comment.

"It's not that bad." He'd made the bed and shoved his dirty clothes in the hamper in preparation.

Not good enough for Caroline, who immediately went to his desk and started to straighten. "I can't work in here if it's not organized." Books, papers, notebooks, pens, were lined up, stacked, and organized while Danny watched from behind her. Satisfied, she'd turned around startled to see him so close.

She'd jumped back with a gasp. Another cliché. She'd tried to move around him but he didn't budge. Her furious blush and nervous lick of her lips told him what he'd hoped all along: despite her ambivalent appearance and apparent disdain for dumb jocks like him, Caroline had it as bad for him as he did for her.

That night was the first time he kissed her. The first of many "tutoring" sessions interrupted by frequent makeout breaks, nights that left him aching and frustrated, relieving himself in the shower after Caroline drove away in her beat up Camry.

Yet he managed to pull his C- up to a B+ by the time the semester was over.

Danny's wry smile faded as he stood in the kitchen Caroline had shared with her murdered husband. What the fuck was he doing, waxing sentimental about a girl who had played him out and dropped him like a bag of shit when she didn't get her way?

He made his rounds through the rooms of the bottom floor, searching the kitchen, the living room, and the media room for any hint of the evidence Caroline had referred to. He searched behind every picture and along the floorboards for any sign of a hidden safe, but found nothing.

When he got to the office, he spent awhile hacking Caroline's password so he could install keystroke tracking software, a sniffer program on her network, and a mirroring program so he could access her computer from his own. Caroline's fastidious organization skills were as evident there as they were in the rest of the house, making the office remarkably easy to search. The contents of desk drawers were meticulously maintained, documents and papers arranged neatly in clearly labeled folders. Unfortunately Danny didn't run across any file folders labeled "Anne Taggart."

But he did find something else that piqued his curiosity. A stack of business cards and brochures promoting Caroline's Custom Closets, offering customized closets and organization systems for busy families. Apparently Caroline had turned her penchant for neatness into a business.

His admiration turned to irritation as he discovered that the office, like the other rooms, had no sign of a safe or other hiding place.

He moved swiftly through the house, avoiding windows in case a neighbor happened to walk by, and ran lightly up the stairs. He checked his watch. He had a good hour and fifteen minutes at least until Caroline would pull back in. He had plenty of time to start on the upstairs rooms.

An oriental runner in a rich green and gold pattern muffled his footsteps as he walked down the upstairs hallway. He paused at a hall table with its careful arrangement of silver framed photographs. The big one in the center caught his attention and he felt his jaw clench.

A younger Caroline than he'd seen at the memorial service smiled for the camera, her smooth, tan shoulders and arms shown off by a sleeveless white dress Her dark curls smoothed into waves rippling over her shoulder, partially covered by a veil of cream lace.

Her fucking wedding day.

James Medford stood behind and slightly to the side of her, a proprietary hand on her narrow waist. His thick hair was more salt than pepper, and deep lines fanned from the corners of his eyes and carved grooves beside his smiling mouth. Danny was sure he saw a smug glint in the guy's eyes, as if to say, "look at the hot piece of ass I scored, boys."

Danny was tempted to put his fist through the picture's glass before he reminded himself he didn't give a flying fuck about Caroline and the guy she'd married. What Danny and Caroline had was ancient history, a couple of kids getting carried away, too stupid to realize their high school romance couldn't begin to go the distance. Whatever bad feelings he had about the breakup were dead and buried, long forgotten, and not worth dredging up now.

Still, as he slipped into the master bedroom and carefully sifted through the contents of Caroline's dresser drawers, the lingering imprint of that photo chased away any last vestiges of guilt he might have had over spying on Caroline after she'd asked for his help.

If Caroline wanted to keep her secrets safe, she shouldn't have dared Danny to come after them.

Let your husband RIP unless you want to end up like him.

Caroline raked a hand towel across her eyes to get rid of the last of the sweat and read the note again.

She'd found it tucked in the door of her locker, sticking out like a white flag. Stomach clenching with dread, she'd known exactly what the note was before she unfolded it.

It was just like the others, printed on plain, white, laser printer paper using a font common to every PC in existence. So generic, so untraceable, that when Caroline had shown the police the first two she received after James's death as proof their suspicion of her was ridiculous, the detectives had accused her of writing them herself to cover up her own guilt.

By the time she'd received the third one, she'd stopped reporting them.

Her fingers shook as she placed the paper in the pocket of her gym bag. Her skin crawled with the sensation of being watched. Only someone with intimate knowledge of her routine would have known the exact time window to slip in, undetected, and put the note in her locker.

Normally she would have showered and dressed there before going to her breakfast with Rachael, but now her breath raced and her heart pounded with the need to flee, to retreat back to the safety and security of her house. Where she could set the alarms and lock the doors and keep out anyone she didn't want coming in.

Her usual bordering on OCD need for organization fled as she shoved her things haphazardly into her shoulder bag. A tiny voice asked her why she didn't interrogate the staff, ask anyone if they'd seen anything, seen someone slip it into her locker.

But she knew it would be the same as always. No one saw anything. No one suspicious around her locker, her car, her mailbox, or the other places she'd found the notes. At that hour of the morning the locker room was humming with estrogen and hairdryers, dozens of women going in and out. For privacy, there were no security cameras in the locker rooms, so even if she did demand to see the security tapes, it wasn't like she'd catch someone red-handed on film.

Caroline raced out of the locker room, ignoring the startled glare of a half dressed woman as she knocked her with her shoulder bag. Normally her workout left her centered and calm, if only for a little while. By the time she reached the parking lot she bordered on a full-fledged panic attack.

Let your husband RIP unless you want to end up like him.

Driven by the need to get to her car and home to safety as quickly as possible, she stepped off the curb and onto the asphalt, oblivious to the people and cars around her.

"Watch out!"

The screech of tires and blare of a horn blocked out the warning, and headlights blinded her as she looked up in terror.

With a sudden burst of clarity and speed, Caroline hurled herself out of the path of the black SUV heading straight for her.

CHAPTER 4

"Jesus Christ lady, look where you're going!" A stocky man in his fifties climbed out of the SUV and slammed the door. "I could have killed you."

"Well maybe if you'd been paying attention instead of looking at your phone you would have seen her. What in the world are you thinking goin' that fast in a goddamn parkin' lot? Caroline, are you okay?"

She looked up to see Melody Easterbrook, Patrick Easterbrook's wife, a look of concern on her face as she helped Caroline get to her feet.

"Are you hurt?" the man asked, slightly contrite after Melody's ass chewing. Caroline recognized his face if not his name. He was a regular at the gym and worked out around the same time she did. He had a red windbreaker over his UC Berkeley T-shirt and his face was red with exertion and anger.

Caroline did a quick assessment of herself. Her knee was a little sore where she'd landed and her right palm had a big gash, but she was otherwise okay. It flashed again, the huge dark SUV bearing down on her.

For a terrifying moment she'd been convinced it had been the killers making good on their threat.

"That wasn't my fault, you know," the man continued. "Lots of people saw you just walk out without looking," he said.

"You were speeding and everyone saw it," Melody broke in. "She'd be totally within her rights to sue you if she's injured."

"I'm fine," Caroline managed to break in, raising her hand to calm Melody down. The last thing she needed that morning was a public altercation. "I'm sorry I wasn't paying attention." Her lips were stiff with cold and it was hard to push the words out.

The man nodded and climbed back in his car.

"I don't know what people are thinkin' bombing through the parkin' lot like it's a NASCAR track," Melody muttered, then turned her attention to Caroline. "Honey, you're shakin' like a leaf." She wrapped an arm around Caroline's shoulders and steered her out of the SUV's way. Even after twenty years in northern California, Melody's voice was heavily laced with a Texas drawl. And though she'd turned forty-five that past December, she still looked the part of the Dallas beauty queen. For Melody, a trip to the gym merited a full face of makeup, sprayed and teased blond hair, and a perfectly coordinated outfit of designer workout wear. "What's got you so out of it you're walkin' into traffic without even lookin'?"

"I think I'm coming down with something," Caroline replied shakily, trying not to shrink away as Melody put a hand on her shoulder. Her skin was tight and too sensitive, and the comforting touch was unpleasant.

"Well, it's freezin' out here," Melody said. "If you're not sick already you'll catch your death out here if you stand out in this cold in those sweaty clothes."

Caroline let out a slightly hysterical laugh at Melody's choice of phrase. Yeah, she was liable to catch her death if she wasn't careful. But now that Melody mentioned it, she was cold, down to her bones, so cold her body trembled and her teeth began to chatter. "I just need to get home," she said, barely able to force the words from between her clacking teeth and trembling lips.

"You better let me drive you."

Caroline tried to fend off Melody's offer, only to find her arm seized in a no-nonsense grip as she was steered gently but firmly across two rows of cars to Melody's powder blue Porsche. "Get in, honey. I couldn't forgive myself if I sent you home like this and found out later you got into an accident."

"Thanks," Caroline said. "I'm sorry about all this. I think the stress is starting to get to me."

Melody clucked and gave her a concerned look as she backed out of her parking space. "You know you can always call us if you need anything."

"I know, but you've already done so much."

"Hey, we trophy wives have to stick together you know. Although," she slanted a look at herself in the rear view mirror, "I'd say this old trophy is due for another polish."

Caroline let out a weak laugh. Part of the reason she and Melody got along was because they were both younger second wives of two best friends and had formed a friendly alliance against the disapproving first wives in their social set. Though they would never be best friends—at the core they were too different for that—Caroline and Melody enjoyed each other's company.

And they'd grown closer over the past six months, as Patrick and Melody stood firmly by her, even when she was accused of murdering Patrick's best friend of over thirty years.

The initial adrenaline spike was wearing off and Caroline's knee and hip started to throb where she'd hit the pavement. She risked a look down and saw a nasty road rash decorating her knee. She shifted in her seat to alleviate the pressure in her hip, which hurt even worse. God knew what she was going to find under there when she took her shower.

Caroline blocked out the pain and leaned against the headrest trying to focus on Melody's chitchat about how their daughter, Jennifer, was coping with her freshman year at UCLA, trying and failing to shove aside thoughts of the note. Shove aside the knowledge that whoever had killed James had her in their sights.

James had been found shot to death in their house while Caroline was away, consulting with a client who wanted Caroline to design the closets in her new vacation home in Sonoma. As the investigation intensified, the police quickly dismissed their initial theory that the murder was a home invasion gone wrong and instead seized on Caroline, the scorned wife, as the prime suspect. Terrified, Caroline had started her own digging, going through every detail of James's life trying to find out who really killed him. She'd told the police about the crying woman and suspicious conversations, but they hadn't wanted to hear any of it.

Caroline knew she'd been on to something, because it wasn't long after she talked to the cops about the mysterious woman that she'd found the first note.

Back off, or we'll finish you like we finished James.

But the cops hadn't cared about that note or the ones that followed, convinced she'd printed them off herself in an amateurish effort to throw them off the trail.

She'd hoped, prayed the notes would stop, that maybe they were a cruel sick joke by someone who wanted to mess with her.

As the weeks since she'd been released lengthened to a month, then two, she half convinced herself it was all a sick hoax. James's killer wasn't really out there, biding his time, waiting for the opportunity to silence her before she discovered whatever secrets she wasn't supposed to find.

"And where they think he's going to come up with two thousand more dollars a month, I have no idea."

Melody's harsh laugh momentarily jolted Caroline from her dark thoughts. Patrick and Melody weren't having an easy time of it lately either, which was part of why Caroline hadn't wanted to bother them. Last year Patrick had been found liable in a medical malpractice suit where a patient had been misdiagnosed and subsequently died in surgery. His malpractice insurance paid out the settlement, but now his already sky high insurance premiums threatened to drive his practice into bankruptcy.

"But I can still pay you for the work you're doing on our closets," Melody said, with a reassuring pat on Caroline's leg.

"Mel, don't worry about it." Despite her skyrocketing legal costs, and decline in business Caroline's bank balance was very healthy. But Melody had hired her, Caroline suspected, out of sympathy since her business had completely dried up.

It seemed most people weren't keen on having a suspected murderer in their homes, organizing their stuff. Go figure.

"You have to finish," Melody said emphatically. "Oh, and I had a great idea—I want you to think about a special way to display Patrick's lab coat from when we first met."

Caroline nodded, inwardly cringing. Unlike Caroline, who liked to purge her closet every season, Melody attached sentimental value to nearly every piece of clothing, making it incredibly difficult for Caroline to design a clean, uncluttered system without it being overwhelmed. She'd managed to get Melody to cull both her and Patrick's closet, at least a little bit. But Melody was inexplicably attached to an ancient physician's coat from St. Luke's hospital.

"I can't possibly toss that," Melody insisted. "It's where Patrick and I met. It represents the foundation of our marriage."

Personally Caroline couldn't see how a swath of white polycotton with a red machine embroidered crest over the left breast pocket could take on such importance, but the customer—especially her only customer—was always right. "I'll think of something, I promise."

But right then her mind was far from functional organization systems. Right then she was wondering how the hell she was going to get herself out of that mess. Despite Mel's loyalty and reassurance, Caroline knew that when it came down to it, she was on her own.

She thought of Danny Taggart, the cold look in his eyes as he'd turned down her request for help. She had no doubt he was investigating James's connection to his mother on his own, and wondered if he'd found anything. Caroline had pored over every page of that date book twice and had come up empty.

But Caroline knew Danny wouldn't stop until he found out the truth about what happened to his mother after she disappeared.

Once upon a time he would have fought just as hard for Caroline. But he turned his back, left her to fend for herself just like before. Shame on her for hoping it could be different.

"We've got a problem," Moreno's voice froze Danny's gloved hand as he was reaching for the middle drawer of James Medford's bureau.

"Yeah, what's that?" he asked, resuming his search, sliding open the drawer to reveal rows of neatly folded and stacked boxer shorts, separated by color and pattern. "Caroline's headed up the front steps."

"She's an hour early," Danny protested. "Why the hell didn't you tell me her car was on the move?"

"Cause she's not in her car," Moreno snapped. "A woman driving a blue Porsche dropped her off at the curb. Better get moving. Her key is in the door."

Fuck. He did a quick mental run-through of the house's layout, trying to come up with the best escape route, something that would go unnoticed by the neighbors. That ruled out the bedroom windows, which were clearly visible from the neighbor's backyard. The neighbor who just happened to be outside playing with her kids.

Ideally he'd go out the way he came in, through the garage, invisible from the street. But that would entail sneaking past her. Not impossible, but not foolproof.

He had to come up with something fast, though, because he could hear the light thump of her footsteps as she started up the stairs. "Hold your position," he said softly into his mic. "I'll take cover until I'm sure I can get out undetected."

Danny needed to get out of James's walk-in closet. It was too open, and attached to the master bath. Even if she didn't walk through the closet, she might catch a glimpse of him if she entered the bathroom.

She was closing in.

He darted out of the walk-in closet, across the room, to the best option for concealment he could come up with under the circumstances. Across the spacious master suite was a sitting area. Two large armchairs were tucked into a corner, a leather ottoman serving as both a table and footrest. One chair was tucked into a corner, its back brushing the heavy drapes that were drawn back to let in the morning light. The heavy upholstered fabric was more than enough to conceal him from view, the chair adding an extra layer of protection to hide his bulk.

And bonus, he could get a clear view of the room and see partially into her walk-in closet, which wouldn't have happened if he'd gone under the bed.

He twitched the thick embroidered fabric into place just as she walked into the room. He barely breathed as he heard her move around the room. The hairs on his arms stood on end, every cell heightened as the room heated with an electric charge. He half expected his earpiece to blow a circuit, he was so switched on.

Danny heard her footsteps move from the muffling surface of the carpet to the echo of hardwood and knew she was in her closet. He heard a thud, then another, as her shoes hit the floor. Then the rustle of fabric as something came off.

Don't do it. This is no time to think with your dick.

His hand moved the curtain a millimeter to the left, offering him a little sliver to see through just as Caroline was slipping a sports bra up and over her head. His mouth went bone dry and every drop of blood rushed to his groin at the tantalizing view of heaven.

Contrary to what he'd said that day at the memorial service, time had served Caroline damn well. Too well. Her lush breasts were still firm and full, their tight, cinnamon colored nipples tilted slightly up. Danny licked his lips at the remembered taste of them against his tongue. It had been over ten years, but he could still conjure up the sweet salty taste of her.

She was thinner than before, whether from the stress of the last few months or the pressure to maintain her trophy wife body, Danny didn't know. When they'd been together she'd never been much for exercise, but now her legs and arms were lean and toned, proving she was getting her money's worth out of those training sessions.

Her hips and ass still curved lushly out from her tiny waist, and his palms itched to run over the smooth, silky skin. His gaze darted to the king size bed with its mountain of pillows and silk duvet cover.

Danny wondered what Caroline would do if he emerged from his hiding place and threw her on the bed. Would she scream for help or would curiosity over what it would be like after all this time take her too? The bed was huge, dominating the room. They could do a lot of damage on that bed.

The bed she shared with her husband, he reminded himself.

His fingers curled into fists and he closed his eyes, shutting out the carnal images that threatened to overwhelm him. As much as the thought of fucking her in her husband's bed revolted him, he was struck with an equally strong urge to take her every way he could think of until he'd banished James Medford from her mind, made her forget what it was like to ever be with any man but him.

He shoved the thought out of his head and forced himself to get a grip. He was a man, totally in control of himself and his libido. It would take more than a glimpse of a naked ex-girlfriend to send him over the edge.

Danny told himself he was immune as she slid the shorts down her legs, revealing that round, perfect ass and a tidy black patch of curls at the apex of her thighs. He forced his breathing to slow as she tugged her hair out of its ponytail, the motion making her back arch and her tits jut out like she was waiting for a lover to come suck on them.

He let out a slow, silent breath as she moved out of sight into the bathroom and he heard the sound of the shower. This was his chance to get out of here, while she was occupied and any noise he made was muffled by the shower. And not a second too soon, he thought as his cock throbbed thickly, insistently, against the fly of his cargo pants. One more second and he was afraid the damn thing was going to bust through the zipper, and to hell with his supposedly ironclad self-control.

He waited several seconds before pushing the drapes aside and grabbing his bag to make a run for it.

The phone rang, cutting like a blade through the silence and Danny had just enough time to duck behind the arm chair before Caroline hurried into the bedroom to grab the handset. She'd thrown on a short cotton robe that barely covered her ass and was belted so loosely the vee dropped nearly to her navel.

She was so fucking hot she should have been illegal.

He hunkered down to wait, holding every cell immobile as he listened to her conversation and prayed she'd get off the phone quick.

"You didn't need to call," she said to whoever was on the other line as she perched on the side of the bed. After a pause, "Really, it wasn't that big of a deal. I just spaced out and stepped into the parking lot without looking. It's a scraped knee, nothing to write home about."

Danny squinted and for the first time noticed the angry red scrape that started on the side of her left calf and decorated the front of her kneecap.

"You'd be upset too if you almost got nailed by a Range Rover."

His heart tripped a beat. She'd nearly been run over?

Caroline swallowed hard and looked up at the ceiling. Her eyelids fluttered, almost like she was holding back tears. "When I got done with my workout there was a note in my locker." A pause. "Yes, one of those notes. . . ."

"Because I knew she'd flip out and want to call the cops

and make a big scene when we both know damn well it won't do any good."

She leaned her head forward and pinched the bridge of her nose. He felt a weird squeezing sensation when he heard her sniff and and swallow hard. Caroline was not a crier. In the six years they'd been together he'd seen her cry maybe four times. And every time it had made Danny's stomach knot and his hands shake with the need to make it stop.

He wiped his hands on his pants and watched her nod as though the person on the other end could see her. "I'm so scared," she said finally. "What about Kate and Mikey? What about you? What if whoever's doing this comes after people I care about?"

Nausea twisted in Danny's gut as he listened, remembering how he'd implied she'd written the notes herself. Her fear was real. The threat was real. And he'd blown her off like everyone else.

She reached for her gym bag, offering a mouthwatering display of a silky shoulder and the top of her breast as she pulled it closer. She pulled a piece of paper from a side pocket. "It's like the other ones. A warning and a threat. I guess they're afraid I'm going to find the real murderer." She shook her head. "If only they knew how far I am from the truth." She let out a humorless laugh. "No, Gemini was a bust. Their caseload is too heavy, they said. Guess my high school connection wasn't enough."

Danny frowned, trying to ignore the pang of guilt as he processed her side of the conversation. Had she told whoever she was talking to about the supposed connection she'd found between James Medford and Anne Taggart? It didn't sound like it.

She rang off with an admonishment not to worry and an assurance she could take care of herself. She put the phone in its cradle and raked her hands through her hair. With a curse, she reached out and snatched the paper from the bed, crumpled it in a ball and hurled it into the wastebasket next to the bed before spinning on her bare heel and stomping back into the bathroom.

He didn't hesitate. Without making a sound he darted from behind the chair, paused at the wastebasket to fish out the note, and moved silently down the stairs. He slipped out the side door and told Moreno to meet him two blocks up. He slipped into the passenger seat of the Lexus and pulled out the ball of paper he'd extracted from Caroline's wastebasket. An icy current ran through his veins as he read the typed words on the plain white paper.

Let your husband RIP unless you want to end up like him.

"What's that?" Moreno asked, nodding at the sheet of paper.

Danny read it out loud. "She told whoever was on the phone she found it in her gym locker."

"So we're not the only ones watching her."

Danny nodded in agreement as protective instincts he didn't know he had anymore swelled in his chest. Someone was threatening a woman—*his woman*—a sinister voice insisted, and every instinct in him screamed for him to go back to her house, shove her in the car, and hide her away somewhere safe until he could figure out who was behind the threats.

No. Caroline wasn't his woman, not even close. And even if he changed his mind and took her case—and that was still a big if—it was all about finding out who was responsible for his mother's death. Whatever Caroline wanted from him came a distant second.

Still, he couldn't get over the sound of her tears, the almost palpable fear coming off her in waves. The Caroline he'd known wasn't a fearful person, didn't back down from a challenge. Now she lived in near seclusion, hiding in her house, not even bothering to report a threatening note to the police because she was so convinced no one would help her.

And didn't you just prove her right, Danny boy?

His cell phone buzzed in his pocket, his guilty conscience growing when he saw his brother Ethan's number on the display. His brother, who had no idea where Danny was or why.

"You're not gonna believe this," Ethan said without preamble. "You know how we couldn't figure out the deed transfers for the cabin near where Mom was found?"

"Yeah?"

"Toni's had Kara working on it, and she's like a pit bull." Kara Kramer was the daughter of one of their former clients. When she'd gone missing the previous summer, Ethan had been hired by Kara's father to track her down, while Toni had been hired by Kara's mother to work on the case. After Toni and Ethan rescued her from her kidnappers and saved her from a truly sick fate, Kara had started helping around the office after school. To Danny's surprise, she wasn't the complete waste of space he feared—far from it. Instead she'd proven to be wily and tenacious, never giving up on a research assignment until she found the answer they needed. Toni was tutoring her in the fine art of cyber investigation and the girl was becoming downright dangerous.

"Anyway, she finally came up with a name: Barbara Sanford."

"Why should that mean anything to me?"

"Because Barbara Sanford was James Medford's former mother-in-law. Her daughter Susan was James's first wife."

* * *

"There's no reason to call off the deal," Marshall Black said as he leaned on his elbows. "My clients are ready, they understand the terms."

"We have another buyer in Portland. I think it would be safer right now, with everything going on."

"Nothing is going on," Marshall slammed his palm against the mahogany surface of his desk. "We can handle this." Marshall had stumbled across James Medford's lucrative side business two and a half years ago. He'd been working late and found inconsistent paperwork that James forgot to shred. James had been shocked when, instead of being horrified, Marshall had insisted on being let in. Since then Marshall had proven his worth to the organization by discreetly recruiting new clients. It pissed him off that they still questioned his ability to handle his part of the business. But he didn't let any of that irritation show in his voice. He ended the call, still without commitment that his clients would receive their delivery as promised.

"Fuck," he said, nothing more than a tight whisper. Gwen, his legal assistant, immediately appeared in the doorway. "Is there a problem, Mr. Black?" she inquired, eyes narrowed suspiciously. She hadn't liked it when she'd been transferred to Marshall after James Medford's death, any more than she'd liked it when she'd had to move Marshall into James's office before, as she put it, the body had even started to stink.

He flashed Gwen a fake smile and and okay sign which turned into the middle finger at her retreating back. Meddling bitch. Marshall had to be careful around her, even going so far as to get a cell phone she didn't know about so he could make calls without her going through the bills to see who he was talking to.

In the part of the business he'd learned from James Medford and taken over since his death, confidentiality was paramount. And God forbid Gwen, the nosy paralegal, should ever find out.

Though it would give Marshall the excuse he needed to get rid of her once and for all.

He turned his attention back to his phone call. "There's no reason you should divert the deal to Portland," he said, choosing his words carefully and keeping any trace of anxiety out of his tone, then hanging up. They couldn't know how badly he needed the commission on this. If this deal got screwed, he'd lose everything. The condo, the Lexus. He'd have to sell his Rolex just to make grocery money.

And forget about ever having a chance with Kate Medford. From the second he'd met her at the firm's family picnic, he'd wanted her. She was everything the stupid sluts he'd grown up with weren't. Beautiful, well bred, educated. It had crushed Marshall when she'd slummed it with that lowlife who knocked her up, but it worked out in the end. Now Kate was adamant about being with a man who could support her, who had no need or desire for her money to shore him up while he figured his shit out.

Marshall was determined to be that man. Or at least do a damn good job of maintaining the illusion that he was that man. James hadn't liked Marshall sniffing around his daughter, but he couldn't say anything, not when he was even deeper into the business than Marshall was.

And now James was dead, and couldn't say anything at all. Marshall wondered what James would think about Marshall's attempts to comfort James's daughter in her grief. Poor bastard was probably rolling in his grave.

But Marshall had bigger worries than what James might be thinking from the great beyond. Namely, Marshall needed to make sure he didn't get boxed out of the business because of the latest complications.

Marshall had figured his shit out enough to make it through Harvard Law School, but the student loans weren't going to pay themselves, not even on his generous senior associate pay. He'd already taken as much equity as he could out of the condo, and without the next few side deals going through, he wouldn't be able to pull himself out of the hole he'd dug.

The discovery of Anne Taggart's body had thrown a huge wrench in the works. Marshall still wasn't entirely clear on James's role in her disappearance and death, but he knew enough to know she'd discovered the truth about James's moonlighting and had paid a heavy price for her snooping.

And James's widow, Caroline, had made an appearance at Anne Taggart's memorial service. Marshall wanted to believe it was a coincidence, but deep down he knew that wasn't the case.

He picked up his cell phone, wrinkling his nose at the cheap plastic casing. The disposable model was purely functional, with none of the cool bells and whistles of the Motorola Marshall normally carried. But the phone had the great advantage of being untraceable. He paid in cash and threw it out when the minutes ran out, so even if anyone were inclined to snoop around his phone records, they'd never be able to tie him to the goons that procured the girls. Or to his other business partner.

His partner picked up on the second ring. "We need to finish this," the man said without preamble.

"Can't we give it a little more time? We just sent her another note, and she hasn't talked to Taggart since—"

"That we know of," the voice broke in. "That she was talking to him at all is too much of a coincidence. Hell, for all we know she found something out and already told Taggart all about it."

"But there's Kate to consider. Besides, there's nothing to

indicate the police have made any connection between James and Anne Taggart's murder."

"It's only a matter of time," the man said. "Caroline is too much of a risk. After what James tried to pull, we need to tie up any loose ends that might lead back to him. We should have taken care of Caroline a long time ago."

Marshall had been hoping to avoid this, convinced Caroline's death would only raise suspicion. It was hard enough to cover up one murder. He'd thought they had it made when the police didn't buy the random break in and turned their attention to the soon to be ex-wife. It hadn't taken too much effort to make sure the police's attention stayed firmly on Caroline. That had bought them some time, but now his partner was pushing to get Caroline out of the picture for good.

"She's been saying all along she didn't kill James. If she turns up dead, won't the police realize she was telling the truth?" Marshall asked.

"We need to figure out a way to make it look like an accident," the man said, then sighed. "But how the fuck we do that, I have no idea."

Marshall looked down at his desk, where the front section of *The San Francisco Tribune* lay partially covering his computer keyboard. The front page featured a full color picture of a small, beaming blond woman in a bright red suit, standing next to a huge African-American man dressed in a five-thousand dollar suit, accessorized with at least a million dollars' worth of diamonds.

Rapper Acquitted of Double Homicide. Weller Sets Record. Immediately beneath the headline was a quote from one of the victim's brothers. *"This is not justice. Furious D murdered my brother, and just because his lawyer got him off doesn't mean he can get away with it."*

Marshall ran his finger across his lips as he studied the

blond woman, smiling her dazzling toothpaste smile as she beamed at the press. "Did she tell you when she's meeting her attorney again?"

"She's seeing Rachael tomorrow."

"I'm going to call Gates," Marshall said. "I think I know a way to do it and have Caroline look like collateral damage."

CHAPTER 5

The heavy thud of a fist against the front door sent coffee sloshing from Caroline's mug onto the front page of the paper. A light brown stain of creamed coffee spread across the day's headlines. From where she was seated at the breakfast bar she could see the clock on the microwave. Who the hell was knocking on her door at eleven-thirty on a Thursday morning?

The fist pounded again, and she slid off the barstool, her ballet flats making no sound as they hit the tile floor. She struggled to contain her apprehension as she walked to the front door. It was probably a neighbor—not that any had offered more than a sheepish nod since she'd returned home. Or maybe the paper delivery.

Whoever it was, it was no cause for panic, she reminded herself in an effort to slow her pounding heart. She really needed to get over this anxiety thing. She'd never been a fearful person, but ever since James had died—been killed—Caroline had suffered from increasing panic attacks and a growing anxiety when it came to going out in public. Now an unexpected knock at the door was enough to send her over the edge.

Then again, considering the note she'd received yesterday, her reaction wasn't completely irrational.

By the time she reached the door she was calm enough that her hand barely shook as she braced it on the door. Raising up on her tiptoes, she looked through the peephole. Her heels hit the floor with a thud when she met Danny Taggart's steely gray stare. She peeked again, just to make sure she wasn't hallucinating.

It was Danny all right, looking all big and bad and dangerous with his almost noon stubble and the collar of his leather jacket turned up against the cold. The fishbowl effect of the peephole did little to soften the hard lines of his face, and nothing to cool the hot flutter that started in her belly at the mere sight of him.

Shock and curiosity moved her to open the door. "What are you doing here?" she asked. After the way he'd blown her off at the memorial service she'd never expected to see him again. She'd gotten the message loud and clear—he wanted nothing to do with her, even when she promised information that might contain some clue about his mother's disappearance.

"Can I come in?" He stepped over the threshold without waiting for her reply. A niggle of irritation broke through her shock. Pushy as ever, he walked through the entry, past the stairs, and through to the kitchen as though he owned the damn place. His leather clad shoulders spanned the hallway and his boots thumped against the floorboards.

She hurried after him, and by the time she reached the kitchen he'd already shucked his jacket and tossed it across the breakfast bar. Under the jacket he wore a French blue broadcloth shirt, a black leather belt and kahki pants. He should have looked like an average office dweller, but somehow Danny managed to look tough and dangerous in Dockers and a button down.

Not to mention hotter than the fires of hell. It should be illegal for a man's ass to look that good in everyday casual wear.

"We need to talk," he said, pinning her again with his icy gaze. She had to clench her fingers in a fist to keep herself from running a self-conscious hand over her hair and pulling her sweater away from her chest. She had a meeting with Rachael in forty-five minutes and had dressed accordingly. Gray wool pants fitted but not tight, paired with a navy cashmere sweater set. A sleek ponytail and pearls completed her ensemble. Every inch the elegant, conservative, affluent housewife. Not the man-eating murderess the press liked to portray.

Color heated her cheeks as he looked her up and down, and felt the fresh sting of his remark about her not aging well. The day of the memorial service she'd dressed carefully to kill. Hair down, lipstick dark red, black dress tastefully hugging every curve. If that look had left Danny cold, it was an easy guess what he thought of her frumpy suburban schoolmarm look.

His gaze meandered back to her face, his expression inscrutable.

"What are you doing here?" she repeated, straightening her shoulders and pulling herself to her full height.

"I came across some interesting information and thought we could talk about it."

"You can't pick up a phone?"

The corner of his mouth lifted in a knowing half grin that used to make her knees watery. "You didn't give me your number and you're not listed."

She put a steadying hand out on the breakfast bar and arched one perfectly waxed eyebrow. "If you can't dig up an unlisted phone number, you're not much of a private investigator. I guess I should count myself lucky you turned down my business."

He raised his big hands it mock surrender. "You got me. I thought this would be a better discussion in person." He leaned back against her breakfast bar and folded his arms across his chest and took a long look around the room. "Nice stove," he said finally. "You finally learn to cook?"

"Nope."

His smile stayed in place but his eyes took on a hard glint. "But you need all the trappings to impress the neighbors, right?"

She didn't bother to explain that James was the one who'd insisted they redo the kitchen two years ago, having decided the old design looked dated. If Danny wanted to think she'd let herself become a piece of useless arm candy who cared for nothing but appearances, let him. "I've learned to accept nothing but the best," she said with a brittle smile as she ran her fingers along her flawless string of pearls. "Do you mind getting on with it? I have a meeting in the city in less than an hour, and I'm sure you didn't come here to discuss my cooking skills or lack thereof."

"James's first wife died, right?"

The question veered out of nowhere. "Yes, before I met him. Of cancer," she said pointedly, in case he planned to imply James had offed his first wife.

"Do you know how her estate was distributed when she died?"

"Everything went into a trust for Kate—James and Susan's daughter. Why do you care about any of this?"

"Why don't you tell me what you found out about James and my mother?" he shot back.

Caroline sucked her tongue against her teeth and shot him an exasperated look. "Danny, I wish I could play your little cat and mouse headgames all day, but I have a very important meeting with my attorney." Blood heated in her veins, urging her on. It had been so long since she'd felt anything other than dull dread or the cold bite of panic, the spark of anger felt good. "So unless you want to stop with the bullshit and tell me why you drove forty-five minutes across the bay to see me, I'm going to have to get going."

Her tell off skills were rusty, she'd spent so long reining in her smart mouth, dulling the sharp side of her tongue. But it felt good to let her rude arrows fly, especially against a target as impervious as Danny.

"I'll go with you."

"To see my attorney? I don't think so."

"If I'm going to help you out, don't you think I should know everything there is to know about your case?"

That brought her up short. "So you're going to help me?" For the first time in a long time a kernel of hope took root. Not just that she'd be found not guilty of murder—having Rachael on her team virtually guaranteed that—but that finally someone was going to help her find the truth. So what if he was an unfeeling ex who would undoubtedly make her pay through the nose for his services? Call her foolish, call her crazy, call her ten kinds of stupid, but deep down Caroline believed in Danny Taggart. If anyone could help her find the truth, it was him.

A little voice warned her that this kind of crazy faith in him had burned her before. But now she was older, wiser, and fully capable of keeping it all business.

"Why don't you let me sit in on your meeting and we'll take it from there? Deal?" He held out his hand for her to shake. Even his hands had gotten bigger and tougher looking in the twelve years since she'd seen him.

She held out her own, let his callused palm swallow it whole, and tried to ignore the flash of heat that singed the skin off her fingers. Her breasts chafed against the silk cups of her bra and her heartbeat throbbed between her thighs.

Hoping her olive complexion hid her blush, she yanked her hand from his. Professional. Businesslike. Right. She could totally do this.

Her perfume was driving him crazy. It smelled like green grass and fresh soap, and, mingled with the too familiar scent of her skin, it all combined to make him so hard it was difficult to keep her silver Mercedes between the lane lines. The perfume was just the tip of the iceberg. In her conservative slacks and sweater set, she was rocking the whole sexy librarian vibe, apparently oblivious to the way her baby soft sweater stretched over her soft, full tits and made it almost impossible for him to keep his hands on the wheel.

Caroline was quiet in the passenger seat, nervous as hell if the pulse beating in her throat was anything to go by. Danny wondered if it was him, or if she was always this anxious when she went to meet her shark of a lawyer. She kept her gaze firmly out the passenger window, staring at the San Francisco Bay, her view impeded by regularly spaced girders of the Bay Bridge. One slender hand rose to her throat to fidget with her single strand of pearls.

Jesus Christ, the pearls. As if the tight why-don't-you-pet-me-to-see-how-soft-I-am-sweater wasn't enough, the pearls sent him right over the edge. They made him want to peel off her clothes, piece by piece, pull her hair out of its sleek ponytail, until she wore nothing but gold kissed skin and creamy pearls.

Danny blinked hard and focused on the traffic in front of him. He'd hoped driving would keep him focused. No such luck. "So why don't you tell me what you found," he said, hoping if he turned his attention to more important matters, his dick might take the hint and stop trying to pop through his zipper.

"Let's wait till after we meet with Rachael," Caroline replied, turning from the window. "No offense, but if you're going to help me, I don't want your mother's . . . situation to distract you. Get off at the next exit," she directed.

He let out an exasperated grunt as he steered the car across two lanes to the exit. Truth was, he still wasn't sure how involved he was going to get in her quest to clear her name. Ethan and Derek were foaming at the mouth to take Caroline's case after they discovered the deed transfer history of the property where Anne had been found. What better way to get access to James Medford's information than to help his widow? And they still didn't know Caroline had other information.

Having found nothing on his own, Danny conceded a more direct approach was needed, so he'd agreed to at least do a preliminary evaluation of Caroline's case, and hope she gave something up in the process. As a matter of course at Gemini Securities, with every new client there was an assessment period, a pre-investigation investigation, if you will. During that time the security specialist assigned to the case dug into the background to make sure it was an area where Gemini's expertise could help, and performed due diligence on the client to make sure the person or the entity was someone they wanted to get into bed with, so to speak.

Caroline crossed and recrossed her legs, and the sound of her wool clad thighs brushing made his knuckles whiten against the steering wheel. No question he wanted to get into bed with Caroline.

Which was one of the main reasons for not working with her. Still, he'd agreed to at least an evaluation period and he had to make good on that. He had to admit he was intrigued, not just by her case, but by her. Why was she so secretive? Since he'd searched her house, he'd read every e-mail and not once had she told anyone about finding something linking Anne Taggart to James Medford. A second search of her house had yielded nothing.

Though some of the correspondence had been otherwise enlightening. In an e-mail to her friend Diana Vasaquez, who Danny remembered well from high school, Caroline mentioned she'd seen Danny at the memorial service. According to her, she'd tried to hire him to help her with her case, but he'd "blown her off like a gnat."

To which Diana had replied, "Sounds like he's still the same self-centered asshole. Nice to know you can count on some things to never change."

He couldn't remember Caroline's reply verbatim, but he remembered it contained words like "dickhead" "douche-bag" and lots of other terms one expected to hear from a fourteen-year-old boy rather than a thirty-four-year-old trophy wife.

Danny shook off the insult. He'd been called a lot worse, and he could come up with a few choice terms about Caroline without breaking a sweat. But why go there?

To his frustration, other than mentioning she'd seen Danny, there was nothing about anything having to do with information or evidence linking Anne and James. Even more strange, other than whoever had called that day he was hiding in her house Caroline hadn't said anything about the threatening note to anyone.

Even if the police were happy to believe she'd paid to have James killed, you'd think she'd at least file a police report and tell anyone who would listen about the note. Instead, the note he'd recovered from her trash can was in his laptop case in the trunk, and most of her e-mails involved trying to convince everyone in her now-limited circle that she was fine. They didn't need to spare a single second worrying about her.

Christ, he hadn't seen her in over a decade, and it only took one look for him to realize she was so far from fine it wasn't even funny.

There it was again, that idiotic protective thing that always popped up around her, second only to the urge to fuck her senseless.

Talk about things that never changed.

He followed her directions through the city into the heart of San Francisco's financial district. Rachael's firm was in a building on the corner of Montgomery and Washington, where the glittering high-rises met the bustle and activity of Chinatown. Pedestrian traffic was thick, forcing Danny to sit through two green light cycles before he could turn into the building's parking garage.

Caroline was silent as they rode the elevator up to the thirtieth floor. The doors opened to reveal a reception area dominated by heavy wood and leather upholstered furniture. The place smelled of money. Danny had heard rumors of what the lawyers at Weller and Bronstein charged, and now he believed it.

The young blond receptionist smiled and nodded at Caroline. "I'll let Ms. Weller know you're here," she said. As she murmured into the phone, Danny caught her sidelong look of interest. Professional to the core, she quickly hid it as soon as Danny caught her staring.

Within a minute, a small, whip thin woman charged into the lobby. Radiating with energy, Rachael Weller was a blond whirlwind in a designer suit. "Caroline," she said, in a tone that had earned her the nickname "the terrier" in the press. "Good to see you. Keep your coat on," she said when Caroline started to remove her trench. "We're going out today to celebrate. Don't know if you heard, but I won a big one this week." Rachael smirked at her own joke. Caroline would have had to be under a rock not to have heard about the big win.

Rachael waved her hand and the receptionist jumped up to retrieve a black winter coat from a coat closet.

"Congratulations," Caroline said. "I would love to help you celebrate, but I want to make sure we—"

Rachael cut her off, raising her hand as she shrugged into her own coat. "We have plenty of time. I cleared my afternoon for you. And don't worry, lunch is off the clock." She straightened her lapels and took her purse back from the receptionist. She looked up at Danny as though she'd just noticed him.

"Who are you?" she demanded, a faint frown line showing between her eyebrows, the only mark on her otherwise unnaturally smooth face.

"Dan Taggart, Gemini Securities," he said, offering his hand.

"Danny's a private investigator," Caroline added.

Rachael's gaze snapped back to Caroline. "I hire my own investigators."

"I know, but Danny's an old friend," Caroline said carefully.

Hm. Not exactly the way he would have characterized their relationship.

She continued, "If I'm going to have to air all my dirty secrets, I thought it would be better to work with someone I know."

What kind of dirty secrets was she referring to, Danny wondered.

"Taggart, Taggart, now why does that name sound familiar?" Rachael said as she nodded for him to punch the down button for the elevator.

The bell dinged and they stepped into the elevator. Danny stayed silent, waiting for Rachael to figure it out as Caroline shifted uncomfortably.

"Your mother," Rachael said bluntly. "That was her body up in the mudslide, wasn't it?"

Danny nodded.

"Big case. Lots of media coverage when she first went missing. I'm sorry for your loss," Rachael said, barking out the condolences without a hint of emotion. "I imagine you must be working closely with the police to find out what happened to her. Must be quite a distraction." Danny didn't miss the look she shot Caroline. Rachael was used to being in charge of her client's cases in every aspect. She didn't like that Caroline had hired him on her own.

They stepped into the building's main lobby, heavy on

marble and chrome. Rachael's heels snapped along the floor as she greeted the security guard with a nod. "You were involved in the Van Weldt scandal too, weren't you?" Rachael said as they stepped onto the sidewalk.

A couple of months ago, Harold Van Weldt, the Chairman of Van Weldt jewelers, had hired Gemini to keep an eye on his black sheep niece, Alyssa Miles. Alyssa just happened to be one of the most popular tabloid targets of the last decade, so when Derek, who had been assigned to the job, discovered a plot to kill Alyssa and a blood diamond scandal that brought down the company, Gemini's name had ended up all over the news.

Danny nodded. "That was mostly my brother Derek though."

"And you were involved in the Kramer kidnapping case weren't you?" Again, Danny nodded.

"I would have killed to get Jerry Kramer as a client, but he went with Morton and Foster," Rachael sighed. "I know I could have gotten him a better deal."

The way Danny saw it, Jerry got off pretty fuckin' easy with the plea bargain he'd struck. Instead of spending the rest of his life in prison without parole, he would most likely be out in ten, maybe sooner with good behavior.

"We're going to Postrio," Rachael said as she turned right and headed up the block. "They serve a delightful steamed halibut. Quite a body count you've amassed in your latest cases," she said, arching an eyebrow at Danny as he and Caroline followed her up the block.

Danny was getting whiplash from the rapid changes in subject. "Nothing like when I was in the Special Forces, ma'am," he deadpanned.

Rachael gave a little sniff. "You better watch it with him, Caroline. This one's dangerous."

"You have no idea," Caroline muttered.

Danny didn't know what it was that made the hairs

stiffen on the back of his neck and raise every sense to high alert. All he knew was that one second he was striding down the street to keep up with Rachael's fast clip, and the next the air was charged with a current, everything in him screaming that something bad was about to go down.

The last time he'd had this feeling was in his last tour in Iraq, when he'd narrowly avoided getting blown in half with an IED. Paying attention then had saved his life. He wasn't about to ignore it now.

The roar of an engine. Screaming pedestrians as a mammoth black SUV blew through the crosswalk.

He grabbed Caroline, ignoring her startled cry. "Get down, now!"

Heavy bass music boomed. Danny pushed Caroline into an open doorway, shoved her to the floor and covered her body with his own. Screams, gunshots, shattering glass. The squeal of tires followed by the engine's fading roar.

Danny was aware of gasps, cries, panicked calls of "are you all right?" But they were drowned out by his keen focus on the woman under him. He could feel Caroline shaking, every sinew vibrating with fear. He pushed away and gripped her by the shoulders, frantic to make sure she was okay. "You're okay, you're okay," he murmured over and over, running his hands over her, lifting her arms, straightening out her legs as he reassured himself that was true.

Her face was a mask of fear, her skin leached of color, lips blue and shaking. The only spot of color on her face was a bead of blood on her cheekbone. A shard of glass had hit her when the front window was shot out. He reached out to brush it away with his thumb and noticed his hand was shaking.

That single drop of blood shook him to his core and nausea rose in his throat, his reaction as bad as when he'd seen his friends shot in front of him.

Still acting on instinct, he pulled her to him, trying to infuse her with his warmth. She wound her arms around him and buried her face against his chest. He cupped the back of her head and buried his face against her hair, trying to slow his heartbeat as he felt hers pounding against his chest. He pulled her to her feet, his sole focus on getting her out of there, getting her someplace safe.

He shoved the emotion back. He needed to keep a clear head, keep his focus on the mission at hand.

"Call 911," someone shouted. "People have been shot!"

Sirens were already sounding in the distance. Caroline pulled slightly away. "Where's Rachael?" she asked, then uttered a sharp cry when she spotted the small blond figure crumpled on the sidewalk, lying in a rapidly growing pool of blood.

Danny uttered a curse and kept his arm tightly around Caroline's shoulder as they hurried to where Rachael lay.

Caroline fell to her knees and called her name. Danny stayed her hand when she went to touch her. "Don't." Rachael had taken several shots to the chest. Her eyes were wide in shock, her face chalk white as a trickle of blood flowed from the corner of her mouth. He reached out, felt the faint flutter of a pulse. She was alive, but barely. He'd be surprised if she made it to the hospital.

"Oh my God," Caroline looked up at him, her dark eyes frantic. "This was for me. I know it."

Rachael Weller had made a lot of enemies in her career, defending everyone from mob types to drug dealers with close ties to international crime syndicates. The rapper she'd gotten off the day before was known to have gang ties, and his alleged victim was part of a rival group.

Still, he couldn't brush off Caroline's fears. James had been murdered and she'd received a threatening note just two days ago. Maybe someone was trying to silence Caroline before she found out the truth. An ambulance careened to a stop next to the curb, followed almost immediately by two police cars.

Danny's arm tightened around Caroline. Any lingering indecision he had about helping her disappeared in an instant. If someone was out to get Caroline, Danny wasn't stopping until he found out who. And why.

Kaylee flinched as the needle sank into the vein in the crook of her elbow. After spending a third day locked in the bedroom with her roommate, early this morning she was pulled out of bed by a short Mexican woman and led downstairs to a room off the kitchen. It looked like it used to be a pantry, but it was set up with a desk and chairs, and a metal filing cabinet. On the floor was a big blue cooler.

Kaylee was shoved into a chair, her arm pulled out to lay across the desk in front of her. Another woman held her arm down while the Mexican woman plunged the needle into her arm.

"What the fuck?" Kaylee yelled as two, then three vials were filled with crimson liquid.

"Hold still," the first woman snapped in heavily accented English, "or we drug you again."

Kaylee sat still for the moment, not wanting to risk being knocked out again. She needed all of her wits if she was going to find a way out of there.

"Okay you answer some questions now, okay?" The second woman said as she capped the vials of Kaylee's blood and labeled them, just like you would if you were sending them off to a lab.

"What are you doing with those?" Kaylee asked, the creep factor ratcheting up another hundred notches as she watched the woman stash the vials in a cooler already filled with similar looking tubes.

The woman scowled, didn't answer, and pulled out a clipboard. "When you have your last period?"

Kaylee wasn't sure she heard right. "My what?"

"Period!" the woman shouted. "When you bleed last?"

Kaylee's face flooded with heat. "A week ago."

"You regular?" the woman asked.

Kaylee frowned in confusion.

The woman muttered and shook her head impatiently. "You bleed same time all the time. Regular?"

"Yeah."

The woman marked something down on her clipboard and conversed with the other in rapid Spanish. Kaylee had only taken a couple years in high school, but she recognized at least one phrase. *Una semana.* One week.

One week till what?

"You ever be pregnant? Have abortion?"

"No." She didn't think her scare last spring, when she'd sweated her period a full two weeks before it came, really mattered. "Why do you care?"

No answer. The first woman slipped her paper off the clipboard and filed it in a big metal cabinet in the corner of the room, while the other motioned for Kaylee to get up. She stood from the table and did a quick look around, wondering if there was a way she could get past them. They were older, heavyset, probably couldn't move very fast. If Kaylee made a run for it she doubted they could catch her.

She was just about to make a break for it when the creepy yellow eyed guy who'd paid Ericka for her appeared in the doorway, flanked by two guys.

He gripped a short brunette girl by the arm. Around the same age as Kaylee, the girl would have been cute if she hadn't looked like she was about to shit her pants in fear. He said something to one of the nurses, the Spanish too rapid for Kaylee to understand.

"*Si*, Senor Gates," the woman replied, and went to retrieve another syringe.

"What's going on?" the girl cried, her dark eyes beseech-
ing Kaylee, as though she could help her. "What did they do
to you? Do you—" her words cut off with a cry, the sharp
smack of a hand on flesh filling the small room.

"You shut the fuck up," the yellow eyed man said through
clenched teeth. "You talk when I tell you to talk. Otherwise
keep your mouth shut. That goes for you too," he said,
turning to Kaylee. She took an instinctive step back, her arms
folding in front of her as he raked her with a cold, snakelike
stare. He spoke to the women again in Spanish.

Una Semana, the women said again. One week.

Kaylee swallowed back the nausea bubbling in her throat.
Something was going down in a week. But Kaylee didn't
plan to be there when it happened.

There were many ways to make money off a woman's body,
and in the course of his career, Gates had found every one.

His real name was Esteban Lucero, but he'd earned the
nickname Gates because he was the gatekeeper to the West
Coast. Drugs, girls, weapons—in the course of his career he'd
risen in power until he controlled some aspect of the distrib-
ution channels. He kept his base in California's capital city of
Sacramento, where he'd emigrated from Venezuela when he
was eight. From that central point he controlled access as far
east as Vegas, as far south as San Diego, as far north as Seat-
tle, and every major city in between.

The blonde was perfect for their purposes, he reflected as
he watched a guard drag her back down the hall. Lately
they'd been coming up short on the Caucasian girls. Too
many girls in varying shades of brown and yellow coming
over the borders and into the ports. The best were the Eastern European girls, as beautiful as they were desperate to

escape their countries in hopes of a better situation in the states. But his last shipment had gotten fucked when that fucking Serb in Chicago had double-crossed him.

Gates would take care of him soon enough, but in the meantime they needed more white girls to fill the backlog of interest they already had. Taking American runaways wasn't his favorite thing. They were more likely to have people looking for them, and there was always the risk of them spilling out their sob story to a John once they were turned out. Luckily most men who visited Gates's girls in their various locations weren't likely to risk their own necks going to the police on behalf of some whore. But just in case, Gates had those girls watched extra closely.

The blonde was a little young, with her long skinny legs and narrow hips, but she looked healthy enough to survive pregnancy and childbirth. Then once she'd crapped out a couple of babies, Gates would turn her out with the others. He'd get another five years out of her, easy.

He hadn't set out to get into the adoption business. Rivers of money poured in from his existing businesses, and he hadn't been looking to expand. Then one of his girls, a particularly beautiful Czech girl named Nadia had ended up knocked up. Gates's girlfriend at the time, Rochelle, said she knew of a lawyer, some rich white guy in San Francisco, who had helped her friend find an adoptive family for her baby. Her friend had received thirty thousand dollars for her healthy, blue eyed baby boy.

Gates had contacted the lawyer, James Medford, and a new business venture was born. Gates had lots of girls, beautiful, young, healthy girls, with different types of looks. There were thousands of infertile couples willing to go to any lengths to get a child. Why make them endure a risky adoption process with some random woman who might pull out of the deal at the last minute? Or worse, deliver an unhealthy baby?

Medford could guarantee to his clients that not only would they receive the baby they so ardently desired, the baby would be healthy, and as an added bonus, he would make every effort to find a birth mother who resembled the adoptive parents.

Gates had put up the capital to build a facility to house the girls, and provide the kinds of medical equipment and capabilities they would need to monitor the girls' health and fertility. It was a low volume, extremely high margin line of business, and had proven to be extremely lucrative to all parties involved. That slick weasel, Marshall, had gotten involved in the last year. Gates hadn't been sure about him at first, the way he'd blackmailed his way into the business by threatening to expose Medford.

But Marshall was no problem—his greed and lack of morals made him easy to control. James was the one who grew a conscience and became a problem in the last year. When he'd threatened to expose the entire operation, Gates had had no choice but to have him killed. As for his widow, Gates wasn't particularly worried about her, but his partners were determined to take her out. Gates was happy to help, in return for a price, of course.

Marshall had come up with a genius idea of how to take care of her and make it look like collateral damage.

His phone rang. Speak of the devil, it had to be his man confirming the hit was done.

"Bad news," Reuben said.

Gates clenched his fist as he heard the wince in the man's voice. "How bad."

"We fucked up," Reuben said bluntly. No use padding the truth. He knew as well as anyone that if he fucked up he better own up to it. The only thing Gates hated worse than a fuckup was a bullshitter. "We took out the lawyer, but we missed the target."

Gates swore, ignoring Reuben's hurried excuses and apologies. He despised incompetence. He'd have to think of an appropriate consequence for Reuben's failure.

In the meantime, they would have to wait for another opportunity to take care of Caroline Medford. His partners were going to have to be patient a little longer.

CHAPTER 6

Gang related revenge shooting. That's the motive the police ascribed to Rachael Weller's murder. "I understand your concerns, Ms. Medford," and by *concerns*, Detective Benson meant *paranoia,* Caroline knew, "but it seems very clear this is some kind of payback for her client's acquittal earlier this week."

No matter what she said, she couldn't convince the police that those bullets had been meant for her, not Rachael. Caroline tried to block out the image of Rachael's bloody, crumpled body. She'd never call Rachael a friend, and had occasionally raised an eyebrow at Rachael's tactics and seeming lack of any sort of moral compass. But Rachael had been a force of nature, a woman whose presence and vibrancy smacked you in the face whether you liked it or not. To see that cut off so fast, so violently, shook Caroline to her core. And Rachael had been an ally, albeit a paid one, but as her circle of supporters rapidly dwindled Caroline had to take whatever she could get.

Even Caroline was forced to admit, if she stood back and looked at the evidence objectively, it stood to reason Rachael had been the victim of a gang-style hit. The drive-by in the black SUV was the same MO used by other members of the gang in previous hits.

As recently as the day before, Furious D's alleged victim's brother had all but threatened Rachael on the front page *of The San Francisco Tribune.*

Yet with all that evidence Caroline knew, *knew* down to her core that she was the one who was supposed to be dead on that sidewalk. Knew it like she knew James was into something deep, something bad enough to get them both killed, even though Caroline would be damned if she could figure out exactly what.

And no one believed her.

Except maybe Danny. After his initial response at the memorial service, even his attitude earlier that day, she would have never pegged him as one of her remaining allies. But without his almost supernatural sense that danger was coming and his superhuman reflexes, Caroline would be lying dead on that sidewalk next to Rachael.

Never in a million years did she imagine she'd be riding next to him, grateful for his presence as he navigated her car through the streets of her neighborhood. Despite any old bitterness, any bad blood between them, he hadn't left her side for a second. And when she told the detective about the note she'd received—and thrown away—Danny looked at her with his steady gray gaze and promised he'd help her find out who was behind it.

"I can't believe I threw away that goddamned note," she said for the hundredth time.

"Maybe it's still in your garbage," Danny said.

"No, they collected yesterday. It's in some landfill somewhere."

"Have you kept the other notes?" he asked.

"Some," she said. "I gave the first few to the police, for all the good that did. After that I stopped handing them over." She slumped against the seat, exhausted after the skyrocketing adrenaline of fear followed by the grueling process of giving her statement to the police.

Not to mention the press, which had descended like a swarm of locusts. Danny turned the car down her street and she swallowed back a surge of nausea when she saw three different news vans blocking access to her driveway.

"Don't worry, I'll get you past them."

Danny parked her car around the corner, got out, and came around to open her door. He tucked her against his side and moved through the throng like a battering ram, using his bulk to move people aside as he barked, "No comment," over and over. Caroline kept her head down and charged through the gauntlet, hiding her face against Danny's chest as he propelled her up the front walkway, reporters dogging their every step.

Caroline hurriedly punched in the alarm code and they ducked inside. A local newswoman with a chin length helmet of brown hair tried to muscle her way inside. Danny planted a big hand in the center of her chest and pushed her back onto the steps. "No fucking comment." The woman barely managed to get her hand out of the way before he slammed the door.

"Thanks," Caroline said, hating the way her voice shook. "I don't think I could have made it in without you." God, when had she become so pathetically fragile? She'd been practically self-sufficient since she was a kid, had learned to watch out for herself at a young age. Between her father's drinking problem and her brother's run-ins with the law, Caroline's mother more than had her hands full. It was up to Caroline to take care of herself and the rest of the family.

Her marriage to James must have made her soft. She'd gotten so accustomed to having her needs—most of them anyway—taken care of by someone else, she'd lost her ability to deal. She needed to get it back, and fast, if she was going to get herself out of trouble. No matter how reassuring she found Danny's presence, she knew she couldn't completely count on him. He had his own reasons for helping her, and they had nothing to do with getting her out of this mess.

She took off her coat, hung it up, and tried to pull herself together.

Danny stood watching her, that damned inscrutable expression on his face. He was so calm, so immovable, Caroline felt embarrassed at the way she'd shivered and clung to him for the majority of the afternoon. "Thanks for staying with me this afternoon," she said. "I'm sure you have a lot to take care of, so if you need to go, we can set up a time to meet later this week to discuss—"

"I'm not going anywhere," he said, shrugging out of his leather coat. He brushed against her as he reached for a hanger, releasing his scent into the air. The combination of leather, musk, and soap made her head swim as she breathed him in. She wasn't sure if his decision to stay was cause for relief or greater panic. When she'd gone to see him at the memorial service, she'd convinced herself that whatever they had was dead and buried. They'd just been a couple of foolish kids who thought they could make a high school romance into happily ever after.

Caroline had told herself she was lucky that they realized they were too immature and too poorly matched before they did something really stupid. Like go through with their engagement and get married. Or God forbid, bring a kid or two into the mix.

Though at the time they broke up, Caroline would have given nearly anything to have had everything turn out differently.

She shoved the well-worn pain aside. It wasn't the time to reopen old wounds. Her past with Danny was just that, and she needed to remember that, no matter how hot the old chemistry threatened to flare.

She led him into the kitchen and gestured for him to take a seat at the breakfast bar. "Do you want something to eat?" she asked, realizing neither of them had eaten since they went to meet Rachael. Unbidden, an image of Rachael's broken, bloody body flashed in her brain. "I'm not very hungry," she said, swallowing back a wave of nausea.

"I'll help myself if I need anything," he replied. "Right now I want to get down to business."

"We need to get everything out on the table," Danny said, trying to keep his attention on business, instead of on the vulnerable curve of Caroline's mouth and the terrified look in her eye. All he wanted to do was pull her close and promise her everything would be okay. But he was afraid if he touched her all bets would be off. He took a deliberate step back. "We need to talk about what you found connecting James and my mother. And I want to see those notes."

She nodded and started out of the kitchen. "Everything's upstairs." He got off his stool and she tried to wave him off. "I'll only be a minute if you want to wait."

"I'll come with you," he said, ignoring her protest. He didn't want to give her the chance to hide anything if she were so inclined.

He followed her up the stairs to the second floor, trying to ignore the soft curve of her ass against the gray wool of her pants. All those mornings at the gym gave her body a honed, tight look. Still, her ass kept its plump roundness, making him want to reach out and give it a squeeze to see if it was as luscious to the touch as he remembered.

He tucked his hands into his pants pockets and followed her down the hall like he had no idea where he was going. The master bedroom was the same as when he'd seen it last, the silk covered comforter pulled up just so, the throw pillows arranged perfectly on the king size bed. Danny watched her walk into her closet heat pooling in his groin as he tried not to remember the last time he'd seen her in that room.

"Big place for two people," he said idly as he stood in the

doorway of her closet and watched her reach for a handbag tucked in the back corner of a high shelf.

"This was James's house with his first wife," Caroline said as she pulled the purse down. Danny didn't bother to tell her he knew that already, having done such a thorough background check on James Medford he knew the guy's blood type. "His daughter Kate was still at home the first few years we were married," she pulled out what looked like a leatherbound book.

"You never wanted to have kids of your own?" Danny could have smacked himself for asking. Why should he care that Caroline, who'd always agreed with Danny that they should have at least three kids, hadn't bothered to have a family. He raked his gaze down a body that was a good fifteen pounds slimmer than when they'd been together. "Then again, I guess you wouldn't want to take the risk that kids would ruin your trophy body."

Caroline's face went even paler and her mouth pulled into a thin, tight line. "Not that it's any of your business, but James had a vasectomy. Something he neglected to tell me until after we were married for five years and I started pressing him for a baby."

Danny shoved back a pang of sympathy. "I guess that's what you get for marrying for money."

Hurt flashed in her eyes, but only for a split second. Eyes narrowed, Caroline straightened, summoned up some of the bravado he remembered so well from their youth, and gave him a sharp half smile. "You know what they say. Every marriage is full of compromise." She held the leather bound book out to him. "Here."

He looked in puzzlement at the book. Something about the light brown color and gold lettering was familiar. He flipped it open, feeling like he'd taken a kick to the chest when he read the inside front cover.

Property of Anne W. Taggart.

10 Stockbridge Rd.
Atherton, CA 94027

He flipped over a page, saw that the book was a planner, with calendar pages for writing in appointments, notes, and daily checklist. He forced himself to focus on the first entry.

January 1, 1991.
Lose ten pounds
Exercise more
Volunteer more
Be more patient with Joe
Get out more

Danny realized he was looking at a list of New Year's resolutions written in his mother's handwriting. It was so . . . ordinary. Yet so surreal at the same time. How strange after all that time to be looking at his mother's handwriting. He flipped through more pages, but couldn't find anything, at first glance, anyway, that would explain how his mother came to be buried alongside another woman in the middle of an open space preserve.

He sat down on the edge of the bed, turning the pages as he felt Caroline's weight settle in beside him. It was his mother's book, but it was full of references to him and his brothers. As though Anne Taggart had no life beyond her husband and her boys. But Danny knew differently. He remembered vividly her mysterious absences, afternoons when she was unreachable and unaccounted for with nothing but a vague explanation.

"Are you okay?" Caroline asked, laying a tentative hand on his arm. "I know it must be really weird to see her handwriting after all this time."

"Weird. Right." Yeah, that was one way to put it. It was like a voice from beyond the fucking grave. He shook off her hand and shoved himself up from the bed. If he stayed there any longer he was afraid he was going to grab her and bury his head in her shoulder. "I'm fine," he snapped. "I dealt with all this shit a long time ago. Now I just want to find out what happened."

Caroline stared at him with wide eyes. Resentment squeezed his chest at her knowing, almost pitying look. Like she knew that underneath his bluster, there was a little boy still crying for his mommy.

Fat fucking chance. "Where did you find this?" he finally asked, careful to keep any shred of emotion from creeping into his voice.

"It was in a box of books Kate had taken from her closet. She brought back a bunch of stuff last week to put in storage."

"And you've never seen this before? In the entire time you were married to James?"

Caroline shook her head.

Danny's eyes narrowed. "Kind of convenient that you only came across it after he was dead."

Caroline glared right back at him. "I would never keep something like this from you."

"Not even if it meant protecting your husband?"

"Danny, I would never do that to you and your family," she said, her voice vibrating with grief that sounded real. He turned away so he could listen without being distracted by those big brown eyes and trembling pink lips. "I know what you went through when your mother disappeared. I never would have kept anything from you, not even to protect my husband. You have to believe that."

Danny nodded. He could hear the truth in her voice and let it go. "But you would use it as bait to get me to help you."

Color flooded her face. "Desperate times," she said, then raised her eyes to his. "I would have given it to you eventually. But I was hoping you would help me."

He smiled without humor. "Maybe you should be careful what you wish for. So tell me where you found it."

"It was only after," she hesitated a few seconds, "he was killed that I really went through everything." She braced her hands on the mattress and leaned back with a sigh. "James saved everything, and I mean everything. We went through all of it, trying to find something that would give us a clue as to who would want him dead. But we never found anything"

"Who's we?" Danny asked.

"Me and Kate. She helped me go through everything. Last week when she brought some stuff over here to store, she found a box of books she realized had belonged to James. That's where I found the date book."

"And Kate knows nothing about it?"

Caroline shook her head. "She may have seen it, but I don't think she would understand the significance."

"Kate was the only one to help you go through James's things?"

Caroline nodded, frowning in confusion. "She was the only one I trusted to go through his personal stuff."

Danny stared at the notes scribbled onto various dates, as though he could will the book to give up secrets that had been buried for nearly two decades. "Someone could easily hide information under the guise of helping you. Sometimes people closest to you are the ones who want to hurt you most."

Caroline sat up straight on the edge of the bed, indignation evident in every line. "Kate would never want to hurt me."

Danny held up his hands. "I'm not accusing her of anything. I'm just trying to get all the information I can."

Caroline's phone rang. "Speak of the devil," she said as she looked at the display, shooting him a glare as she picked up the phone. "Hi Kate."

He listened to her half of the conversation with one ear as he continued to scan the appointment book. Nothing but notes on groceries for the housekeeper to pick up, errands to run, appointments, various sports games Danny and his brothers had scheduled that she probably wouldn't attend. Normal, everyday things you'd expect to find in the calendar of an affluent stay-at-home-mother.

"No, I'm okay. Really. No, you don't have to stay with me. I don't want to put you out." Caroline's eyes flicked in Danny's direction. "It had nothing to do with me. Just the wrong place at the wrong time." She rang off and met Danny's questioning look.

"You haven't told her about the notes?"

"Not the most recent one." Caroline pocketed her phone and twisted her fingers in front of her. "She's got enough on her plate with school and Michael. I don't want to worry her anymore. Did you find anything in there?" She tilted her chin toward the book. "I've already been through it twice, but couldn't find anything about James, or anything related to James. Maybe it's just a dead end." Her shoulders slumped, and he fought the urge to give them an encouraging rub.

Or even better, he could close the last few inches between them, lay her across that big bed and spend the next few hours making them both forget the rest of the world. Heat pooled between his legs and he licked his lips as the idea took hold. Maybe he could get some extra benefits out of their renewed acquaintance.

He saw the flash of awareness in her eyes right before they flicked nervously from his gaze. Her fingers shook a little as she brushed back a curl that had escaped from her sleek ponytail.

Yeah, she was feeling it too, the crazy chemistry that had erupted long ago in his teenage bedroom and had lain dormant until then. All it needed was a whiff of oxygen and it was roaring to life, white hot and undeniable.

Don't do it, man. She's nothing but trouble for you. She

ate you up and spit you out before. What makes you think she won't do it again?

But he was older by over a decade and infinitely wiser. He knew the difference between sex and love. Mainly that sex was an enjoyable way to pass some time with a woman and did a decent job keeping his thoughts from creeping over to the dark side, while love was a word people liked to throw around and use as an excuse for acting like a bunch of jackasses.

He'd been there, done that, and sure as shit wasn't going back for more.

So why not add another dimension to his working relationship with Caroline? He hadn't had a problem walking away from a woman since she'd left him. She wouldn't be any different.

She knew exactly what was on his mind if the pulse beating in her throat and the flush across her cheekbones was any indication. Danny was pierced by a sudden, vivid memory of that same flush staining the creamy skin of Caroline's stomach as her orgasm hit. By the time she'd finished coming, her tits would be suffused in the same rosy pink, the perfect backdrop to her diamond hard nipples.

He started to reach for her but before he could even get his hand up she darted away, skittering toward the door with her hands in her pockets, her eyes fastened to the floor like some secret to the universe was hidden in the pattern of her area rug. "You said you found some information too, about my husband. Maybe if we go through the book and you tell me what you found, we'll figure out the connection."

My husband. Two words, and his cock shriveled like a prune. Danny thought of James Medford, his aging hands all over Caroline's body on that enormous bed, and was afraid his balls were going to climb into his abdominal cavity. "Let's go downstairs and I'll tell you what we found."

* * *

Caroline fought the urge to fan herself as she led him back downstairs. Her whole body felt lit from within. Amazing how his gray eyes could go from stone cold to liquid mercury in a split second. And that look still had the same devastating effect it had had on her when she was sixteen. Innocently wandering into his bedroom like a baby deer into a lion's den. He'd lured her over under the guise of tutoring him in calculus, but Caroline was the one who'd received an education. Up until that night, she'd barely been kissed, awkward, mildly pleasant interactions of lips and tongue. By the time she left Danny's room that night she'd been throbbing in places she didn't even know she had, clinging to her virginity by the skin of her teeth.

Dwelling on memories like that could only lead to trouble. She needed to get away from him, away from the *bed* for God's sake, before she did something royally stupid. It was a below the belt shot to bring up James, but thank God it had worked to distract him. Caroline liked to think she was older, wiser, and much more in control of her libido than she'd been as a hormonal sixteen-year-old. But she knew if Danny pushed it, she'd end up naked under him, over him, any which way he wanted her.

She ordered her body to cool down as she led him back to the kitchen and gestured for him toward the loveseat and armchairs that made up a sitting area in one corner. During the day, light flooded the kitchen through the windows and skylight, creating a sunny pocket of warmth where Caroline loved to sit and read or sketch plans for her latest project.

Danny ignored her and went straight for the refrigerator. "Do you mind?" he said over his shoulder as he pulled out a package of chicken breasts and a head of broccoli from the refrigerator. "All of a sudden I'm starving."

"Can I help you find something?" Caroline called as he opened and shut cabinets, banging around in her kitchen like he owned the place. He ignored her, bent to open a door, and straightened with her spaghetti pot, which he quickly filled with water and put on the stove.

"I have some frozen lasagna and other stuff in the freezer if that's easier."

But Danny was rummaging in her pantry for more supplies. "Don't tell me you still eat that shit," he grimaced. "I told you that shit's worse than army chow."

Caroline couldn't hold back a smile at the memory. Danny had been appalled when Caroline had opened the freezer at her parents' house to reveal shelf after shelf filled with TV Dinners and Hot Pockets, and barely any other food in the house. Danny was obviously still an avid, though messy—she winced as a glug of oil sloshed over the side of the sautee pan onto her immaculate stove—cook.

Within minutes the water was heating and her kitchen was full of the aroma of garlic, chicken, broccoli, and whatever herbs he'd dug out of her spice cabinet. Her stomach, previously sour from stress and too much police station coffee, grumbled in appreciation.

"Did you know that James's wife had land up in the Santa Cruz mountains?" Danny said and came to take a seat across from her.

Caroline frowned, trying to keep up with the swift change in subject. "No. Like I told you, after she died everything went into a trust for Kate to be managed by James." Upon his death, control of the trust had passed to Caroline. "I haven't looked at it closely recently, but I don't remember any other property in the trust."

Danny nodded. Dark stubble shadowed his chin. Even as a teenager he'd had a thick beard, and she'd loved to run her fingers along the raspy skin. She shoved her hands in her pockets to keep her tingling fingertips from venturing out on their own. "The area where the bodies were found is part of an open space preserve. There was a cabin up there, taken out by the landslide. It took a little digging, but we discovered that before it became open space, the title was held by Barbara Sanford. It was donated in 1991."

Caroline's stomach sank as she sat back against the cushions. First the book. Now the bodies were found on land that belonged to James's first wife. "Jesus," she shook her head in disbelief. "I thought James was hiding something towards the end, but I thought it was an affair." Could he really have been responsible for those two bodies?

Could he really have—no she didn't want to go there yet. The pang of hunger that had reared at Danny's cooking died a swift death as her stomach fisted inside her.

There had to be another explanation, other than that she'd spent a decade married to a murderer.

"I never heard about any land, or any donation," Caroline said. "We can ask Kate."

Danny went to the stove, stirred his chicken and broccoli concoction and dumped pasta into the now boiling water. "Not yet. I don't want to clue anyone in until we know who to trust."

"We can trust Kate. I told you."

Slabs of muscle shifted under his shirt as he shrugged. "We just got off a case where a woman killed her parents and plotted to kill her sister in a fake drug overdose."

Caroline rolled her eyes. "Yeah, and the woman was Alyssa Miles and there were millions of dollars in blood diamonds to cover up."

"Why would someone be after James and after you, if not to cover something up?"

"Kate has nothing to do with James's death, and besides, she was too young when your mother disappeared to have had anything to do with that."

Danny forked up a bite of chicken from the pan, chewed thoughtfully, then grabbed one of the dozen spice jars he'd unearthed from her pantry and threw in a pinch of something. "Maybe she was helping her mother cover something up. James and Anne were having an affair. Susan got angry, killed Anne, hid the bodies in the cabin."

Caroline frowned, his emotionless theorizing sending a chill through her. How could he be so cold, referring to his mother as Anne, like she was a stranger. Then again, Danny had always been good at cutting off his emotions, separating himself, shutting out anything that distracted him from his duty. She had no doubt it had made him an awesome captain when he was in the Army.

But it had eventually made it impossible to have a relationship with him.

"What about the other body?" Caroline said.

"Was James into threesomes?"

"No!" Even the thought made her squirm.

"Not that you know of."

"Besides, I thought the other woman died after your mother." She watched to see if he reacted to her reminder of exactly who one of the victims was. Not even an eyelash quivered.

"Maybe. It's hard to know for sure." He opened a drawer and rifled through it. Caroline tried not to wince at the thought of him messing up her carefully organized utensils. She looked up and caught him watching her, his lips curved into the barest of smiles. Bastard was doing it on purpose, knowing how much it bugged her.

He used to do the same thing whenever he came over to her house. He'd pick a perfectly organized drawer and make a mess of its contents and ignore her pleas to stop. Only when she physically tackled him would he give in, and then because he was too distracted fooling around to mess with her anymore.

She wondered what he'd do if she tackled him now. Renewed heat pooled low in her belly, and she deliberately turned her back on him.

"Look, all I'm saying is in a situation like this, you can never rule anyone out. You never really know anyone as well as you think you do." He deposited a plate on the low table in front of her chair and set the other in his lap as he settled onto the love seat. A size twelve black shoe thumped on the table and he shoveled a mouthful of garlic scented pasta and chicken into his mouth.

She thought of James as she picked up her plate and twirled the fork tines through the pasta. She'd been shocked enough when she believed he was cheating on her. The thought that he could be a murderer . . . She set the plate back down, unable to muster any appetite.

"What I don't understand is why," Danny said as he polished off his mountain of pasta in a matter of seconds.

"I don't know why James would be involved with your mother, either," she replied.

"Not that," he shook his head and pinned her with an intent stare. "I want to know why you married him in the first place."

Oh God, she so didn't want to get into this with him. "I don't think it's appropriate for me to discuss the details of my marriage with you."

"Why?" he scoffed. "You already admitted you thought he was playing hide the salami with another woman. He may have killed my mother. It's not like you're going to dishonor his memory."

She bristled. Even if he hadn't been a perfect husband, James had been good to her. And it wasn't like she was wife of the decade either, marrying a man because he represented a safety net at a time when she was in a free-fall.

"Was it the money?" He sat back against the love seat in a casual sprawl, but she could see the tension rippling through every sinew. Danny was a predator, ready to pounce if she made one wrong move.

"Yes," she said bluntly, shoving down the hurt at the disappointment in his eyes. He'd lost the right to judge her a long time ago. "At least that was part of it." Caroline struggled to explain how weak she'd felt to a man who didn't understand the meaning of the word. "He was safe, stable."

"Since when did you need someone to take care of you? You were always kicking ass and taking names, keeping it together when everything else fell apart."

Yeah, but that was before you broke me. She wasn't even going to touch that. "I'm not superhuman like you, Danny. You remember everything that was going on," and was still going on. "Ricky had gone back to jail, Dad was out of work again, and Mom," she shook her head. There were no words for her mother. That was one of the things she and Danny had bonded over, beyond mutual teenage lust. Like Anne Taggart, Lena Palomares was an unhappy woman, from the roots of her silver streaked black hair to the callused bottoms of her feet. Unlike Anne, Lena may have had cause. Caroline could see how a delinquent son and an alcoholic husband could grind a woman down.

Her mother found no joy in anything. Not even a daughter who snagged herself a scholarship to an exclusive private high school, then put off her plans for college indefinitely to keep her parents from losing their house. Lena's unhappiness fueled her hypochondria. Every headache was a brain tumor, every bout of heartburn a heart attack or a gastric perforation. Her multiple trips to the urgent care clinic—sans health insurance, of course—nearly sank them, no matter how many tips Caroline pulled in working as a bartender at a chic San Francisco restaurant.

Danny knew all that. She didn't need to go into detail. Just as she wasn't about to lay out how he'd devastated her. How the long absences, how not knowing where he was or if he was coming back ground her down, even though she tried to put on a strong front, be the supportive girlfriend back home since he was out there saving the world after all.

Yeah, that had worked out well.

She'd limped along for nearly two years after they broke up, convincing herself it was for the best. Caroline wasn't cut out to be a military wife, holding strong at home while Danny was out there dodging bullets. And she couldn't spend the next fifty years needing a man who refused to be needed, much less ever let himself need her back.

"It was nice to lean on someone else for a change, instead of having to handle everything by myself. But it wasn't just money," she continued. She picked her plate up and took it to the sink, eager for an excuse to get away from him. "We had a lot of similar interests in books, literature and art. He loved to travel and took me all over the world."

"So you talked and read and looked at pretty pictures?" His eyebrow cocked skeptically. "That, along with a big fat bank account was enough to make you happy?"

"Yes," she said, avoiding his eyes so he wouldn't see the lie in hers. She rinsed her dish and bent to put it in the dishwasher.

"Bullshit."

She straightened and jumped back when she realized he was right next to her. How could a man his size make it across the room so fast and without her hearing him? "I was happy," she said, backing away until her butt hit the edge of the kitchen island.

"James was about to divorce you," he countered.

And she'd been happy about that too, but she wasn't about to admit it. "We'd grown apart."

"I can't imagine why," Danny leaned forward and braced his hands on the counter on either side of her hips. "You need more than friendship from a man, Caroline, and we both know it."

"You never know anyone as well as you think you do. You said it yourself."

"I know you well enough to know you need more than a polite tumble once or twice a year."

He was so close she could see each individual whisker on his dark skin. His eyes were liquid silver, framed by heavy dark lashes. "James and I had a fine sex life," she managed. Total lie. James had a fine sex life. Caroline put on a good show and gave a prayer of thanks when James's doctor told him he couldn't take Viagra anymore once he started his new heart medication. "Besides, sex isn't everything."

"Said like a woman who hasn't gotten it like she needs it in a good twelve years or so."

"You have no idea what I need." Oh, but he did. And judging by the thick column of flesh tenting out the front of his pants, he was just the one to give it to her.

"You need passion, Caroline," he said. One hand came off the counter to wrap around the base of her ponytail. He pulled, tilting her face up to his. "You're lying to yourself if you think you don't."

She felt his breath across her face, his grip tightening almost painfully in her hair. But his kiss wasn't the voracious, hungry assault she'd braced herself for. Danny was surprisingly gentle, his lips firm but soft, sucking, nipping as his tongue flicked out to tease the seam of her lips. She made a last ditch effort at retreat. "This will complicate things."

"I like complicated," he whispered.

She almost laughed. That was a load of crap and he knew it. Danny was the most black and white, you're in or you're out person she'd ever met. He didn't even like to admit his eyes were gray.

But she couldn't keep herself from responding to the stroking of his lips and tongue, the gentle nip of teeth. She knew exactly what he was doing. Holding back, asking to be let in, making her want it so much she would be the one to make it happen.

He still knew how to play her. Her lips parted, her tongue stole out to slide against his, and heat exploded between them like a nuclear bomb. Danny held her head still as he took her mouth.

She'd spent years trying to forget. The taste of his mouth, dark and rich and spicy, the smell of his skin. The feel of him, his lips hot and sweet against hers, the thick silk of his hair tangling around her fingers, the leather and cedar scent of him.

It was so good, so awesomely familiar, tears stung the backs of her eyes. He was right. She needed this. But she'd spent so long convincing herself that part of her was dead she'd forgotten how much.

Danny groaned against her mouth and wrapped his hands around her waist to lift her up onto the counter. Both hands came up to cup her face, his thumbs stroking across her cheekbones, tracing their way along her hairline as his mouth devoured her. God, she'd always loved the way he kissed her, like he couldn't get enough of her taste, like he could kiss her for the next hundred years and not care if it went any farther.

Desire tightened between her legs, so intense it was almost painful. She wrapped her arms around his back and pulled him closer, her breath quickening as his hips settled between her legs. His cock was a hard ridge against her throbbing sex, and even through their clothes, the heat of him was enough to burn her alive. She knew exactly how he'd feel inside her, hard and thick, stretching her almost to the point of pain as he worked himself inside.

This is such a bad idea. But she couldn't make herself push him away, especially when he was rocking his hips against her in a too familiar rhythm. And not when his big hand skated up her torso to cover her breast. And not when he pulled away from her mouth to fasten his lips on the exact spot on her neck guaranteed to send her into the stratosphere.

His fingers pinched her nipple through her sweater and she almost jumped out of her skin.

Danny Taggart was about to make her come in her kitchen and she wasn't going to do a single thing to stop it.

CHAPTER 7

Bells. That was a new one. Danny had never heard bells while kissing a woman before. Bombs, fireworks, a roaring in his head like a tsunami was coming in—he'd heard all of those in his head at one time or another. Especially with Caroline.

But never bells. Until now.

And why fucking not? She tasted even better than he remembered. Sweet, spicy, hot, her own unique taste custom made to drive him wild. He closed his mouth over a patch of skin on her neck, right under her ear, and groaned when she shuddered like she'd been hit with an electric current.

She still loved that. He remembered the first time he'd discovered the spot on her neck that he now licked, nipped, sucked. Back before she'd let him get past third base. He'd had his hand in her panties, his fingers soaked with her juice as he stroked her. Using every last bit of control he had to resist the urge to strip off his own clothes and beg her to please, please, just let him get inside her. Frustrated, he'd nipped Caroline's neck on that exact spot and she'd gone off like a rocket, jerking and moaning and shuddering against him.

Danny's cock got even harder at the little groans she was making in the back of her throat. God, he'd always loved those sounds, the way she couldn't hold back her pleasure. Now they were almost enough to make him unload in his pants. Her hands were all over him, rubbing up and down his back, over his ass, pulling him close until he could feel the heat of her pussy through her clothes and his. Her nipple was hard as a bullet beneath his fingers, driving him insane with the need to suck it into his mouth.

Bells. He wondered what sound he would hear when he finally got inside her.

But her hands stopped stroking him, and instead of pulling him closer she was pushing him away. He settled more firmly against her. No way was she stopping, not when he was this far gone.

He tried to cover her mouth with his and let out a frustrated grunt when she pulled away and flattened her hands against his chest.

"Doorbell," she said, half gasp, half moan. "Someone's at the door."

Danny shook his head, clearing away the red lust haze as her words registered.

Bells. The bells in his head were nothing but the doorbell. And what he'd thought was the sound of his heart beating out of his chest was someone pounding on the front door.

He stepped back and tried to slow his breath as she jumped off the counter and started for the door. He grabbed her arm to stay her. "Let me," he said. "After what happened today, I don't want you answering the door by yourself."

Danny walked to the entryway, forcing his mind back into some semblance of calm when all he wanted to do was grab Caroline, throw her to the floor, and finish what they'd started. She was only a step behind him, so close he could hear her agitated breathing, smell the combined scents of her perfume and arousal coming off her skin.

Yet another thing that hadn't changed. For Danny, being around Caroline meant pretty much a perpetual hard-on.

"Caroline, are you okay?" A female voice sounded through the door. "I know you're home—I saw your car in the garage. Please open the door. I'm worried about you." The speaker's accent thickened at the end. *Ahm wurried abay-out yew.*

"It's my friend Melody," Caroline said, trying to brush past him to open the door. He grabbed her hand before she could slide the deadbolt free and gave her a stern look.

"Let me make sure she's alone." He looked through the peephole and saw a blond woman whose big fake hair rivaled her big fake tits, but no one else. He nodded for Caroline to open the door.

"Oh my gawd, Caroline are you okay?" The woman hurled herself through the door on a wave of perfume and pulled Caroline into a fierce hug.

"I'm fine, Melody, really." Caroline gave her friend a brief squeeze and pulled out of her embrace.

Danny recognized the name from both the news coverage of the murder and the handful of e-mails she and Caroline had exchanged. Melody Easterbrook, the wife of Patrick Easterbrook, who had been portrayed in the press as James Medford's oldest, closest friend.

Danny had found it intriguing that while everyone seemed eager to buy into the idea of Caroline as a murderer, those closest to James had rallied around her.

"I saw what happened on the news. That's just terrible about Rachael and you were right there! You must have been so terrified," Melody's face pulled into a mask of sympathy. "I've been trying to call you all afternoon, and when you didn't answer I got so worried I decided to come over." Melody's heavily lined blue eyes locked on his. "But I see you're not alone."

"Melody, this is Danny Taggart. He's uh, an old friend of mine who's a private investigator. I hired him to help me look into James's case."

"An old friend, huh?" Melody quirked a perfectly arched brow and held out her hand. It was soft, smooth skinned, and tipped with lethal looking pinkish-orange nails.

He could see why Melody was skeptical. He'd totally wrecked Caroline's neat ponytail, and her hair lay in a messy tangle around her shoulders. Her cheeks were still flushed, her lips red and puffy from kissing. And he was pretty sure that was a scrape of whisker burn along her jaw. "Nice to meet you, Melody."

"Likewise, Danny Taggart." She shook his hand slowly, deliberately, before she released it.

He forced himself to stand still, impervious as she looked him over. He fought the urge to cup his hands in front of his crotch. Caroline wasn't the only one bearing signs of their little tussle in the kitchen.

"You're a private investigator, you said?" Melody asked, looking between him and Caroline like she didn't believe it for a second.

He pulled a card out of his wallet and held it out to her. "We specialize in private investigations as well as personal and corporate security," he said as she studied the card.

"Danny was with me today when . . ." Caroline stopped short and swallowed heavily. "He saved my life."

"Well thank God and the Baby Jesus he was there," Melody said.

"Can I offer you a drink or something, Melody?" Caroline asked, her hostess instinct making Danny want to grit his teeth. If it had been left up to him, he would have kicked Melody out on her pampered ass and gotten back down to business.

"That's sweet, honey, but I need to get back home before Patrick calls. He had to go out of town on business or he'd be here too. I was thinking I'd take you home with me since I don't want you to be alone tonight after what happened."

Her gaze flicked back to Danny. "But it looks like you're in good hands."

Danny nodded. "I'll stay with her tonight."

"If you do it will be in the guest room." Caroline interjected.

Melody patted her on the arm and gave her a knowing grin. "Whatever you say, sugar. I know it's awful, what happened to Rachael and all, but don't you worry. She wasn't the only high-powered attorney Patrick knows. We'll get you all squared away in no time, this time with someone who hasn't made so many enemies." Melody gave Caroline another quick squeeze and a kiss on the cheek and floated out the door on a perfumed cloud.

Caroline slid the deadbolt home and started back to the kitchen.

"Alarm?" he said. If her life was in danger, and he was pretty damn sure it was, she needed to be a lot more careful. Not that her alarm was even close to foolproof, as he'd discovered himself. He watched her key in the code. "How many people have the code?"

"Me, Kate, the cleaning lady, I think."

He shook his head impatiently. "Change it. From now on, the only one who knows it is you. Better yet, I'm going to call the office tomorrow and have someone replace your antiquated system."

"I just had this installed six months ago," she protested. "The guy assured me it was top of the line."

"And I'm telling you it's too easily compromised. You need to install infared motion detectors that will give you enough warning if someone breaks in. Right now all anyone has to do is cut the wires on the doors or windows and you're screwed." He struggled to keep himself calm as he was assaulted by images of Caroline lying vulnerable, alone in her bed, ignorant of the fact that someone was in her house and on his way to hurt her.

He knew it was crazy, getting close to her again, but in that moment he knew he wasn't letting her out of his sight until he knew she was safe.

"Right," she said. He could see her visibly choke back her fear, force herself to remain calm as she no doubt entertained visions that were as scary—or scarier than his. "Whatever you say."

Now that was an interesting proposition, he thought as he followed her back into the kitchen. As quickly as his brain jumped to terrifying visions of Caroline alone, vulnerable, and under attack, it jumped right back to where they'd been about ten minutes ago, before Melody's unwelcome interruption.

Caroline grabbed his mother's datebook off the breakfast bar and took a seat in one of the armchairs. "Like I said before, I've been through this a bunch of times and nothing popped up."

With her rounded shoulders and tightly crossed legs, Caroline's body language practically screamed, "Go away."

No problem. If she wanted to go back to the starting line and pretend he hadn't been about to lay her back on her breakfast bar and fuck her into oblivion, he'd let her. For now.

He ignored his cock, throbbing like a caged beast behind his zipper. *Patience grasshopper.* If he made good on his plan not to let Caroline out of his sight, he'd have plenty of opportunity to wear down her defenses.

He sat across from her and took the book from her hands, immediately sobering when he flipped the book open to June, 1991. A month before his mother disappeared. He flipped over another page.

"There was one entry with an address—" Caroline started.

"Where?" he cut her off and flipped through a couple of pages.

"Sometime in May, I think." She got up from her chair

and looked over his shoulder. A lock of her hair fell forward and teased his hand. He fought the urge to bring it to his nose for a deep, satisfying inhale. "There," she tapped her fingertip against the entry.

HH. 1223 Harper Ave. San Mateo.

His brain started going a thousand miles an hour and he got that weird prickly feeling in between his shoulders like he did whenever he was on to something.

"I looked it up," Caroline said, "but it's just a dentist's office. They've only been there for a little over five years."

"But what was it before?"

"No idea," she replied with a frown. Then understanding dawned on her face, followed by a look of self-recrimination. "Right. We need to find out what was there before, that would have interested your mom. Duh."

"Not quite as quick on the uptake as you once were," he chided, but his tone was teasing.

"Never had days like this before," she said with a tired smile, immediately followed by a jawcracking yawn. "Speaking of which, I think I need to go to bed." Her gaze flicked from his. "You're planning to stay tonight, right?"

He nodded, holding her stare with his, willing her to invite him to stay in that great big bed with her. Right now, he didn't give a shit that she'd shared it with another man. Besides, after Danny was done with her, any other man would be obliterated from her memory. Her pupils dilated slightly and her sweet little tongue flicked her plump bottom lip.

She shot up from the chair so quickly she staggered a little. "Good then. There are three empty bedrooms, pick whichever one you want. You probably don't want Kate's room because she still has the pink canopy bed she got when she was nine," she said in a nervous rush. "There are clean towels in the guest bathroom . . ." she trailed off.

"I'll be fine," he said. "Go get some sleep."

Fine. Yeah, he was pretty fucking fine all right, he thought forty-five minutes later. Still hard as a rock, trying to keep his mind off the woman upstairs by poring over the notes and scribblings that represented the last days of his mother's life.

His body was tired but his brain was doing its usual pinging around. He knew he wouldn't sleep, not with his brain on overdrive and Caroline upstairs tempting him like s siren. He went out to his car to retrieve his laptop, and settled in at the breakfast bar to start his search.

Bleary eyed after a restless night, Caroline was jolted to full awareness when she ran into a massive, damp, muscular chest in her upstairs hallway. Danny reached out to steady her as she bounced off him. The touch, combined with the awesome display of male near nudity was enough to make every nerve ending in her body sit up and say hello.

Why? Why did he have to look even better than he had at twenty-three? And why did he have to parade around almost naked, showing off his perfection and blowing apart her already shaky resolve? She'd barely been able to restrain herself the night before, and knew that if Melody hadn't shown up when she did, Caroline would have found herself naked and spread under Danny.

Even as she warned herself to steer clear, she couldn't tear her eyes away. Through clothes, she could see that Danny had packed on at least twenty pounds since they'd been together. Naked, it was clear it was all pure, powerful muscle. Bunching and rippling under acres of tanned skin. Skin that was covered in goosebumps.

"Is the hot water working?" She dragged her gaze up to his face, not that that was much better. His hair stood up in damp clumps, making her fingers itch to smooth it down. His jaw was scraped clean of stubble. She wanted to rub her cheek against it to see if it was as smooth as it looked. His wet eyelashes stuck together in pointy clumps, and the look in his gray eyes told her he'd noticed her lustful stare.

"It's working fine. Why?"

"You're covered in goosebumps, like you're cold." She, on the other hand was going to have a core meltdown if she didn't get away from him soon. She wanted to trace her tongue down the deep groove of muscle bisecting his abs, pull away the towel, take him in her mouth. Rediscover the hot, musky taste of him. The towel twitched before her eyes, tenting out in front as a skyscraper of an erection threatened to pull the towel from his waist.

"So much for my cold shower," he muttered. He stomped past her into one of the guest rooms and slammed the door.

By the time he joined her downstairs forty-five minutes later—fully dressed, thank God—Caroline had managed to pull herself together. After her shower she'd pulled on jeans, a turtleneck, and a thick knit wool sweater, as much a barrier against him as to the cold.

"Did James ever mention Harmony House?" he asked as he poured himself a cup of coffee from the stainless steel carafe.

"Doesn't ring a bell. Why?"

"That's what the HH stands for in Anne's book," he replied. "The address used to be the location for Harmony House, a home for teenage girls who were pregnant. They've since moved to a bigger facility."

"I can't imagine James had anything to do with a shelter for pregnant teens." Not that he hadn't been philanthropic, but his charities of choice usually centered around disease. Caroline was the one who'd been involved in various community groups, and James had never shown any interest whatsoever in helping kids of any flavor in the community.

"Well we're going to pay them a visit and find out."

Harmony House's new headquarters was a massive

craftsman style house in a neighborhood just off the freeway in San Mateo. Danny parked next to the tree lined sidewalk across the street from the house. A concrete walkway
bisected a patch of lawn, leading to the front steps of a
house that, while homey and inviting, looked a little frayed
around the edges. A slat was missing from the railing on the
stairs, and the paint curled in a couple of spots near the
door.

Their knock was answered by a girl with strawberry
blond hair and freckles, who couldn't have been older than
fourteen. She sized them up with eyes as jaded as any thirty-
year-old's.

"Yeah?" she said in a tone that would have gotten Caroline smacked in the mouth at the same age.

"We need to ask some questions about someone who
might have worked here," Danny said.

"You the police?" The muscles in the girl's arms tensed,
poised to slam the door in their faces.

"We're not the police," Caroline said quickly. "We're trying to find information about someone who disappeared a
long time ago. It has nothing to do with anyone who lives
here now," she added, when the mulish curve of the girl's lip
told Caroline she was about to get blown off.

The girl finally shrugged and turned around with a vague
motion for them to follow. Her pregnancy was so advanced,
her belly so huge, Caroline couldn't imagine how she even
managed the awkward waddle as she made her way down a
dark hallway.

The sound of television and girls talking rang through the
halls as they followed the girl. Caroline peeked into the
doorway of a sitting room and saw two girls sitting on a
couch. One was nearly as pregnant as their guide. The other
was cradling a baby wrapped in a blanket. Both had their
heads bent over the baby, whispering as they took turns
stroking the baby with gentle hands.

That could have been me. Caroline's throat went tight at the thought. Of course, she had been older than these girls. And she wouldn't have been alone.

It could have all been so different.

"Caroline, are you coming?" Danny's voice snapped her back to reality and she hurried to catch up.

The girl knocked on a door marked simply, "Office," and opened the door at the muffled, "come in."

An African-American woman with elaborate braids and a no nonsense attitude looked up at their entry. She sat behind a cheap laminate desk, covered in such a mess of paper it made Caroline's fingers twitch with the need to straighten everything into neat, organized piles. A name plate on the front edge indicated her name was LaTanya Jackson.

"What is it, Ginger?" LaTanya asked.

"People to see you," Ginger said, indicating Danny and Caroline with a thumb over her shoulder. Without another word, the girl turned and waddled back down the hall.

Danny introduced them both and cut right to the chase. "We're private investigators working on a missing persons case, possibly a homicide, and we're hoping you can help us out."

The woman gestured, indicating for them to take a seat in the hard plastic chairs opposite her desk, her brow knit with concern. "Is this regarding one of our residents?"

"We think it was someone who might have volunteered here, or worked here in some capacity."

"When did she work here?"

"It would have been sometime back in 1991," Danny said.

LaTanya shook her head. "I've been here a long time, but not that long. I'm afraid I wouldn't have known your friend."

"Did they keep records of all the volunteers?" Caroline asked, shifting to get comfortabe in the hard plastic seat.

"Maybe we could take a look, just to make sure we're on the right track."

LaTanya barked out a humorless laugh. "Records? Let's just say the former director wasn't too keen on paperwork. She barely kept up with the residents, much less anyone coming in and out."

Danny's jaw tightened in frustration. "Where is the former director now? I'd like to talk to her, see if she recognizes the woman we're looking for."

Again LaTanya shook her head. "She'd be the one to talk to, but unfortunately Christine Williams died in a car accident fifteen years ago. I came in to replace her, and let me tell you she left this place a god-awful mess. It took me six months just to get the bookkeeping worked out and get the girls' information into the computer system." She launched into a laundry list of all the things Christine Williams had left undone. Losing track of the volunteers wasn't even the half of it.

Caroline jumped in when she paused to take a breath. "What about former residents? You said she kept their information on file. If we could talk to some of the girls who were living here then—"

LaTanya cut her off. "No can do. We have strict confidentiality rules. A lot of the girls who come through here don't want anyone to know they've ever been pregnant or had babies. I'm afraid I can't share any of that information with you."

"The information would be used to solve a crime," Danny said, and Caroline could tell he was barely keeping his temper in check. "Surely that's good reason to bend the rules." Danny sat forward in his chair, leaning into the desk, using his sheer size to will LaTanya into compliance.

LaTanya just leaned forward herself, not batting so much as an eyelash as she met Danny's hostile gray stare head on. "I don't bend the rules for anybody. My job is to protect these girls, and unless the police show up with a warrant to search through my records, I'm keeping them sealed."

Danny nodded and pushed up from his chair. Caroline rose as well, offered her hand to LaTanya and thanked her for her time. LaTanya ushered them back into the hall and closed the office door with a decisive click.

"Well that was a bust," Caroline muttered. Damn, why did everything have to lead to a dead end?

"Not entirely."

"We didn't find out squat. We still don't know if your mother has ever even been here."

"There's more than one way to get information," Danny said.

"Like what?"

"I'd tell you but then I'd have to kill you." It was said with a cocked eyebrow and a half smile that hit Caroline straight in the chest. She knew that look, a look that said he was up to no good but that she was going to love the results.

As he started down the dim hallway, Caroline caught sight of a small figure hovering in the first doorway down from LaTanya's office. When she realized she'd been spotted, she immediately made herself busy sweeping nonexistent dirt from the hardwood floor.

She looked to be in her late forties or early fifties, and Latina. It was obvious she'd been eavesdropping. "Excuse me," Caroline said. "I was wondering, how long have you worked here?"

The woman shook her head. "No Ingles," and started to retreat down the hall.

Caroline repeated the question in Spanish.

"*Veinte anos,*" the woman replied somewhat reluctantly.

She looked up at Danny to see if he understood. "Twenty years. So she would have been here."

Caroline nodded. "How's your Spanish?" she asked.

"Not as good as yours, but if you ask her some questions I can follow along."

Caroline introduced herself and learned the woman's name was Ines. Ines had worked as a cook and a cleaning lady for the shelter for over twenty years. Though the girls had to help with chores as part of their board, Ines made sure everything got done.

"Do you have time to answer a few questions about someone who might have worked here?"

Ines's brown eyes were wide and wary. "Are you the police?"

"No," Danny said in his own stilted Spanish. "We're trying to find out what happened to someone. Someone who was lost, and now she's dead."

Ines's eyes flashed with panic, immediately followed by resolve. She swallowed hard and nodded. "I think I know who you are talking about. You're talking about the blond lady who disappeared, and everyone thinks she ran away from her family."

Every muscle in Danny's face seemed to tighten as he held out Anne's picture to Ines. Ines studied it for several long seconds, then handed it back to Danny with a nod. "I remember her. She volunteered here for a little while, and then one day she didn't come back."

Chapter 8

The girl writhed in pain, sweat soaking her hairline as she let out another low, almost bovine moan. Patrick Easterbrook checked the girl's IV and nodded for the nurse to pump another dose of fentanyl into the line. It wouldn't come close to the relief that an epidural would provide, but it would take the edge off the contractions. He only had limited doses of the epidurals, and needed to save those for the C-sections.

Besides, he was a radiologist, not an anesthesiologist, so in theory he had no business putting in a spinal block on anyone. Then again, he shouldn't be delivering babies, but here he was.

He snapped on a fresh pair of gloves and reached up under the girl's gown, avoiding her accusing stare as he did so. She said something and spat at him. He didn't understand the language—it sounded vaguely Eastern European to his uneducated ear, but the sentiment was clear.

"She's nine centimeters dilated and 100 percent effaced," he said to the nurse, who also kept her eyes averted from the girl's angry stare. Patrick didn't know the nurse's name— didn't want to know her name. It was better that way. He didn't want to know any of the other employees in Gates's enterprise. "It should happen in the next hour or so."

The nurse nodded and offered the girl a cup. Ice chips littered the floor as the girl smacked the cup out of the nurse's hand, her body convulsing with another contraction.

"You have to breathe," the nurse said to the girl in heavily accented English. "Breathe through the pain."

The girl's only response was a low sob as pain overtook her.

Patrick's cell phone buzzed inside his scrub pocket. He looked at the display and stepped out to take the call. "Hey Mel," trying to keep his tone light. He was supposed to be at a radiology conference in Los Angeles, and his wife had an uncanny knack for picking up any tension over the phone lines. "Can we keep this short? I'm about to step into another session."

"Okay, but I was hoping you could chat since you missed our call last night." He could hear the pout in her voice. Still, just her voice was enough to make his tension ease a couple of degrees, reminding him of why this was all worth it. He'd do whatever it took to give his wife and daughter everything they wanted.

But it wasn't just about money. Hadn't been for a long time. Patrick would protect this operation at all costs if it meant keeping Melody and Jennifer safe.

"I know, but dinner ran late." In truth, he'd been monitoring the girl whose water had broken late yesterday afternoon. In a stroke of good luck, Patrick was there anyway, checking up on the status of the other girls so he could report back on upcoming inventory.

Another lowing moan came from the room across the hall.

"What in the world was that noise?" Melody asked as Patrick hurried away from the noise, down the corridor into another section of the house.

"Just the TV in the hotel lobby," Patrick explained. "Now did you have something you wanted to talk about, because really, honey, I have to run." He was next to the lab now, where the nurses drew blood and monitored the girls' hormone levels in preparation. Patrick had to hand it to Gates. Looking at the rambling farmhouse and barn from the outside, no one would ever imagine it contained a fully equipped blood analysis lab, two labor and delivery suites, and accommodations for up to thirty girls in various stages of pregnancy.

When he and James had first connected with Gates five years ago, it had been an ad hoc operation. If one of Gates's girls got knocked up, James worked to find an adoptive family while Patrick made sure the girl and the baby were healthy until the baby was delivered. But they had quickly seen the potential upside of matching birth mothers and fathers who resembled the adoptive parents. Gates had put in the capital investment to build the facility and made sure he maintained a steady, healthy supply of girls of varying ethnicities and coloring. Before that, it had been a fluke when the birth mother so strongly resembled the adoptive parents. Now Gates had it worked out so adoptive families could practically custom order a baby that would fit perfectly within their family.

A tall blond girl was escorted past him by a woman who held her arm in an iron grip. With her blond hair almost to her waist and long limbs, she had the kind of Nordic perfection so many of their clients desired. Her issue would get them close to half a million, he had no doubt.

"Oh fine," Melody said. "I just wanted to tell you I went over to check on Caroline last night. I still can't believe what happened to Rachael."

Patrick's gut clenched as he listened to Mel rattle on. Yeah, he couldn't believe it either. Couldn't believe that, for a second time, Caroline had somehow survived unscathed. The woman had more lives than a damned cat.

"Did you know she hired a private investigator?"

Patrick's stomach sank somewhere down around his knees. "She mentioned something about talking to someone." *Please don't tell me Taggart decided to help her.*

"Some great big hunk of man meat—no offense sweetie— named Danny Taggart. She says he's helping her investigate James's death, but I think she's helping him with something else if you know what I mean." Her tinkling laughter usually brought a smile to his face but right now it was like nails on a chalkboard. Danny Taggart. Of all the fucking bad luck.

For eighteen years Patrick and James's secrets had remained safe. Now Caroline had invited Anne Taggart's son to dig into her life and James's, and God help him if they managed to uncover the truth.

"Even so, this guy is legitimate," Melody continued. "I Googled him, and it turns out his firm is the one that found that kidnapped girl over in Atherton, and his brother uncovered the plot to kill Alyssa Miles."

Patrick closed his eyes as a cold sweat of panic bloomed across his shoulders. Yeah, he knew all about Danny Taggart and Gemini Securities and their uncanny ability to get to the heart of the truth, no matter what the evidence said.

They had to find those records James was stupid enough to keep, the ones he was stupid enough to threaten to use against Gates and Patrick when they refused to let him out of the operation. James always did have more of a guilty conscience about the operation, but in the past four years since his grandson had been born, the guilt had kicked into high gear. It was different before Gates came into the picture, he insisted. Back then, they were finding better situations.

Patrick had hated to see him killed, but he agreed with Gates and Marshall that it was the only way. They couldn't let James's newfound misgivings ruin them all.

He felt a soft brush against his arm. He looked down at the nurse.

"It's coming," she mouthed.

"Honey, I really need to go," he said. "I'll be home tonight."

Half an hour later he placed another call, this time to Marshall, on an untraceable prepaid cell phone. "The shipment has arrived. Seven pounds, five ounces, baby girl as requested."

The nurse walked by with a blanket-wrapped bundle in her arms, and Patrick ignored the wails coming from the delivery room. She'd known she wouldn't keep her baby. She'd get over it.

"Great," Marshall said, and Patrick could almost see his green eyes light up with greed. "I'll tell them to wire the funds tomorrow. You'll get your cut within the week."

In time to pay his malpractice premium, his mortgage, Jennifer's college tuition, and alimony to his bitch of a first wife whose extravagance got him into this business in the first place. She'd been sucking him dry ever since Patrick announced he was leaving her for Mel, making sure he could never get out from under Gates's thumb, even if he wanted to.

No matter. There were lots of childless couples all over the country with deep pockets, willing to pay anything to get a healthy baby, especially one likely to resemble one or both of the adoptive parents. Business was good, his cut was generous, and as long as they kept Caroline Medford from screwing everything up, the business showed no signs of slowing down.

"I don't understand why it was such a big secret," Caroline huddled against the damp January chill as they walked to her car. Danny was about a millisecond from taking off his heavy leather coat and draping it over her shoulders before he stopped himself.

That was too much of a lover-like, boyfriendy gesture, something he would have done in the past. Danny wanted to get back in her pants, sure, but he didn't want to create any confusion about their relationship in the meantime. Instead he opened the passenger door for her, settled himself in the driver's seat and cranked up the heat.

She didn't even question that he'd drive her car. Just like before.

He forced himself to get his mind out of the past and back to what they were dealing with, namely his mother's volunteer work at the girls' shelter, and why she was so determined to keep it secret. According to Ines, Anne had started volunteering there in May, around the date they found in her appointment book. It was there that she met James Medford.

James had been coming to the shelter regularly for a couple of years, according to Ines. He'd show up every once in a while and meet with the director and various residents. Ines had no idea what the meetings were about. They were always conducted behind closed doors, and since her English wasn't very good, she wouldn't have been able to understand anyway.

"So why didn't you or the director ever go to the police when Anne turned up missing?" Danny had asked. Between the news stories and his father's own publicity, Anne's picture had been plastered across the state for the first six months after she disappeared. Ines would have had to have seen it.

Ines looked at him like he was crazy. "I couldn't risk getting deported. I didn't have my green card then, and I needed this job to send money back home to my kids."

Danny tried not to let his anger show—nothing they could do about it anyway. But it was maddening, to think all the time they'd been searching for her, someone had been holding back one tiny, but critical piece of information.

"Who knows what she was thinking?" he said as he pulled into the street. "Maybe she wanted to stick it to Dad with her secret life, make him squirm, wondering where she was, who she was with, when really she was doing volunteer work. You tell me why women play the games they do," he said as he turned onto the highway.

Caroline's dark eyes narrowed into a glare. "I have no idea what was going on in your parents' relationship. But it was obvious to anyone she was unhappy. Not all women play games, Danny."

"Right. They just tell you they want one thing when really they want something else entirely." He could have bitten his tongue in half. That didn't sound like a guy who was indifferent to what happened in the past. He needed to stop being such a chick and get over it already. "So now we know the connection between James and Anne—"

"Do you think they were sleeping together?" Caroline said, distaste at the idea apparent in her tone.

He'd second that. Even though he had suspected his mom of having affairs, he didn't want to think about her actually sleeping with anyone. "No idea, and I don't really want to go there. For now let's focus on what we know—that they knew each other—and figure out what was going on before she died."

"We need to talk to the girls who lived there."

Danny took the exit off the freeway near Gemini's offices. "If LaTanya has the records in a networked computer Toni will have them in minutes. If not, there are other ways to get access." If the shelter received money from the county, they would most likely have records of who had lived there over the years. Barring that, Danny was always up for a little B&E, providing it was in the name of a good cause.

He turned the Mercedes into the Gemini parking lot and

braced himself. His brothers had been on his ass, leaving messages left and right ever since they'd learned he was with Caroline the day before when Rachael Weller was killed.

Not only did they want to know if there was anything to the land connection, thanks to the GPS locators all three brothers wore at all times, Derek and Ethan knew damn well he'd slept over at Caroline's last night.

He took Caroline's arm in an unconscious gesture and guided her up the stairs and into the building. Kara Kramer looked up from the receptionist desk. Danny checked his watch. It was only twelve-fifteen.

"Shouldn't you still be in school or something?"

Kara sat back in her seat. "I'm doing my work-study program in criminal justice. Toni signed off on it."

"As long as you're making yourself useful."

Kara rolled her eyes and held up a ball of wadded up papers. "Ben has me working on his expense reports."

Danny didn't envy her for a second. Moreno was great in the field, but his organization in the office majorly sucked. Then again, it was no secret Kara was nursing a giant crush on the security specialist, leftover from the fall morning when Ben had helped rescue Kara from kidnappers who would have sold her to a bunch of wealthy perverts willing to pay top dollar to deflower virgins.

Ben, who loved female attention in all its forms, indulged Kara but was careful never to cross the line, even though Kara made a big deal of reminding everyone she was eighteen now.

Ethan was in the lobby waiting for them, having seen them on the video monitors as they approached. "So Danny, what's the sitch?" His laser-blue eyes flicked meaningfully to Danny's hand resting on Caroline's arm.

Danny tamped down the urge to snatch his hand back like he was afraid of getting cooties. Let Ethan speculate all he wanted about what was going on with him and Caroline. If it wasn't true yet, it would be soon.

"Go get Derek and meet me in the conference room."

Five minutes later, both Ethan and Derek were glaring daggers at him. Anne's appointment book lay in the middle of the polished wood table.

"Why the fuck didn't you tell us about this?" Ethan yelled, slamming his hand down on the table.

"The real question," Derek said, his quiet tone somehow more menacing than Ethan's explosion, "is how long have you been keeping this from us to protect your husband?"

"What are you talking about?" Caroline asked, her head tilting forward like she wasn't sure what she'd just heard.

"It's quite a coincidence," Derek said, walking around the table until he stood next to Caroline's chair, "that the book would suddenly turn up when we find Mom's body. And well after your husband is dead and unavailable to answer questions."

"Derek, back off," Danny growled. He'd had his initial doubts, but he knew in his bones Caroline wouldn't have kept evidence like that from them, no matter how angry she was at Danny.

Caroline jumped in to defend herself. "Are you kidding me, Derek?" Danny had to give it to Caroline. There weren't too many women who could go head to head with Derek when he was turning on the cold menace, but Caroline was too pissed to be nervous. "Do you really think I would keep something like that from you?"

"If it meant protecting your husband. You dumped Danny flat on his ass. Why should we think you'd have any loyalty?"

That stung, Danny could tell. Caroline closed her eyes and swallowed hard, and when she opened them up they were shiny with tears. "Whatever you think happened between me and Danny, I loved him," she kept her eyes carefully averted from his, and Danny felt something twist open in his chest. "And you guys were like little brothers to me. I never would have done that to you."

Derek and Ethan looked at each other. Their expressions didn't change, but Danny knew they were having one of their annoying twin to twin telepathyfests, deciding what to do about Caroline. They needed to understand the decision had already been made, case closed.

"Caroline, will you excuse us a minute?" Danny asked. He walked over to her chair and muscled Derek out of the way so he could help her stand. "I need to talk to my brothers in private."

"Why, so you can talk about me and how you think I hid evidence that would help you find your mother until it was convenient for me to reveal it?" Caroline tried to jerk her arm out of his grip as he steered her to the door. "You told me you believed me, Danny." Her eyes were dark, pleading for him to trust her.

And the hell of it was, he did. In this anyway. He had from the moment she'd first shown him the book. "And I meant that," he said, so soft it was almost inaudible. But it was enough to send a wash of relief across her face, for her to reach up and squeeze his arm in reassurance. Sometimes, like right then with her smiling up at him, her beauty hit him like a sucker punch to the nose, taking away his breath, making him dizzy as stars exploded behind his eyes. With her creamy, flawless skin and soft pink mouth, her hair tumbling in waves around her shoulders, she could have easily been the sixteen-year-old he'd fallen in love with practically at first sight.

Danny used every shred of restraint to keep himself from bending his head and covering her mouth with his. But he knew he'd never hear the end of it from Derek and Ethan. Hell, he was in for a major ass chewing as it was. "Go wait in my office—second door on the left. You'll see my name on the door."

He turned to face Ethan and Derek, their hostile stances almost identical.

The best defense was a good offense with these two. He walked over to where they stood and got right in their faces. "Lay the fuck off her. She's been through enough lately without you two jumping all over her."

"Is this the same guy who accused *me* of thinking with *my* dick not too long ago?" Ethan asked, catching Danny with an openhanded blow to the chest for emphasis.

"You've got to admit it looks bad, Danny," Derek said. "She was married to that guy for ten years, and she never came across it?"

"You both told me I should help her," he reminded them.

"That was before we knew she was hiding evidence that could have helped us find Mom."

"She found it right before the funeral," Danny said. "I know she's telling the truth."

"Really?" Ethan said. "The last time you saw her before the memorial service was twelve years ago when she dumped you for not calling her right when you got into town. You really think you still know her well enough to know if she's lying? Or are you protecting her for the opportunity to dip your wick in an old pot?"

Danny winced at the crudity. "Come on, this is Caroline. Don't talk about her like that."

Ethan and Derek's eyes widened. Yeah, yeah, Danny knew what they were thinking. They were remembering every one of the locker room type comments he'd had about both their girlfriends until it became clear the women were there to stay. Not to mention the crude comments Danny had made about Caroline after she dumped him.

Still, he didn't want anyone badmouthing Carrie, not even his brothers.

"Besides," he continued, "I'm not dipping my wick any-where—"

"Yet," Derek and Ethan interrupted in unison.

Okay, he'd give them that. "I'm treating her like a regular case." *Liar. You've never had a client you wanted to strip naked and bend over your desk.* "Someone killed her husband and, based on what happened yesterday, is trying to kill her too. In the meantime, she's helping me figure out what James Medford had to do with Anne's disappearance."

"Fine, assume she's telling the truth," Derek said. "Why the fuck would you keep something like this from us?"

"I wanted to wait and see if there was anything to it."

"How could you not think there was anything to it, when we already know about his first wife owning the land where the bodies were found?" Ethan said.

"I didn't want to get anyone's hopes up." The excuse sounded lame to his own ears. They knew he was working with Caroline, knew about the connection to James's first wife. He had a bad feeling he knew the answer, and it wasn't one he liked. He'd hidden it from his brothers because he'd wanted to avoid this conversation. Didn't want them to question his judgment about the only woman who'd ever been able to get under his skin. "And I knew the second I told you anything, you'd drop everything else. We have clients who have hired us, and we can't ignore them to focus on this investigation."

"Controlling son of a bitch," Ethan bit out. "You had no right to keep us in the dark. And while you were off playing cowboy, we could have been helping you."

"And that's why I'm here now," Danny said. "You guys are pissed. I get it. But we can either keep yapping about this like a bunch of blue hairs at a bridge game, or we can get down to business."

Caroline did another circle around Danny's office, too keyed up to sit still. The furnishings were spare. A wide maple desk topped with a flat screen monitor. A leather rolling desk chair and a built in bookshelf full of books about World War II. The only decorations were a picture of him with his father and brothers. All three Taggart boys were dressed in their military dress uniforms, Danny and Derek in olive green, Ethan shining in Navy whites. Tall and strong and every girl's soldier fantasy come to life.

Caroline had been devastated when Danny told her he was going to West Point. But she still remembered how the sight of him in his dress uniform made everything below her wasit perk up and say hello.

Don't go there. She turned away from the picture and focused her attention on the desk. Papers and files covered the surface in haphazard stacks. She started straightening to give herself something to do. Within seconds a familiar calm came over her. Her world might be spinning out of control, but she could create order, no matter how insignificant.

"Were you really engaged to Danny?"

Caroline looked up from her organizing to see Toni, the tall, dark haired woman she'd seen with Ethan at the memorial service. The woman was beautiful, with Snow White coloring and a lean, athletic body. Her heavy dark rimmed glasses, severe haircut, and outfit of skinny jeans, T-shirt, and hoodie gave her the look of an indie-rock star.

Caroline lined up a stack of files so the edge was parallel to the edge of the desk. "It was a long time ago."

"I just can't believe Danny was ever close to getting married. I mean, he barely has any friends, much less girlfriends."

"He was a lot different back then. We both were."

Toni cocked a dark brow over her glasses. "Yeah? How so?"

"We were high school sweethearts. Really young." *Really dumb. Really naïve. Really foolish.* She thought about the last year of her life. *Maybe I haven't really changed that much.*

"They've been talking about you since you showed up at the memorial service," the woman said, staring at Caroline like she was a particularly exotic animal in the zoo.

"I didn't realize you worked here too," Caroline said in an attempt to ease the awkward silence.

"Danny calls me the nerd patrol," she said with a smile. "I specialize in electronic investigations. I'm also Ethan's girlfriend."

"Now there's a guy I never thought would settle down." Even as a teenager, Ethan had been a Lothario in training.

"Exactly my impression when I first met him," Toni said, her red lips slanting in a grin. "But within a week he'd saved my life and moved me into his place, and the rest is history." Her smile took on a dreamy, satisfied look that left no doubt Ethan was taking *very* good care of Toni in every way that counted. "Back to Danny," Toni said. "Were you seriously high school sweethearts? Personally I can't imagine Danny ever being sweet to anybody."

Caroline's mouth stretched into a smile at the woman's brazen curiosity. "Sweet? No Danny was never sweet. But he was—"

"Huge? Hot? A total stud in the sack?"

Hot color flooded Caroline's face when she heard Danny's voice. *All of the above.* "I was going to say intense," she said and he arched his left eyebrow. "And you can take that however you want to."

"Toni, if you're done trying to pry into my love life, I have a system I need you to hack."

Toni gave Danny a mock salute and clicked her heels. "Aye, aye, *mein führer*. Let me get my system up and I'll get on it."

Danny rolled his eyes but didn't say anything as Toni disappeared down the hall. Caroline made to follow but was stopped by Danny's hand on her arm. She could feel the heat of that touch all the way through her wool sweater and cotton T-shirt underneath.

"Intense, huh?" He stood with his head bent intimately over hers, so close she could feel his hot breath tease her hairline. Her nipples chafed inside her bra, and she fought the crazy urge to rub up against his chest for some relief.

Danny's office was suddenly ten degrees warmer. She wanted to strip off at least one layer of clothing. What was wrong with her? They were supposed to be investigating a murder, if not two, and she was letting herself get carried away by memories of the past.

And the present, she thought, unable to get the taste of his kiss from the night before out of her mouth. It was exactly the same, and completely different, and part of her— the foolish, impulsive part of her that never seemed to learn its lesson with him—wanted to strip him down and catalog all the ways he was the same and different after all those years. She gave herself a mental shake and pulled herself out of it. "There were a lot of things I could have said," Caroline said, deliberately stepping back and pulling her arm from his grip. "But I get the feeling Toni likes you, and I didn't want to badmouth you to a friend."

His full lips quirked into that sexy half smile and she knew he wasn't buying it for an instant. He let her walk past him down the hall, but she knew her reprieve was only temporary.

Danny pointed her a few doors down. She stepped into an office where Toni sat behind a desk outfitted with half a dozen computer monitors and a laptop. Two standard tower units hummed under the desk. Ethan stood behind Toni. His hand rested on her shoulder, his thumb moving back and forth in an absentminded caress that spoke volumes.

"Okay, I'm all fired up. Tell me what we're looking for."

"I need you to get into the records for Harmony House. It's a shelter for pregnant teens in San Mateo. We need to know who the residents were in the six month window around when Anne disappeared."

Irritation pricked at the back of Caroline's shoulders at his continued use of his mother's first name, as though he could keep his distance, forget he was emotionally invested in the case as long as he didn't acknowledge their relationship. "We know your mother," she emphasized the syllables, "started in May, and according to Ines she stopped showing up in July."

To Caroline's astonishment, Toni had the records within minutes. There were six names on the list. Toni quickly printed out the list and handed it to Danny.

"Okay, let's divide and conquer. I'll take these two, Ethan, you take these, and Derek," he said to his brother who had joined them, "take these. Let's find these girls and try to set up face to face meetings if they're still local. We need to know everything they remember about Anne and James Medford."

Within a few hours they had located all but one of the girls. Two lived out of state—Amber Tomkins lived in Tacoma, Washington, and Maria Lopez lived outside of Phoenix. Another, Serena Washington, had relocated south to Los Angeles, and Constance Morales lived outside of Sacramento. Only one—Lauren Adams, now Lauren Schiffer—was local. She lived about five miles away in Palo Alto.

There was no sign of the sixth girl, Emily Parrish. According to the records, she'd moved out of Harmony House on June 26, and vanished into thin air.

"Doesn't look like anyone was too worried about her though," Derek said. "No missing persons reports were ever filed.

"Okay, let's try to get everyone to talk over the phone. I'm going to try to set up a meeting with Lauren Schiffer."

According to their research, Lauren lived in Palo Alto with her husband, a professor at nearby Stanford University, and her two school-age sons. It hadn't been easy to get Lauren to agree to talk to them. At first she'd insisted she'd never lived at Harmony House—they must have the wrong woman.

"I'm investigating the disappearance of Anne Taggart," Danny said. "I promise I won't take up much of your time."

Silence poured over the phone line and he could feel her weighing whether or not to talk to them. It was clear from her initial reaction, she didn't want anyone to know she'd once lived at the shelter.

"Maybe we should just swing by your husband's office and ask him if he knows anything," Danny said.

Lauren agreed to meet them in a coffee shop two towns over. "But I have to be back by eight," she said.

He parked the car and followed Caroline across the street, his hand resting in the small of her back. When she tried to inch away, he slid his hand more firmly around her waist. She might as well get used to him having his hands on her again. The curve of her waist was just the start.

A rush of warm, coffee scented air hit them as he opened the door. It was easy to spot Lauren, as she was the only woman over the age of twenty-five in the place. She sat alone, her eyes fixed on the door, her hands wrapped around the paper cup in front of her.

As they approached her table she stood up and nervously stuck out her hand. Around his age of thirty-five, give or take a year on either side, Lauren was pretty in a kind of matronly way. Fine lines fanned out from clear blue eyes, and her auburn hair was straight and grazed her chin. Jeans and a cardigan showed off a body that had done moderately well through the rigors of having two children.

Well, three, assuming the one she had as a teenager made it to term.

"I don't have much time," Lauren said as she sat down and motioned for them to do the same. "My husband took the boys to a movie, but I have to be back when he gets home."

Danny nodded. "This shouldn't take much time. We just need to ask you about a few people you might have come in contact with while you were living at Harmony House."

Tension carved deep lines around Lauren's mouth. "If I answer your questions you have to swear you won't tell anyone I ever lived there," she said, her voice barely audible. Her lips pressed into a tight line. "No one has any idea I ever lived there, that I ever had another—" she stopped and shook her head, unable to force the word "baby" out. "He can never know."

Caroline reached out and laid her hand over Lauren's. "I'm sorry we have to force you revisit what's obviously a painful subject, but we wouldn't be here if it weren't really important."

Lauren nodded.

"Do you recognize this woman?" Danny held out his cell phone with Anne's picture on the screen. "We think she was a volunteer at Harmony House while you were a resident."

"Yes," Lauren nodded. "That's Anne. I can't remember her last name, but I remember she was really nice, always trying to help us figure out what we were going to do once we had to leave the shelter."

"Her last name is Taggart. Anne Taggart."

"She's Danny's mother," Caroline interjected.

Danny watched Lauren's face for understanding to dawn,

for her to put the name together with the one she'd been hearing in the news lately.

Nothing. Instead she asked, "Really? How is she?"

"Do you follow the news, Lauren?" Caroline asked gently.

"Not really, why?"

"Because Anne Taggart went missing eighteen years ago, and her body was recently discovered outside of La Honda."

Lauren covered her mouth in horror, then looked around to make sure no one was listening to their conversation. "I'm so sorry. I had no idea. All I knew was that Anne stopped showing up one week, and after that I moved out of the area. I never heard anything about her disappearing. I'm really sorry I can't help you—" she started to stand up.

Danny caught her hand and gently forced her back down. He called up another picture on his phone. "We're not finished yet. How about this man? Do you recognize him?" He held out his phone so she could look at an older picture of James Medford.

Lauren's already pale complexion turned the color of chalk. "Yes," she said after several seconds of silence. "I recognize him. That's Jack Murphy. He's the man who convinced me to sell my baby."

CHAPTER 9

"He what?" Caroline felt like she'd taken a fist to the stomach. There had to be some mistake.

"He paid me twenty thousand dollars to give up my baby for adoption," Lauren said, her voice a whisper as she leaned closer.

Caroline was going to be sick. There was no way James could have been involved in something like that. "But you said his name was Jack Murphy. This man's name is James Medford. He is—was my husband. Maybe it's not the same man." She was grasping at straws and she knew it.

Lauren shook her head. In the low light of the coffee bar, Caroline could see the sheen of tears in her eyes, the faint tremble in her mouth. Lauren's fingers twisted around her cup and she held herself perfectly still as the story came spilling out. "I was only sixteen, and I had run away to live with my boyfriend, who was twenty. We were going to get married and keep the baby, but he was killed in a liquor store robbery."

"I'm so sorry," Caroline said.

Lauren let out a humorless laugh. "Don't be. He was the one doing the robbing. Stupid idiot tried to rob a liquor store with a toy gun. The manager's wasn't a toy. God, we were so stupid."

"How did you meet Jack?" Danny asked gently.

Lauren took a deep breath and collected herself. "I'd seen him at the shelter before, and I knew he helped some of the girls find adoptive parents for their babies. The girls he helped were always really secretive about it—said it was really important that no one else knew any details. All I knew was that the adoptions were closed—no future contact with the kids, records sealed tight, all that stuff. When I was about seven months pregnant, the director called me into her office one day. Jack was there, and he wanted to make a deal."

"What kind of a deal?" Caroline asked through lips that had gone numb.

"He said he worked with wealthy, childless couples who would do anything to have a healthy baby. They would pay any amount. If I agreed to give up my baby after it was born, I would get twenty thousand dollars."

Caroline wasn't overly familiar with California's adoption laws, but she knew paying a mother for her child was illegal. Big time.

James had brokered the deal himself. She looked up to see Danny studying her with a funny look on his face. Almost compassionate.

"I know how awful it sounds," Lauren said and scrubbed at her eyes. "But it was the best choice. I had nothing, there was no way I could have supported us. My baby girl went to live with a rich couple who wanted her. That money helped me make something of my life. Now I have a great husband and two perfect little boys, and I never would have had that if I'd kept her."

Caroline swallowed back a lump in her throat as she heard Lauren repeat the words she must have said to herself millions of times. Like when she woke up in the middle of the night, stared into the dark and wondered about what might have been.

Caroline could relate. She'd done a lot of dark of night second-guessing herself in the past decade.

"Really, it all worked out for the best," Lauren said.

James would have been a hero for helping a young girl with an impossible choice, had it not been clear he'd profited from the venture, too. Not for a second did Caroline believe twenty thousand dollars was the end of it.

"I don't understand though," Lauren asked. "Why would he say his name is Jack Murphy?"

"Cover his tracks," Danny said. "Adoption records are sealed in some counties in California—where was the baby born?"

"St. Luke's. Up in South San Francisco."

Danny nodded. "But in some cases adoptees can get their records unsealed. He filed the papers under a false identity so no one could ever trace it back to him."

False identities and fake adoption records? This was getting more sickening by the second. "How many other girls did he . . . help?" Caroline wasn't sure she wanted to hear the answer.

"There was one other girl while I was there. Emily Parrish. Her parents were religious freaks and threw her out when she got pregnant. Jack wanted her to give up her baby, too."

"The files showed there were four other girls living at Harmony House at that time. James wasn't working with any of them?"

Lauren licked her lips, taking care to choose her words. "Two of the other girls were Mexican, one was black, and one was," she paused, looking sheepish, "really ugly."

"James only wanted pretty white babies for his clients," Danny bit out.

"It wasn't Emily's fault she was beautiful, and I may not look it now, but I was a lot cuter as a sixteen-year-old. James made us swear the babies' fathers were white too, and told us the deal was off if the babies came out looking, how did he put it? Ethnic."

Caroline swallowed back a surge of bile. She pushed it away, forcing herself to focus. They still didn't really know how or if Anne Taggart was involved. "So was Anne helping him with any of this? Was she involved at all?"

"No," Lauren said. "I mean, I talked to her about giving the baby up, and she thought Jack was a great guy for helping us, but I never told her about the money part. He made us swear."

"She thought he was a great guy?" Danny asked, and only someone who knew him well would pick up on the hostility vibrating through his voice. "Do you think they were having a relationship?"

Lauren's wide eyes darted nervously between Danny and Caroline, as though it had just dawned on her that they were discussing Danny's mother and Caroline's husband. "They were friendly," she said carefully. "They seemed to like each other, but I don't know anything that happened outside of Harmony House." She shook her head and held her hands up as though to fend off a predator.

Caroline couldn't blame her. Danny's eyes were narrowed into icy gray slits and his whole body was tense. She put her hand on his arm and gave him a warning squeeze.

"I remember them arguing though, about Emily. It was right before Emily left."

"Left?"

Lauren nodded. "I wasn't supposed to know, but Emily wanted to back out of the adoption. She wanted to keep her baby. She and the director and Jack had a meeting and he was really pissed. Afterward, Emily told Anne what happened. Anne promised to help her smooth things over with Jack. They got in a huge argument. He told her it was none of her fucking business, and she said he had no right to force her to give up the baby if she didn't want to."

"What happened to Emily? We can't seem to find any record of her anywhere after she left the shelter," Danny said.

Lauren shrugged. "After she decided she wanted to keep her baby she left. She moved back with her parents, at least that's what Christine told us. I remember Anne was really upset. She'd heard about Emily's family and was worried about how they'd treat her. After that she quit showing up for her volunteer shifts. I figure she was pissed at the director and Jack and didn't want anything to do with any of us."

"She didn't show up because she disappeared," Danny said bluntly. "What about Jack? Did you see him after that?"

Lauren closed her eyes and nodded. A big fat tear escaped to roll down her cheek. "The day after my daughter was born. He had me sign some papers and gave me my check. Then he took my daughter to her new family."

Lauren looked at her watch and her eyes widened in horror. "I have to go now." She jumped from her seat. "Good luck with everything," she said awkwardly and practically ran to the door.

Danny held Caroline's arm as they walked to her car. She knew she should pull away, but it felt too good to have his big, strong hand on her, his muscular presence at her side.

She climbed in the car and waited for the accusations to fly. With every new discovery, it became more clear James had something to do with Anne's death. He had probably killed her to keep his secret. Her mind flinched away from acknowledging the possibility.

Instead of voicing her worst fears, all Danny said was, "If this goes the way I think it's going to go, that woman's going to have to tell her husband what happened. She should have told him a long time ago."

"She wanted a new life. A clean slate. I can appreciate that."

"She claims to love her husband, but she keeps something like that from him? That's not cool."

"Some secrets get too big to share," Caroline said. She should know, she was choking on hers, and she never made it past the twelfth week of her pregnancy.

"Not if you're going to spend the rest of your life with someone."

"Right. Says the expert in romantic relationships who is always so open about everything."

"Not wanting to spill my guts all over the table for everyone and keeping big secrets like, say, having a baby, are two very different things. But you're right. I'm certainly no expert on romance. Good thing we figured that out early."

Caroline ignored the pinch of grief and pulled out her cell phone as Danny guided her car out of Lauren's neighborhood. She needed to talk to Patrick. He was James's closest friend. If James had been up to something, chances were Patrick would have had an idea. He had to have been suspicious, even if he hadn't known exactly what James had been involved with.

Melody answered on the first ring. "Hey Caroline. I've been wondering how you are. Are you still hanging out with that fine—"

"Mel, sorry to cut you off, but I really need to talk to Patrick. Is he home?"

Danny started to say something, and she held her hand up for silence.

"Sure, I'll get him."

"I'd really rather talk to him in person. Will he still be home in about an hour?"

"Yes, but you can't stay long. Patrick has to get up early again tomorrow to catch a flight."

Caroline promised they wouldn't take too much time and hung up.

"What do you think you're doing?" Danny's harsh voice cut through the car's dark interior like a steel blade.

"Patrick has been James's best friend since they were freshmen in college. I can't believe James would have all of this going on without Patrick knowing something."

"That may be true, but if he hasn't said anything in all this time, why would he say anything now?"

"Maybe he doesn't realize what he knows. But he could remember something from that time that could help us."

"What are you hoping to find out, Caroline?"

She wasn't sure. "I don't know. Another explanation? An accomplice who held a gun to James's head and forced him into this?" Anything but what the truth was shaping up to be. "Let me talk to Patrick, okay? He and Mel have done so much to help me, and if nothing else I don't want them blindsided when the truth comes out."

Danny finally agreed. "But you follow my lead. I'll ask the questions, I'll manage the information. Got it."

"Sir yes sir," she snapped.

He made a detour to his house to pick up a few changes of clothes. They left the lights of town behind and traveled up a windy, unlit road into the hills. As they climbed, the twists grew sharper and the trees grew bigger until Danny turned down a narrow, gravel drive and pulled up in front of a woodframe structure that was more cabin than house. To her intense disappointment he instructed her to wait in the car as he ran inside to grab his things.

After years of trying not to think about Danny at all, suddenly she was intensely curious about every aspect of his life, including his house. Though Joe Taggart had made a fortune as an investment banker, Danny and his brothers were no trust fund babies. Even if they were, Danny wouldn't have spent his money on a lavish home. The house was small, cozy looking from what she could see of it from the single porch light casting its glow across the front. Intensely private, it was set back deep in the trees. It suited Danny perfectly.

She bet if she went inside, she'd find it sparsely, but comfortably furnished, with Danny's typical piles of clothes and magazines littering every surface.

Danny emerged from the house and tossed a small black duffel in the backseat. He was largely silent on the drive across the bay, other than to ask Caroline exactly where they were headed so he could punch it into the Mercedes' navigation system.

Caroline couldn't get Lauren's grief stricken face out of her head. Imagining the other woman's pain cut her to the core. Money aside, Caroline understood the other woman's choice. She'd learned through her experience with Kate that raising a child was hard even when there was family support and plenty of money. A scared, broke teenager with no one to fall back on barely stood a chance.

Yet she couldn't imagine how painful it must have been, to carry a child, give birth to a healthy, perfect baby, then let someone else walk away with her, knowing you'd never see her again.

Caroline took a shaky breath and swallowed the baseball that had taken up permanent residence in her throat.

"You okay?"

"I can't stop thinking about Lauren. About her baby." *About my baby.* "How hard it must have been to give her up." She swallowed back a sob.

"You're pretty broken up over a stranger's baby."

"That my husband apparently helped her sell on the black market," she reminded him. "I'm still a little shell-shocked from that. Besides, hearing Lauren made me think about Kate." *And me.*

"Your stepdaughter, right. She's got a kid."

Caroline didn't remember telling him that, but didn't bother asking how he knew. It seemed no secret in the world was safe from Gemini Securities. "She got pregnant when she was nineteen. She'd just started her freshman year and she hooked up with a loser named Spike." At Danny's snort she said, "Seriously. That's what he called himself. After Kate got pregnant, it was clear he was hoping to cash in on her trust fund. Instead, James cut them both off. Spike was out of there the first time Kate's credit card was declined."

"Sounds like exactly the kind of guy you want to blend DNA with."

"It was another two months before I could convince Kate to move back in. She was so mad at James for running Spike off."

"You wanted her to move back in? Why not let James write a check and let her live on her own?"

"I wanted her and the baby with us. She was young and scared and still needed her parents." *I was young and scared and needed someone to lean on.* "And then when the baby came, I was able to help her." She closed her eyes and breathed through her nose, able to conjure up the sweet baby smell of Mikey's head.

Until Mikey, Caroline hadn't had much experience with babies, but she took on the role of nursemaid like she'd been trained for it. The first year and a half of his life she'd seen him every day. Squeezed his plump little thighs when she changed his diaper. Walked him up and down the hall, singing "Twinkle Twinkle Little Star" on an endless loop. Imagined what it would have been like with her own baby.

Kate and Mikey had moved out two and a half years ago, and Caroline understood Kate needed to be closer to school and they needed to have their own space.

That didn't mean it didn't break her heart.

"So you're a grandmother then, aren't you? What does that make you? A GILF?" Danny asked.

"A what?"

"Never mind," he chuckled. Caroline wanted to press him but they had reached Melody and Patrick's house, a beautiful Mediterranean style stucco house tucked back from the street.

Patrick answered the door when Caroline rang the doorbell. She couldn't help returning his broad, friendly smile. He was a big, strapping Irishman with thick silver hair and a weathered, ruddy complexion. Like James, he'd aged extremely well. On the north side of fifty he was still fit, his belly flat, the muscles of his arms evident in the sleeves of his polo shirt.

She'd met Patrick a little over ten years ago, after she and James had been seeing each other for several months, and she'd liked him as soon as she met him. Unlike most of the friends and colleagues that she'd met, Patrick didn't look her over like she was on an auction stage and follow it with a look at James so blatant it might as well have been a high five. Of all of James's friends and colleagues, Patrick was the only one who seemed more interested in her brain than her bustline. He'd grilled her about where she was from, why she hadn't gone to college, and if she thought she was prepared to be a stepmother to then thirteen-year-old Kate. Apparently satisfied with her answers, Patrick, and by association, Melody, had taken her under their collective wing and insured her acceptance into the country club social circles James ran in.

Since James's death, Patrick had been Caroline's rock, a big brother type who helped her with everything from funeral arrangements to using his influence to get Rachael Weller to represent her. As Caroline stepped over the threshold, Patrick opened his arms, and Caroline didn't hesitate to step into his embrace.

"How are you doing, kid?" he asked as he released her with a warm pat on her shoulder. "Melody said you wanted to talk to us? About James?" Caroline nodded and he looked over her shoulder. "And this must be the private investigator you were talking about."

Danny introduced himself and offered his hand. Patrick took it, and Caroline could see the muscles in his forearm tense as he squeezed Danny's hand in an aggressive grip. The men locked stares, gray to blue, sizing each other up as they shook hands several seconds beyond courtesy.

"Ease up boys, okay?" Caroline said. "No need to break each other's wrists."

Patrick's face creased in a grin that didn't quite reach his eyes. Caroline chalked up Patrick's suspicious vibe to being protective of her. Patrick gave Danny's hand one last pump before releasing it. "Melody's waiting for us in the living room," he said, motioning for Caroline to lead the way. "You'll have to forgive me for not offering you a drink," he said, his voice echoing off the high ceilings and hardwood floors, "but I have to get up early tomorrow to drive to Sacramento."

"Another seminar?" Caroline asked. In addition to his busy radiology practice, Patrick also taught seminars in cutting-edge ultrasound and X-ray techniques.

Melody was curled up in the corner of the sofa with a book when they entered the living room. She smiled and put down her book before she stood and gave Caroline and Danny a dazzling smile. She wore leopard print silk lounging pajamas, and her usual full face of makeup. Her smile melted into a concerned frown when she got a closer look at Caroline. "Caroline honey, you look like you're about to drop. Sit down." She pushed Caroline onto the love seat and resumed her position on the couch.

Danny took the seat next to Caroline, his broad frame swallowing up the remainder of the small sofa. He rested his ankle on his knee and spread his arms across the padded back. His fingers barely grazed her shoulder.

She shifted as far away as possible and gained about an inch of extra space. She barely took a breath before Danny shifted imperceptibly and closed the gap. Caroline gave him a sidelong glance, but he was looking at Melody, his expression bland as Wonder Bread.

Bastard knew exactly what he was doing, crowding her like that, getting in her space.

"What did you want to talk about?" Patrick had taken a seat on the cushion next to his wife. His hand rested on her spotted, silk clad knee.

Caroline licked her lips and tried to figure out how to start. But Danny's deep voice cut through the room before she could utter a syllable.

"As you know, I'm helping Caroline look into her husband's murder," he began. "We're exploring a connection he may have had to a shelter in San Mateo about eighteen years ago."

"What kind of a shelter?" Melody asked.

"It's a shelter for pregnant teens," Danny said.

"I don't understand what relevance James's work at a shelter for pregnant teens would have on his murder investigation," Patrick said, giving Caroline a confused frown.

"In a case like this, we need to follow every lead, no matter how obscure it seems," Danny said. "We think James may have helped some of the girls find adoptive homes for their babies. Did he ever mention anything like that to you?"

Patrick shook his head. "James did a lot of family law, and I know he handled adoptions on occasion, but it was never anything we discussed in depth."

"He never talked to you about his work at the shelter?" Danny asked.

Again, Patrick shook his head. "This is the first I've ever heard of it. When did you say this was again?"

"The time frame we're looking at is between May and July of 1991."

Melody rolled her eyes and she and Patrick exchanged a knowing look. "The year of hell," Patrick said. "I barely saw James at all that year."

"That was the year Susan was diagnosed for the first time," Melody explained. "I didn't know her that well then—Patrick and I had been married for about a year."

"Mel was getting ready to have Jennifer, and I was picking up extra shifts at all the area hospitals. My ex-wife sued me for additional alimony—"

"We call her the leech," Melody piped in, her smile straining around the edges.

Danny smiled faintly as they chuckled, but his eyes stayed locked on Patrick.

"But if she wasn't such a money sucker, I might not have met you," Patrick said with a smile for his wife. "I met Mel on one of my many extra shifts about a year before."

"I remember Mel mentioning that," Caroline said.

"Anyway," Patrick continued, "James and I were both so busy, we barely saw each other for at least six months." Patrick scratched his chin thoughtfully. "I'm trying to think if I saw him at all that summer." He shook his head regretfully. "I wish I could help you." His bushy gray eyebrows knit together over his bold beak of a nose. "Now explain to me again what you think this has to do with his murder."

"I'm still working on a theory," Danny said. "But we'll let you know as soon as we know something."

Patrick returned his grin, his chilly blue eyes belying the warmth of his expression. He opened his mouth to speak, but the trill of a cell phone interrupted. He pulled his phone out of his pocket and checked the display. "I need to take this. Sorry I couldn't be more help." He nodded to Caroline as he got up from the couch, flipped open the phone, and exited the room.

"Sorry," Mel said, twisting and untwisting her fingers in her lap. "I wish I could help, but like Patrick said, I was getting ready to have Jennifer, and I certainly wouldn't have any idea about James being involved in something like that."

"It's okay," Caroline said. "Like Danny said, we're not even sure if there's a connection." *Not to James's murder anyway.* "We're just covering all our bases." And not like Danny hadn't left a few holes in the information he provided. He hadn't mentioned anything about his mother's connection to James or the shelter.

As Melody walked them to the door, Caroline felt a strange sensation, like something scratching at the back of her brain. A faint, tingling itch, like she was missing something but she couldn't quite put her finger on it.

"Tell me none of this has anything to do with Jennifer," Melody said as soon as she'd locked the door behind Caroline and Danny.

Patrick felt his mouth go dry and his heart squeeze at the panic he saw in Mel's face. "Of course not, sweetheart."

Mel's hand shook as she smoothed her already impeccable bob. "Please tell me you didn't know anything about this. Please tell me we didn't do anything illegal."

Patrick pulled her tense form into his arms. "Mel, we didn't do anything wrong," he lied. "It's just like James told us, there was a girl who wanted to put her baby up for adoption. There's nothing illegal about what we did."

"What if Jennifer finds out we've been lying to her all of this time?" Melody said, the catch in her voice nearly breaking his heart.

"She won't," he vowed. "The records are sealed, and

James made sure the birth mother could never contact us." With Patrick's help. He would do anything to protect his wife, even perpetrate the fiction that Jennifer was their biological child. Even kill his best friend who threatened to reveal their secrets.

"It's all going to be fine, Mel," he promised. "I'll never let anything happen to our family."

As they drove back to her house Danny called to check in with Derek and Ethan and compare notes on what they'd found. Caroline took in as much as she could from his side of the conversation, and he filled her in on the rest after he parked her car and followed her into the house.

"The other women corroborate Lauren's story," he said as he dropped his duffel bag on her kitchen floor and draped his leather coat over a kitchen chair. "They all remembered Anne and James, aka Jack Murphy, but none of them were approached by James to give their babies up for adoption."

"What about Emily? Does anyone know what happened to her?" Caroline asked. There was that niggling feeling again, combined with a twist of dread in her gut that she couldn't shake off.

Danny shook his head. "None of the other girls know what happened to her either. Like Lauren said, as far as they know she moved back with her parents. Speaking of which, Toni got an address. They're completely off the grid in a little town in the Sierras, no phone, nothing. I think we should pay them a visit in person tomorrow. It's about a three hour drive from here."

Caroline nodded and glanced at the clock. It was already after eleven. "In that case, we better get to bed so we can rest up."

Danny's full lips curved into a half smile and his gray eyes turned to molten silver. "Sounds good to me," he said and took a step closer.

She'd been chilled from the damp night, but now Caroline's core temperature rose a good five degrees. "I mean, I need to get to sleep. In my bed."

He took another step. "Any bed is good with me." His lips were firm and smooth, framed by the dark outline of stubble. He stepped closer, blocking out the light from the overhead fixture as he bent closer. Backlit, he was a huge, dark, silhouette coming toward her, his intent clear in every line of his massive body. "And I promise I'll let you sleep after." He was so close she could feel his breath ruffling her hair, smell the spicy scent of his skin. Head bent, he stopped just short of kissing her.

Waiting for her to make the next move.

Making sure she was clear that ultimately, the choice was hers.

It would be so easy. Take one half step forward. Slide her palms up his chest, feel the granite hard lines of his body as she twined her arms around his neck and pressed herself against him. Breast to chest. Soft to hard. Tilt her head back to take his kiss. Part her lips, open to him, give up every last shred of resistance.

He'd carry her upstairs and strip her. Lay her across the bed and run his hands and lips over every square inch of her. He'd part her legs and drive his thick cock all the way inside her. Within minutes she'd be writhing, whimpering, screaming her way to an orgasm the likes of which she hadn't experienced in a decade.

All she had to do was move. One. Half. Step.

Lust and fear warred in her chest as she contemplated that one half step.

She squeezed her eyes shut. "You can sleep in the guest

room," she took a half step back, whirled, and practically sprinted up the stairs.

His low chuckle vibrated along her nerve endings and her heart picked up speed as his heavy footsteps pounded behind her. She hurried to her room and slammed the door shut without a backward glance. One look was all it would take to grind her resolve into a fine dust.

She leaned back against the door, panting, heart pounding as she heard him stop in front of her door.

"You sure you want me to stay in the guest room, Caroline?"

No. "Yes, I'm sure. Good night, Danny."

"Good night, Caroline." He laughed softly and she could see him perfectly in her mind's eye. White teeth flashing against dark skin. Fine lines crinkling at the corners of his eyes. An expression of amusement and frustrated desire in his eyes. "Sleep tight."

She leaned against the door, stifling a moan as she listened to his retreating footsteps.

Fear and self-preservation had won out over lust, but barely. Caroline didn't know how much longer she could take it. She remembered—too well—how easily Danny could move past her defenses. Every second she spent with him it became more and more difficult for her to resist. She was so terrifyingly close to giving in.

She couldn't let that happen. Couldn't let him break her again.

CHAPTER 10

Kaylee's knees shook as she was led to a doorway. Two of the nurse types had retrieved her from her bed that morning. Ignoring her protests, they stripped her of her jeans and T-shirt and dressed her in what looked like a hospital gown. Kaylee had protested, slapping and kicking, but the two women had subdued her and tied her hands in front of her with a plastic strap.

As she was half led, half dragged down the hall, another girl emerged through the doorway. She was a short brunette with wide, brown eyes. She was hugely pregnant, her belly swelling against her hospital gown. "What are they going to do to me?" Kaylee asked the girl as she passed, earning her a pinch on the tender skin of her inner arm. The girl just shook her head. "They're jus' gonna look at you," the girl replied in a thick southern drawl.

Kaylee was momentarily stunned to hear the girl speak English. In the few days she'd been there all the other girls she'd seen were foreign. In addition to her Thai roommate, she'd encountered a couple other girls, but none of them spoke English. She wanted to stop, ask the girl more about how she'd gotten here and how they might get out, but she was shoved through the doorway before she could form a sentence.

Kaylee's heart lurched to her throat when she saw three men speaking in low voices in the corner. She shrank back, her bare feet making slapping sounds on the linoleum floor as she scrambled for an escape. Ruthless fingers dug into her arms and pushed her forward.

The men turned to stare at her, three cold pairs of eyes running over her. She recognized two of them. One was the man she knew only as Gates, the man who had paid Ericka for her. The other she'd seen a couple of days ago, on her way back to her room after she'd been taken down so another nurse—a Chinese woman that time, could drain her of several more vials of blood. He was an old guy, big and tall with thick gray hair. He'd been wearing surgical scrubs, but today he wore a white lab coat over his shirt and khaki pants. His blue eyes were bright against the reddish flush of his skin and they raked over her with all the emotion of a snake before he turned back to say something to Gates she couldn't hear.

The third guy she didn't recognize. He wore an expensive looking suit and a heavy gold watch and he was really good looking, like actor handsome with dark blond hair and green eyes. But his slick good looks didn't stop her skin from crawling or keep the nausea from bubbling in her throat as he looked her up and down.

"Nice," he said to Gates.

Kaylee's knees shook and she was afraid she was going to wet her pants. She swallowed back a surge of vomit. Were the two men there to have sex with her? Here, in this weird, clinical room with only a padded plastic table and horrible fluorescent lights?

Gates nodded at the two women holding her. One untied the back of her gown. Kaylee squawked as it fell down, exposing her breasts to the men. Tears pricked her eyes and she shook with panic as she struggled to put the gown back in place with her bound hands.

"We need to see her," Gates snapped, and one of the nurses cut the tie binding her hands while the other stripped the gown from her.

"No!" Kaylee lashed out with her arms and legs, catching one of the nurses in the stomach. The woman's breath left her in a whoosh and she bent double as Kaylee jerked free of the other woman's hold. Naked, she ran for the door, but a brutal hand grabbed her by the hair. She was yanked against a hard chest. She struggled, then felt her vision dim as a thumb dug into the side of her neck.

"If you do not do exactly as you are told, it will go much worse for you."

A tiny voice in Kaylee's head urged her to take her chances. What was worse than being gang raped, which she was pretty sure was going to happen in about five minutes. But the voice was drowned out by something horrible, awful, inhuman promised in Gates's voice.

He pulled her back to the center of the room.

"Her blood work is all clear?" the doctor guy asked.

"Perfectly healthy. She's totally clean."

They were worried about what they were going to catch from her? What was going to protect her from them?

"She's perfect," the good looking one said, and Kaylee closed her eyes against his assessing stare. "She's got the hair, the height. Great bone structure. I know of at least four couples who would be interested, especially if we can match her with a similar type."

Her heart pounded in her ears until his voice became muffled. She braced herself for their touch, told herself to float away, close off her mind where no one could touch her.

"Put her up on the table."

Oh, God, she was going to throw up. But maybe that would repulse them enough to stop.

She heaved, her meager breakfast spattering against the linoleum.

She opened her eyes to see the slickster and the doctor frantically backpedaling to avoid the spray while Gates shook his head in disgust. He glared at the nurse types.

"Get her up on the table and clean this up."

The nurses glared at her and yanked her over to the padded table and pushed her to lie flat. She heard a ripping noise and thick velcro straps were fastened around her upper arms and wrists.

Kaylee was afraid the force of her heartbeat was going to break her ribs as the big man in the doctor coat pulled a pair of latex gloves from his pocket and snapped them on. He nodded at the nurses, who came over to hold Kaylee's legs. Forcing her to bend at the knees, they held her legs open as the doctor approached.

"Just relax. I promise to get this over with as quickly as possible."

Sobs tore at her throat as she struggled against the straps and the women holding her. Tears blurred her eyes as she stared up at the man. "Please let me go. Please don't hurt me."

"I'm not going to hurt you. I just need to take a look at you."

Somehow through her panicked haze she realized there was no lust in his gaze, just a cold, clinical detachment. She remembered the other girl's words. "They jus' wanna take a look at you."

That didn't calm her or stop her body from revolting as a gloved finger was pushed inside of her. She froze, her entire body paralyzed by fear and disgust as she endured the exam. It was no different than the exam she'd had last year when she wanted to go on the pill.

Yet as the doctor withdrew his hand, stripped off his gloves and dropped them into the garbage, she felt ill and hollow, like someone had scooped out her guts and tossed them to the floor.

She didn't bother to struggle as the nurses unstrapped her and forced her arms back into the gown.

"She's in great shape," she heard the doctor say, but she couldn't bring herself to lift her head to glare at him. "We'll know for sure in a few days after an ultrasound to do a follicle count," he continued, and Kaylee started to tune him out, not understanding what the hell he was talking about.

But his next words snapped her back to attention and froze the blood in her veins.

". . . and I see no reason why she would have any problem conceiving this month."

It took her a few seconds to process what he was saying. But as realization dawned, she felt the blood drain from her face in such a rush she thought she was going to faint. All of the questions about her period, the blood tests, the pregnant girls she'd seen in the house. It all made sense now.

I know of at least four couples who would be interested.

They weren't going to just sell her for sex. They were going to get her pregnant and sell her baby.

Marshall blocked out the stunned look on the girl's face as he followed Patrick out of the examination room. Unlike many of the girls, this one was American born and bred, a native English speaker. It took her a minute, but after Patrick delivered his prognosis, understanding had leached the remaining color from her already pale face. She knew exactly what was in store for her in the coming months.

Guilt coiled its way through his belly, but he shoved it aside. Guilt was what got James Medford killed. Guilt and stupidity. First for not covering his tracks well enough, and then for trying to threaten them all—including Gates—into letting him out of the business. Everyone knew you didn't mess with Gates.

Patrick was no pussycat either. And from the look in his icy blue eyes, he was still on the warpath over Marshall's inability to get Caroline Medford out of the picture earlier that week. Apparently not even the successful delivery of a healthy baby girl, which promised to earn both Marshall and Patrick healthy commissions, or the promise shown by their latest recruit was enough to cool him off.

They left the shaking girl behind in the exam room and went out in the hallway. "We'll get her scheduled for a shoot," Gates said. "You're welcome to observe, as always," he said to Marshall.

His face heated. But even through his embarrassment he couldn't deny a spike of lust at the thought of watching the beautiful blonde get fucked. He only wished he could be the one doing it, but the risks were too high. He had to content himself with watching.

Patrick shook his head in disgust. "Pervert."

Marshall didn't get it. The doctor had no qualms about impregnating girls on purpose to sell their babies to unsuspecting, desperate couples. No hesitation about killing his best friend and trying to kill his best friend's wife. But somehow Marshall was less moral because he liked to watch the girls when they made their debuts.

Gates's phone rang and he excused himself to take the call. Marshall took that as his cue to make his exit, but Patrick caught him by the shoulder. "We need to talk."

"Watch the suit," Marshall said, wrenching away from Patrick's grip. He winced at the way the doctor's meaty fist had crumpled the fabric. "Look, I'm sorry about what happened to Rachael Weller. It's not my fault the guy's aim was off and Taggart was able to pull Caroline to safety."

Marshall had been watching from across the street, out of sight, to make sure everything happened according to plan. Taggart had grabbed Caroline before the Escalade had even rounded the corner. Like he could sniff the threat on the wind. Like he was some fucking psychic.

"Thanks to your so-called perfect plan, we've got bigger problems. Last night Caroline came to my house and asked me about James being involved with Harmony House. Specifically helping girls find adoptive families."

Marshall's face paled. Even though he hadn't been involved in what happened eighteen years ago, it didn't take a genius to realize if they kept following that thread, it would eventually lead them to Patrick. And to himself. "What did she find?"

"She didn't say specifically. But it was enough to lead them there. We can't take any more chances. We need to find out what they know, what they found, and take them both out before they dig any deeper."

Marshall nodded. Easier said than done. In the months since James had died, he and Patrick had been over every inch of James's house, his office, his car, even Kate's apartment, without finding a single shred of the evidence James claimed to be keeping. Insurance, he'd claimed.

It had turned out to be a death sentence. Marshall had convinced himself that meant they were fine, James must have been lying, bluffing to cut himself free of a business he could no longer stomach.

"I'll take care of it," Marshall said.

"That's what you said last time."

"Yeah, well this time I mean it. Just make sure Gates stays in the dark about all of this. If he thinks we're a liability—"

"We're both dead," Patrick finished.

"You weren't kidding when you said off the grid," Caroline said as she stepped carefully out of Danny's Jeep which he'd driven in deference to the weather. It had been pouring in

Piedmont when they left, meaning snow in the Sierras, and the tiny town of Whiskey Creek didn't disappoint.

By the time they got to Emily Parrish's parents' house, a good six inches of snow had accumulated on the dirt and gravel driveway, and it showed no signs of slowing. Danny was beginning to wonder if they'd make it out of the mountains even with four-wheel drive and chains.

The Parrishes lived in an A-frame house three miles outside of Whiskey Creek. The green metal of the roof showed through where the snow had slid along the sides to the ground. A carport on the right of the house sheltered an ancient Ford F-150 pickup and about a decade's worth of chopped wood. Thick smoke curled from the chimney, lending a sharp salty bite to the frigid air.

Caroline took a step forward and cursed as her boots slid out from under her. Danny caught her before she hit the ground. "I told you to go with hiking boots," he griped. "Or better yet, a pair of these," he stomped his own black army issue winter boots for emphasis.

Caroline had insisted on wearing a pair of clunky, fleece lined suede boots, thinking they'd keep her feet warmer. "Sorry, I threw out my combat boots last season." She pulled from his hold and took another step, nearly falling on her ass as she hit a patch of slick gravel hiding under the snow.

Danny lunged forward and wrapped his arm around her to steady her. Snow dusted her dark hair, releasing the fresh scent of her shampoo. His cock, already in a state of semi-arousal just from being cooped up in a car with her, thickened to full hardness.

Something had to happen, soon. He was trying to be patient, hang back, let her come to him, an approach that had worked so well with her years before. But last night had nearly done him in. Danny didn't think he could take another night of having her sleep just down the hall from him while he jacked off like a loser in her designer sheet draped guest bed.

Something definitely needed to happen. But later, because right now he needed to get his mind off the way Caroline's luscious round ass filled out her jeans and on whether or not Emily's parents knew anything about her connection to Anne Taggart and James Medford.

Danny let his arm slide from Caroline's shoulders as he knocked. A rangy, rawboned man who could have been anywhere from fifty-five to seventy-five answered. His thinning gray hair was cut military short, his white beard was neatly trimmed. His flannel shirt was cleanly pressed and tucked neatly into a pair of heavy canvas work pants. "Are you lost son?" the man asked, his blue eyes showing a mix of confusion and concern behind his wire rimmed glasses.

"I'm looking for Edward and Nora Parrish," Danny said.

"You've found us," the man said. His expression was guarded and he used his tall frame to block the doorway.

Danny quickly introduced himself, then Caroline. "We want to ask you a few questions related to a case we're working on."

"If you're a cop you better show me some ID."

"I'm not a police officer sir, I'm a private investigator." The wind whipped the snow into a vortex and he felt Caroline shiver next to him. "Please sir, it's really cold out here. If we could just come in and ask you and your wife some questions, I promise not to take too much of your time."

Caroline gave an exaggerated shiver for emphasis. The man raked her up and down, his mouth taking on a disapproving cast as he looked her over. But finally he stepped back and motioned them inside.

The bottom floor of the house consisted of only one big room, which held the kitchen, a dining area, and a sitting area with a worn small sofa and a padded armchair. A narrow wooden staircase in the far corner led to the second floor. Though the house was lit with electricity there was no sign of a TV, a phone, or even a radio.

A Bible was displayed prominently on the small table in front of the sofa and a magazine with the headline "Is the End of Days Nigh? What You Need to Be Ready!" lay discarded on one of the sofa cushions. The man motioned for Danny and Caroline to sit and called for his wife. "Mrs. Parrish, can you come down here please?"

The interior of the house was almost uncomfortably warm, thanks to the giant wood stove tucked into one corner of the kitchen. An old fashioned coffee pot sat on top, steam curling from its spout.

Mrs. Parrish—Nora—came down the stairs and Danny could see Caroline trying to school her face into impassivity. He knew exactly why—Mrs. Parrish was dressed like an escapee from *Little House on the Prairie*. Danny introduced himself and Caroline, and she responded with a quick nod. "Let me just get the coffee and I'll be right with you."

"Please don't go to any trouble," Caroline said, but Nora had already retrieved four ceramic mugs and filled a plate with some kind of dark bread. She loaded everything onto a tray and brought it over, serving Danny and Mr. Parrish first, before offering Caroline coffee and taking a cup for herself.

Only he could detect the subtle arch in Caroline's brow as it cocked in disapproval.

"How can we help you, young man?" Mr. Parrish asked after he'd taken a sip of coffee.

"We're working on a missing persons case, and we believe the woman may have had a connection to your daughter, Emily. We were hoping you could help us track her down."

While Edward Parrish's demeanor hadn't been exactly

warm up to that point, it had at least been cordial. Now it turned downright glacial. "I have no daughter."

"Sir, I understand you may have had a falling out with Emily—" Caroline began.

"Do not say that name in this house!" Edward boomed.

Caroline's eyes widened as she sat back, while Nora Parrish stared at a point across the room.

"Sir, if you could just tell us when you last spoke to her, if she ever mentioned a woman named Anne Taggart—"

Edward slammed his coffee mug down on the table. Steaming black liquid sloshed across his hand but he didn't seem to notice. "You've defiled my home with her name as she defiled it with her presence. She died the day she decided to become a whore. I repeat, I have no daughter. Now take your painted Jezebel," he pointed at Caroline with a snarl, "and get out of my home."

Danny stood up and gave Edward a look that had made dozens of new recruits wet their pants in fear. "I need to know where your daughter is, sir."

Edward turned his back, marched across the room, and went up the stairs.

"Oh dear," Nora's soft voice trembled slightly, "you'd better go. I'm afraid he's fetching the Remington."

"Shotgun," Danny said in response to Caroline's confused look. Her eyes widened as she heard the thumping of footsteps overhead.

"Maybe we should go," Caroline said.

Danny ignored her, and pinned Nora with a hard stare. Nora's watery brown eyes darted furtively to the stairs.

"I haven't seen her in nearly twenty years. Not since she told us she'd gotten herself in trouble." Her eyes filled with tears and her chin wobbled. "She'd sinned," she said like a woman trying to convince herself.

"She didn't come back to live with you and have her baby?" Caroline pressed.

"Edward wouldn't abide a bastard in this house."

Booted feet were approaching the staircase overhead, and Caroline edged toward the door.

"Do you have a picture of her?" Danny said, staying Caroline with a hand on her arm. She was vibrating like a hummingbird, terrified Edward was going to march downstairs and open fire.

"We got rid of everything," Nora said, but Danny could tell from her downcast eyes she was lying.

"Please. Anything taken around the time she left would be helpful."

With another nervous look at the stairs, Nora hurried into the kitchen where she opened a cabinet stocked floor to ceiling with canned goods. She knelt down and stuck her arm all the way back and pulled a snapshot out of an envelope. "This was one of the few I was able to save."

Danny took the picture, thanked her, and started for the door as Edward's foot hit the first step.

Nora grabbed his arm and whispered frantically, "If you find her—"

The metallic click of a rifle cocking rang through the air. "I told you to get out of my house," Edward bellowed as he swung the barrel in their direction.

Maybe Caroline was right to be so nervous.

Danny grabbed Caroline's arm and yanked her through the front door. Cold air stole their breath as they hurried down the front steps. The blast of a shotgun cut through the thick snowy silence, followed by Edward yelling what Danny thought might be a Bible verse. Caroline gave a yelp of fear and dove for cover. Danny yanked her to her feet and rushed her to the Jeep, shoving her in through the driver's seat before climbing in after her.

Danny hazarded a look back at Edward just in time to see the man fire into the air.

Caroline dove for the floor and screamed as the blast reverberated around the Jeep.

"Relax," Danny said as he started the car and put it into gear. "He's just firing into the air."

"Well excuse me," Caroline said, her voice shrill, "if having a gun pulled on me scares the shit out of me. You may be used to people trying to kill you, but the experience is still relatively new to me."

"Edward wasn't trying to kill you," Danny said as he carefully negotiated the Parrishes' drive. In the brief time they'd been inside, the storm had increased in intensity. He could barely see through the windshield as the wipers struggled to keep pace with the dumping snow.

"Says you. You weren't the one he called a painted Jezebel," Caroline said, grunting a little as she pulled herself from the floor.

"Now that he mentions it, you could lighten up on the lipstick there, Tammy Faye."

"Go fuck yourself."

"But it's so much better when you do it."

She responded with a disgusted noise and turned her attention pointedly out the window.

As Danny turned onto the main road, it became evident that Edward Parrish's shotgun wasn't their only worry. The snow lay in a thick blanket, and as they inched along, the wind buffeted the Jeep until Danny had to use all of his strength and concentration to keep the car on course. After a few miles he pulled off to put chains on his tires, but all the tire traction in the world couldn't help anyone navigate in zero visibilty.

He kept their pace to a crawl as they passed through Whiskey Creek, knowing that the only hope of escaping the snow was to get to a lower elevation. As he reached the outskirts of town, flashing lights barely penetrated the thick curtain of snow.

"What's happening?" Caroline asked as the Jeep crawled a few more yards.

A sheriff's SUV blocked the road ahead, positioned in front of a closed metal gate. Yellow lights flashed where the two sides of the gate met. "The pass is closed because of the snow," Danny said.

"Maybe they'll let us through—"

Before Caroline could even finish her sentence the sheriff tweaked his siren at them, signaling them to stop. A thickset man in a wide brimmed hat and fur trimmed parka climbed from the SUV. He stomped through the snow and Danny lowered the driver's side window.

"Sorry folks, road's closed."

"Well how are we supposed to get home?" Caroline snapped as she leaned across the console to the driver's side.

"Sorry ma'am, I'm afraid you'll have to turn around and wait it out until we can get the roads cleared."

"How long will that take?" Caroline asked, exasperated.

"Can't say, ma'am," the officer said, getting irritated and no doubt yearning for the warmth of his car. "But seeing as this is the only road out of here, I suggest you turn around and wait it out."

"Wait it out? Where the hell are we supposed to wait it out? There's nothing there."

Danny rolled up the window mid tirade and gave the officer a friendly wave before turning the Jeep around. "Will you give it a rest already? So the road is closed. We'll deal with it."

"What are we going to do? Sit in the car for the next twelve hours?"

"No," Danny said, slowing as a truck pulled out of a parking lot in front of him. He signaled and turned right into the driveway. "I figure this place will do."

"We're going to spend the night in the 7-Eleven?" Caroline asked.

"No," Danny drove past the 7-Eleven toward the dimly lit sign that was barely visible through the snow. "We're staying at the Whiskey Creek Motor Inn. We're in luck. The VACANCY sign is on."

The Whiskey Creek Motor Inn was a squat, two story building painted a color that was probably once white or cream but had turned to a dirty putty color over the years. The rooms opened to the outside and offered an unobstructed view of the parking lot. The lot was full of trucks pulling trailers loaded with snowmobiles on the back.

Danny pulled under the awning in front of the motel's office and got out. Caroline followed with a faintly disgusted pull to her mouth. "We're going to stay here?"

"Unless you want to stay in the car, princess, this is our only option."

They entered an office that smelled of old coffee and stale cigarette smoke. An ancient TV, complete with rabbit ears, displayed a picture even snowier than the storm outside. A worn rust colored couch flanked by two Naugahyde arm chairs completed the retro seventies feel.

No one was at the reception desk, but when Danny rang the bell a hacking cough, followed by a husky, "Be right with you," sounded from the back. The hacking started up again, and a woman with an iron gray beehive emerged from a room behind the desk. Her face was as weathered as an old boot, a slash of scarlet lipstick the only color in a complexion roughly the color of her hair. Her thin shoulders were covered by a thick wool sweater with puffy birds sewn on the front. She paused long enough in her coughing to ask, "How can I help you?"

"We need a couple rooms for tonight," Danny replied.

"You have a reservation?" the woman asked in a voice that sounded like she'd been swallowing gravel.

"No," Caroline said, "we got stranded by the storm."

The woman tapped on the keyboard of a vintage IBM

machine and squinted at the monitor. "Afraid we only have one room," the woman said.

"Are you sure?" Caroline asked. "Maybe if you check again—"

"There's a big snowmobile rally this weekend over in Lake Alpine and we're full up." Danny saw Caroline wince as the woman paused to hack up another quart of phlegm. "You're lucky we have anything available, but someone canceled at the last minute."

"We'll take it." Danny drew his money clip out of his pocket and pulled out his credit card.

"But we can't share a room," Caroline sputtered, her dark eyes wide with alarm.

"It's all we have," the woman repeated as she snatched up the card in arthritic fingers. "Don't worry hon," she said as she ran the card through an old fashioned manual credit card imprinter, "there are two beds. I'm sure your virtue is safe with him," she said with a sly wink at Danny and handed over the key.

CHAPTER 11

Caroline followed Danny into their second floor room and chafed her arms against the chill. Danny switched on the light and quickly located the thermostat. "Wood paneling. Nice touch," she said over the low hiss of the wall heater.

Danny threw his leather coat across an armchair in the corner. Caroline snatched it up and hung it with her own in the closet, then took a closer look at their accommodations. Next to the lumpy, worn armchair was a round table coated in wood laminate with a table lamp on top. Two double beds were covered in polyester bedspreads in shades of green, orange, and gold, divided by a bedside table that held another lamp. She could feel Danny standing beside her, too warm, too close, and the shiver that ran through her had nothing to do with the cold.

She moved away and heard the thump of Danny's duffel bag hitting the thinly carpeted floor. Unlike her, Danny carried an overnight bag with him everywhere, so he was prepared for an event like getting stranded in a hotel overnight.

With someone he used to have sex with.

Really, really, amazingly awesome sex.

She pulled back a bedspread to distract herself and fingered the rough sheets. "Ooh, what is this, like, twenty threadcount? How luxurious." She injected as much snottiness into her tone as she could muster, trying to remind herself that there was nothing sexy or provocative about being stuck in a dive of a motel with Danny Taggart.

"You didn't used to be so particular," Danny said from right behind her, so close she could feel the heat of him against her back. And there she was, so close to the bed her thighs brushed the edge. Why had she moved so close to the bed? She froze, willing him to move away, promising herself that as soon as he did she would sit her ass in that armchair and not move until morning.

But Danny got even closer. "In fact, this kind of reminds me of something." Her eyes fluttered closed as she felt him brush her hair to the side. Warm breath wafted against her cheek as he bent his head to that ultra sensitive spot right below her ear. "Remember that hotel in Spring Lake?"

Oh God, she did. The hot press of his mouth on her skin sent warmth pooling between her thighs. Danny had been stationed at Fort Bragg, North Carolina, and she'd managed to get a few days off. Danny got a three day furlough and took her to a hotel in nearby Spring Lake. It was the last time she'd gone to visit Danny, right before he'd been deployed on yet another mission she couldn't know anything about.

"Remember how bad it stormed?" His hands curved over her hips, up to circle her waist, his touch burning her through the weave of her sweater.

That time it had been rain instead of snow. She and Danny had locked themselves in a room similar to this one. Caroline hadn't cared about the rain, or the cheap sheets, or the ugly décor. All she'd cared about was having Danny and a bed. They'd gone at each other voraciously, made love until they were both sore and tired and could barely move. Then one of them would run a hand up the other's thigh, or circle a nipple with a finger, or kiss the other's neck, and it would start all over again.

Still, it wasn't enough. She hadn't seen him for six months before that, and had no idea when the next time would be. They parted with desperate kisses and whispered "I love you"s.

Three weeks later Caroline had realized she was pregnant.

That was enough to snap her out of it. She pushed away from Danny and walked on shaky legs to the other side of the room.

Danny followed her like a tiger on the prowl.

"This is a really bad idea," she said, as much to herself as to him.

He ignored her, of course. "Come on Caroline. Don't try to tell me you're not curious what it would be like now."

"Curiosity is a really bad reason to have sex with an ex," she replied, hating the way her voice shook as much as she hated the way her sex throbbed between her legs.

He moved closer and she took another step back, then another, until he had her pinned up against the room's door. Her breath caught as he leaned into her, letting her feel the weight of him, the heat of him. The hardness of him pressing insistently against her belly. "I want to know if you still like it when I suck your tits while I fuck you."

Caroline closed her eyes and let out a low moan as her nipples hardened at the thought.

He braced his hands on either side of her head, trapping her.

Not that she wanted to escape. He kissed her then, rough, hungry. "I want to know if your pussy is still as hot and tight as a wet little fist, squeezing around me." His tongue swept the seam of her lips, and she couldn't stop herself from sucking him inside. *Stupid,* her brain tried to warn. *This is so stupid.*

One hand slid under the hem of her sweater and he rocked his hips against her. "I want to know," he said, his breath coming faster, "if you still yell so loud when you come that the people next door will worry that I'm killing you."

Caroline let out a low whimper and slid her arms around his waist. She should be angry, offended, or at the very least, embarrassed by the things he was saying, but God help her, she wanted to know, too. Need pumped through her veins like warm honey. It had been so long since she'd felt anything like this, she'd almost convinced herself she'd never felt it at all.

But as Danny pulled her sweater over her head and pulled off his own shirt, it was like the years melted away. Caroline was back in that hotel room in North Carolina, running hot and wet with the need to have Danny fucking her hard and deep.

He unhooked her bra and slid the straps down her arms. He leaned into her, and they both hissed at the first skin to skin contact. The skin of his chest was hot and smooth, and the dusting of rough hair brushed her nipples into achy peaks. It was so familiar, yet so new. He was bigger, harder, leaner. Mountains of muscle rippled under her fingers and she wanted to explore every ridge with her lips and tongue.

"From that first day I saw you again," he muttered against her mouth, "I haven't stopped thinking about you, about all the ways I want to make you come." He bent his head and sucked her nipple into his mouth. She laced her fingers through his hair and pressed him close, urging him on.

"Tell me," she moaned. "Tell me everything you've been thinking about." Heat flooded her face at her own boldness, but this is what Danny did to her. Made her crazy. Made her lose control.

"How about I show you instead," he said, his breath hot against her other breast as he slid one hand down the back of her jeans. His fingers slid against the silky fabric of her panties and he insinuated one thigh between hers. She moaned and hitched her leg up over his hip so she could ride the hard muscle. His mouth abandoned her breasts and he straightened. His hands slid down to the button of her jeans and buzzed the zipper down.

Caroline's head tipped back against the door and her breath came in sharp pants as he slid one hand down the front of her panties. Thick, callused fingers caressed her slit, parting her so he could tease the ripe bud of her clit.

"I remember the first time I made you come with my fingers," Danny murmured, increasing the pressure up, down, around as she braced herself against the door and tried to keep her legs from buckling under her. "You were so wet, just like you are now." His lips brushed hers. "By the time I got your pants off your panties were soaked, and you were so embarrassed. But you're not embarrassed now, are you?" He kissed her again, thrust his tongue inside before retreating.

"No," she moaned, arching against his fingers, a silent plea for him to increase the pressure.

He ran his fingers up her slit in a firm stroke while his other hand shoved her jeans down her hips. She clumsily kicked off her boots and pulled her legs free, eagerly parting them as his hand slid down further. A low groan escaped her throat as he circled her clit with his thumb and slid one, then two fingers inside her.

"You're even tighter than I remembered," he groaned against her mouth, sinking his fingers in and out until the hot stretch and slide was enough to make her scream.

She clung to his shoulders for balance as her entire universe centered around that pleasure giving hand. Her muscles clenched and she rocked against him. His low words of encouragement against her lips pushed her higher and higher.

"That's it, Carrie. I can feel you, so tight around my fingers. I can't wait to get my cock inside you."

The thought was enough to send her over the edge. A harsh, high pitched cry pushed through her lips, and he quickly swallowed it with his mouth over hers.

"Mmm, don't want anyone calling the cops just yet," he said, as he scooped her up and carried her to one of the beds. He pulled the tacky bedspread down and onto the floor before laying her across the sheets.

Caroline didn't notice the roughness of the sheets against her bare skin as she looked at him. The room was dim, lit only by the single lamp on the table across the room. Danny was a dark, shadowy figure above her, a study in light and shadow, golden skin and rippling muscle. His face was partially obscured, but she could feel him looking at her as he stripped off his pants and boxers. His cock stood stiffly at attention, jutting up between his legs. Jesus, she'd remembered him being big, but not that big.

It seemed to swell before her eyes as she stared, transfixed. Veins traced along the thick shaft and a drop of moisture beaded on the swollen head. She sat up a little and reached out, a thrill coursing through her at the feel of silky hot skin over steel. He stood frozen, every muscle locked and trembling as she wrapped her fist around him and pumped, once, twice. Bits and pieces flooded back as she stroked and squeezed, memories of what he liked, how he wanted to be touched. How to make him shudder and groan until he spun out of control.

After only a few seconds Danny grabbed her wrist and wrenched her hand away. He collapsed on the bed beside her and pressed a surprisingly tender kiss to her palm. "I'm so jacked up right now, if you keep touching me like that

I'm gonna blow. And I want to make you come about a half a dozen more times before that happens."

A thrill ran through her as he rolled her underneath him, his weight pressing her into the mattress. She would have thought any other man was bluffing about the half dozen orgasms. But she knew what Danny was capable of. Knew what *she* was capable of when Danny took control of her pleasure.

She could only pray she made it out of this room in one piece.

The last flutters of her orgasm had barely faded, but already the heat of his skin, the weight of him against her, made her clench in renewed need. His hands were everywhere, sliding up and down her sides, the curve of her ass, fisting in her hair to take his kiss, parting her legs so she could feel the firm press of his abs against her sex. Over her breasts, squeezing, pinching, his mouth sucking at the tips as he murmured how beautiful she was.

God, it was so good, just like it had always been. Under Danny's hands, Danny's lips, she lost herself in a vortex of pure pleasure. He knew exactly what to do, exactly what to say, to spin her up until she exploded into a million shimmering pieces. His mouth trailed down her belly, pressing a line of hot, sucking kisses to her skin until he was between her legs.

He hovered over her, teasing her with his hot breath. "I've been dying to taste you again," he murmured as he spread her pussy lips with his thumbs. "Wanting to see if you're as salty sweet as I remember."

Caroline arched off the bed, nearly coming at the first, teasing lick of his tongue.

"So sweet," he said and ran his tongue up one side and down the other before ducking down so he could dip inside. In, out in a wet velvet slide, he fucked her with his tongue until she thought she'd lose her mind. Then he withdrew to trace lazy circles around her clit. He hooked his hands under her knees and guided them over his shoulders so she was completely open, completely vulnerable to his touch.

"God I love going down on you."

Caroline could only moan as he licked and sucked, feasting on her like she was the most delicious thing he'd ever tasted. The first time he'd done this she'd nearly died of embarrassment, unable to believe that a guy could really enjoy it. Danny had pleaded and pushed, promised her that all she had to do was pull on his hair and he'd stop. She'd yanked on his hair at the first flick of his tongue, but of course he hadn't stopped like he'd promised. But soon she'd had her fingers twisted in his hair as she writhed underneath him, embarrassment forgotten as he sucked her clit into his mouth with firm pulls of his lips.

Just like he was doing now. Sucking her hard as his tongue stroked her. Her heels dug into his back as her orgasm tightened and built, more fiercely than before.

"Mmmm, that's it baby, come in my mouth. You know I love to taste your sweet pussy juice running over my tongue."

She arched her head back into the pillow, her hands fisting in the cheap sheets, too turned on to be embarrassed by the hot, filthy things he whispered against her swollen flesh. Pleasure broke over her in a dizzying wave, even more intense than before. She was dimly aware of him moving off the bed. She wanted to reach for him, keep him with her, but her arms were rubbery dead weights.

She watched him walk across the room, his naked, muscular body moving with predatory grace. He knelt on one knee in front of his duffel bag and rustled around. Finding what he was looking for, he straightened and turned back to the bed.

Caroline's boneless satisfaction receded when her gaze dipped between his legs. He was still rock hard. Unsatisfied sexual heat rolled off him in waves. Her mouth went dry and she licked her lips at the thought of satisfying his need.

Renewed desire pulsed through her. She sat up against the pillow and parted her knees wider in invitation. She could see the flash of white teeth as he smiled in anticipation.

She heard the rip of foil and watched him smooth the condom down the length of his cock. Her pussy fluttered at the remembered feel of him sinking deep inside her. After twelve years, she was going to have him inside her again.

The thought terrified her as much as it thrilled her.

Danny climbed on the bed and knelt between her legs. "Brace yourself baby," he said with a cocky grin as he positioned the head of his cock at her entrance. "You're about to get the ride of your life."

"Promise?"

Danny's breath caught at her low, husky voice and her sultry smile. She let out a little gasp as he squeezed the tip of his cock inside. His own breath hitched and he squeezed his eyes at the slick heat. *So tight.* She'd come twice, was so wet the pale, smooth skin of her inner thighs was shiny with juice, but she was still so tight he could barely squeeze inside.

Almost as tight as the first time he took her.

No, don't go there. That night had been a near religious experience. He'd felt empty, broken. *Needy.* And Caroline had come to him, given herself to him in complete love and trust, and for a moment at least, filled the black hole inside him that threatened to swallow him up.

This is different. He took a deep breath and eased up, giving her a chance to get used to him. He hitched her knee over his elbow and folded it up against her chest, opening her wide so he could sink in another few inches. This was fucking, pure and simple. Tab A in slot B.

She moaned, arched her hips and slid her hands down to cover his ass. "God, Danny you feel so good."

His hips flexed under her hands; he sank all the way in, so deep his balls nestled up against the curve of her ass. *So good.* The fucking understatement of the year.

It's just a fuck, he reminded himself as he pulled out almost all the way before sinking back home in one smooth, gliding stroke.

But this is Caroline. Caroline's beautiful brown eyes narrowed into slits as she stared up at him. Caroline's little pink tongue circling her plump red lips. Caroline's sweet, soft tits bouncing with every jolting thrust he delivered. Arching her hips, taking everything he gave her, giving it right back.

She was so beautiful, still so gorgeous it made his chest squeeze just to look at her. Something inside him seemed to tear, a weak spot in the scar tissue that held back everything he'd managed to shove back over the past twelve years. Now it was breaking through in a slow, steady leak.

"Danny," she called his name in a high, startled cry and started to buck frantically under him.

Yes, this was what he wanted. Caroline, who had become so cool and reserved under her shell of sophistication, hot and wet, writhing out of control underneath him. To show her that no matter how she tried to keep him at a distance, he had the power to make her half insane with lust and need.

He sped up his thrusts, reveling in the power he still had over her. Loving that he could still make her scream, make her beg. He hooked her other knee over his elbow, spreading her wide, pinning her like a butterfly to the mattress with the force of his thrusts. Caroline's hands were frantic, sliding along the sweat slick skin of his back. The sharp prick of her nails urged him on, the pain sending currents of pleasure straight to his balls. His vision went red as he felt her stiffen and convulse around him, heard her wail her pleasure up to the ceiling as her pussy milked him in greedy pulses.

He held himself still inside her, as deep as he could go, relishing every last tremor. He stared down at her face, watching her eyes focus as she came back to herself. She gave him a sleepy, satisfied smile that punched him right in the chest.

Closer. He wanted to get closer. Breath to breath. Mouth to mouth. Every inch of him covering her until she was absorbed into his skin.

A warning bell went off in the back of his head penetrating the fog of lust and need. *No.* He couldn't give into the hold she still had on him.

He rose up on his knees and closed his eyes, caught her hand and pressed it back down to the mattress when she would have curled it around his neck. But even with his eyes closed, her beautiful face, her expression of sexual satisfaction was burned on his brain. He forced his mind away from it, focusing instead on the base, carnal sensations of her pussy gloving his cock, so hot it threatened to burn him alive. So tight around him, pulling and squeezing him to his own oblivion.

Just sex, he chanted to himself, even as every sinew went tight and he was swept up in one of the most intense orgasms he'd ever had in his life. It started at the base of his spine, working up and out, tightening his balls almost painfully before he exploded with such force he was sure the condom would break. On and on, his body jerked convulsively, as what felt like every drop of moisture came spurting out the tip of his cock.

He collapsed beside her, eyes closed, air sawing in and out of his lungs as he struggled to get oxygen back to his brain.

Jesus. What a fucking disaster.

He felt the mattress shift as she rolled toward him. Her slender hand rested tentatively on his chest and her soft kiss on his shoulder burned him like a brand.

Without hesitation he brushed her hand from his chest and rolled off the bed.

Caroline stared at his retreating back and watched him disappear into the bathroom, feeling like she'd been kicked in the gut.

She didn't know what she'd expected. She was a grown up, after all, and a realist. Not to mention she'd gone too many rounds with Danny in her life to expect that he'd go all ooey gooey after sex. She didn't really expect him to curl his big body around her as he had in the past, snuggle her back to his front while they spoke in whispers about everything from what movie they should go see that weekend to what kind of house they would live in after they were married.

But she also didn't expect him to literally brush her off like an annoying fly and hightail it from the bed like the mattress was on fire.

And she didn't expect that such callous behavior would hurt so much.

The bathroom door clicked open and she sat up, clutching the sheet to her chin. Danny emerged into the dimly lit room. Asshole or not, he was still the most gorgeous male animal Caroline had ever had the pleasure to see or to touch.

Even now her fingers itched to trace the ridges in his abdomen, to follow the trail of coarse hair that led to . . . she jerked her eyes guiltily to his face to see if she'd been caught staring.

He wasn't even looking at her, and didn't spare her a glance as he pulled on his pants, socks, and shirt. He pulled on his boots and turned to her, finally deigning to acknowledge she was in the room. "I'm going to see if I can find us something to eat and make a few phone calls."

He didn't bother to wait for a reply before he left. Icy wind blustered through the room as the door shut behind him. But the shudder that coursed through Caroline's veins had nothing to do with the temperature outside.

Idiot. She was such an idiot to ever let that happen.

She put her forehead to her sheet covered knees. Five minutes. That's all she was giving herself to wallow and kick herself for her own stupidity. Not so much for letting herself sleep with him. Really, who could blame her? Caroline and James hadn't had sex for nearly a year before he'd been killed, and even before that it was nothing worth bragging to the tennis group about.

Unlike some of her set, Caroline was faithful with a capital F, and never considered finding satisfaction with the poolboy, or the masseur, or the tennis instructor, or any of the other young, good looking, easy going guys some of her acquaintances seemed to collect like stamps.

So when met with a full frontal assault from the one man who had always been able to make her wet and willing by just looking at her the right way, it should be expected that she would be a little vulnerable. That she would indulge.

What she couldn't forgive herself for, she thought as she stepped into a shower hot enough to peel off a layer of skin, was allowing herself to think, even for a second, that maybe . . . maybe this still raging sexual connection meant that something deeper existed between them. He remembered things from when they'd been together and he hadn't hesitated to use them to get to her. Maybe that meant something.

Right. As if that would be enough for her to get over him for tearing her heart out, him to get over his own anger at her. If they managed that, there would still be the issue of her dead husband's involvement in his mother's death to work through.

If they could only accomplish all that, maybe they could find their way back to each other. Just thinking it through was enough to make her hysterical laughter echo off the shower stall. It was either that or sob uncontrollably.

She scrubbed herself with the tiny, cheap bar of soap, and lathered her hair with an envelope of two in one shampoo and conditioner, but she couldn't get the scent of sex, of *him* off of her. She lathered herself twice from head to toe, but it was as though he'd marked her. It didn't help that every time she closed her eyes she was back in the damn hotel that was just like that one, the one he'd forced her to remember before proving to her once again that while the sex they had was off the charts, beyond compare, as a couple they were irretrievably broken.

They had been broken twelve years ago, and one hot round between the sheets wasn't going to change that.

Caroline emerged from the bathroom, relieved to find Danny still gone. She pulled her clothes on and borrowed a comb from his toiletry kit to untangle her hair. She checked her phone and saw that Kate had called twice.

Caroline, I haven't heard from you in two days, and I'm starting to get worried.

She winced guiltily. She'd been so caught up in everything lately she hadn't returned Kate's calls. She knew Kate must be worried, especially after what happened to Rachael.

She hit CALL REPLY, but her phone beeped a warning and died before the call could go through.

Crap. She'd forgotten to charge her battery. She used the

hotel phone to call, not surprised when Kate didn't pick up at the unfamiliar number. Caroline left a message explaining the phone issue and telling Kate to call her back.

The room phone rang less than a minute later. "What's going on with you?" Kate asked before Caroline could even get out a "hello." "Why haven't you called me back? I was getting worried."

Caroline apologized. "We've been really busy. We've found some new information—"

"We? You mean you and the private investigator guy? What have you found out? Any more information about Dad?" Kate asked in her typical breathless manner.

Guilt pricked Caroline as she struggled with how much to reveal. She hated keeping Kate in the dark, but like Danny, she didn't want to inadvertently give too much away until they knew who they were up against. "We're following some leads, that's all I can say right now. I just wanted to let you know I'm safe."

"Where are you, anyway? I don't recognize the area code."

"Believe it or not, we got stuck in a blizzard in some little town you've probably never heard of."

Kate asked what kind of lead would take them up there, but Caroline blew her off. "It's too much to go into right now. We'll be heading back as soon as the roads clear, and I'll fill you in next time I see you."

"Fine," Kate said, her annoyance at Caroline's continued evasiveness evident in her voice.

"Can I talk to Mikey real quick?"

"Actually I need to get going. I'm dropping off Mikey at the sitter's a little early so I can have dinner with someone before class."

Caroline shoved back her disappointment, along with the suspicion that Kate's refusal to let her talk to Michael was a punishment for not telling her everything they'd discovered.

She was probably just in a hurry. Since when had everyone's motives become suspect?

Since your husband was killed, someone tried to pin the murder on you, and then tried to kill you, that's when.

Maybe a little caution was justified.

"Really? Anyone special?" Caroline asked, trying to inject a little enthusiasm in her voice. Kate hadn't dated much at all since Michael was born. She had been so messed up by what Spike had put her through she'd been totally gun-shy about dating anyone since Michael's birth four years ago.

"Maybe. But I don't want to jinx it by talking too much about it. I gotta run."

Caroline hung up, a little miffed Kate wouldn't share the details of her date. Maybe she wasn't sharing because she was afraid Caroline wouldn't approve. She hoped not. Thanks to Spike, the bar was pretty low. As far as Caroline was concerned, anyone with a brain, a job, and an appreciation for Kate was fine with her.

For awhile Caroline thought there might be something going on between Kate and Marshall, one of James's associates at Medford and Kingston. He'd been sniffing hopefully around Kate ever since he'd joined the firm five years ago, and even Kate's relationship with Spike and the birth of Michael hadn't seemed to dampen his enthusiasm.

It would be good for her to date a guy like Marshall. Stable, steady, and obviously smitten.

Unlike some *other* men Caroline could think of. Maybe she should take a page from Kate's book and avoid any emotional entanglements with big tough bad boys who were nothing but bad news.

Caroline turned her attention to putting the room back in order, her resolve strengthening as she went through the comforting ritual of straightening up. First the bed, stripped then remade with precise hospital corners. Then the bathroom, towels draped evenly over the rack, counters wiped down. She even folded the end of the toilet paper roll into a point. She emptied out Danny's duffel bag, folded, and repacked it. And even managed to stop herself from lifting his T-shirt to her nose and taking a deep inhale.

She looked at the neatly made bed and forced herself to relive every second. Especially at the end, when he had pulled away, pushed her hand from his neck, closed his eyes and gone at her like a battering ram. Broken any connection with her until she became nothing but a means to release. She'd felt it, even then, her stomach sinking, the rosy glow of orgasmic bliss fading as she felt him distance himself even before he'd finished.

But that hadn't been enough. She had to push it, reach out, knowing full well he was going to push her away.

The bad taste she was swallowing back was her own damn fault. But in its own twisted way, that was good. From the beginning, she'd been sure Danny was flirting, teasing, pushing her to make a point. And he'd made it. He could still make her come.

And he didn't have any lingering tenderness for her and what they had.

Message received, loud and clear.

But he didn't realize that Caroline wasn't the same girl who'd loved him so mindlessly years ago. She was tough, she was practical, and she could take anything he dished out. She was just as capable of having hot, sweaty, mean-ingless sex as he was. If he wanted to use sex to prove that the past was the past and there was nothing left between them . . .

Bring it on.

Kate felt a rush of anticipation as she spotted Marshall across the crowded cafe. He'd tried to convince her to meet him at a fancier place near his office, but she'd held firm on meeting him someplace casual near campus.

Several people took a second look as he wound his way through the tables, flashing her his killer grin. It wasn't just his soap star good looks that drew attention his way. In his gray suit, pressed white dress shirt and red tie, he stood out like a sore thumb in a sea of casually dressed students.

As he reached her table he leaned over and gave her a quick kiss on the cheek. Her nose filled with the scent of hair gel and expensive cologne. She wasn't sure she liked it.

Which was, she supposed, the problem with Marshall in general.

Still, she couldn't help but return his smile as he took the seat across from her. "Thanks for meeting me," he said, his teeth flashing whitely against skin so perfectly brown she wondered if he got a professional spray tan.

"No, thank you for giving me a reason to have a meal that doesn't involve hot dogs, mac n' cheese, or any food that comes in a nugget form." She smiled up at the waitress as she dropped off Kate's glass of chardonnay. She winked at Marshall's cocked eyebrow. "Trust me, Feminist Tropes in Victorian Literature will seem a lot more interesting after I have a couple of these."

Fine lines fanned out from Marshall's crystal blue eyes as he returned her grin. "I'm really glad we have a chance to catch up. It's been too long since I've seen you."

Kate's cheeks warmed under his frankly admiring gaze and she took a sip of her wine to ease her discomfort. She knew Marshall was attracted to her. She'd known it from the first time she'd met him five years ago when he was starting as a new associate at her father's law firm.

At the time she'd dismissed perfect, polished Marshall with his soap opera actor good looks as too old, too boring, too *lame* to be anything other than entertaining eye candy.

Why in the world would she want to date a lawyer, especially one who worked with her father? But since her father's death, Marshall had shown himself to be a surprisingly good friend, quietly supportive, always available for a quick drink, coffee, meal, whatever, when she was craving a little male attention. And unlike the handful of other guys she'd tried to date in recent years, he didn't leave skid marks when she mentioned she had a little boy waiting for her at home.

Friendship aside, she knew Marshall wanted more. There was something really flattering about having a guy like Marshall, gorgeous, successful, eminently eligible, willing to put up with her cat and mouse game after all that time. Especially when more and more lately she was feeling less like a young, sexually attractive woman, and more like a tired old mom, stuck in the grind of life as a single parent and a full time student. Between the constant low level fatigue and the ten plus pounds of baby weight she still carried—although, to be fair, after four years, she supposed the weight was officially hers—she felt about as sexy as the pair of granny panties she was sporting under her jeans.

So it was nice, she reflected as she admired the broad set of Marshall's shoulders as he slipped off his suit coat, to be reminded that a man—especially a man as physically perfect as Marshall—found her attractive.

So what was wrong with her that she couldn't just dive in head first? On paper, he was perfect. And therein lay the problem. There were no rough edges, no visible flaws, and something about that made Kate extremely nervous. She couldn't shake the feeling he was hiding something under all that perfection, though there was certainly no evidence to show her otherwise.

Maybe she was just being paranoid.

"How's Michael?" Marshall asked, looking at her expectantly.

That was another thing. Though he tried to look all interested and engaged, Kate knew he didn't really want to hear about Mikey's latest preschool exploits. She'd seen the zoned out look in his eyes often and knew better not to go into any deep detail. "He's great. He's almost mastered the alphabet."

Marshall nodded absently and took a sip of his drink. Kate shoved back the disappointment. Could she really expect anyone to be as impressed as she was that her four-year-old could almost read already? Maybe like Caroline said, she was being too hard on him.

As though he'd read her thoughts, Marshall asked, "How's Caroline doing? Is she okay after what happened to Rachael Weller?"

Kate put down her fork as her stomach knotted with dread. Despite Caroline's assurances that she was fine, not to mention safe, with the private investigator she'd hired, Kate couldn't stop worrying. "I don't know. I talked to her earlier. Did I tell you she's hired some private investigator?"

Marshall leaned forward and rested his elbows on the table. "I think you might have mentioned that. What do you know about this guy?"

"Do you remember that whole thing with Alyssa Miles a couple of months ago?" Marshall nodded. "It was his firm that was involved, his brother, actually, who rescued her from her kidnappers. So I guess they know what they're doing but . . ."

"What?"

Kate shook her head, hating having to explain away her unsubstantiated hunches to Marshall. He was a typical lawyer, all analytical and demanding evidence. "I don't know. They're looking into my father's murder, and she won't tell me anything about what she's been doing for the past week. Which makes me worry that what they've found is bad, because Caroline and I usually talk at least once a day, and she tells me everything."

"Maybe they haven't found anything yet."

Kate shook her head and drained her wine glass. "They found enough to drive up to the mountains and get stuck in a blizzard. She finally called me back from some random number in the 209 area code after I left her like ten messages." She closed her mouth, realized she'd been babbling as she had a tendency to do. "Sorry, I don't mean to unload on you. It's just really driving me crazy, not knowing what's going on with her, especially after everything that's happened."

He laid his hand on hers and leaned across the table. "You can always talk to me, Kate. That's what I'm here for."

I should kiss him. It would be the perfect moment. Just lay one on him, get this show on the road and quit dancing around the do I or don't I question. His thumb stroked across the back of her hand. Smooth, uncalloused, almost as soft as her own. She pushed back in her chair. "I'm going to hit the ladies room," she said and withdrew her hand as unobtrusively as possible. "If the waitress comes back, will you order me a refill?"

Jackpot. Marshall watched Kate's lush, denim clad ass disappear through the heavy black curtains hiding the door to the cafe's unisex bathroom.

He grabbed Kate's phone off the table and quickly scrolled through the caller ID until he found the number she was talking about. Then he took a phone out of his pocket. Not his regular cell, but the prepaid one he used to communicate with Patrick and Gates. Though the display said, "unknown caller," a quick call to the number got him the front desk of the Whiskey Creek Motor Inn.

Shit. Marshall diconnected and quickly dialed again.

Patrick answered on the first ring. "What do you want? I'm about to go in with a patient."

"Just thought you might like to know Caroline and Taggart are up in Whiskey Creek. As of six p.m. they were at the Whiskey Creek Motor Inn."

"Son of a bitch. We're fucked."

"Not necessarily. Remember, there's nothing linking you to Anne Taggart or Emily Parrish. Anything they have to go on points at James."

"That we know of. We still haven't found the evidence James said he kept."

Marshall made a scoffing sound and kept an eye on the bathroom for Kate. "I have serious doubts any evidence exists. James was bluffing."

"I knew James for thirty years. The man didn't bluff. It's somewhere. We need to find it. And we need to take care of Caroline and Taggart."

Marshall thought of Kate with a twinge of guilt. He knew how close Kate and her stepmother were, knew it would kill her if something happened to Caroline. "Maybe we should lay low, see how this plays out."

"We can't afford to waste any more time. Thanks to you and your so called clever cover-up, Caroline's still alive, and she and Taggart have already learned too much. Once the cops figure out James was involved with Anne and Emily's deaths, don't you think they'll take a harder look at who killed him? Maybe they won't be able to brush Caroline off like they have been. And if they keep looking, what do you think they'll find?"

"Nothing," Marshall said firmly. "We have nothing to worry about. We've covered our tracks too well."

"Right, until James's 'insurance policy' gets out. Then

we're all screwed. We have no choice. We need to find that
evidence, and get Caroline and Taggart out of the picture
before they do any more damage. I'll go back to Caroline's
house, you rip apart the office one more time and take another look at Kate's place. And call Gates. Tell him where
Caroline is, have him take care of it. And tell him we need it
to look like an accident."

Marshall didn't bother pointing out that he could tell
Gates whatever he wanted, but the scary motherfucker
would take care of it in whatever way he deemed best.

He disconnected and tucked the phone back in his pocket
as Kate rejoined him at the table. It wasn't hard to conjure
up a look of regret as he told her he had to cut dinner short.
In addition to finding out what he could about Caroline and
her investigation into James's murder, he'd been looking
forward to making more progress in his quest to get into
Kate's pants.

Instead of ending the evening with at least a kiss and a
promise of another date—a real one—in the next couple of
days, he was going to make an urgent call to ensure someone else Kate loved was taken care of once and for all.

"Really? You can't even finish your dinner?" Kate's full
bottom lip stuck out in a pretend little girl pout. Marshall
wondered what she'd do if he leaned across the table and
nipped her lip the way he was dying to.

"Sorry. Urgent situation with a client," he said and rose
from the table.

Kate sighed and rose to give him a hug. He closed his
eyes and took a deep breath, savoring her scent as much as
the soft press of her body against him.

Not tonight, but soon.

He consoled himself with the fact that he would be the
first one there to comfort her when the shit went down. He

could feel it now. Kate warm and lush and soft in his arms as Marshall kissed away her tears. She'd turn to him in her grief, defenses down, and he would finally get what he'd wanted from the first day he'd set eyes on Kate Medford.

He was on the phone to Gates by the time the cafe door closed behind him.

CHAPTER 12

D anny slogged through shin deep powder as he walked
along the edge of the road to the diner down the street.
The woman working the desk at the motel had assured him
he could get a decent meal to take back to the room for
himself and Caroline.

It would have been easier to get something at the conve-
nience store next to the motel, but he needed something
more sustaining than a bag of chips or a hot dog that had
spent days sweating on the roller.

Besides, he needed more time to put himself back together before he went back in that room with Caroline.

Snow was trickling down the tops of his boots and chilling his feet. He sucked in a lungful of freezing air, taking in
the cold, hoping it would bring down his core temperature
a few hundred degrees.

After all this time, she still burned him alive. He came to
the diner and ordered a cheeseburger for himself and a
chicken sandwich for Caroline, remembering her thing about
ground beef. She'd always contended that it, like hotdogs,
was a clearing house for all the parts of the cow they couldn't
use in "real" meat, and refused to touch the stuff.

It bugged him that he remembered that about her. It
bugged him that he remembered lots of little shit like that

about her. Because it reinforced what he'd already realized was true. Caroline wasn't like one of the nameless, faceless fucks he'd had over the years, and he was an idiot for thinking she ever could be.

He'd been so cockily sure that there was nothing left but a big empty space where his feelings for Caroline used to live. There was a big space all right, but he'd realized it was crammed full with a thick dark mass of stuff he didn't even want to begin to look at.

He had a bad feeling there were more masses like that lurking under his surface. Big emotional tumors he needed to excise before they destroyed him from the inside out.

Speaking of bad feelings, there was a call he couldn't put off making any longer. Even before they'd come up here and spoken with Emily's parents, the bad feeling had gnawed at his gut. Danny had always had keen instincts, especially when something bad was about to go down. It had gotten to the point that the men he used to command joked that he was psychic.

Now that he knew for sure Emily hadn't returned to live with her parents after she'd left Harmony House, his instincts were screaming that hers was the body found near his mother's. There was only one way to know for sure.

Detective DeLuca answered on the second ring. A twenty-five year veteran with the San Mateo County Sheriff's department, he'd worked on Anne Taggart's case after she'd initially disappeared, and had unofficially helped the Taggarts over the years as they'd continued their search privately. When the bodies had been found a little over six weeks ago, DeLuca had tipped them off that one of them could be Anne.

Danny was returning the favor, morbid though it was. "Hank, I think I have a lead on that second Jane Doe you found. Emily Parrish. You should be able to check dental records."

"How did you come up with the name?"

He wasn't ready to give that information up. He didn't give a shit about protecting James Medford or anyone else connected to Harmony House, but he had a gut feeling that if word got out the police were investigating James Medford's connection to this case, Caroline would be in even more danger than she already was. "I'll promise to give you all the details as soon as I can," Danny replied. "But for now, the name is all I've got."

Hank's heavy sigh echoed over the phone line. "You know I can only coast on an anonymous tip for so long. Eventually I'll have to bring you in for questioning."

"That won't be necessary," Danny promised. "I have some loose ends to wrap up," *oh like a thousand,* "and I promise I'll hand the whole thing over in a neat little package."

"I'll hold you to that. So Emily Parrish?"

"Yeah, two r's, grew up in Whiskey Creek. That should narrow your search."

Danny hung up with DeLuca and immediately dialed Derek.

"We were expecting you to check in several hours ago," Derek said without bothering with a greeting.

"I've been busy. Besides, I'm wearing my watch. You know where I am." Ever since they'd started Gemini, Danny, Derek, and Ethan wore GPS tracking devices in their watches. At any given time, they could locate one another by the exact latitude and longitude anywhere on the map.

"We still need an update on Emily Parrish."

"Like I said," Danny said, smiling through clenched teeth as he took his bag of food from the waitress, "I had some things to take care of."

Derek barked a laugh into the phone. "Yeah, I bet you did. According to your chip, you left the Parrishes' nearly three hours ago, and have spent the last two at the Whiskey

Creek Motor Inn. Now you're at the local diner. Let me guess. Caroline's back in the room resting up and you're getting a burger to refuel for round two."

Dammit. Sometimes Danny really resented the hell out of this accountability bullshit. "Well I'm calling you now, aren't I? At least unlike some people, I don't blow off my clients for more than twenty-four hours and fail to check in so I can chase a hot piece of ass to the beach."

"That 'hot piece of ass' is my fiancee, dickhead, and point taken."

Danny quickly filled in Derek on what they'd learned. "You're sure it's her?" he asked soberly when Danny told him his hunch about the body.

"Like I said, it's a hunch, but—"

"In the past your hunches have kicked ass over most of our careful analysis."

Danny didn't argue, but he took no pride in it. For all the accuracy of his hunches, most of the time they didn't come in time to prevent disaster. His feeling that it was Emily up on that hillside with his mother certainly wasn't going to help her or her baby at this point. "De Luca's on the ID," he continued. "But I want you and Ethan to go back up to La Honda, ask around about Emily and James Medford this time. See if you can put them there near the time Anne disappeared."

"We'll get on it."

"How's Dad?" Danny asked, not sure he wanted to know the answer.

"The same," Derek said after a pause.

Danny pinched the bridge of his nose. He knew what that meant. Joe was still closed up in his den, drinking vodka by the bottle, the TV tuned to a channel he wasn't watching as he tried to drown out the outside world. "Did you tell him what we found out?" Danny had hoped that news of progress on Anne's case would start to pull his dad out of a nosedive.

"He doesn't want to hear about it," Derek said. Though his inflection barely changed, Danny could hear the repressed grief in his brother's voice. Since Anne's body had been identified, their father had done a complete one eighty. For eighteen years he'd searched tirelessly, single-mindedly, as focused on his mission as he'd ever been as a soldier. But when the news came down that Anne was dead, it was as if all the life drained out of him.

All those years Danny had resented his father for his futile quest to find a woman who didn't want to be found. He remembered all the fights, all the arguments, all the times he told his father he was an idiot to keep up his search. He never realized the search was the only thing that kept his father going.

And now everything Danny thought he knew about his mother's disappearance was unraveling. He could only hope that by finding out the truth of what happened to Anne, he could give his father some peace and comfort.

As for himself, it was too late.

By the time he got back to the motel with their dinner, Danny's hair was soaked with snow and any warmth he'd soaked in from the diner was long gone. Caroline had showered and dressed. Her damp hair rippled down her back and her face was scrubbed clean of makeup. She nodded briefly when he walked in, then turned back to the news program she'd turned on, giving no indication that less than an hour ago she'd been naked underneath him and digging her nails into his ass, silently begging him to fuck her harder.

She'd made the bed too, obliterating any physical sign of their tussle. The bedspread was smooth, pillows fluffed, not a single crease visible in the cases. His duffel bag was zipped and stashed in a corner, and all the towels were hung perfectly straight in the bathroom. Everything was in perfect order, the room untouched, pristine, as though the last few hours hadn't happened.

It pissed him off.

Danny tossed the bags of food on the little table. "I got you a sandwich."

She raised an eyebrow and caught a bag before it slid to the floor. She opened the bag and wrinkled her nose as she pulled out a chicken sandwich and fries. "Ooh, breaded and fried and mayonnaise. My cardiologist will love this."

He sat down in the opposite chair and pulled out his burger. "Sorry it's not five star, but it was either this or gas station food."

"You could have at least ordered me a salad," she huffed.

"Or I could have skipped going out in a blizzard and let you starve," he said and ripped a bite out of his burger. He watched her pull apart her sandwich and wipe off most of the mayo with a napkin.

By the time he polished off his burger, she was still picking the breading off her chicken breast. He tossed the bag into the garbage and paced, restlessness vibrating through his limbs until he couldn't sit still. Usually after a good, lusty, fuck he could count on the relaxed satisfaction carrying through for at least a few hours, sometimes even a few days.

But he couldn't shake the sensation that his skin was too tight for his body, like if he didn't blow off some of the excess energy he was liable to combust. Leave it to Caroline to change the game on him. He didn't even have to look at her. All he had to do was smell her from across the room, think about how good she'd tasted, coming against his lips and tongue, how hot and tight she was around him after all that time, and he was right back where he'd been for the last few days. Hard as a spike and pissed the hell off.

Meanwhile, Caroline sat there picking at her sandwich as though she didn't even realize he was there.

"Just eat it already! Jesus, when the hell did you get so fucking picky?" Christ, it bugged him. The way his practical no nonsense Caroline had turned into such a snob.

Scratch that. She's not your Caroline, and never was.

The thought jarred him back to reality, reminding him what they were doing out there in the middle of bumfuck nowhere in the first place. "I think the other body is Emily's," he said without preamble.

Caroline was shocked enough by the abrupt change in subject that she froze in the act of chewing the bite of sandwich she'd finally deigned to take. Her face went chalk white. She set the rest of the sandwich on the table and pushed it away and nodded slowly. "As much as I hate to think about it, it makes sense."

"They're checking dental records and should know for sure within a couple days. In the meantime, I asked Derek if he and Ethan can go back to La Honda, see if anyone can put Emily and James there around the same time Anne's car was seen up there."

"Why do you keep calling her Anne?" The anger in her tone was enough to stop his pacing. Caroline sat back in the armchair, arms folded, her dark eyes narrowed in a glare.

"Because that's her name."

Caroline pushed up from her chair. "She's your mother, Danny."

A fact he had no intention of dealing with, not here, not in front of her. Still, hazy memories forced their way into his mind. A soft hand in his hair. The smell of her face cream as she pressed a good night kiss to his cheek. A soft, slightly off key voice singing "Puff the Magic Dragon." Little expressions of love, memories he'd buried in the time since she disappeared and he'd convinced himself she couldn't have cared much about them at all.

He couldn't let them in until he'd closed the case. If he let them in, he'd drown under the weight of his guilt, his grief.

"Right now she's a case," he said harshly, reminding himself as much as Caroline. "Just like you're a case. Nothing more, nothing less."

Caroline's mouth pulled tight. "Right. Nothing touches you, does it? Not even the fact that your mother is dead and my husband might have killed her, and maybe killed another girl too." Her voice caught on a sob and she wrapped her arms around her waist as though she was holding herself together. "How did you get so cold, Danny? How did it happen, and how did I not see it coming? Even after your mom first disappeared, you weren't like this. You need to deal with this, Danny. You can't pretend this is just another case, because it's not. I know you still care about her—"

"You don't know shit!" he yelled. Her words battered him, cracking the barriers he'd put up so long ago. He couldn't deal with this, couldn't deal with her, and the dark soupy mess she threatened to unleash inside of him. He turned on her with a snarl. "You think because we fucked around when we were a couple of stupid kids, you know me? You think because I got you off a few times, you get to go all Dr. Phil and pry into my head? You don't know anything about me, what I care about. And if you think what happened in this room changes any of that, you're not nearly as smart as I gave you credit for."

He waited in dark anticipation for his words to find their mark. A sick, twisted side of him wanted to see her flinch, wanted to see the hurt and devastation on her face. She shook him to his core. All he wanted to do was mete out his own destruction.

Her slow smile and laugh sent a shock wave through him. For the first time it occurred to him that maybe she cared as little about him as he pretended to care about her. "Don't worry, Danny, I'm not the same idiot who convinced herself she was in love with the first guy she slept with and spent six years fighting tooth and nail for a relationship that should never have moved past high school graduation." He felt his mouth drop open as she stripped her sweater over her head. "I was too young then, and too guilty, I suppose, to realize sex was the only thing we had between us."

That young, idealistic idiot inside him wanted to scream in protest. That dumb kid who'd loved Caroline with every cell of his body fought to reject what she was saying.

But Danny shoved that kid right back into the hole he'd been living in for the past twelve years.

Lust raged as she came closer, her breasts swelling over the cups of her lacy black bra.

"What the fuck are you doing?"

Her eyes widened in feigned surprise as her hands stilled on the button of her jeans. "You don't want to talk, and we can either sit here in silence, stewing about all the shit going on around us, or we can pass the time doing the one thing we're good at. Unless you're too tired from before?" Her fingers flicked open the button of her jeans and her zipper was as loud as a buzz saw as she eased it down.

God damn Caroline, always changing the game. This was the woman he remembered, always standing up to him, giving as good as she got. A surge of affection bubbled through his veins, and he shoved it aside. He couldn't afford to like her, couldn't afford to admire her, couldn't afford to rehash all the reasons he'd once thought she was the only woman on the planet for him.

Black lace peeked through the vee of her jeans as she sauntered over, all smoldering dark eyes and slinky curves. She stopped close enough for him to feel the soft warmth of her satin and lace clad breasts through his T-shirt. His cock hardened another inch, straining behind his zipper like it hadn't gone off like a geyser less than an hour ago. His stomach muscles jerked like he'd been shocked as Caroline hooked a finger in the hem of his shirt and drew it up a couple of inches. "Come on Danny, what do you say? One more round for old time's sake?"

She was calling his bluff, daring him to prove they were nothing more than two animals fucking for mutual satisfaction, and had never been anything but.

He whipped his shirt over his head and kicked his boots off. Caroline better watch out. If she remembered anything about him, she knew Danny Taggart never turned down a dare.

Caroline watched him strip in quick, angry motions. She swallowed hard, cursing the wild impulse that made her goad him on. She'd grabbed the tiger by the tail but she didn't dare back down. She shoved her jeans off her hips and down her legs and watched him do the same.

His cock was rock hard, bulging with veins as it stood at attention between his thighs. His heavy sac was pulled up tight against his body. "All for me," she murmured, proud of the way her hand didn't shake as she reached out to stroke him.

"For now anyway," he said.

She shot him a glare, but his attention was riveted on the sight of her slender fingers circling his cock. She squeezed her fist up and down his length and reached out her other hand to cup his balls. "For as long as I want it." She pumped him again, pausing to run her thumb over the smooth head. He let out a harsh groan and her pussy clenched in anticipation.

Caroline leaned in and licked at a bead of sweat that was charting a course down his abdomen. His skin was hot, salty, intoxicating against her tongue. His groan echoed in her ears as she covered his torso with wet, sucking kisses. She slid lower, sinking to her knees, rubbing his cock against her belly as she slid to the floor.

He stood stock still in front of her, practically shaking with need. She could feel the faint tremor of his fingers as he laced them through her hair. But to give him credit, he didn't tighten his fist and shove her where he wanted her to go.

As much as she appreciated that, Caroline wasn't ready to stop the torture. Keeping a firm hand on his cock, she leaned forward to press a kiss to his inner thigh. He widened his stance, arched his hips into her hand. She rewarded him with a nuzzle to his lower abdomen. Licks, sucks, soft, wispy butterfly kisses, landing everywhere but where he wanted them.

She was so caught up in her torment that she didn't hear his throaty growl until it was too late. Suddenly she found herself lifted off the floor and landing face down on one of the beds.

"Little tease," he murmured, his breath hot against her ear. "You should know better than to tease me, Carrie."

She felt a tug, heard a ripping sound, and what was left of her panties flew across the room. Her bra was next, unhooked and jerked down her arms. She tried to roll over but was stayed by a firm hand on the small of her back. Desire flooded through her, along with a little curl of uncertainty. He was so big, so hard, almost menacing behind her.

It was always part of the turn on, the idea that he could so easily overpower her and do whatever he wanted to her. But his big, hard body had never delivered anything but pleasure.

But that was before. What if she'd pushed him too far?

She'd barely completed the thought before she felt his big hand slide between her legs from behind. Long, thick fingers parted her lips, came to rest on either side of her clit and stroked back and forth. Caroline drew her knees up under her to give him better access.

His legs brushed the backs of her thighs as he knelt behind her, and she felt his cock like an iron brand against the curve of her ass. She rocked her hips back, rubbing herself against his fingers, urging him to come inside her.

"You want me to fuck you, Caroline?" He slid his cock between her thighs, replacing his fingers with his hard length. He dragged himself back and forth against her drenched slit. "Or do you want to play your little games?" He drew back and slid just the head of his cock inside. She reared back, trying to take him deeper, but he wrapped one hand around his cock and the other around her hip, tormenting her with just that shallow penetration.

"How much do you want me to fuck you?" He slid out, then in, barely entering her.

Damn him. She'd meant to call his bluff, teach him a little lesson She should have known she would be the one who ended up begging. Still . . .

She wasn't conceding defeat just yet.

"I'm dying for you to fuck me," she said with a secret grin he couldn't see. She circled her ass and rocked her hips against him. "I want you to fuck me hard and deep, slide your cock in me so deep I can feel you in the back of my throat." She heard his breath hitch and was glad she was facing away so he wouldn't see the heat of embarrassment in her face. "I need you to fuck me so much I'm afraid I'm going to come before you get all the way inside me," she moaned, feeling the dirty talk roll off her tongue now that her head was full of the images she was describing.

And it was working for Danny too. His grip on her hips tightened as he squeezed himself all the way in and held himself there. Caroline's words dropped off with a cry as he buried himself deep.

So wet. So tight. Danny struggled for control as Caroline rocked her ass back against him, taking his whole, aching length into her body with a loud moan of pleasure. *Still screaming the rafters down after all these years.* His hands tightened on her hips as he held her still, struggling to get a hold of himself.

"Don't slow down," she panted, struggling against his hold as she tried to work herself on his thick length. "Fuck me like you mean it." Heat shot through his body, singeing its way to the head of his cock as he struggled not to come immediately. The raw demand in her throaty voice was enough to send him over the edge. The feel of her hot, slick, clenching around him, was so good he was on the verge of incinerating.

"Jesus, where'd you learn to talk like that?" he asked as he flexed his hips, withdrawing inch by torturous inch, savoring the feel of her all the way. Then back inside, showing her, showing himself, dammit, that she could whip him into a frenzy but he would never lose control.

She tossed him a naughty smile over her shoulder. "You like it? I learned from the best."

He paused, thrown off kilter as he wondered for an agonizing second who the fuck the "best" was.

She moaned, arching like a cat, pushing back to take him deeper. "Remember the first time you told me how good my pussy felt around your cock?"

His balls tightened and his dick pulsed inside her wet heat.

"I was so embarrassed." Another moan, another swivel of her hips, one he met with a counter swivel of his own. Her dark eyes met his eyes over her shoulder. Her mouth was plump and red. "I'm not embarrassed now. Especially when I know talking like this makes you so *hard* . . ." her words ended on a groan as he thrust inside her, unable to control himself under her onslaught. "God, Danny, I've never felt anything like your cock in me."

A groan tore from his chest as he began to thrust hard and fast. His fingers sank into the soft flesh of her hips as the sounds of sex mingled with their increasing groans.

Nothing had ever felt like her pussy, so hot and tight and wet around him, like he'd developed a trillion additional nerve endings in the head of his cock.

A tiny part of his brain still possessing common sense recognized why.

No condom.

He was in her, totally bare, nothing separating them.

He'd never fucked a woman without a condom. Not even Caroline back in the day. He'd never felt the hot slick grip of a woman's pussy against his unsheathed cock. And it was better than he'd ever imagined.

And some sick, stupid part of himself—that dumb kid he tried to keep locked in the root cellar—took savage satisfaction that this first time was with Caroline. Her bare flesh yielding around him. Her juice glistening on his cock as he thrust and withdrew, pummeling her into the mattress as she pushed back against him, taking him as deep as he could possibly go.

He should stop, now, pull out and go get a condom before things really got messy. It was a good measure of how far gone he was that he didn't even pause in his thrusts.

He didn't think he'd stop if someone put a gun to his head. It was too good, too much, he needed to savor every second. His eyes were locked on her, unable to look away. It should have been dirty, primitive, animalistic. He was taking her in the basest way possible, fucking her from behind, not even looking at her face.

Even so, he couldn't stop thinking how beautiful she was, how beautiful *they* were as he watched his cock disappearing inside her. The lines of her back, the curve of her hips, the silkiness of her skin under his fingers struck him as uniquely gorgeous, even as he tried with everything in him to see her as a body, a sex object, another gray cat in the dark.

Her cries grew louder and she spread her knees wider as

she rocked back against him. A surge of triumph coursed through his veins as she stiffened and convulsed around him. He rode her through it, never easing up on his pace as her cunt flexed and released around him.

Danny felt his own climax building, gathering steam as her body milked him. Every instinct screamed for him to come inside her, hold himself deep until she'd wrung him dry of every last drop.

As the first wave of his climax hit him, he somehow conjured up a shred of restraint. He pulled out, his cock jerking and pulsing as he shot thick jets of come across the lush curve of her ass. He collapsed onto the mattress, half on top of her, feeling like he'd been blown into a million pieces and scattered across the room.

What the fuck had just happened here?

The little crack in the wall was threatening to spread wide open. In his effort to bring his relationship with Caroline back to its most base, meaningless level, he'd inadvertently uncovered a cache of emotional baggage he didn't even know he'd been carrying around. Now it wanted to spill out, the huge colossal mess he didn't even want to acknowledge much less deal with.

Caroline stirred beside him and he braced himself, keeping his face partially hidden by the pillow so she couldn't see him watching her. She rose to a kneeling position and reached back, tracing her fingers through the sticky fluid on her left butt cheek. She held her hand up and stared at it for a moment, her expression unreadable.

"Thanks for pulling out. Wouldn't want this to get any more complicated," she said before sliding from the bed and heading for the bathroom.

She emerged a few minutes later, freshly showered and wrapped in a towel. Without asking his permission she unzipped his duffel bag, withdrew a T-shirt and pulled it over her head. He tingled with anticipation and dread, waiting for her to come back to bed. Would she want to talk? Would she want to cuddle?

Would she want to fuck again?

His cock twitched, apparently approving of that idea.

He watched with mingled relief and disappointment as she pulled back the bedspread on the other bed and slid between the sheets.

She took the remote off the table, clicked on the TV, and settled back against the pillows as though he wasn't naked in a bed less than three feet away.

They stayed like that all night, staring at the TV, not talking.

When they finally got tired they turned off the lights and slept facing away from each other in their separate beds. Two combatants retreating to their separate corners.

"I'll take care of it," Gates said, "but tell Patrick he's going to owe me for cleaning up his messes."

He hung up on Marshall and made another quick call to make the arrangements. Fucking idiot James Medford was coming back to haunt them from the grave. Unlike Patrick, Gates had been convinced James Medford's secrets had died with him. They'd searched his house—discreetly, so Caroline wouldn't suspect—and found nothing.

But even without the evidence James claimed to have been keeping, Caroline Medford and Taggart were getting too close.

Not to Gates, of course. The thing with Anne Taggart had happened well before Gates' involvement with Medford and Easterbrook. Gates had only learned of the connection when Anne Taggart's body was identified and Easterbrook started to get antsy all over again.

The last thing he needed was for the cops to come sniffing around Easterbrook and stumble across him in the process. If the evidence James Medford had saved really did exist, they needed to find it before it led the authorities straight to Gates.

"Tear Medford's place apart," he said. He was finished being careful and discreet. He had a business to protect.

When dealing with drugs and whores, it was easy enough to move the merchandise when the Feds got too close. But there was too much invested in the facility, too many people in the network for the adoption ring to reestablish itself easily. If he lost it, it would take years to recoup his losses.

Gates hadn't been too concerned when the first attempt on Caroline Medford's life had failed. But she and Taggart were getting too close to the truth, getting too close to him, and that was unacceptable.

Whatever secrets they'd learned needed to die with them.

CHAPTER 13

The next morning dawned clear and cold. The sky was a bright, cerulean blue against the mountains and the sun bounced so brightly off the white snow Caroline squinted at it even through sunglasses. In the bright alpine wilderness Whiskey Creek was transformed from a shabby, worn down dot on a map into a secret mountain paradise.

She focused on the cold air in her lungs and the breathtaking beauty of the mountains. Anything to keep her attention from the man striding across the parking lot, his breath steaming around a face as hard and cold as the mountain peaks surrounding her. Dark wraparound shades hid his cool gray eyes and his mouth was set in a tight line.

He paused as a truck pulling a trailer with a snow machine on it passed in front of him, then continued to where she was waiting under the awning in front of the motel's office. Danny handed her a cup without a word.

She murmured thanks and took a sip, impressed in spite of herself that he'd remembered exactly how she liked her coffee. Light but not too light. Sweet but not too sweet. "Are the roads clear?" she asked as she followed him to his Jeep.

"They just finished plowing the last stretch," he said as

he unlocked the driver's side door. "Weather's supposed to be good so we should be fine to get home." He got in and leaned over to pop the lock on her side.

"You know, in my century they make cars with things called automatic locks," she couldn't help sniping. Anything to penetrate the oppressive silence that had enveloped them from the moment they woke up.

She'd taken one look at him, laying awake in his separate bed, and the tension between them had gone way beyond awkward, straight to excruciating, and hadn't abated a bit as they'd dressed, and packed up to leave.

She couldn't decide what was worse. Looking at him and remembering in vivid, unsparing detail exactly what had gone on in that room. Or looking at him and knowing with dread and certainty, that the body with Anne Taggart's had been that of Emily Parrish, and that James had most likely killed them both.

Caroline opted not to dwell on either.

Danny's only response to her swipe was a grunt as he backed out of the parking space. Caroline stared out the window as Danny drove for several miles on the freshly plowed road. The view of the mountains was quickly obscured by the thick pine forest edging either side of the road. "It's beautiful up here," she murmured. Almost beautiful enough to make her forget the ugliness she would have to somehow come to terms with.

"I ran a race up around here a couple years ago. It's even more beautiful fifty miles into the backcountry."

"Like a marathon kind of a race?" She turned her attention away from the view to look at him. When Danny played football in high school and when he'd joined the military, he'd done the necessary conditioning runs, but she'd never known him to run for pleasure. Especially not at those distances. It seemed too boring, too repetitive, for someone like Danny.

He let out a humorless laugh. "Not just a marathon, an ultramarathon. The race I did through this area was one hundred ten miles with over twelve thousand feet of elevation gain."

Her mouth dropped open. "You ran one hundred miles? In a row?" No one could be that psycho.

She looked at the man sitting across the seat from her. Maybe Danny could be that psycho.

"Some people do yoga and meditate, some people drink or do drugs. I run. It takes the edge off and calms the demons for a little while."

What demons do you have, Danny? Are some of them the same as mine?

Caroline didn't dare ask those questions. "How much do you have to run to train for something like that?"

"I usually run fifteen miles or so a day," he said and rolled his shoulders restlessly.

"That explains it."

"What?"

"Why you're so lean." Running fifteen miles a day shaved any spare flesh from his body. "You don't have a single ounce of fat anywhere on your body." Heat rose to her cheeks as he cocked a knowing brow at her. She snapped her mouth shut, cursing herself for mentioning his body, even thinking about his body, because that brought up a whole slew of images reminding her of exactly how she knew he was all lean, hard muscle. Everywhere.

He turned back to the road while a smile that was annoyingly close to a smirk tugged at his mouth. "You're looking pretty good yourself."

Her face flamed hotter as she thought about all of the different angles from which he'd been able to make that assessment.

The smile faded from Danny's mouth as he glanced in the rearview mirror. He shifted the Jeep into fifth and pressed on the gas. He glanced in the mirror again and his brow furrowed as he sped up even more.

Caroline looked back to see a blue sedan following closely. Two men were in the car, their faces partially hidden by dark sunglasses, their heads covered in knit skullcaps.

Danny took a curve at stomach lurching speed. "Why don't you pull over and let them pass?"

"I have a feeling that would be a really bad idea."

The Jeep's tires squealed as Danny took another curve. Caroline watched as the sedan fishtailed on the wet pavement behind them, but didn't give up any ground. She gave a little cry as the sedan knocked into the bumper of the Jeep. "What's happening?"

"Trying to knock us off the road, I imagine," Danny replied, totally calm. For once, Caroline was grateful for Danny's ability to suppress any sign of emotion. They only needed one person freaking out in the car, and that person was definitely her.

Caroline dug her fingers into the dashboard as the Jeep whipped around another curve. They were near the top of a pass, and the forest broke as the road wound its way around the side of the mountain. A thousand foot deep canyon opened up beside them, nothing but a single guardrail keeping the Jeep from plunging to the jagged rocks below.

The driver of the sedan crossed the double yellow line and turned sharply into the Jeep, sending it into the rail. Caroline gave a little scream and closed her eyes. That way her last sight would be of the beautiful mountains and the blue sky, not the ground rushing up to meet her.

Miraculously, the Jeep kept its grip on the road and shot

forward, gaining ground as the sedan was forced to slow to avoid going through the guard rail. Blood roared in her ears as Danny, grim, silent, focused, negotiated the sharp, exposed curves until they were once again surrounded by forest. It was small relief, but Caroline figured they had a better chance of surviving a collision with a tree than a plunge down a cliff face.

Caroline heard a loud pop and the back window of Danny's Jeep exploded.

"What happened?"

"Motherfucker's shooting at us," Danny said grimly as he slid lower in his seat. "I want you to get your head down and stay there."

Caroline ducked down and pressed her face against the upholstered seat. She moved to unbuckle her seatbelt so she could slide all the way to the floor.

"Don't. You're going to need that."

The Jeep veered sharply to the right, jerking and bucking as Danny steered it off the road and into the woods.

"Are you insane?" she asked, popping her head up to see nothing but snowdrifts and thick trunks of trees.

"According to the GPS we'll hook up with a forest service road in 500 meters."

A tree branch exploded next to her window a millisecond before Caroline heard the crack of the gunshot.

"Get the fuck down!" Danny grabbed her head without taking his eyes off the windshield and shoved her face back to the seat.

Cold air rushed in through the back window of the Jeep and Caroline's heart threatened to beat through her chest as the Jeep spun and lurched through the snow. There was a loud thump and a scraping sound on her side of the car. She watched veins bulge and sinews flex as Danny shoved at the gear shift.

Any second they were going to hit a tree or slam into a snowdrift. She wondered how fast she'd be able to run in her stupid boots in the knee deep snow.

Caroline heard a crash of metal but was shocked to feel no impact.

"Ha ha!" Danny's triumphant laugh echoed through the Jeep a second before a series of shots rang out. He ducked low in his seat and floored the accelerator.

The tires whined as they spun against the snow, then suddenly, miraculously, she felt the ground smooth beneath them. She risked a peek over the dash to see they'd hit a road of some type. Though not plowed, it had seen enough recent traffic that the snow was packed down enough for them to pick up speed. The cold air through the back whipped her hair around her face. "Where are they?" She looked through the blown out back window, ready to duck as soon as she caught sight of their pursuer.

"Crunched against a big sequoia, ass deep in snow," Danny said, satisfaction evident as he navigated the Jeep along the road's snowpacked surface.

Caroline sat up and leaned her head back against the seat, wrapping her arms around herself as her body started to register the chill. She looked at Danny, who looked like a real-life action star with his dark glasses, square jaw, and full lips hitched to the side in a satisfied smile.

Unable to quell the urge, she leaned over and gave him a quick kiss on his lean, stubbled cheek. "Nice driving. Remind me never to insult your car again." She patted the dashboard of the Jeep like it was a faithful dog.

The other corner of Danny's mouth hitched up.

He drove without stopping, consulting the GPS until he found a route through the forest roads to another spur of the highway. Then he drove another hour south to hook up with another highway in case anyone else was watching their predicted route home. When they finally got to Caroline's neighborhood six hours later, she was exhausted and chilled to the bone from riding in an open car for so long. They'd stopped briefly so Caroline could put on every extra item of clothing Danny had in his duffel bag. The hat, sweatshirt, sweatpants, and socks were barely enough to keep her from hypothermia.

Caroline was fantasizing about a steam-filled shower before the Jeep came to a complete stop.

"We're not staying," Danny said, as though reading her mind. "I want you to go in, pack a bag for the next several days, and we're out of here."

She didn't protest. As they'd discussed in their hours in the car, it didn't take a genius to see someone didn't want the truth about Anne Taggart's and Emily Parrish's deaths to come out.

"But who?" Caroline had asked, more thinking aloud than expecting Danny to have an answer.

"Someone who was working with James who's afraid his number is finally up."

Too bad Caroline had no clue who that was. But until they found out, she was on board with Danny's plan to clear out of her house.

She handed Danny her key and watched him punch in the alarm code. She scanned the street, wondering if they were watching her. She eased a little closer to Danny and was brought up short by his vicious curse.

Caroline's mouth fell open in horror as she looked past him into her entryway.

Trashed didn't even begin to describe it. The little table in the entryway was on its side, the contents of the drawers scattered across the hardwood floor. To the right she could see into the living room. Furniture was smashed, cushions had been sliced open. Numbness overtook her and without thinking she pushed past Danny and rushed headlong up the stairs.

"Wait," Danny yelled after her. The fine hairs on his neck stood up and he moved to the left. Air whistled in his ear as something—a pipe or a police baton—narrowly missed his head. Danny caught his attacker's wrist in one hand and jabbed his other fist into his assailant's elbow. A cry of pain and the snap of bone echoed through Caroline's entryway. A jab to the man's face and he was down. Danny quickly frisked the guy, pocketing a switchblade and a small hand- gun. Then he reached out to rip the ski mask from his at- tacker's head.

Caroline's shriek reverberated from upstairs. Without hesitating Danny charged up the stairs, slipping his glock from his shoulder holster as he went. He burst into Caro- line's bedroom, relief nearly flooring him when he saw her on the floor sitting up and very much alive.

He knelt down next to her. "Are you hurt?" he asked, trying to keep the frantic note out of his voice as he quickly examined her for signs of injury.

"I'm okay," she said. "He surprised me when I came in and pushed me over, but he went out the window as soon as he heard you coming." She nodded to the open window that overlooked her backyard.

Danny rushed over to take a look. It was a good drop, about twenty feet, but there was no sign of Caroline's in- truder. "Did you get a look at him?"

She shook her head. "He was wearing a mask."

"Same as the guy downstairs."

Assured Caroline was unharmed, Danny let his fear morph into fury at her carelessness. He grabbed her by the shoulders and gave her a little shake. "What were you thinking, running into the house like that? Do you have any idea what could have happened to you?"

Her eyes went wide in her pale face and her throat convulsed. "I'm sorry. I wasn't thinking—"

"Damn right you weren't. From now on, you follow my lead, no matter what. I don't want you to so much as sneeze without my say-so!"

"Don't yell at me!" Her shaky tone snapped Danny from his temper, forcing him to take a good look at her. So pale she was almost gray, her lips blue and quivering as shock threatened to set in.

His anger fled as quickly as it had surged and he pulled her against his chest. "Just promise you'll be more careful, okay?" He pressed a kiss to the top of her head, closing his eyes against the images of what could have happened to her if the guy downstairs had managed to get the jump on him.

He eased back and cupped her cheek, tilting her head up to meet his gaze. He was relieved to see a little splash of pink warming her face as her panic abated. "I need to take a look around, and I want you to stay right behind me."

Caroline's fingers were icy as they wrapped around his, but she nodded and let him pull her to her feet.

Danny quickly dialed 911 and started a sweep of the house. He would have preferred to look around without Caroline glued to his back, but he wasn't about to leave her alone until he knew no one else was in the house.

And judging from her fast, agitated breath in his ear as she trailed him through every room, up the stairs and down the halls, she wasn't in any hurry to go off by herself.

The guy who had tried to jump Danny was long gone, of course, and no one else seemed to be waiting in the shadows.

"We're all clear," he said in the most reassuring tone that he could muster. Caroline nodded, her face white, her eyes dilated with fear. Still he had to give it to her. She was remarkably calm, considering what had just happened.

Seemed the resilient core he'd always admired hadn't completely disappeared during her years as a trophy wife.

"Why would someone do this?" Caroline asked as she looked around the master bedroom, seeming to take in its condition for the first time. It was in the same shape as the rest of the house. The king size mattress was on the floor and slashed open. The drawers of the nightstands were up-ended, the contents strewn across the floor. Clothes from both closets were all over the place, the dressers in both hers and James's closets pulled out from the wall, emptied of their drawers, and turned on their sides.

"Is anything missing?" Danny asked after he'd satisfied himself that they were alone in the house.

Caroline's fingers only shook a little as she sifted through the piles of clothes, shoes and purses littering the floor of her closet. "My jewelry's gone." She walked through the adjoining bathroom into what had been James's closet. "And James's watch. But there's so much stuff they could have taken." She picked up a high-end digital camera from the corner where it had been tossed. "But we surprised them. Maybe they didn't have time . . ." her voice trailed off.

But they'd had plenty of time to tear the place apart. Plenty of time to load things like a flat screen TV or a computer into a waiting car. No, the robbery was incidental, a smokescreen to cover up their search.

Caroline was a smart woman. Danny didn't need to spell it out for her. "Do you think they found what they were looking for?" A police siren sounded in the distance and she let out a peal of semi-hysterical laughter. "Maybe this is a good thing. Maybe they got what they needed and now they'll leave me alone."

A knock sounded on the front door and he reached out to guide her out of the room and down the stairs. "I suppose that's in the realm of possibility, but I wouldn't bank on it. In the meantime, as far as the police are concerned, this is a standard B&E. Don't tell them anything about what we've been working on."

Caroline nodded. "No reason to lay all our cards out, right?"

"Right."

The officer was in and out in a little over an hour. Danny handed over the knife and the gun he'd taken off his attacker and told the officer they should be looking for a guy with a badly broken arm, not that he thought it would help much. The officer took Caroline's report, left her a copy for her insurance, and left to canvass the neighbors. "In this economy we're seeing a lot more property crimes," he said as he left. "You should really look into upgrading your security system."

Danny didn't bother pointing out that whoever had done this either had enough skill to circumvent the alarm system, or was familiar enough with Caroline's house to know the weak spots. "Who knew where we were yesterday? Who knew you were leaving town?"

Caroline pulled her dazed stare from the pile of wood, upholstery and stuffing that in no way resembled a couch. "No one. Well, I called Kate yesterday to tell her I was okay but she would never—"

"Are you sure?"

Her mouth drew tight with irritation and she folded her arm across her chest. "You asked about her before, and my answer is still the same. No way would she do this."

"But would she tell anyone? Maybe inadvertently? Mention it in passing to someone not realizing who she's talking to?"

Caroline let out a frustrated sigh and went down the hall to James's office. The locked desk drawers had been pried open. A sea of papers and file folders carpeted the room, topped by a mountain of books that had been pulled from the shelves. "I don't know. I can't even think right now."

He backed off, for the time being anyway.

"I've been over and over every inch of this house, gone through every single bit of data on the computers and I never found anything until Kate brought over that stupid box. I can't imagine what they thought they would find." Caroline's voice was low, defeated, and she wavered on her feet as her unfocused gaze drifted across the room. Danny knew she was starting to shut down, her body and brain unable to deal with one more ounce of stress.

"Come on," he said, as gently as he could given his current level of frustration. "We don't need to do this right now. You need a hot meal and a good night's sleep."

She shook her head and dropped to her knees. She gathered papers in her hand, lining their edges and stacking them carefully. "I need to clean this up. I can't leave the house like this—"

He knelt down beside her and placed his hands over hers. "We'll come back tomorrow and put the house back together." His voice was soft but his tone was steeped in authority.

Like all the green recruits Danny had trained over the years, she nodded without protest.

She let go of the papers and sat back on her heels, shoulders slumped. Exhausted. Dejected. It made him want to wrap his arms around those fragile shoulders, pull her into his lap, and promise he would make everything okay.

He shoved the thought away as he stood and guided her

to her feet with a firm hand on her wrist. It wasn't his job to give her reassurance and a shoulder to cry on.

Even when they'd been together, Caroline had stood firmly on her own two feet. She'd taken care of herself and her family and never asked him for anything. Self-sufficient, and unlike his mother, not too emotionally needy.

Not until the end, anyway. He watched her walk down the hall and climb the stairs to the bedroom, trying not to focus on the sway of her round ass in her tight jeans. Trying to remind himself of all the reasons it was good she'd dumped him a hundred years ago when he'd made it clear he wasn't the kind of guy who dealt well with a lot of sharing and needing and all that other emotionally contrived bullshit.

"There's a leather wheeled suitcase in James's closet if you can find it in that mess," she said wearily as she entered her own. He heard the shift of fabric and the thump of shoes dropping as she went through the piles on the floor. Even he, with his untrained eye, knew Caroline probably had tens of thousands of dollars worth of designer goods in there. Most women would be throwing a hissy fit seeing them thrown to the floor, stomped on, and in some cases, torn apart. Caroline simply picked up each piece, hung it carefully on a hanger, and placed it back in its designated spot.

Danny kicked piles of clothes and shoes out of the way until he found the suitcase Caroline was talking about. There was a deep slash in the leather and the inner lining was torn out, but it would still hold her belongings and survive a ride across the bay. Danny moved an empty dresser drawer aside and pulled the suitcase to the door.

Something caught his eye, so small he wasn't sure he saw it at first. He backed away so his shadow didn't fall over the section of the hardwood floor he was studying. He bent down and squinted for a closer look, then cleared the area of scattered clothes. He ran a fingertip across the wood floor panel. Right there in the middle, lost in the graininess of the oak, was a crack.

Or was it a seam?

He traced the crack with his finger. Thin and remarkably straight, it ran midway through the panel next to it.

Definitely a seam. Another ran perpendicular from the corner, crossed five panels, then turned again to run parallel, then back up, forming a rectangle about ten by twenty inches in size. He pulled his Randall Knife out of the sheath strapped to his calf and slid the tip in one of the seams. The panel came up without resistance.

"Like they didn't do enough damage? Why are you tearing up my floor?"

He looked up to see Caroline staring down at him, hands on her hips, and an expression that said she thought he'd lost his mind. From her angle he was blocking her view of what was under the panel.

He moved back so she could see the metal door embedded into the floor.

"You think anyone else knows about James's floor safe?"

Caroline braced herself with one hand on his shoulder as she leaned down to look. He heard her breath catch in her chest. "I had no idea that existed."

"No reason you would. It's one of the better jobs I've seen. It wouldn't be obvious to anyone not trained to look for it."

"Like you."

He shrugged. "Even I wouldn't have noticed it if the dresser hadn't been shoved aside." When he'd searched Caroline's house before, the dresser had been flush with the corner, totally obscuring the panel. He gave himself a mental kick for not being more thorough in his initial searches.

"Can you open it?" Her voice was breathy with anticipation.

He nodded. "Don't get your hopes up. It's possible who-ever was here already cleaned it out."

She nodded. "Open it," she repeated.

It took him a few minutes to bypass the code, then the lock slid free with a metallic snick. Danny flipped the door open and peered inside.

Not empty.

His mouth pulled into a grin.

He reached in and pulled out a DVD, a thick sheaf of pa-pers, and a computer flash drive.

CHAPTER 14

"These look like bank statements, numbered accounts," Caroline called over the wind whipping through the battered Jeep.

"Put those away," Danny barked. "That's all we need is for them to blow away."

She rolled her eyes, but obediently tucked them back in Danny's computer bag, then tucked the bag under the seat for good measure. After all that, the last thing she wanted was for the contents of the safe to go blowing across Highway 80.

A floor safe. How could she have been so clueless? Granted, it must have been installed well before she married James and was damn well hidden. But still. After all that time, the truth about James's death had been right there under the floor of his walk-in closet.

Maybe. Danny cautioned her repeatedly not to get her hopes up.

Too late. Caroline had been nearly crushed with defeat when she'd walked into her house to find it trashed. Any last shred of security or sanity to be found in her home was gone. She just wanted all of it to be over.

But she was flying high on a second wind. Squirming like a puppy to find out what was in those bank records, what was on that flash drive, convinced they held the key to the hell her life had become over the past year.

She managed to make it to Danny's house without badgering him to death. She knew he was as eager to look into the evidence as she was, but was more concerned with getting her somewhere safe first.

"We're not doing anything until I know you're somewhere they can't find you," was exactly how he put it. It was enough to give her a little rush of pleasure, amidst all the chaos.

Finally they pulled into his driveway. "Aren't you worried they'll follow us here?" she asked as she picked her way across the gravel drive and followed him up the two stairs that led to his wood porch.

He set her bag down beside him, keyed in the code for his alarm, and answered without looking. "I would have seen a tail, and no one but my family knows I live here."

She cocked an eyebrow and looked around. "Who exactly do you think is going to come looking for you?"

His massive shoulders shrugged. "You never know. But count yourself lucky you get to stay here with me instead of in one of the piece of shit safe houses."

Danny's cell phone rang before she could reply

She drank in the small house's cabin-like interior, even as she told herself she had no business caring what Danny's house looked like, how he lived, or what clues it might give about the man he'd become.

She was no expert, but the heavy leather furniture, massive flat screen TV, and walls bare of any other sort of decoration screamed *confirmed bachelor*. She told herself firmly she was not happy or relieved in any way, and wandered over to a built-in bookcase crammed full of books, heavy on spy thrillers and military history.

Immediately off the front room was a small eat-in kitchen with a simple pine table and two chairs. A mountain of mail was piled on the table. Caroline flexed her fingers, fighting the urge to straighten and sort.

As Danny paced the sitting room, speaking in grim mono-syllables to the caller, Caroline looked past him down a short, dark hallway. One that undoubtedly led to bedrooms.

Danny's bedroom.

Don't go there.

But of course she did. There, and back to the motel last night, and all the things she said and did. Things she couldn't seem to keep herself from doing when she spent too much time alone with Danny Taggart.

She swallowed hard. *Evidence.* They were going to go over the information they found in James's safe. That was the priority, not the sharp ache that was forming between her thighs.

At this rate, it would be over so fast, it's not like it would be much of a delay—

"They identified Emily's body."

Danny's words had the effect of a cold shower.

"And Derek has an eye witness up in La Honda who says she remembers a man who looked like James coming into her store shortly before Anne disappeared. And she remembers seeing him get into a car with a young woman who looked like Emily."

The cold shower had turned into an icy deluge. Caroline's heart seized in her chest and her stomach churned as she struggled to process the truth, even as her brain tried to reject the explanation.

James had killed Danny's mother, and Emily Parrish along with her.

It shouldn't have been so shocking. All evidence had pointed in that direction.

But somehow, even as they'd gone further down that path, Caroline had hoped there was another explanation. "Someone else was involved, someone else who doesn't want the truth to come out," she scrambled, grasping at straws.

Danny nodded, grim. She knew exactly what he was thinking. Sure, someone else had been involved. Someone who killed James to keep the secrets safe. Someone who would kill her to keep her from finding out the truth.

But in the end, her husband had been there. Through a twisted game of fate, Caroline had inadvertently ended up married to Anne Taggart's murderer.

How could she have been married to James for a decade and have not seen, have had no clue that he was capable of something like that? Was James so very skilled at deception? Or had Caroline been so eager for security that she didn't bother to ever really get to know the man who was her husband?

It was like a crazy Greek tragedy, playing out in her own life.

"Danny, I'm so sorry," she said, feeling helpless, stupid for being unable to think of anything else to say.

"Don't." The single, cold syllable stopped her short, as did the glacial look in his gray eyes. Caroline, already chilled from riding around in the dead of winter in a windowless car, felt icy fingers creep into her very bones.

He was going to tell her to fuck off, to get out. She could see it in the hard set of his shoulders and muscle throbbing in his jaw. She'd been shut out by Danny enough in the past to know the signs. Back then, she knew how to deal with it, knew how to wheedle and charm him back from his black moods, his cold silences.

Now she didn't have a leg to stand on. She was still the enemy, had been when she showed up at Anne's memorial service. Was even more so now.

Contrary to her panicked musings, Danny wordlessly pulled out his laptop and turned it on. Caroline took a risk and sat on the leather sofa next to him. She made sure to leave plenty of space between them.

"Let's see what's on this flash drive," he said, his voice remarkably steady for a man sitting next to the wife of the man who had probably murdered his mother.

Caroline took a deep breath. She was spiraling out of control. She couldn't let herself do that again, not with him. She was the queen of capable, the master of keeping it together when the shit went down.

She could not hit one of her walls now.

She focused on the screen of Danny's laptop, taking a second to admire his desktop picture of the eastern Sierras in all their flinty, snowcapped majesty. Danny slipped in the flash drive and clicked on the icon to open the drive. The file names were all gibberish as far as Caroline could tell. He clicked open one and was prompted for a password.

Her fingers clenched in frustration. "How are we going to figure out the password?"

"Don't worry. There's always a back door." Danny closed the dialog box and executed a few quick keystrokes.

Suddenly the screen went blue. Danny yelled, "No, no, son of a bitch," at his computer. His fingers flew across the keyboard, but nothing happened. The screen stayed that same flat, annoying, royal blue, an unmistakable sign to any PC user that he or she was royally screwed.

She watched helplessly as Danny thumped at the keyboard a few more times. He tried to restart, only to be greeted by that same blue screen.

"God*dammit*," Danny said viciously. "Fucking cyber booby trap!"

"What, like a virus or something?"

He nodded. "When I didn't enter the password it fried my hard drive."

"What are we going to do now?" Her voice was getting

that annoyingly frantic tone, but she couldn't make herself calm down. Out of nowhere it seemed they'd been given the key to James's murder, only to be tripped up by his cyber-terrorism.

Danny made a sound of disgust and closed his laptop. "I'll have Toni take a look. That's what I should have done in the first place."

He pushed up from the sofa and walked the few steps to the kitchen. Caroline watched in disbelief as he pulled out two bottles of beer and silently offered her one.

"What are you doing? Why aren't you calling her?" she said, ignoring the beer.

Danny closed the refrigerator and ran a hand through his hair. "I'm not calling because it's after eleven, she's probably in bed, and we could both use some rest. There's nothing on that drive that can't wait until tomorrow."

"Someone trashed my house and tried to kill me for what's on that disk drive."

Danny dug a bottle opener out of a drawer, flipped off the cap, and took a deep drink of his beer before he replied. "As long as you're here with me, you'll be safe. Come on Caroline, it's late, we're both exhausted, and we'll be able to deal with all of this a hell of a lot better after a decent meal and a good night's sleep."

He turned his back and started rummaging through his pantry. He seriously wasn't going to call Toni. He was actually pulling steaks out of his refrigerator and seasoning them like the key to her future wasn't sitting on the coffee table three feet away.

She stomped over to the kitchen table where she'd left her purse and pulled out her phone. "What's Toni's number? I'll call her myself."

"I'm not giving you the number." A cast iron grill pan hit the cooktop with a metallic thud.

"You're seriously going to just eat steak and drink beer and not do anything to find out what's on that flash drive?"

"That's the plan."

A red haze covered her vision as something inside her snapped. Without conscious thought her phone flew from her hand and smacked him in the back of his head.

He turned without flinching and pinned her with a steely glare. "What the fuck is wrong with you?"

"You're a selfish dickhead, that's what's wrong with me. It's always all about you, isn't it, Danny? Whatever you say goes, your way or the highway. I should have seen this coming. You're not even going to help me, are you?" She couldn't stop the words from spilling out of her mouth. She couldn't hold herself together any longer. She was sick of feeling powerless, sick of watching her life career out of control while she was helpless to do anything about it. She wanted answers, now, once and for all, and Danny was willfully withholding them because he wanted to drink his beer and eat his goddamn steak. "You probably never had any intention of helping me, did you?" She heard her voice raise an octave, knew she was verging on hysteria, but couldn't make herself calm down as all of her fear, tension, and old, festering anger came roaring out. Helpless to stop the words from pouring out of her, she lashed out at Danny. "You just wanted to you use me for the information I had, and now that you know what happened to your mother, you're going to leave me to fend for myself, just like you always did."

She knew her accusations were unfair, irrational, but she couldn't escape the gut-wrenching fear that he was going to stop helping her. As scared as she was, she couldn't blame him. She'd married his mother's murderer, for God's sake. Lived in his house. Slept in his bed. So what if she'd had no idea. In Danny's world, black was black and white was white. There was no room in his world for forgiveness or redemption.

The spatula in his hand hit the floor with a clatter. "Me? Leave you to fend for yourself? Funny, I remember it being the other way around."

"Yeah, well, you would. But then you only ever see your side of things anyway."

"Really? Enlighten me. Because from where I was standing, there was only one side. I came home for a few days of leave and you dumped me for no reason."

"You didn't call, and you went out and got drunk—" her voice cracked. She didn't want to rehash the past. None of it should matter, not after all this time. But the pain of that night slashed at her, as fresh and raw as it had been in the moment she realized it was over between the two of them.

He rolled his eyes and threw up his hands. "I needed to blow off some steam before I saw you. Are we seriously going to rehash this right now? 'Cause unless you have some new explanation for why you went mental and over-reacted, I don't want to hear it." He paused, scratched his chin as though in deep thought. "Scratch that. On second thought, even if you do have a new explanation, I don't want to hear that either. I'm just glad the needy psycho bitch you were so good at hiding reared her head before I was dumb enough to marry you."

Caroline staggered back as though she'd been slapped. She'd had a pretty good idea what he thought of her, but somehow having him say it out loud hit her like a ton of bricks. After everything she'd done for him, all she'd given him, the way she'd stood up to him and stood by him through all the ways he tried to push her away.

Needy psycho bitch.

That was the one line descriptor she got in the story of Danny Taggart's life.

"I had a miscarriage," she spat out, before she had even a

second to weigh the impact of finally launching that grenade after holding on to it for twelve long years.

He froze, then shook his head, blinking like he hadn't heard her right. "I thought you said James had a vasectomy."

"It wasn't James's, Danny. A month after I came home from visiting you in Fort Bragg, I found out I was pregnant."

She could practically hear his thoughts careening through his head as he remembered their lust filled weekend in that cheap hotel room.

His lips moved but no sound came out, and for the first time since she'd seen him again at the memorial service, Danny Taggart actually looked unsure of himself. He leaned against the counter and took a deep drink of his beer. "Why didn't you tell me you were pregnant?" he said the last word almost hesitantly.

"When? During the one five minute phone conversation we had after I found out?"

His dark eyelashes cast shadows on his cheeks as he broke their stare.

"Or how about after you were deployed for three months," she continued, "when I had no idea where you were and if you were ever coming back?" And knowing that when he did come back, he'd be even more closed off than before. It would take her weeks, months, to chip away at his defenses and get him to let her back in. By then he'd be deployed again, and they'd have to start all over.

But she would have dealt with that, would have dealt with almost anything to be with him. Because she loved him, and she loved the baby growing inside her.

Tears stung her eyes and she angrily wiped them away. "I was going to tell you in person when you came out to visit. And then when I had the miscarriage . . . it," *was awful, and scary and left me feeling like someone had sucked the joy out of me.* "It wasn't something I wanted to drop on you over the phone."

She waited for him to say something. Offer an excuse for his behavior, both that night and the months before. Hell, maybe even offer an apology for her loss.

Their loss.

But he didn't say anything, just stared silently, his gray eyes flat and lifeless, his mouth pulled in a tight, grim line.

The silence was awful, and soon words came spilling out to fill it. "After your mom disappeared it was like everything was a test. You wanted to see how hard you could push me, always making me prove that I wouldn't crack like she did." Caroline thought about what they'd discovered in the past few days and gave a short, humorless laugh. "Like you *thought* she did. And I took it. I took all of it because I loved you, and I thought I was strong enough to change you back into the person I fell in love with." She thought he flinched, a subtle tightening of his muscles, but it happened so fast she must have been imagining it.

He drained the last of his beer and wordlessly opened another.

"You want to know the really stupid thing? After I left you that morning, I kept thinking you would come after me. I'd always been the one to smooth things over after a fight, make everything okay again, but I thought maybe if you realized you were going to lose me forever you'd care enough to come after me." The pain in her chest was so fierce she was surprised her shirt wasn't soaked with blood. She shouldn't be talking about this. And it shouldn't hurt this much anymore. His continued silence only made it more severe. She lashed out, wanting to find some hidden chink in his armor. "But I guess you were glad to rid yourself of the needy psycho bitch before I could do to you what your mom did to your dad. Oh, wait, I guess you were wrong about her too."

She searched his face for any reaction and got none. A brick wall had come down around him, hard and impervious.

What was she expecting? That suddenly Danny would see her side of the story and beg her forgiveness?

Would she give in if he did?

Luckily it didn't look like she'd have to answer that question because Danny had turned away without a word to stare out the window over the kitchen sink.

Unable to bear being in the same room with him, Caroline retrieved her suitcase and retreated to the spare bedroom to try to stem the bitter flow of blood that came from picking old wounds.

Stop her. Grab her. Hold her. Tell her you're sorry. Tell her if you only knew, if she'd told you. Stop her. Grab her.

Danny couldn't make his body obey his brain's frantic orders as he watched Caroline disappear down the short, dark hallway. He felt like he'd been hit by a Taser, Caroline's revelation so jolting it left him paralyzed, unable to move or speak.

Pregnant. She'd been pregnant. With his baby. Their baby. And she'd lost it. Alone.

Jesus.

He wanted to scream and cry and smash things, but all he could do was sink to to the floor as his legs buckled underneath him.

Wrong. Fuck. He was so wrong about so many things.

So many choices he'd made based on things that weren't true. And he'd been so convinced he was right. Thought he knew the score everywhere, all the time. Because of his mom's disappearance, he'd let himself believe that any woman, anywhere, could up and leave her husband and children.

Caroline was right. He'd tested her. Pushed hard to see what she'd put up with. Even though she'd stuck by him and pulled him through one of the hardest times in his life, he didn't trust she'd be around for the long haul. And even though he was just a kid, he'd known, deep in his gut, that Caroline was the one for the the long haul. But that didn't stop him from trying to push her away, to test her mettle to see if she could really hack it.

He'd let it be known that he was doing what he wanted with his life, and she could either come along for the ride or get off the train. Despite her misgivings about him joining the Army Rangers, and later the Special Forces, she'd stuck by him then, too.

Jesus, he was such a jackass.

A baby.

Blood roared in his ears and the wood paneled walls of his house seemed to close in on him. He staggered to his feet and lurched for the door, needing an escape, knowing there was none. He couldn't get away from Caroline and leave her unprotected.

And he sure as shit couldn't escape from his own mistakes.

He burst out the sliding glass door to his deck. He looked out at the redwood forest, haloed in silver by the light of the nearly full moon. Through the trees he could make out the lights of the valley below, and beyond that the bay and the hills across the water.

It was the exact same view he'd seen every day and every night in the four years that he'd lived there. How could the world look the same when everything felt so different? There was a hot, aching sensation in his chest, like he was being stabbed from the inside out.

Everything he'd packed away, pain at his mother's apparent betrayal, his hurt that Caroline could shove him aside for something as trivial as him going on a bender with his brothers, came shooting to the surface like a geyser. Made all the more painful because he'd been wrong about all of it.

His mother he could almost forgive himself for. Even the police had been convinced she'd left of her own accord. Hell, even his father had accepted that Anne had left them. She'd taken off with a suitcase and a wad of cash, for fuck's sake.

Cash and clothes that he now realized were meant to help Emily Parrish and her unborn child. Guilt threatened to rip him apart. His mother had died trying to help a young girl in a terrible bind, and Danny had spent the past eighteen years convincing himself and anyone else who would listen that his mother wasn't worth a second thought.

I'm sorry, Mom, for everything I said, everything I thought. You deserved better than that. Better than me.

As did Caroline.

He replayed that last visit home as the knot in his stomach tightened another notch. He'd just gotten back from a grueling mission in Central America, one where one of his guys had died. By the time he was on his flight to San Francisco, he still hadn't come down from combat mode, still edgy and alert and ready for a fight. When Caroline had pressed him on when he was coming back, when he was going to pick her up, he'd snapped at her and told her to get off his ass about it.

He'd immediately regretted it, but asshole that he was, of course he couldn't apologize. He knew he needed to calm down, get hold of himself before he saw her, or who knew what he was liable to say. He didn't want to explain why he was so messed up after that mission, didn't want to tell Caroline about how the memory of his buddy lying on the ground with his intestines spilling out kept him from sleeping.

What he saw out there was ugly and evil, and he didn't want to bring it home to Caroline. So instead he'd gone out with Derek and Ethan who'd managed to coordinate their leaves with his. They were in the military too, they understood the need to go out and get shitfaced and tell gory tales to offset the horror of what he'd seen.

Caroline hadn't understood. And when she'd lashed out, he'd lashed right back. *"I don't need any of your emotionally needy bullshit."*

A lump swelled in his throat.

"I thought maybe if you realized you were going to lose me forever you'd care enough to come after me."

Arrogant fuck that he was, he'd expected her to call him within a couple hours of their fight. When he'd boarded a plane back to Fort Bragg four days later, he still couldn't believe he hadn't heard from her.

Twelve years later he wished he could go back and kick his own ass for being such a dipshit.

It all could have been so different. It *should* have been so different.

For once Danny was forced to acknowledge that there was nothing he could do to fix it. He couldn't change the past and take away Caroline's hurt and make things turn out the way they should have. So he sat on his deck and stared unseeing into the night as his world imploded around him.

Caroline tossed and turned in the double bed for a few hours before she finally gave up and threw back the covers. She didn't hear Danny moving around the house. Maybe she could sneak into the kitchen and find a bottle of vodka or scotch—anything to help her shut her mind down and go to sleep.

Goosebumps popped up on her skin as soon as she stepped into the hall. Danny's house was like a meat locker.

Figured. He was so cold blooded he probably didn't even feel it. She was still reeling from his response—or non-response—to her revelation. She wanted to kick herself for telling him at all. But she'd needed to strike out, shake him up, let him know that she didn't deserve all the blame in breaking them up.

Turned out she didn't shake him up. And she hurt even worse knowing how little he cared about her and the baby she'd lost.

She blinked back tears as she walked into the front room. Her teeth chattered as a cold wind blew through the room. The curtains shading the sliding glass door fluttered. At some point Danny had left the door wide open.

Weird, since he was such a stickler for security, even way out here in the boondocks. She went to the door and looked outside. A large, dark form was seated in a deck chair, and she gave a startled gasp before her brain registered it was Danny. She started to duck back inside, but was halted by his quiet, almost stilted voice.

"Did you know what it was?" He turned to face her, the hard planes of his face illuminated by the silver glow of the moon. "The baby? Did you know if it was a boy or a girl?" His voice sounded tight, like he was being choked.

Or fighting back tears.

But this was Danny Taggart, a man who would sooner pluck his eyes from his head than let a single tear fall.

She took a step onto the deck without thinking. "It was too early, only twelve weeks."

"Were you uh, okay? I mean, was James's vasectomy the only reason—"

"I'm perfectly healthy," she reassured, taking another step closer to his chair. "My eggs might be getting a little stale, but otherwise I should be able to have children if I want."

"Good." She could see his dark head nod jerkily. "That's good." He was dressed only in a long sleeved T-shirt and jeans, but he didn't seem to notice the cold as he stared off into the moonlit forest surrounding his house. He turned to face her then, and even in the darkness she could feel the intensity of his stare. "You should be a mom, Caroline. You should have been one already." His voice caught and he turned away, but she didn't miss the telltale scrubbing of his fists against his eyes.

Crying? No way. Had she finally gotten to him?

She didn't feel anything close to triumph at the knowledge. All she felt was a deep, black ache that threatened to consume her. Old pain she'd struggled to keep at bay from the moment she saw him again came bubbling to the surface, washing over her. Worse because she could feel his pain too, rolling off him in dark waves.

He rested his elbows on his knees and dropped his head to his hands. "I thought I had it all figured out. I knew exactly what was going on. With my mom. With you." He sat up and shook his head. "I didn't know a fucking thing. Not a goddamn thing."

For a man like Danny who thought he knew everything, it must feel like his world was ending. Caroline stepped closer, unable to help herself. She prided herself on being smarter than average, and a smart woman would have left him to his brooding. A smart woman would have known she didn't owe him a lick of comfort or sympathy, that he'd lost that right when he'd closed himself off and pushed her away. His ignorance was no excuse.

But Caroline had always been monumentally stupid when it came to Danny Taggart. She'd always been drawn to him, especially when he got like this. He was like a big battle scarred jungle cat, tempting her to pull his head into her lap, stroke his hair, do whatever she could to take away his pain. Never mind that he could kill her with one careless swipe of his paw.

So when he reached out one, big, shaking hand like he was reaching for a lifeline, she released a helpless sob and let him pull her over to him. He grabbed her around the waist in a desperate grip and buried his face against her stomach. He burrowed his head like a little kid seeking comfort.

Tears burned at the backs of her eyes as Caroline folded herself over him, wrapping her arms around his shoulders and bending until her face was buried against his hair. Huge muscles bunched tight under her fingers, like he was afraid if he relaxed even one sinew he'd fly apart.

She knew the feeling well.

"Caroline," he said, his voice muffled against her tank top, "I'm so fucking sorry."

Caroline straightened a little, struggling not to burst into sobs. Twelve years. For twelve years she'd waited for that apology. She felt like she was being ripped down the middle.

In a last ditch effort at self-preservation she tried to break free of his hold. She needed to get away from him. Sleeping with him was bad enough. She was afraid if she stayed with him she'd start remembering all the reasons she'd loved Danny Taggart to the point of madness, and all the reasons he still had this crazy pull on her.

But he clutched her closer when she would have pulled away. "Please, Caroline," he tilted his head up to look at her, his arms like iron bands around her middle. "Don't go. Please Carrie." Begging. Danny Taggart was begging her, his voice low, throbbing with pain and something else. Something she couldn't resist.

Then he dealt the death blow to any resistance she might have been able to muster. "I need you, I need you so much."

Chapter 15

Danny had only said those words to Caroline one other time. The night she'd given him her virginity. When it became clear his mother was gone and not coming back, and he'd fallen into a black hole that threatened to suck him under. Then, as now, he'd reached out to her to help him claw his way back out.

Now, as then, she was helpless to resist the siren's call of a big, tough, brutal warrior like Danny needing her.

"Need you," he murmured again as he rained kisses along the neckline of her pajama tank top and slid one hand in the elastic waistband of her knit pants. His big, warm hand sliding over her ass made warmth pool low in her belly. With every stroke of his hand, every press of his lips the warmth grew, until it drowned out everything. The voices in her head telling her to run away were silenced. The ache subsided until all she cared about was Danny.

Touching her, kissing her, needing her.

But she needed him too. Needed him to make her forget the grief she'd been carrying around. Needed him to make her forget that she'd spent ten years married to a man she didn't really know.

She threaded her fingers in the rough silk of his hair and tipped his head back. She slid one knee on his lap and bent to kiss him. Tongues thrust and lips sucked and desire poured through her veins like thick, hot, honey.

Danny. No one tasted like him, she thought as she cupped his face in her hands and thrust her tongue against his.

No one touched her like him, she thought as he slid his hand up under her tank top to cup and caress her breasts. She'd always marveled at the sheer power and strength of him, and he'd only grown bigger, harder, and tougher over the years. But he touched her with tenderness, sensitivity, seeming to know exactly how to touch her. Like he had a connection with her body that told him to flick his thumb across her nipple and to pinch the tight little bud with a firm pressure that danced on the edge of pain.

She slid her other knee onto his chair and settled into his lap, straddling him so she could feel the thick bulge of his cock between her thighs. She was drenched, the crotch of her pajama pants soaked as she ground herself against him.

"Sweet Carrie," he muttered as he whipped her tank top up over her head. "So sweet," he said as he closed his mouth over the tip of one breast and sucked hard. The heat of his touch chased away the chill of the night. His mouth devoured her breasts and he caressed her back and sides with hands that still held a faint tremble.

He shifted under her, grinding his cock against her sex. Moans erupted from her throat, increasing in volume as the knot of arousal between her legs drew tighter with every surge of his hips under her. Caroline's hands shifted restlessly, touching every part of him she could reach. Broad cotton clad shoulders rippling with muscles; his bare corded arms and their dusting of wiry black hair; the soft, tender skin of his ears and neck.

All hers. At least for tonight.

* * *

Danny struggled to get a grip as Caroline circled her hips over him again. He was caught between pleasure and pain as his cock strained at the confines of his pants. He could feel her damp heat even through the layers of clothes, and the friction of her grinding against him had him close to bursting in his pants. That, combined with the sweet taste of her tits on his tongue and the sexy musk of her filling his nostrils, was all so good he was afraid to stop, afraid she would vanish into the moonlight like some elusive dream.

Caroline. The night before he'd tried to pretend it didn't matter, that she didn't matter. He buried his head between her breasts, breathing in her scent like oxygen. He didn't kid himself. She was everything.

He'd hurt her. He shoved the thought away, knowing if he dwelt on that he'd get sucked right back into the hole that had threatened to swallow him before she'd walked out onto the deck.

Caroline. Everything in him called to her, begged for her, even though he didn't deserve anything from her anymore. He wanted to tell her he was sorry again, to beg her forgiveness, but all he could get out was her name as he kissed every bare patch of skin he could reach.

She was the only one. The only one who could unknot his insides and keep his demons at bay. Even as he knew he should be comforting her, he should be begging her forgiveness, greedy bastard that he was, he couldn't stop taking from her. Taking everything she had to give in a selfish bid to save his sanity, save his soul. He wanted to lose himself in her and the way she made him feel. He wanted to give her so much pleasure she'd forget he ever caused her pain.

He lifted her from the deck chair and walked her inside, his arm under her ass supporting her weight as she wrapped her arms and legs around him. He tangled his fist in her hair and pulled her head back for his kiss. He swallowed her groan as he devoured her mouth, drinking in her taste, rubbing his tongue against hers as she clutched at his shoulders.

Danny lay her on the bed. The sight of her, with her creamy skin and hard nipples, her dark hair spread across the comforter as she gazed up at him with heavy lidded eyes, hit him with the force of a roundhouse kick to the chest.

Right. Caroline in his house, in his bed, looking up at him with puffy lips parted and eyes dark with arousal. Nothing in his world had been this right since the day she walked out on him.

With that memory, and the knowledge of why she'd really left, came another surge of grief, so bleak and strong it made his knees buckle.

But Caroline chased it away, coming up on her knees to tug his shirt over his head and unbutton his pants with deft strokes of her fingers. He thought he was going to explode when she burrowed her face against his chest with a hungry little moan and started trailing hot, sucking kisses down his abdomen. He helped her shove his pants and boxers off and joined her on the bed. She pushed him onto his back and a groan ripped from his chest as she bent her head. Hot sweeps of her tongue teased the tip of his cock until he felt like he was going to burst out of his skin.

Jesus, she was going to kill him, running that soft pink tongue up and down his shaft, circling around the tip and greedily lapping up the thick pearls of precome that formed. He fisted his hands in the sheets to keep from grabbing the back of her head and shoving himself down her throat. "Please, Carrie, please." He was begging again, but he didn't care. Because Caroline sucked him into her mouth, over and over, taking him as far into her throat as she could. Sucking and stroking him until he knew he had to pull away.

He flipped her onto her back, stripped off her pajama pants and pinned her to the mattress with his hips between hers. He braced his hands on either side of her head and came down over her, mouth to mouth, skin to skin, the soft silky feel of her tits against his chest almost as good as the feel of her mouth around his dick.

Almost.

"I want to make you come," he said, breaking from her mouth so he could kiss the spot on her neck that would make her gasp and sigh and shiver against him. "I want to make you feel so good." He slid his hand between her thighs and his eyes rolled back in his head at the feel of her. Wet, hot, perfect. The hard bud of her clit pulsed against his circling fingers. He spread her lips and delved lower so he could sink his fingers into her giving warmth.

His cock jerked against the bedspread, anticipating the grip of her tight, willing heat as he sank into her body.

"Carrie," he couldn't stop saying her name as he slid his mouth and hands over her body. Like he had to keep reassuring himself she was real, she was here, giving herself to him. He couldn't be this lucky.

He didn't *deserve* to be this lucky.

"Ah, sweet, you're so fucking gorgeous," he said as he hooked her knees over his shoulders and took a long, appreciative look at her pretty pink pussy. He closed his mouth over her like a starving man and her loud, high cry rippled along his nerve endings. God he loved going down on her, the sweet salty taste of her, the feel of her hot and wet against his tongue. The way she pulled at his hair and rocked her hips and dug her heels into his back as he pushed her higher and higher. The firm clench of muscles rippling, her loud siren's wail echoing through the bedroom as she came.

He licked and stroked her until the last aftershock pulsed through her. He rolled and pulled her on top of him until his cock was slipping and sliding against her slit. She spread her knees and he felt her body stretch as she took the tip of his cock inside.

No condom.

And it felt just as good—no better—as it had the night before. He slid in another inch, gritting his teeth at the silky hot feel of her stretching to take him.

He wanted to thrust home, stroking and pumping until he came.

Inside her.

With nothing between them.

He could get her pregnant. Right now. Tonight. Then no matter what happened later on, after they found out who was really behind James's death, she would always be tied to him.

She would always be his.

He slid deeper, groaning as her hips rocked back to take him all the way.

"Oh my God, we forgot the condom again," she gasped and came up on her knees. As his cock slipped from her body it took every shred of restraint to keep from grabbing her hips and thrusting her back down. Gritting his teeth, he rolled off the bed and walked stiffly to his bathroom and retrieved a condom from the box under his sink.

He cheered himself with the thought that he'd had that box of rubbers for so long, it was possible they were expired.

Was he an asshole for hoping the condom broke? Probably. But he was practical enough—maybe even desperate enough—to want to tie Caroline to him by any means necessary.

Danny returned to his bed and gathered her against him, kissing her mouth as he pulled her on top of him. She sat up and gripped his cock, staring into his eyes as she positioned herself and sank down over him. She was the most beautiful woman he'd ever seen, her head thrown back, red lips parted on a moan as she took his cock all the way inside her.

Tight. Hot. Perfect. She eased her way down, nice and slow, then back up until she held only the tip inside her. Then back down, and up, a slow, steady rhythm as her body gripped him like a hot wet fist. He leaned up to catch a nipple between his lips, sucking hard. The answering clench of her body nearly sent him over the edge.

He slid his hand down until his thumb rested against her clit. He circled it in time with her slow up and down strokes, increasing the pressure and pace as she moved faster on him. She came hard and fast, looking almost shocked by the force of her orgasm as she braced her hands on his chest and ground her hips against him.

Danny sat up and wrapped his arms around her, wanting to taste every moan and sigh as she rippled and pulsed around him. He held her tight and sucked her tongue into his mouth as he held himself inside her. He couldn't seem to get close enough, deep enough.

Caroline. His destruction. His salvation.

His own orgasm built in force, until his thigh muscles were rock hard, quivering in readiness as his balls pulled high and tight against his body.

"Oh, Danny, I love it when you come inside me," her hot whisper against his ear threw him over the edge. He buried his face in her neck and thrust against her as his body was wracked with shudders. Even as he shook with pleasure, he couldn't shake the feeling of resentment that he was shooting into a condom instead of inside her.

He could still give her a baby.

It was crazy to even entertain the thought, but he couldn't let it go. Just like he'd never let her go. Not completely. All he'd done was shove her way, way back in his memory bank and pretended to himself and the world that what they'd been was nothing more than a couple of dumb kids clinging to something familiar as the rest of their world spun into chaos. But it had been a lot more than that.

As Danny pulled Caroline's back to his front and curled around her body, the emotions he'd held in check for so long came spilling through the cracks. The love, the lust, the anger poured through him in a torrent until all he could do was hold onto Caroline to keep from getting swept away.

Yeah, they'd been more than a couple of dumb kids planning too far ahead. They still were.

But how were they ever supposed to put all the broken pieces back together again?

"There was nothing there," Patrick snarled into the phone. "Taggart almost fucking caught us, and for what?" Shit, if only Taggart hadn't come pounding down the hall, Patrick could have taken care of Caroline himself.

Another fuckup in a seemingly endless chain.

As he paced, his footsteps were muffled by the twenty thousand dollar oriental carpet Melody had recently bought for his home office. Usually he enjoyed the feel of the thick weave under his feet, the smug pride that came from being able to afford to walk all over a piece of art.

Tonight it felt like another burden. Like everything else in this house. Like Mel herself and her need to upgrade and update the house as often as she upgraded and updated herself.

What would she do if the money stopped coming in? Because there was no question that he had to cut all ties with Marshall and Gates. With his malpractice insurance costs skyrocketing after the lawsuit, there was no way he could continue to support Mel in the style to which she'd become accustomed.

Fuck, he was so deep in the hole with Gates, he didn't even have enough money to clear out and disappear. Which was exactly how Gates wanted it. At this point, Patrick owed him so much money, they could sell a thousand babies and Patrick's share wouldn't cover his debt. If Patrick tried to take off, he knew Gates wouldn't hesitate to come after Melody and Jennifer.

And he had the added worry that once the truth about Anne Taggart and Emily Parrish came out, the trail would eventually lead back to him.

He had to keep that from happening.

"There's nothing at the office either," Marshall said. "I told you there wouldn't be. I've been through James's old files dozens of times in the last six months. Any evidence he kept, it was never there. But I don't think there's anything to find. If there was, we would have found it, or it would have turned up by now. Caroline hasn't—"

"Caroline's still looking, thanks to the idiots you hired to take her out."

"They were Gates's guys. I gave them the location, that's it."

"Well now she and Taggart are more suspicious than ever. They're not going to stop until they figure out what happened to James."

"We have nothing to worry about. No one knows anything, except for Gates, and you think he's going to rat us out?"

Patrick wouldn't put it past Gates to let it slip with an anonymous tip to the police before disappearing into the ether. Gates was a wily, scary fucker who had a knack for getting rid of any complications.

Except for one gigantic complication named Caroline Medford.

"All we have to do is sit back and let Taggart and Caroline come to their own conclusions, that James killed them both. I don't understand why it's so complicated."

For a guy who went to Harvard, Marshall could be a

complete idiot. "If they keep digging around, it's possible they'll find a connection to me." He'd always worn a surgical mask when he delivered the babies, so he wasn't worried about any of the girls recognizing him. But Caroline and Taggart had managed to connect the dots this far, far enough to prove to Patrick that after eighteen years of thinking they'd gotten away with it, no one was safe from the truth.

"I didn't—"

Patrick knew what Marshall was going to say before he uttered the words. "I know you weren't around back then, but if you think I'm going to quietly take the fall while you and Gates go on your merry way, you're even stupider than I thought."

Marshall was quiet except for an audible swallow. "So what do we do?"

"We take out Caroline and Taggart before they can do any more damage."

"What about our deal with Gates? We have two deliveries pending in the next two days. Money has already changed hands."

And Mel had already spent a substantial portion on new furniture for the formal dining room. "That will all happen as planned. And there's that new girl Gates has scheduled for a shoot day after tomorrow."

"The blonde?" There was no mistaking the lustful undertone in Marshall's voice.

"Yes. As long as we take care of Caroline and Taggart, we'll be able to keep anyone from finding out James's connection to us or to Gates," he said with more conviction than he felt.

"We'll have to find them first," Marshall said. "You couldn't get to her at the house and Taggart shook your tail after they left."

"They'll have to surface eventually, and when they do Gates's guys will take them out. No fancy shit, but they need to disappear. Make it look like Caroline ran off with her lover to avoid going on trial for James's murder." So much easier said than done, he knew. How were they supposed to pull that off, when they'd failed so many times already? Patrick felt like the little Dutch boy, sticking his finger in the crack in the dike, only to have another bigger one form in its place. He'd feel so much better if he could just find the evidence James alluded to. He'd known his friend well enough to know when he was lying, and he knew James had been telling the truth about that.

Even with Caroline and her pit bull out of the way, as long as that evidence existed, waiting to be discovered, he, Marshall, Gates—the whole operation would never be safe.

Before he hung up Marshall said he'd call Gates. Patrick slipped his prepaid, untraceable cell phone in his pocket as Melody poked her head in the door.

"Everything okay, honey?" she asked, her perfectly groomed brows knit into a concerned frown. "Who on earth are you talking to at this hour?"

Patrick forced the stress from his face and voice and answered, "Everything's fine. I needed to clear up a few loose ends for my seminar the day after tomorrow, but everything's going to be just fine."

He looped his arm around Mel's shoulders and guided her upstairs to the master bedroom. *Everything's going to be just fine.* As he stretched out next to his beautiful, pampered wife he willed it to be true.

This is so good. Dangerously good, Caroline thought as she lay in Danny's bed, staring out his window into the moonlit night. He spooned her from behind, his chest pressed against her back, his thighs tucked up under hers and his pelvis cradled the curve of her butt. Against one cheek she could feel the hard weight of his cock, not completely hard but far from soft. She knew all she had to do was turn and give him one hot open mouth kiss and he'd be rock hard and ready to go.

But then she'd have to give up the blissful comfort of lying quietly in his arms, in an embrace that was somehow more intimate than sex. They hadn't slept together much back when they'd been together, mostly because they'd lived with their parents, precluding sleepovers. They stole every moment alone that they could, but beds for them had been about sex, not sleep. Only on the rare occasions when Caroline went to visit Danny at school or later, when he could get a weekend away from base were they able to actually spend the night together in the same bed.

She'd always loved the way it felt to drift off to sleep with Danny's big, warm body beside her.

Warm. Safe. Cared for.

It was the same now as then.

Danny's warm protective presence wrapped around her like a thick quilt, and for the first time in a long time she felt like she had someone to lean on. Someone to share her burden and help her clean up the mess her life had become.

She'd never imagined feeling that way ever again, and certainly not with Danny. But it was like the impenetrable wall between them had crumbled, for the moment at least. She wasn't naïve enough to think it wouldn't spring right back up in the harsh light of the morning.

Even before, when things had been good between them, Danny had hated to show any hint of vulnerability. On the rare occasions he did let his guard down he always pretended it never happened.

Except for that one night. The night that was excruciatingly similar to this night, when they'd had sex for the first time. After his mother's disappearance, when the darkness threatened to consume him. He hadn't been able to hold her like this after—she'd had to be home by curfew.

The next day, Danny had pulled her into his arms, kissed

her so sweetly she'd nearly melted into a puddle at his feet, and told her he loved her for the first time.

She had no illusions of a repeat performance.

He must have felt her stiffen because he shifted, pulled her tighter against him and pressed a soft kiss to her bare shoulder.

She closed her eyes and savored the warmth that coursed through her. The man was so dangerous to her equilibrium he should wear a hazard sign.

His warm breath tickled her ear as he spoke. "You would have married me, right? Like we'd planned"

Caroline's eyes flew open. She definitely hadn't seen that one coming. "You mean if the baby had—" she didn't want to finish.

"Yeah."

"Yes, I would have married you."

She heard him swallow hard as his fingers tightened on her hip. He didn't say anything for a long time. Finally Caroline broke the silence. "Did you ever think about marrying anyone else?" It was easier to ask those questions in the dark, turned away so she couldn't see his face. Those questions she wasn't sure she wanted the answers to.

"No. You were the only woman I ever wanted to marry."

She wanted to kick herself for the burst of relief that exploded in her chest. "Do you think you will someday?"

He was quiet for so long she thought maybe he'd fallen asleep. "I don't know that I'm cut out to be anybody's husband," he finally whispered. "Considering the piss-poor job I did as a fiancé, I don't think I've earned the promotion."

Something in his voice made her throat tighten and her chest ache. There was a sadness there, almost a wistfulness, not at all in keeping with his character. She turned in his arms so she faced him and lifted her hand to rest against the side of his face. His stubble scraped against her fingers and she could feel the hard lines of his jaw and cheekbone under her palm. He was so tough, so hard, keeping himself locked in a granite hard shell.

But tonight he was giving her a rare look at the soft spot underneath. So small it was a pinprick, so easy for him to hide. And yet he was showing it to her. She kissed him, tasting her own salty tears as she ached for everything they'd lost, the pain they'd caused each other. And the pain that was still to come.

He rolled her to her back and swept his tongue into her mouth. Though his touch was gentler, slower since they'd taken the edge off, she could still feel the raw need emanating from him, bordering on desperation. It was in the trembling of his hands, the hitch of his breath, the almost tortured sounding groans ripping from his throat as his hands cupped her breasts and pinched her nipples.

He rolled her to her side so they lay breast to breast, belly to belly, while he took her mouth over and over in those deep, drugging kisses. He hooked her leg over his hip and she could feel his cock, thick and hard as a club pressing against the curve of her stomach.

"Carrie." The sound of her name on his lips sent a hot shiver down her spine. "I never stopped wanting you," he whispered as his lips traced a hot path across her cheek before settling on the wildly sensitive skin of her neck.

Wet heat flooded between her thighs as he slipped on a condom. He rubbed the broad head around the knot of her clit, spreading her juice before sliding inside.

One slow glide and he was buried to the hilt. Deeper inside her than any man had ever been. As close to her as anyone could possibly be. He didn't move, simply held himself inside her, kissing her, touching her, like he was in no hurry to ever have it end. She was lost in a haze of sensation, where the only things that existed were his lips on her mouth, his hands on her skin, and his cock buried high and hard inside her.

His fingers tweaked her nipples and she felt an answering pull inside her. He let out a groan as her muscles clenched around him.

"Oh do that again," he whispered, his muscles pulling tight as she squeezed around him. She did it again and he sucked her tongue into his mouth. "You feel so good, squeezing my cock like a tight little fist."

He slid his hand between their bodies and rested his thumb on her clit. He stroked it in slow, gentle circles, while with the other hand he held her still to keep her from moving. "Like this," he said, tracing another circle. "Every time I do this, your hot little pussy squeezes me," he let out a groan as she clamped down around him. "So tight and hot, you're going to make me come and I don't even have to move."

Another pass at her clit, and he seemed to swell even bigger and harder inside her. Oh, God, she wanted him to move, needed him to move. But he kept his firm grip on her hips as his thumb slipped and slid around the apex of her sex.

"Jesus, Caroline. You drive me crazy. There's never been anyone like you." His thumb was moving faster, firmer, but he still wouldn't let her move like her body craved.

A sob ripped from her throat. "Please," she moaned, not caring that she was begging. "I need you, need you to move."

He flexed his hips, pumping inside her in short strokes that kept him buried deep but gave her the friction she craved. "Like this, baby, is this what you need?"

Her only answer was a muffled moan as he increased his pace. "Whatever you want baby," he panted between hot kisses, "whatever you need. I want to give you everything."

He swiveled his hips, twisting inside her, touching places that had never been touched as his thumb kept a firm steady pressure on her sex. Inside, outside, he touched her everywhere from mouth to toes and everywhere in between.

"Anything baby," he repeated, his voice strained now. She could feel him struggling to hold back his release. "Anything you want."

"You," she whispered before she could stop herself. "All I ever wanted was you."

"All yours," he said, locking his sex hazed gray stare to hers. "Always all yours." Then he stiffened and cried out, his muscles jerking and trembling beneath her hands as his release rumbled through him.

She followed him headlong into the abyss, arching and straining against him as she trembled and pulsed around his cock.

Always all yours.

She knew better than to give any weight to careless words spoken during the heat of sex. But she wanted to.

Through the pleasure, a pit of dread formed in her stomach at how badly she wanted this all to mean . . . something. But she'd been slammed by Danny Taggart before, and no matter how much he needed her tonight, there was no telling how he'd act tomorrow. Just because they'd cleared up some misunderstandings about the past didn't mean she should start hoping for a future.

But that couldn't stop her from indulging in the bliss of cuddling up against Danny's broad, muscular chest as she slipped into a restless sleep.

Her dreams were frenetic and disjointed. Full of images of the white walled rooms and bright lights of a hospital. Somewhere in the distance a baby cried and Caroline felt an answering sob. Her baby. Her baby was crying somewhere.

In her dream she turned and saw another girl. Blond, her heavily pregnant stomach rounding the sheet as James stood next to her. Emily Parrish. Emily Parrish delivering her baby while a nameless, faceless doctor stood at the foot of the bed in a white doctor's coat. The only splash of color was the bright red insignia embroidered over the left breast.

In her dream Caroline turned to see Lauren Schiffer in a hospital gown, cradling an infant to her shoulder.

A baby cried in a high thin wail and Caroline put her hand to her own flat stomach. She felt the sobs heaving in her chest but they made no sound as hot tears leaked down her cheeks.

Masculine hands closed over her shoulders and a deep voice called her name.

She awoke, startled at first to see a huge male form hovering over her in the dim morning light. She relaxed a degree when she saw it was Danny, but she couldn't calm her frantically beating heart or shake off the raw edge of grief.

"You were crying in your sleep," he said as he pulled her against him. "What were you dreaming about?"

She buried her face in his neck and held off a fresh wave of tears. "I don't really remember," she lied. She lay there in the dark as her mind touched on the pieces of her dream. That niggling feeling was back, like someone was scratching the back of her brain, trying to get her attention.

CHAPTER 16

Danny sat back and watched a little regretfully as Caroline pulled away and yanked on one of his T-shirts. "Are you sure you're okay?"

"Yeah," she said, scrubbing at her eyes. "Just a weird dream."

He threw his legs over the side of the bed and stood up. A blush rose up in Caroline's cheeks and her gaze slid away from his naked form. She turned her back and pretended to hunt for her clothes.

So that was how she wanted to play it, huh? He'd ripped himself open and let his guts spill out last night, and now she wanted to act like it was no big deal.

Served him right, not that he was going to let her get away with it. It was a big deal. A very big deal. His brain shied away from defining exactly what was going on just yet, but there was no way he could pretend something important hadn't happened. Danny walked up behind her and turned her gently but firmly to face him.

"We should call Toni as soon as possible, and see if there's any information—"

Whatever she was going to say was swallowed by his mouth. She was stiff at first, every muscle going rigid and her lips stayed glued shut in a thin, tight line. He wore her down with teasing sucks and licks, and within a few seconds she was sighing into his mouth and curling her fingers into the hair of his nape.

Much better.

"Good morning," he whispered and gave her a final, soft peck. "I'll call Toni ASAP to tell her to meet us at the office, okay?" Danny smiled at her dazed nod as he sauntered past her into the bathroom. His morning erection throbbed a protest over Caroline not joining him in the shower, but he figured there would be time enough to fool around after she was completely safe.

When he emerged, showered and dressed, he found Caroline on the couch, her hands curled around a steaming cup of coffee. With her hunched shoulders swallowed up in his giant T-shirt and her hair spilling down her back, she looked like a lost little girl.

He poured coffee into a heavy ceramic mug and joined her on the couch. "It's going to be okay."

She shook her head. "So much has happened. I'm just not sure who I can trust anymore."

He ran a soothing hand down her back. "You can trust me. You can trust Derek, Ethan, and Toni," he said firmly. "Don't ever doubt that."

Her eyes narrowed and she looked like she was going to say something, but stopped herself. Finally, she said, "I guess I don't have much choice."

Something about that stuck in his craw, and he shoved the uneasiness aside. "Why don't you go get cleaned up. I'll make some phone calls and take you into the office."

An hour later they met Toni, Ethan and Derek at the office.

"Now what about the flash drive that melted your laptop?" Toni said, holding out her hand.

Danny handed it over, along with the DVD that had been

in the safe. "We found this too, but after what happened with the flash drive, I wasn't about to slip it into my Bose."

Toni's eyes rolled behind the lenses of her heavy framed glasses. "Viruses don't work on stereo equipment, Danny."

Danny and Caroline followed her back to her office, which was a good five degrees warmer than the rest of the space from the sheer volume of computer equipment. She stuck the flash drive into a Mac laptop and executed a few keystrokes . "I'm running a deep scan antivirus program," she explained as the computer hummed. "Although since most viruses are written for Windows machines, whatever James loaded his data with is a lot less likely to hurt the Mac." She patted the computer as though it were a loyal pet.

Caroline took a seat in one of Toni's guest chairs while Danny resisted the urge to pace.

"Tapping your feet and squirming like a four-year-old who needs the potty isn't going to make me go any faster," Toni said without looking up.

Caroline gave a tired little laugh and Danny felt an answering smile tug at his mouth. He willed himself to stay still, even as restless energy sparked through his veins.

For several minutes the only sound was the white noise hum of computers and the clack of Toni's fingers on the keyboard. Finally she sat back. "Eughh." She grimaced as though a foul smell were emanating from the computer.

"Eugh? What does eugh mean?" Caroline asked, jumping from her seat and coming around so she could see Toni's screen.

Toni slouched a little in her seat and she pulled at her lip. "It's pretty well encrypted."

Danny's stomach sank. "You can't read it?"

Toni sat up straight. "Of course I can read it," she snapped. "But it might take me awhile."

Impatience bubbled in his chest and he struggled to keep his tone calm. "How long is awhile?"

Toni's eyes narrowed and she typed something. She shook her head. "At least a few hours."

"No problem," he said, biting back his disappointment. "We know a hell of a lot more than we did a few days ago. We can wait a few hours." He met Caroline's eyes and she nodded in agreement. "We'll leave you to it," he said to Toni. "I'll have Derek take a look at the DVD and see if we can get any more info on these bank records." Toni barely nodded, her focus already on cracking the code of the incomprehensible characters on her screen.

They caught Derek and Ethan in the break room, their dark heads bent as they spoke in low, serious tones. They both looked up when Danny and Caroline walked in. Two pairs of eyes, one striking blue, one dark and fathomless locked on them in speculative stares. They looked back at each other and exchanged a series of nods and facial expressions that had meaning only to them.

Fucking stupid twin shit. "We need to take a look at this," Danny held up the disc in its clear jewel case. "But we need to be careful in case it's loaded like the flash drive."

"Got it," Derek said and motioned them to follow him to his office. Like Toni, he didn't load the disk into his regular computer, but pulled out a spare laptop and loaded the CD into the drive.

Caroline and Danny crowded around the back of the desk to see Derek's screen. Almost immediately the screen went black.

"Oh, no," Caroline said. "It's going to be just like the last one. Since when did James know how to booby trap computer files?" Her voice took on a high, frantic tone.

"No, wait," Danny held up a hand. "It's just launching a video file."

A guitar lick with a heavy base line started to play as a series of computer generated credits flashed across the screen. The scene cut to the living room of a house, where a young woman in a tank top and shorts so tight you could see the outline of her sex lounged against the cushions of a couch. A heavily muscled man walked in, his face obscured by the camera angle. A few lines of improbable dialog provided the only setup before the guy was thrusting his tongue in the girl's mouth and twisting her nipples like he was trying to tune in Tokyo.

Danny felt his face heat as realization dawned.

Caroline got it at about the same time. "Oh my God, is this a porno?"

"Yep," Derek said all cool and matter of fact as he sat back in his chair. The man on the screen stripped off the girl's shorts, cursing when he bumped into an off camera microphone. "Nice to see they didn't spare any expense on production value."

"Maybe I should watch this by myself," Danny said.

Caroline gave him an appalled look.

"I don't mean it like that," he said. "But if it was in James's safe, it has to be important. So someone should watch it."

"Maybe that someone would be me," Caroline said, "since I'm less likely to be distracted by . . . ew," her nose wrinkled and her head recoiled. Then she leaned over Derek's shoulder and peered closer at the screen. "I know that guy."

Had he not been resting his hand on the back of Derek's chair, Danny would have fallen on his ass.

"You know porn stars?" He was glad Derek asked the question because Caroline's comment had rendered Danny speechless.

"No," Caroline said. "That's the guy from that reality show. You know, the fighter one—"

Danny squinted at the screen. "She's right. It's Curtis

Thomson from *Last Fighter Standing*." Thomson had been a contestant last season on a trashy reality show focused on the ultimate fighting world.

"He was voted off in round six," Caroline said.

"You watched that show?" He knew it was stupid, but that small area of compatibility made him smile.

An answering smile teased the corners of her mouth as she shrugged. "A girl's gotta ogle her man meat." Then her eyes widened as the light shifted enough to fully reveal the girl's features. She was beautiful in a faintly exotic way. If her sleepy expression and bored moans were anything to go by, Curtis Thomson wasn't any better in the sack than he was in the Octagon.

"She was at my house," Caroline said, an undercurrent of disbelief in her voice. "A month before James was killed.

"I thought they were having an affair," Caroline said as she accepted a bottle of water and let Danny guide her to one of the leather club chairs on the other side of Derek's desk. Derek had thankfully stopped the DVD so Caroline wouldn't have to hear the squirm inducing fake moans and cheesy music.

"Tell us everything you remember about her."

"I didn't get her name," Caroline said.

"According to the credits her name is Lanie Deep," Derek said, "but I'm gonna go out on a limb and say that's a stage name."

"I came home early from a weekend with Kate." She looked at Danny to see if he'd roll his eyes, but his expression remained serious, focused on what she had to say. "I heard James arguing with someone in his office. The door was open and I waited outside to see if I could hear anything. She had a really heavy accent—Eastern European, I'd guess."

Caroline frowned, trying to remember every detail of the few seconds of conversation she'd heard. Between the hysteria and the thick accent, the woman had been nearly incomprehensible. "James was angry, telling her there was nothing he could do. I must have made some noise because he came out into the hall and found me." James's face had drained of color when he'd found her out there. At the time Caroline had been convinced she'd just walked in on her husband and his distraught mistress. "He tried to cover it up and say she was a client having problems. He made her leave. I asked him point blank if he was having an affair. He didn't try to deny it. Three days later he filed for divorce."

The woman's sobs echoed in Caroline's head as she lowered her face to her hands. At the time, all she'd seen was a beautiful young woman upset with her husband and jumped to the obvious conclusion. She realized the truth could be much, much worse. "Do you think he took her baby? Is that why she tracked him down?" Her stomach twisted and her eyes burned at the thought.

"We won't know until we talk to her," Danny said. But she could see the suspicion in his stormy eyes. "Do you know what happened to her?" he asked and handed her a tissue.

Caroline dabbed at her nose and eyes, struggling to regain her composure. There would be plenty of time to lament her stupidity for marrying a man she never really knew. A man who was capable of doing something so horrific. "I have no idea. James wouldn't give me any information, and I had no idea where to start looking. But if he took her baby for illegal adoption, wouldn't she go to the police?"

"Not necessarily," Derek said. "You said she sounded Eastern European?"

Caroline nodded.

"You'd be surprised how many people are trafficked from overseas," Derek said. "They take these girls, promise them jobs, then sell them into forced labor or prostitution."

"But she escaped and managed to track down James. She would have to tell somebody—"

"These women are terrified," Danny said. "When they get here their passports are confiscated and their pimps put a scare into them about going to the police. Most of them are convinced they'll go to prison and that no one here will help them."

"Then there's always the possibility she didn't just disappear," Derek said.

A sense of foreboding swept through Caroline at his words. She had a terrible feeling, deep in her gut, that the beautiful girl in the movie, the same distraught woman who had been at her house, had met the same fate as Anne Taggart and Emily Parrish. Whether directly by James's hand, she wasn't sure. She still couldn't see him actually killing anyone with his own hands.

Not because she had any remaining belief in James's inherent goodness, but because she simply didn't see him having the balls to do it himself.

"How do we find out for sure?"

Danny leaned his butt on Derek's desk and rubbed absently at his chin. He was only a foot or so away. Close enough for her to pick up the woodsy scent of his soap and the salty tang of his skin. Close enough to make it hard to resist the urge to throw her arms around his waist and bury her head in his chest so he could whisper that no matter how fucked up all this seemed, everything was going to be all right.

Caroline curled her fingers into the armrests to keep herself anchored.

"Curtis Thomson was from around here, wasn't he?"

"He's from Dublin," Caroline said, smiling in spite of everything as she saw where Danny was going with this.

She could hear Derek typing at his keyboard. "Already have an address," he said.

Danny offered his hand to Caroline and pulled her up from the chair. "How about it? Want to pay a visit to your favorite Ultimate Fighter?"

Thomson wasn't at home when they got there but his room-mate was happy to direct them to the auto shop where he worked as a mechanic. At six feet, Thomson was tall for a fighter, with all-American blue-eyed, blond hair good looks. The kind of kid you expected to see sitting on a tractor in the middle of a corn field. Not a kid you expected to be beating the crap out of someone in a metal cage.

Or starring in a one step up from homemade porno.

Thomson wiped his hands on a rag before offering one to Danny to shake. Danny suppressed a smile as the kid assessed him and squeezed his hand a little too hard. He faked a wince. Let the kid think he could take him if it made him a little more talkative.

"Thanks so much for talking to us," Caroline said, all fluttering eyelashes and pouty red lips.

The kid flashed her a cocky grin. "Let me guess, you two were fans of *Fighter*?"

Caroline cocked an eyebrow and gave Danny a look.

"Actually," Danny said, "it's your other work we wanted to ask you about."

The smile faded from Curtis's face. "I don't follow." But the slash of red on Curtis's cheekbones told Danny the kid knew exactly what he was talking about.

"What can you tell me about the girl you worked with in *Mutiny on the Booty*?"

Curtis took a couple steps back and faked another smile.

"Like I said man, I don't know what you're talking about. Now if you don't mind, I need to get back to work—"

"What's the matter, you don't want anyone to know about your porn career?" Danny said, raising his voice enough to get a double take from one of the other mechanics."

"Shut up, dude," Curtis hissed. "The guy who runs this shop is super conservative. You're gonna get me fired."

"Then talk to us, or I'll see to it personally that he gets his very own copy of your latest work."

Curtis glared and clenched his fists. Danny rolled his weight to the balls of his feet and held his hands loosely at his sides in case the kid made any sudden moves. Though he was smaller than Danny, the guy was whipcord lean under his overalls. He may not have been the last fighter standing, but he'd give Danny a workout before Danny took him down.

Danny was almost disappointed when Curtis loosened his fists and said, "Fine. Let me tell them I'm taking a break and I'll meet you outside."

"He's a lot cuter in person than he was on TV," Caroline mused as they walked outside.

Something suspiciously close to jealousy clawed at Danny's stomach. "He's not even close to being man enough for you."

"Were you watching the same movie I was? Not that I could ever go there, after . . ." she trailed off with a mock shudder, squinching her nose in distaste. Then she covered her mouth, her dark eyes widening in horror. "I can't believe I just made light of this. If what we think is true—"

He grabbed her in a quick hug. "Don't worry about it. I know it seems sick, but sometimes in the worst situation, all you can do is joke about it." When he'd been in the military, sometimes the gallows humor of him and his men was the only thing that kept them all from losing their shit.

Curtis joined them then and suggested they move to the coffee shop across the street.

They took their coffees to a small round table. Curtis took a sip of his drink and shook his head. "I was hoping to keep all this on the lowdown, you know?"

"You were on national television. You didn't think someone might recognize you?" Caroline asked.

Curtis shrugged. "*Fighter* didn't have huge ratings, and besides, the lighting is so bad in those movies . . ." He looked up to meet Caroline's stare and his face went bright red. "Look, I'm not proud of it, or anything, but they pay good money, and I needed a little extra to cover some medical bills over the past couple of years."

"How many movies have you been in?"

"You get paid by the scene, not the movie," Curtis said.

Danny rolled his eyes. He didn't need a primer on the inner workings of the porn industry. "Fine. How many scenes then?"

Curtis stared at the ceiling and his lips moved silently. "Fifty? Give or take a few?" Caroline's expression went from disgusted to horrified.

"Always with different girls?" Danny asked.

"Not always. Sometimes they put me with the same girl two, three times in a row."

Caroline looked like she was having trouble keeping her latte down. "What about the girl in *Mutiny*?"

"Remind me again which one she is."

Caroline's lips pressed together in a tight line. "Dark hair. Very pretty."

"Spoke with a Russian or Eastern European accent," Danny added. "Her name in the credits was listed as Lanie Deep."

A smile of recognition spread across Curtis's face. "Oh yeah, now I remember her. She was one of my first scenes."

He stared off in the distance like he was actually getting nostalgic. He pulled back to reality with a look of concern. "Did something happen to her?"

"We're not sure," Danny replied. "But we were hoping to track her down and ask her some questions. Is there anything you can remember that might help us?"

"All I remember is that she seemed kind of nervous. Not as nervous as I was. I almost ruined the scene and was afraid I wouldn't get paid."

"I'm not sure I want to know, but how?"

"I uh messed up the, you know," Curtis's gaze flicked uncomfortably to Caroline, "the money shot."

"The what shot?" Caroline asked.

"I'll tell you later. Better yet, I'll show you later," Danny said.

"It's the, uh, climax shot," Curtis supplied helpfully.

Danny met Caroline's glare with a smirk.

"Anyway," Curtis said with a laugh, getting over his embarrassment for the moment, "I did what I thought they'd want and did it all over her tits. But the director got all pissed and told me I was supposed to finish inside her. Like how was I supposed to know that?"

"I sure wouldn't," Caroline said in a high strained voice. "What can you tell us about the girl?"

"Nothing much. She barely spoke English. A lot of them don't."

"What about the girls who do? Do they ever talk about where they came from, how they ended up in the movies?"

Curtis shook his head. "I know it sounds weird, but we don't really get personal on set. We show up, do our thing, and take off. And to be honest, a lot of times the girls were kind of out of it."

"Like they'd been drugged?"

"I think some of them took something to take the edge off, but I never saw anyone force anyone to take anything."

Not that he saw anyway. Danny rolled his neck in frustration. This was going nowhere. "Okay. What about the producers, the directors? Would they know anything? How do we get in touch with them?"

"No clue."

"Wait, you've had sex in front of these people at least fifty times," Caroline bit out, "but you don't know how to get in touch with them?"

He shook his head. "I don't ask, they don't tell. Everyone's on a first name basis."

"So how did you ever get involved in this anyway?"

Curtis looked around, as though checking for eavesdroppers. "A buddy of mine—I'm not going to say who—gave me a call. He knew I needed the money and said I had the right look, whatever that meant. I met with some people, they made me take a blood test and I shot my first scene six weeks later. They paid me in cash. A few weeks later, a new girl, a new scene. All I have to do is turn in clean labs every six weeks."

"But you don't know anything about the company or the producers, anything?" Caroline asked.

Curtis drained the last of his coffee and gave Caroline a long look. "I'm a fighter. That means I get hurt. I don't have insurance. That means I pay a lot. I needed cash. They had it. I didn't ask questions. I was just happy I got to fuck girls and not take it up the dirt road, if you know what I mean. Now if you'll excuse me—"

"Wait," Danny grabbed him by the arm, tightening his hold when he would have pulled away.

"You don't wanna fuck with me, big guy," Curtis said and moved to strike with his other hand.

Danny shifted his grip so his thumb dug into a pressure point at the base of Curtis's palm, which immediately went slack. "Settle down there, junior. We're not done with our chat. Now how do they contact you?"

"Phone," Curtis wheezed. "But it's a blocked number. They tell me when to be there, and I show up."

"Be where?" Danny increased the pressure on Curtis's wrist.

"Wherever they shoot," Curtis said.

"Which is where?" Caroline bit out.

"Different places. They rent out different houses or locations depending on the shoot."

"You have a shoot coming up?"

Curtis looked away. "Tomorrow. But they haven't told me where yet. Please man, don't fuck this up. I need the money. One last chunk of change and I'm done, I swear."

Danny sat back and pasted a smile on his face. "Don't worry, man. I won't mess anything up for you. Thanks for your help."

Curtis looked a little puzzled at Danny's sudden change in demeanor. "I better get back to work."

They watched Curtis jog across the street. "We need to do something. If what you think is true, that those girls are trafficked here and somehow being forced—"

"Don't worry," he told her. "We're going to keep an eye on junior, and when it comes time to film his next money shot, we'll be there. And if James had anything to do with these guys, we'll find out, okay?"

"Okay."

As they walked back to the car, Danny pulled out his phone to call Toni to see how she was progressing on the data decryption.

"I don't know who did this code for him," Toni said, a combination of awe and frustration in her voice, "but he's good. They used a code string I've never even seen before—"

"Toni you can have your nerdfest later. How long before you know what's on that drive?"

She was silent for several seconds, and he could practically see her chewing her lip in contemplation. "Tomorrow?"

Not the answer he wanted to hear. "Keep on it, and transfer me to Derek."

He quickly filled in his brother on what they'd learned from Curtis. "Fuck if I know what's going on," Danny said. He flashed what he hoped was a reassuring look at Caroline, whose face was getting more pinched by the day. "But if there's a link between James Medford, and bad porn, we're going to find it."

CHAPTER 17

"**P**ut these on."

Kaylee winced as the woman's stinking cigarettes and cabbage breath hit her in the face. Unlike the other women who'd been yanking her around and sticking her with needles for the past week, this woman had a different accent. Something harsher and European sounding. She wasn't dressed like a nurse, either. Her hair was dyed a dark maroon color, and she wore so much eyeliner that the black color leaked into her crow's-feet.

If she hadn't been so freaked out, Kaylee would have told her the Amy Winehouse look didn't work once you hit thirty. This woman was a good twenty hard years past that.

"Why? What is it?" she asked, even though she knew it wouldn't make any difference.

"Is wardrobe," the woman surprised her by actually answering. "Then we do makeup."

Wardrobe and makeup?

Why the hell did she need wardrobe and makeup for what was going to happen if she didn't find some way to escape in the next few hours? After the horrible, invasive, humiliating exam, the big doctor guy had done another test, with an ultrasound. Whatever he saw among the smudges of white and black had made everyone happy, even as Kaylee felt the growing horror threaten to choke her.

"Perfect. Just what we want to see," he'd said. "Three more days and she'll be totally ready."

That had been three days ago, and Kaylee hadn't figured out how to get out of there. They guarded all the girls heavily, but after the exam she'd been kept confined to the bedroom, her arm cuffed to the bed. She was back in a room with girls who didn't speak any English and didn't seem inclined to help her even if they could understand her. She wasn't allowed downstairs for meals, and was only uncuffed from the bed long enough to use the bathroom.

She stood uncuffed before the woman waving a piece of fabric no bigger than a handkerchief in front of her. A gangbanger looking thug stood guard at the door as always, ready to catch her if she made a break for it.

Could she get past him?

She thought about the Thai girl, of the "many men" who used her. She thought of the pretty brunette girl, sobbing incoherently as she wrapped her hands around her waist.

If she didn't get out of there, she'd end up like them.

The woman heaved herself up from her metal folding chair and advanced on her. "If you no take off your clothes yourself, I do it for you. Maybe I let him help," she said, giving a meaningful look to the guard at the door.

Feigning cooperation, Kaylee took a step toward the woman and held her hand out as though to take the clothes. At the last minute she lunged for the chair, picked it up and swung.

It landed with a satisfying clang against the woman's head. She hit the ground like a felled tree, flat on her ass, groaning as she brought her hand up to the deep gash across her forehead.

"Drop it, bitch," the thug said. The bottom dropped out

of Kaylee's stomach as she saw the gun pointed straight at her.

They want me pregnant, not dead, she reminded herself and charged straight ahead, the metal chair held high over her head. But unlike the woman, the thug was prepared for her charge. He ducked down and took her out at the knees.

A desperate "No!" exploded from her lungs as she was knocked to the floor and the chair was kicked out of the way. Her ears rang as he slammed her head into the floor, a warning blow meant to stun. She heard him yelling something in Spanish, felt his heavy weight settle on her torso as he pinned her arms above her head.

Her head was spinning but she bucked and twisted, thrashing as hard as she could to get out of his hold. Footsteps thundered across the hard linoleum floor and the plain, stern face of one of the Spanish speaking nurse types swam into her line of vision.

A sharp sting bit into the crook of her arm, and almost immediately her body went all weak and floaty.

Oh, God, she'd failed.

Caroline swallowed back a wave of nausea as Danny guided the car through the streets of an upscale suburban development about an hour east of San Francisco. It was the kind of development where all of the homes were huge, sprawling variations on a Mediterranean theme. Each stuccoed and terra cottaed mcmansion perched squarely in the middle of its own picture-perfect square of grass.

As shiny new and beautiful as the houses were, the multiple FOR SALE—PRICE REDUCED, signs and the one foreclosure sign she saw indicated it was a neighborhood hit hard by the recent housing crash. It was so easy to imagine the streets and cul de sacs filled with kids riding bikes and scooters in the neighborhood.

It was not where you expected to find a porn movie being shot. But it was where Curtis Thomson had led them.

"There's his car," Danny said, spotting Curtis's small truck. Another vehicle was already in the driveway, a utility van which Caroline imagined had transported all of the equipment. Although from what she'd seen of the DVD the production values hadn't gone much past a hand held video camera and a poorly positioned microphone.

There were no other cars on the street or in front of any of the other houses, giving the street the feel of a ghost town. If nothing else, Caroline supposed it offered lots of privacy for whatever was about to go on in there.

Danny parked around the block where their car wouldn't be seen. "You stay put while I go take a look around." He'd already unclipped his seatbelt and was halfway out the door, expecting her to blindly obey.

"Oh, right, like I'm really going to wait here twiddling my thumbs." She opened her door to get out, only to have her way blocked by a very large male body.

"We don't know what we're going to find in there, Caroline."

She rolled her eyes. "I may not be well versed in porn, but I think I can handle what we're going to see." She tried to push him out of the way. Which of course didn't work, and of course she got distracted by the hard ripple of his ab muscles under his shirt and remembering how they'd flexed tight as he'd held himself over her the night before.

"If we're dealing with the kind of people I think we are, they could be armed. They could be willing to do anything to protect this little enterprise."

Any hazy memories of last night's indulgence fled in the face of cold, harsh reality. Still, Curtis hadn't mentioned anything about guns or feeling threatened, which she pointed out to Danny.

"Just let me come with you to see what's going on. If you

decide it's too risky, *we'll* come back to the car and call for help." Like she would let him face a bunch of gun toting bad guys alone while she went scurrying back to the car.

His grunt wasn't exactly an agreement but he moved a little bit out of her way. As they walked to the house, he took her arm in a firm grip and bent to speak quietly in her ear. "You follow my lead completely, got it? Don't talk unless I talk first. Don't move unless I tell you. Hell, don't breathe unless I say it's okay. Got it?"

"Sir yes sir," she nodded.

His eyes narrowed and his mouth pulled into a rueful half smile. His hand came up to cup her cheek and his lips came down to cover hers in a deep kiss that was somehow as calming as it was arousing. He lifted his head, shaking it as he looked at her with unreadable gray eyes. "I should have left you at home today."

She couldn't argue the point because he lifted his finger to his lips, signaling the demand for silence. She obliged and followed after him, doing her best to follow his lead and make sure her running shoes didn't make any sound as they cut through the neighboring yard up to the side of the house. Danny motioned for her to stop as he looked in a window.

After several seconds, he motioned for her to join him. Caroline peered through a crack in the wooden blinds. From the window she had a view of a small dining room that led into a larger great room. A bed had been moved into the room, she imagined to take advantage of the natural light coming in from sliding glass doors and skylights in the ceiling. A lone male figure sat on the bed. Curtis, she supposed, but the blinds blocked the view of his face. A man was setting up a tripod while another moved around the bed holding a boom microphone. Crew members, probably. Their voices were nothing but low murmurs through the glass.

"Doesn't look too menacing," Caroline whispered, earning her a glare and a "zip it" signal from Danny.

He pulled her back, away from the window, and spoke in a whisper so low she had to strain to hear. "We're going to go around to the front. You let me do all the talking, okay?"

Caroline nodded and followed him around the side of the house. Just as they rounded the corner a black SUV screeched to a stop in front of the driveway.

Panic pulled her chest tight as she saw that it was identical to the car driven by Rachael Weller's killers. She wanted to believe it was a coincidence, that those people had nothing to do with whoever had killed her defense attorney, but she'd learned the hard way the past year that coincidences were seldom what they seemed.

Danny grabbed her and pressed them both against the side of the house as they watched the occupants of the car get out. Three men, decidedly tougher and scarier looking than the guys working inside. Two of them scanned the empty street while the third went around to the rear passenger door.

A few seconds later a female form half stumbled and was half pulled onto the sidewalk. A fierce gust of winter wind blew her coat open. She didn't seem to notice, even though all she had on underneath was a short, belly baring halter top and a pair of shorts so tiny they may as well have been a pair of denim underpants. She had long, straight, golden blond hair. Her body was tall and almost coltishly thin.

The guy helping her jostled her and her head fell back, revealing her face. She was beautiful, with classic, delicate features.

Startlingly beautiful, just like the girl in the movie.

Curtis hadn't seemed to think that the girls were being forced into it. Nevertheless, Derek and Danny's talk about human trafficking and forced prostitution rang in her head.

The girl took a clumsy step forward and staggered, then

tried to pull away from the man's grip. He gave her arm a rough yank and pulled her partway up the walk. "Bitch, if you don't get your ass inside this house . . ." the threat trailed off and the girl made another clumsy attempt to pull away.

"Don' wanna do this," the girl said, her meaning clear even if her words were slurred. "Don' make me—" the girl cried out as the man's hand caught her openhanded on the side of the head.

"You do whatever we say you do, else you'll get turned out on some street corner somewhere, got it?"

Despite Danny's order of silence, Caroline couldn't hold back her protest any longer. She clawed frantically at Danny's arm. "We have to help her. You heard her. She doesn't want this. They drugged her. They're going to rape her and film it. We have to—"

"Shut up," Danny bit out. "I know. I'm not going to let them do anything to her. You go back to the car, and call the police. I'm going to try to stall them."

She opened her mouth, but Danny clapped his hand over it before she could utter a single syllable. "Do not fucking argue with me."

She pressed herself against the side of the house, her heart pounding in her throat as Danny continued up to the front. She heard his firm knock on the door, the murmur of low male voices. Her breath froze when she heard what sounded like a scuffle, but from where she was she couldn't see anything.

She heard another car pull up as she scooted around to the back of the house to go back the way she came. She wondered how long Danny could stall them without getting in serious danger and how long it would take the police to get there.

Caroline had gone a few steps when she heard a crash and the sound of voices yelling. *Do exactly what I say.*

Danny's words rang in her ears even as she found herself running back to the house. She looked in the same window as before, scrambling for a glimpse of what was happening inside.

Through the slats she could see a lamp had smashed on the floor. The girl was a lanky lump in the middle of the bed. There were lots of male bodies gesturing and a lot of yelling and swearing. Danny stood in the middle of it all, hands raised as though to calm everyone down.

He had a handle on the situation, and she wasn't helping anything by peeking through windows. She was about to turn and spring back to the car when something round and hard pressed into the middle of her back.

Horror and shock paralyzed her as a familiar voice spoke directly into her ear. "You couldn't keep your nose out of it, could you, Caroline. At least this time we'll be able to take care of you and Taggart once and for all."

A hard blow caught her on the back of the head with sickening force a split second before her vision went black.

Aww, shit. It had the feel of a clusterfuck the second he stepped inside the house. Danny knew he should have turned tail and run back to the car and called for backup. But he couldn't let them force the girl. She might have done it a thousand times before for all he knew, but that day she didn't want to. He wasn't about to let a girl be drugged and raped while he ran around the block and did nothing.

The only problem with his do-gooder streak was that it landed him situations like this. Stuck in the middle of a pack of meatheads whose guns were bigger than their brains with strict orders from the boss, whoever that was, to make sure the filming went on as scheduled.

The only bright spot so far was that Curtis, for whatever reason, picked up on Danny's cue not to give Danny up. He'd since retreated to a far corner of the room and was keeping a nervous eye on the Glock one of the goons was casually holding at his side.

"Guys, there's no reason to wave those around," Danny said, nodding at the guns while he held his hands up in front of him. "Like I said, we've formed a new neighborhood watch, and I came over to see what was going on." As he spoke a fourth man entered the room from the kitchen. Danny feigned an uncomfortable smile and let his gaze dart from the girl on the bed to the camera, all while doing some quick mental math on how long it should take Caroline to get back to the car and call the cops.

He expected sirens any time in the next few minutes.

"Listen man," the new guy said, taking charge, his fake smile showing off gold capped teeth. "Why don't you forget about what you saw here today, and go tell your friends at the neighborhood association that everything here is all good." He gave Danny a not so friendly squeeze on his shoulder and pulled a roll of bills from his pocket. "You understand the need for discretion."

Danny grinned and reached for the cash. "Consider my lips sealed."

The guy gave him a pat on the back. "Hey, maybe you want to stay and watch?"

The thought made Danny want to barf, but he needed to stall. Where the hell were the police? "That might be, uh, kind of cool," he stammered. He met Curtis's eyes and subtly shook his head. Curtis nodded back. Yeah, he got it. No performance, not today.

"Hey, she seems kind of out of it," Curtis said. "Maybe we should wait for her to come around a little more."

The thug next to Danny dropped his smile and leveled a hard stare at Curtis. "We're not waiting on anything. Camera's ready, lights are going, let's get down to business."

Curtis shook his head. "No way man," he said, casting a

look at the girl, who was trying to sit up on the bed, only to be pulled back down by the weight of her own head. "I didn't sign on to fuck no corpse."

The thug walked over to Curtis and pulled up to his full height, which was a good six inches less than Danny and a couple inches shorter than Curtis. But the sidearm that peeked out when he pulled aside his jacket leveled the playing field. "You're a hired dick. You signed on to fuck when we say fuck, not—" he was cut off by the ring of a cell phone.

As he listened intently to the man's quick, monosyllabic conversation with whoever was on the line, Danny's internal alarm system started to shoot off in sharp bursts.

Something was up there, a suspicion confirmed when the man hung up and gave Danny a slow, evil grin. He pulled his Glock out of his shoulder holster and pointed it straight at Danny's chest. The other three thugs followed suit as Curtis jumped back into the corner. "It appears Mr. Neighborhood Watch isn't who he appears to be."

Fuck. He'd been made.

Caroline. Panic squeezed his chest. Fuck, they'd gotten to her, and that was why the police weren't there yet. Every instinct screamed for him to charge out the door and find her. Images of Caroline hurt, maybe even dead, ripped through him. He couldn't lose her, couldn't let go of her again, couldn't . . .

Couldn't lose his focus, or he'd end up with a bullet in his brain and no help to her at all. He forced the terror down deep and shut it up in a black box. The mission. Only by focusing on the mission could he get everyone out alive.

Every muscle tensed in readiness as Danny held up his hands in mock supplication. "Oh yeah, what did they tell you?"

"Just that they need you taken care of. That's all the information I need. Now turn around and walk to the kitchen with your hands on your head. I don't want no bloodstains on the carpet."

"What the fuck? You can't just kill him!" Curtis said, a panicked note entering his voice. The two unarmed crew members looked away, on board with whatever needed to happen.

One of the gangsters leveled his gun at Curtis's nose. "You do your job and you don't worry so much, kid. Then you won't end up dead like him."

Danny caught Curtis's terrified gaze. They both knew Curtis was as dead as Danny was whether he did his command performance or not. Before Danny turned around, he gazed around the room, quickly cataloging every armed man's position and body language. They all held their guns out of the holsters, loosely at their sides. It was clear none of them were fighters; they all let their guns, not their muscles do the work for them. A fact Danny planned to use to his advantage.

"Go." The thug prodded him in the back with the barrel of the gun.

Dammit. He really wasn't in the mood to kill anyone.

Danny took a half step forward and pivoted, taking the thug by surprise as he caught him with a sharp blow across the forearm, sending his gun skidding across the floor. At the same time, Danny caught him in a leg sweep that landed him flat on his back.

He heard shouts, curses, and out of the corner of his eye saw one of the other guys raise his gun. Danny grabbed the thug off the floor and rolled to one knee, using the guy as a shield as the other guy pulled the trigger, catching his buddy in the shoulder. Danny dropped his shield and pulled his own Glock from his ankle holster in one seamless move. A shot, a scream, and the thug's gun hand was hamburger.

The third thug aimed his gun at Danny. Danny iced him

with a side kick to the jaw. The wounded man lay groaning on the floor, and Danny fired at the one guy left standing. His shot went wide and he rolled to the side to avoid return fire. The guy turned and made a run for the stairs.

Curtis came out of his panicked daze as he stepped into the guy's path and clocked him with a sharp jab to the face. Before the guy could recover enough to lift his gun Curtis caught him with a punch to the back of the head, hard enough to render the guy unconscious.

Danny ignored the pain in his shoulder as he surveyed the damage. One wounded, one out cold, one cradling a broken jaw, and the fourth screaming as he clutched his hand and looked at the bloody gap where two fingers used to be. The two crew members had run at the first shot.

"Chill out," Danny snapped. "You'll live." He sent Curtis to get a rope while he kept a gun leveled on all four.

Danny and Curtis quickly secured them as the girl stirred on the bed. He had a lot of questions for those assholes, but first things first.

Caroline.

The panic he'd managed to beat back earlier surged back with even more force. He forced his hand to stay steady as he handed Curtis a gun, who took it with a little too much eagerness and not a shred of skill. "You ever shoot one of these?" Danny asked.

Curtis shook his head.

"Hold it like this, not like in the movies." Danny did a quick lesson in operating the Glock. "Keep your thumb on the side, or the slide will kick back and snap it."

Curtis swallowed hard and gave him a dubious look. "Anything else?"

"Make sure you only shoot the bad guys," Danny said before he darted out the front door.

He skirted around the house, cut through the neighboring yard back the way they'd come and arrived at the car.

No Caroline.

He wanted to believe she'd fled to safety. But he knew she would have come back to the car to call the police like he'd told her to, and she hadn't been there.

Christ, someone had her, he knew it. Someone had her and he had no idea who, no idea where, and a very bad idea of what they meant to do with her.

Chapter 18

Caroline came to with a nose full of dust and a sensation in her head like someone was in there with a sledge hammer.

She started to sit up and found that her hands and feet were bound by plastic flex ties. She rolled to her stomach and managed to wriggle her way into a seated position. She jerked her head to try to get her hair out of her face, wincing as the motion sent a stab of pain through her head.

Marshall had kidnapped her.

Her husband's former associate had pressed a gun in her back and knocked her unconscious and taken her . . . where?

She pushed through the pain in her head and forced her vision to focus. It was dimly lit, wherever he'd taken her. She shifted so she could get a three sixty view, taking in the thick wooden slat walls and and the gate at one end. She was being kept in a stall in a barn. It must have been vacant because she didn't hear any animal sounds or smell any evidence of livestock.

None of that information was important, but cataloging the details helped to calm her. And distract her from what was happening to Danny, and that poor, drugged out girl who obviously wanted nothing to do with whatever movie-making those assholes had planned.

Danny. A sick feeling grew in the pit of her stomach. Danny outnumbered five to one, and at least three of them had guns. Sure she'd seen him slip his own gun in his ankle holster, but what were the odds that he'd be able to take out three armed men on his own?

Her chest seized at the thought of losing him. In the past week and especially in the last few days she'd done everything she could to downplay the connection between them. Tried to convince herself that what they'd resurrected was nothing but old chemistry sparked by being thrown together in a highly charged situation. But then she thought of the way he'd reached out to her, the way everything in him had needed her. The way everything in her had needed him. God, she'd never gotten over him, never stopped loving him. And she was going to lose him before they could get a second chance.

Hot tears leaked down her cheeks and a keening sob rose up in her chest. It froze there as she heard the squeal of the old barn door being opened, the sound of masculine voices arguing and getting closer.

"I don't see why you think that was necessary." She recognized Marshall's sharp, clipped voice. "There was no reason to bring them into it."

"Shut up," another voice, another shockingly familiar voice growled. "This isn't your operation—it never has been. I make the decisions."

No, it couldn't be.

"I think Gates would have something to say about that." Caroline could hear the sneer in Marshall's voice.

She stared through the bars of the stall gate as the muffled footsteps came closer, hoping against hope she was wrong. Praying her ears had played a trick on her.

Her stomach bottomed out as a ruddy face topped by

thick salt and pepper hair appeared between the bars. "Patrick," she managed to choke out.

St. Luke's. The insignia flashed in her brain. *We all gave birth at St. Luke's,* Lauren had said. Caroline saw the physician's coat hanging in Melody's closet, clear as day. Too late, her brain made the connection that had been floating around back there, waiting for Caroline to take notice. "Are you going to kill me now?"

His mouth stretched in a smile that didn't reach his blue eyes. Eyes she'd always seen as glowing with humor were now flat and cold as ice chips. "Not yet. First you're going to tell me everything you know, and how much damage you've done in your idiotic quest to clear your name."

"Who are you working for?" Danny said to the thug in charge, whose name, Danny discovered when he pulled out his ID, was Antonio. He and Curtis had moved the three stooges to the couch. The fourth was still on the floor where he landed, unconscious. The girl had finally managed to haul herself into a seated position but was still too out of it to do more than stare at them in a slack jawed daze.

"Fuck you, man, I'm not telling you shit," he slurred as blood seeped from the wound in his shoulder.

"Shouldn't we call the cops or something?" Curtis asked, his eyes widening nervously as Danny pressed the barrel of his gun against Antonio's cheek.

"Not till I get some answers." As soon as the police got there, the whole thing would be locked up and lawyered up and Danny wouldn't get anything from them. "Maybe you can tell me something," Danny said, keeping the gun trained on the couch as he slipped his Randall Model One from its sheath on his right calf. He smiled tightly as the goon with the shot off fingers watched him twirl the blade.

Danny reached out and clamped his hand around the man's wrist. The guy had no ID. Sticky blood soaked his wrist and the cuff of his shirt. The man struggled, but Danny's grip was like a vice as he brought the knife closer to the raw, jagged wounds. "Come on, Stumps. Who are you working with? Who wants Caroline dead?"

"Don't you fucking tell him shit, or I'll kill you myself," Antonio shouted.

The other guy was screaming and Danny hadn't even touched him yet, while the third sat silently, his face ashen as he fingered his broken jaw.

Danny pressed the tip of the blade against a raw finger stump and twisted. The man screamed and thrashed. "You feel that? And I'm barely applying any pressure." He dug in a little with the blade, twisted harder. The man twisted and moaned, but didn't give up any information.

Time to try a new tactic.

He shifted his attention back to Antonio. "Maybe you'll be more talkative if you've got something to lose."

The man's lips curled back in a sneer. "I've been shot nine times. You think I give a fuck about a couple of fingers?"

"Who said anything about fingers?" He nodded at Curtis to catch his attention. "Take off his pants and hold his legs."

Curtis looked uncertain, but moved to obey.

"What the fuck?" the goon yelled, thrashing and trying to worm his way off the couch. It took some doing, but Curtis got him in a leg lock and wrestled the guy's pants off his hips.

He screamed and froze at the first icy touch of Danny's blade against his scrotum.

"No man, no," finally the guy had lost some of his bravado. Now they were getting somewhere.

"Don't worry, I'm not going to cut the whole thing off." The man's scream was loud and startlingly shrill as Danny let the razor sharp edge of the knife barely kiss the man's skin as the others looked on in horror. "Just the balls. You'll still be able to piss normally and everything." He pressed harder with the blade, enough to coax a tiny bead of blood to trickle down the man's thigh.

"Please man, please don't do this."

"I'd love to drag this out," Danny said, his voice turning deadly, "but someone I care very deeply about is in danger, and I think whoever you're working for has something to do with it. Now tell me who he is and where I can find him, or come this Sunday you'll be singing soprano in the church choir."

"Gates!" the man yelled. "Please, we work for Esteban Lucero, but he goes by the name Gates. He moves women and drugs out of Sacramento."

Danny eased up the pressure on the blade. "Why does he want Caroline Medford dead?"

"I don't know, man, I swear. We're just muscle, get called in on jobs when we're needed. We don't ask no questions."

"Where can I find him?"

"I don't know."

"Wrong answer." He pushed the tip of the blade against the underside of the guy's scrotum.

Sweat poured down his face and his chest heaved in quick, panicked breaths.

"He's telling the truth," the third guy, who had remained silent up until then, slurred. The guy was staring at his buddy's junk like he couldn't tear his eyes away, his face even paler as he saw the smudges of blood on Danny's blade. The thug swallowed hard like he was trying not to barf. "We get our orders on the phone. We never meet Gates in the same place. He could be anywhere."

Danny put aside his anger, fear, and frustration over Caroline's disappearance to take careful assessment of their reactions.

Through the stink of sweat, fear, and blood, he could smell the truth. He could cut their dicks off one by one, but that wouldn't give him the answers he needed.

"Got the call, they told us to pick up the girl at the hotel to take her to the shoot," the head goon said, now apparently in a talkative mood. "But Gates wasn't there. He never is."

"What hotel?" Danny pressed, scrambling for something, anything that might lead him to Caroline.

"The Motel Six off exit eight. It's just an exchange point. I don't know where they bring the girls from and I don't ask. Usually we just make sure nothing fucks up the shoot and get the girl back to the hotel. But today the creeper didn't show up, he just called to say you was sniffing around and we had to take you out. You ask me, he's the one who has your woman."

"The creeper?" Tiny hairs stood up on the back of his neck.

"Creepy dude who likes to watch the shoots," Curtis said. "He told me he was a producer, but he just gets off on watching."

"Who is this guy?"

"He said I could call him John Smith," Curtis said.

A fake name if Danny had ever heard one.

He reached for the goon's pants, which were still down around his thighs, ignoring the yells as he rooted around in the pockets. He quickly scrolled through the calls received list. Maybe he'd get a break and at least get a cell phone number to connect to John "Creeper" Smith.

Unknown Caller
Unknown Caller

Over and over again until the list of stored calls ran out. The list of outgoing calls had been cleared, and no names were stored in the address book. Same with the other two phones.

"How the fuck am I going to find her?" he asked the room at large.

He didn't expect a small, wavering female voice to answer. "I think I know how to find Gates."

"Why are you doing this, Patrick?" She still couldn't quite believe what was happening, that she wouldn't wake up and realize it was a very bizarre, very bad dream.

But the hard look in his eyes was real all right, as was the hard metal gun in his hand, currently pointing straight at her.

Marshall stood a little behind him, dressed more casually than Caroline had ever seen him in a fleece pullover and jeans. Still, the jeans sported a knife like crease and the pullover boasted an expensive designer label.

And what the hell was wrong with her that she was noticing details like that when Patrick was pointing a gun at her face?

"Why don't you tell me, Caroline? Why don't you tell me everything you know. Why you and Taggart were nosing around the Harmony House, and how you ended up on the set of Gates's latest production?"

"Why does it matter what I know if you're going to kill me anyway?"

She didn't think Patrick's stare could get any colder, but the reptilian smirk that pulled at his mouth sent a chill straight to her soul. "I can also keep you alive, wishing you were dead, for as long as I need to."

Caroline swallowed back a surge of bile. She could see in his eyes he wasn't bluffing. This man, a man she'd considered a friend for the last decade, was fully willing to torture her to death if necessary.

"Now, I need to know how much damage you've done," Patrick said, and for the first time a flash of emotion flickered in his eyes. "If you've ruined everything or if I can still salvage something."

"I've ruined everything?" Caroline scoffed. On some level she acknowledged how stupid it was to argue with someone holding a gun to her head, but the certainty that he was going to kill her regardless made her bold. "You ruined it yourself. You and James. Forcing girls like Emily Parrish to give up their babies for adoption—"

"Those poor girls were very well compensated, and the kids ended up a hell of a lot better off than if those teenage sluts had kept them. We did a great thing for everyone—"

"Like Emily Parrish? And Anne Taggart? What great thing ended up with them both dead and buried for the past eighteen years?"

"Anne never should have been harmed, but she couldn't let it go. Just like you," he sneered. "It was her own damn fault for following James up there. We couldn't let her leave after she saw where we were keeping Emily."

"So you and James killed her?"

"We did what we needed to do." Why had she never seen the icy core that lay at his soul?

"And Emily?" Her voice thickened as she imagined the pregnant girl at the mercy of this man. This monster she'd never realized was lurking behind his genial facade.

"If Emily had been smarter, things would have gone differently. But instead she stupidly listened to Anne Taggart, and let her talk her into backing out of the deal. If she'd listened to us she would have walked away with a lot of money, enough to start a new life and have as many babies as she wanted. But we couldn't risk her telling anyone the truth. We did what we had to do to protect everyone involved."

Caroline swallowed back another surge of bile.

"Now tell me what else you found," Patrick said, once

again leveling the gun at her. "How much more do you know?"

She raised her chin. "Why does it matter? The police already know about Anne and Emily. And the Taggarts will make damn sure the truth comes out."

Patrick's smile was a vicious baring of teeth. "And right now the only one they can pin it on is James. Unless you found James's so called insurance policy that tells a different story."

Sweat beaded on his forehead and she could see the gun start to waver. He was scared. He had no idea what they knew or how many people knew it. For all he knew, her death was all the insurance he needed.

She thought of Danny, Toni, Ethan, and Derek. All the people who might be endangered if she told Patrick the truth.

She'd told herself she was done taking care of everyone else when she'd married James. *I guess my martyr streak runs deeper than I thought.*

"The only thing I ever found was Anne Taggart's personal calendar," she said, figuring she'd be more convincing telling a partial truth than an outright lie. "That's what led us to the shelter and to Emily. But there was never any mention of you." Not in the calendar anyway. She still had no idea what was on the flash drive they'd found. "The calendar is at my house, in James's desk," she lied. "You can get it yourself, and you'll be in the clear."

The blow to her cheek was stunning as much for its force as its unexpectedness. Pain exploded across her cheekbone as he hit her with his wide open palm.

"Don't you lie to me, you little cunt."

She heard him through the ringing in her head. She looked over at Marshall, who stood in the corner, eyes averted, as though if he didn't look at her he could pretend it wasn't happening.

"I know you found something!" Patrick roared. He grabbed her hair in his fist and pulled her to her knees. "How else did you find out we were filming! That sure as hell wasn't in Anne Taggart's day planner."

Shit. She'd forgotten that little detail. "Danny won't let up, you know. Killing me will have him on your ass so hard you won't know what hit you. He—"

"He's dead," Marshall bit out. "The guys at the house took care of it."

Caroline hung her head as pain exploded in her chest. She'd known it was likely. He was outnumbered. But she'd hoped . . .

She squeezed her eyes shut and remembered the feel of his shaking arms wrapping around you. *Carrie, I need you. I never got over you.*

All that week she'd been trying to protect herself from him, to not let him back into her heart. Now her heart burst into a million pieces as she faced the reality that he was gone, and even if she got out alive, they'd never have a second chance to get things right.

"I'm not telling you shit. Go ahead and kill me like you killed Anne and Emily. Like you killed James. You've wanted me dead all along. Now finish it."

"It's not that easy anymore," Patrick said, calmer now. "Marshall, go get them."

A prick of fear permeated her haze of grief. Who, exactly, was "them."

"Patrick, I don't see what good this is going to do," Marshall said, his voice low but not so low she couldn't hear. "We should just do it and—"

"You don't get it, do you? I need to know how much damage has been done, how far he went—"

"Just assume we're fucked, okay?" Marshall bit out. "Gates will help us go underground—"

"You think I'll just give up my wife, my family, if it's not totally necessary? There are bigger things at stake here."

A panicked note reverberated in Patrick's voice. He was a man at the edge, trying desperately to climb out of the hole he'd dug for himself, trying to convince himself his life could go back to normal. "Now go get them."

"No."

Patrick's mouth fell open at Marshall's refusal. "You don't tell me no, you little shit." Without warning he lifted his gun and fired. Marshall didn't have time to move even a finger to his own gun before Patrick's bullet caught him in the middle of the forehead.

Caroline's cry of horror choked in her throat. She couldn't make herself turn away from the gruesome sight of Marshall, dead, his blue eyes wide with shock as a thick crimson puddle formed under his head.

She barely heard Patrick mutter about doing something himself as he took Marshall's gun from his waistband and left the stall. Left her alone with Marshall's dead body.

He'd killed Danny. Maybe not with his own hand, but he might as well have. It tore at her guts to think of a fierce warrior like Danny being taken out by a slick weasel like Marshall. She was glad Marshall was dead. Would have been happier if it had been by her own hand.

Caroline squeezed herself into the corner, as far away as possible from the corpse. She had to think. There had to be some way out. She pulled at the bonds of the plastic ties, wincing as they cut into her wrists.

Before, she'd cavalierly thought about martyring herself. Now she saw the face of death in Marshall. Imagined it in Danny. Anne Taggart. Emily Parrish. Rachael Weller.

She wasn't going to let that be her fate, too.

Caroline's gaze darted around the stall, looking for anything she could use to cut the ties. Dust and hay were all she saw.

She looked at Marshall, his sightless stare aimed at the ceiling. Maybe he had a knife, or even a key. Swallowing back her revulsion, she scooted back over to him. Her bound hands ran clumsily over his pockets and found a lump in the right one. She managed to get two almost numb fingers in and felt the edge of a key.

The barn door was squealing, signaling Patrick's return. Caroline's fumbling grew more desperate.

"Patrick, what's going on?"

Every muscle froze at the sound of the panicked, feminine voice.

Please no.

A child started to cry.

"Shh, Michael, it's okay."

Caroline sobbed as she tried to extract the keys from Marshall's pocket.

The stall door slid open, and a rough hand grabbed her by the hair to pull her away from Marshall's body. Patrick was back. And with him were Kate and Michael.

Kate's face went white when she saw Marshall. She tried, too late, to keep Michael from seeing. His blue eyes went saucer wide and filled with tears.

"Now Caroline," Patrick said, raising the gun so it pointed at the back of Michael's head. "Let's start this conversation over, and this time try being a little more cooperative."

CHAPTER 19

"Are you sure it was this way?" Danny tried to keep the
frustration out of his voice as he pulled onto the state
route headed north. The last thing this poor girl needed was
him biting her head off when she was his only hope of finding Caroline. He was an asshole for taking her with him instead of leaving her to be taken with the others by the
police. It had quickly become apparent that she wasn't able
to tell him how to get to Gates, but she insisted that if she
rode with him she would recognize landmarks.

He forced himself to travel at a few miles under the speed
limit so Kaylee could focus on every detail and keep an eye
out for anything familiar. Danny had little hope she'd remembered much of the trip in her drugged out haze, but,
sixteen-year-old Kaylee was the only hope he had. Toni still
hadn't managed to pull any information off the flash drive
and so far Derek could only trace the bank accounts back to
James. Ethan, Alex Novascelic, and Ben Moreno were on
their way to meet up with Danny to offer backup and get
Kaylee to safety once they'd determined Caroline's location.

"Yes," she insisted. "I remember this road when Ericka
first brought me out here." He'd taken her back to the
motel where the thugs had picked her up, as good a starting
point as any. In the fifteen or so minutes it had taken to get

to the motel Kaylee had told him a story that made his stomach churn and his blood run cold.

A story he might not have believed had he not discovered the truth about what had happened to his mother and why. James Medford and whoever he'd been working with had taken their operation to a new level of sinister sophistication.

A fucking baby factory. Danny had seen terrible things in some of the darkest corners of the planet, including girls younger than Kaylee kidnapped and forced into prostitution. But he'd never heard of girls, some illegal immigrants who came to the states on promises of good jobs and new opportunities, some runaways like Kaylee, being forcibly impregnated so wealthy infertile couples could adopt a custom ordered baby.

"Do the parents know?" Danny asked, struggling to imagine how any adoptive couple, no matter how desperate, could knowingly take part in such an exchange.

"I don't know," Kaylee said. "I only figured out what they were doing after my exam. Today was supposed to be—"

Danny didn't need her to finish. "And they make money off of the . . ." he didn't know what to call it, "by filming it and selling it as porn."

Kaylee gave a shudder next to him, her coltish frame swallowed up by the oversize T-shirt and sweatpants he'd dug out of his gym bag. She sniffed and wrapped her arms tightly around herself. "They make some of the girls do it a bunch of times with a bunch of different guys. One of the girls told me it's better once you get pregnant, because you don't have to have sex with anyone and they take good care of you until the baby comes."

"You don't have to worry about any of that now," Danny strove for a reassuring tone, even though his helpless frustration mounted with every slowly passing mile.

Caroline.

Her name was like a drumbeat in his head, driving him forward. He couldn't lose her again. He thought of his father, and finally understood his unceasing need to believe that his wife was alive, to cling to that last shred of hope that it wasn't all over.

Caroline.

He struggled to contain his helpless rage. If he wanted to find her, he needed direction, and the only help he was getting was from the remarkably brave but slightly foggy-headed girl next to him.

"A couple more guys are going to be here soon, and as soon as we find Gates's place, we'll get you away from there where you'll be safe."

Kaylee nodded silently and stared intently out the window.

"Anything?"

"Not yet. I have a feeling we were on this road for a while."

A familiar silver BMW appeared in Danny's rearview mirror, tailed closely by a red Mustang. His cell phone rang a second later.

"I take it since you're traveling at grandma speed she hasn't zeroed in on the location yet," Ethan said.

"Not yet. What did Toni find?"

"In a ten mile radius there are about thirty properties that could be described as 'big old houses with what kinda looks like a barn,'" Ethan said, using Kaylee's description of what Gates's compound looked like from the outside. "But nothing registered to anyone named Gates or to Esteban Lucero. Not that we expected it to be that easy."

In the meantime all Danny could do was travel slowly up State Route 12, followed closely by his brother and colleagues and hope something jogged Kaylee's memory pretty damn quick.

* * *

"You have to let them go," Caroline said. "Kate doesn't know anything about what James was involved in, and Michael," her sob caught in her throat as she looked at his sweet, terrified face as he pressed himself against his mother's side.

"Tell me what I want to know and they won't suffer," Patrick said.

Kate let out a whimper as if she, too, absorbed his words.

"We found a floor safe," Caroline said, all bets off as the words came spilling out. She was out of ideas, but maybe if she talked and stalled something would come to her. "There was a DVD. That's how we found the movie shoot. I recognized the woman in the movie from when she was at our house."

"What movie? What woman?" Kate asked, bewildered. "Someone tell me what's going on here."

"Goddamn her," Patrick said. "That bitch was the beginning of the end."

"Who was she?" Caroline asked.

Patrick shrugged. "Some Russian slut. Who cares? She escaped a couple days after she gave birth, and somehow she got hold of one of James's business cards. The baby had already been transferred—"

"Don't you mean sold to the highest bidder?" Caroline snapped.

"Transferred to her new family," Patrick continued as though she hadn't spoken. "James was an idiot. I told him to be more careful about bringing anything with him that gave any clue to his identity, but he never listened."

"Selling babies?" Kate whispered. "Are you saying my dad—"

"Shut up, Kate," Patrick snapped, pushing the barrel of the gun harder against Michael's head for emphasis. "Your dad did what he had to do to keep you and your stepmother in high style. Just like I did what I had to do to provide for my family. Now tell me what else you found in that safe, Caroline!"

"What happened to the girl?" Caroline countered.

"I expect the same thing that's going to happen to you. Killed, her body stripped of any identifying marks before being suitably disposed of. Now what was in the safe?"

He was crazy. She could see it in his wild blue eyes. "The only things we found were a flash drive and some printouts that looked like bank statements, but there were no names on the accounts, just numbers."

"And what's on the flash drive?"

"We don't know yet."

Kate yelped in pain as Patrick brought the butt of the gun down on her head.

"I swear!" Caroline yelled. "It had something on it, a virus or something, like a booby trap. And all the data is encrypted."

"You're lying. What was on it?"

"We couldn't get any information off it before I left. I have no idea what's on there."

"You swear. You swear on his life," he yanked Michael away from Kate and pressed the gun to the little boy's temple. "There was no information on there about me, or my family? Anything about Jennifer?"

"I don't know if there is or not," she said, pleading. Through the fear and rush of adrenaline that stole the warmth from her veins, she finally saw the truth. "Jennifer isn't yours."

Patrick's mouth tightened. "She's as much mine and Melody's as any child. She looks enough like Melody that no one ever questioned it. I made sure of that."

He was right. Melody's blond hair and small, fine features were so similar to her daughter's it had never occurred to Caroline that Jennifer wasn't their biological child.

Then another blonde with pretty, delicate features flashed in her head. "You took Emily Parrish's baby. That's why you wouldn't let her back out of the deal."

"It was all Melody wanted." Pain flashed across Patrick's face and for a moment, Caroline caught a glimpse of the man she'd thought was her friend. "I would have done anything to make her happy." His mouth tightened and his eyes narrowed. "Who has the flash drive, Caroline?" Patrick pressed.

Caroline swallowed hard. If she told him, she was likely putting Toni Crawford in danger. Caroline knew Patrick wasn't working alone, and some of his colleagues were ruthless killers. But if she didn't tell Patrick, she was going to put Kate and Michael through more pain. At least Toni had all those big strapping ex-military types to watch her back. "It's at the Gemini Securities office. They're working on it right now."

Patrick's face relaxed a little and he released a sobbing Michael. He came to stand over Caroline, his legs spread in a sickeningly triumphant stance. "We better hope I get my hands on it before they crack the code. But thanks to your cooperation, I'll keep my promise and make it quick for them."

She could barely hear Kate and Michael's sobs through the roar in her head. She had to do something. Caroline leaned back on her elbows, and using every bit of core strength she'd built up in endless hours with her personal trainer, she brought her bound, booted feet up squarely between Patrick's legs.

He emitted a choked groan and fell to his knees.

"Run, Kate! Get out of here!" she yelled, rolling to the side as Patrick squeezed off a wild shot. "Go!"

Kate staggered to her feet and grabbed Mikey's bound hands in her own as she slipped through the stall door Patrick had left partially open.

Caroline squeezed her eyes shut and said a little prayer. *Please please please let them get away.* She opened her eyes to the sight of Patrick's gun, trained straight at her face.

"What the fuck do you think you're doing, Easterbrook?"

Patrick's eyes widened with what looked like fear at the clipped, accented voice. Caroline dragged her gaze away from the gun and saw a tall, lean man with caramel colored skin and the coldest yellow eyes she'd ever seen. He held Kate by one arm, Michael by another and was flanked by two goons that closely resembled the three she'd seen earlier on the porn set.

"I think we're getting close," Kaylee said as she peered out at the rain soaked hills that lined the road. "I definitely remember that rocky field."

The fenced off pasture on the east side of the road was dotted with gray boulders that stood out against the deep green grass like giant moon rocks.

"You got that?" Danny asked Ethan, Alex and Ben who were still on the line. They all answered in the affirmative."

"Let me check in with Toni, see if she can come up with something," Ethan said and clicked over. A few seconds later he clicked back on the line. "Danny I've got Toni on with me."

"Where do we need to go, Toni?"

"I don't have the house," she said, excitement evident in her voice, "but I managed to get into the documents on the flash drive. James Medford was working with Patrick Easterbrook. He was the doctor who delivers all the babies and falsifies their birth certificates."

Son of a bitch. And they'd gone straight to Easterbrook's house and tipped their hand. "Kaylee, what did the doctor who examined you look like?"

Kaylee's eyes were wide and haunted. "Old, with a lot of

gray hair. Blue eyes. And big. Not fat, but like a big guy who maybe used to play football. I saw him a couple times before that too, when he was there doing deliveries."

"There's some stuff in here too about someone named Marshall who worked at James's law firm, along with a list of names, birthdates, hair and eye color of the birth mothers." Toni's voice grew more serious. "There are a lot of names on this list, Danny, going back a lot of years."

An ugly legacy Patrick Easterbrook was willing to kill to keep quiet.

"Any mention of anyone named Gates?" Danny asked.

"Hold on," he heard her click. "I haven't had a chance to go through all the documentation." There were a few seconds of silence and then a soft, horrified, "Oh, God. He's described as the 'supplier.' James wrote that Gates set up a facility to keep 'selected gestational carriers'. He describes the procedure—"

"Yeah, I have a good idea what's going on," Danny said as he swallowed back bile. "Where's the facility?"

"It doesn't say. James wasn't allowed to go on site. Patrick met James or Marshall at another location to hand off the baby. . . .

"There's one other thing, Danny," Toni said. "According to James's notes, not all of the babies were adopted by outside families. At least one stayed in the inner circle. Eighteen years ago Patrick Easterbrook and his wife kept a baby girl for themselves."

Dread curled in his gut as the answer hit him full force. But just to be sure, he asked. "Does it list a birth date?"

"Just a month and a year. June 1991." If money wasn't enough to motivate Patrick to kill, protecting the circumstances of his daughter's birth certainly was.

Patrick Easterbrook and James Medford had taken Emily Parrish's baby and killed Anne Taggart to keep their secret.

Rage burned in Danny's veins. At the years he'd lost hating his mother, thinking she'd left him. Letting that lie fuck up his entire world and costing him the only woman he'd ever loved.

Rage for the pain he, his brothers, and especially his father had endured in their exhausting, fruitless searches.

Every sinew screamed for revenge. James was dead. It was too late to do anything about him. But Patrick was about to learn the hard way that you don't fuck with the Taggarts or their women.

"We have to find Patrick Easterbrook, now."

"On it," Toni said and clicked off.

Danny switched lines and called Melody Easterbrook. "Where's your husband?" he said, barely giving her a chance to say hello.

"Who is this?"

"It's Danny Taggart. We spoke the other night. I need to know where your husband is."

"He's out of town on business," she said testily, "and I don't think I appreciate your tone."

"And I don't appreciate that he killed James Medford and tried to pin it on Caroline, so we're even."

Shocked silence echoed over the line. "I have no idea what you're talking about."

"Come on, Melody, the game's up. I know who your daughter's real mother is."

"Sh-she was a single mother who wanted to give her baby up for adoption," she protested, voice cracking.

"Her name was Emily Parrish and your husband and James Medford kidnapped her and killed my mother to keep it a secret. Then once the baby was born, they killed Emily, too."

"No, no. James helped us with the adoption, but Patrick would never have been involved in anything like that."

He could hear the doubt creeping into her voice. "Then why keep Jennifer's adoption a secret, if you and Patrick don't have anything to hide?"

Melody's voice broke on a sob. "I didn't want anyone to know that I was . . . deficient in that way. When James said he knew a girl who wanted to give her baby up for adoption who looked exactly like me, we immediately said yes and promised to keep it a secret. But it was all James, it had to be," she protested. "Patrick would never—"

"I need to know where he is," Danny said firmly, trying to keep Melody from disintegrating into full-blown hysteria.

"Fine, talk to him yourself. But I'll have to call his office to find out exactly where he's giving his seminar today."

Danny bit back a curse. He had no time to wait to retrieve what was no doubt bogus information. Maybe they could use his cell phone to track him, or—"Does his car have a built-in navigation system?"

"Yes," Melody said, confused.

He already knew Patrick drove a BMW 5 Series. "What's the license number?" Melody quickly told him.

"Thanks. That's all I need to know—" he was about to hang up when she interrupted him.

"Wait. You're not going to tell anyone about Jennifer, are you? She has no idea, and if what you say is true . . ."

Danny grimaced. He believed in his gut that Melody didn't know the truth about where her miracle baby had come from and knew this was going to be painful for her and her daughter. But he couldn't protect them anymore. "I think you need to get yourself a good attorney and prepare yourself for a long, hard discussion with your daughter."

He quickly dialed Toni and relayed the information. He pulled over and stopped his slow cruise up the Highway. Ethan, Alex, and Ben quickly followed suit. Once Toni hacked into the network, they'd be able to pinpoint Patrick's location. He prayed Caroline was with him, and still alive by the time they got there.

Caroline inchwormed her way to where Kate and Michael sat huddled in the corner. All three watched tensely as the man Patrick called Gates laid into Patrick. "Why am I getting calls that the shoot is going bad? And what the fuck happened to him?" Gates said, toeing Marshall's body as though it were a sack of meat. "Although I suppose I should thank you for saving me the trouble. I swear to God, the three of you have caused me nothing but trouble this past year. First James thinks he can blackmail me into letting him out, then we have her," Caroline flinched as his cold yellow gaze landed on her huddled form, "with more fucking lives than a cat. What is she doing here, anyway? What are they doing here?" he asked, indicating a trembling Kate and a sobbing Michael.

"I needed to know how much she knows. If James was telling the truth."

"I think it's safe to assume if she and Taggart found their way to the set, they know too much." He nodded to one of his goons. His gaze pulled back to Caroline. "I'm going to do something I haven't done for a long time and kill you myself. I should have done you myself a long time ago and saved all of us a bunch of trouble. Now get those two," he said, indicating Kate and Michael, "inside, and get them ready to transport with the others."

Toni had quickly homed in on Patrick's location, only five miles from where Kaylee had led them. As they approached, Kaylee's already pale face had gone chalk white. "That's it. Right down that drive." She pointed to a narrow dirt driveway marked only by a mailbox, destroyed a long time ago.

Brush grew thick on either side, making it difficult to see from the road and discouraging anyone who might be inclined to investigate.

They pulled their cars off the road about a quarter mile past the drive and got out. "Ethan's going to take you to the police station, and you tell them everything you told me," Danny said.

Kaylee nodded, wide eyed as she watched Danny, Alex, and Moreno load up with their arsenal. In addition to the knife strapped to his right calf and his Glock tucked into his shoulder holster, Danny also carried a Taser, and a derringer in an ankle holster. Alex and Moreno were similarly armed, their muscular bodies bristling with weapons.

Danny squatted down next to his car. Taking direction from what Kaylee remembered, he drew a diagram of the huge house and surrounding grounds and went over the plan one last time. "We need to go in as quick and quiet as possible," Danny said, though he didn't need to remind Alex or Moreno of anything. The big Latino and even bigger half Croat were two of the best soldiers he'd ever worked with. They'd performed similar extractions in a lot scarier places. Despite their size, they could move as swiftly and silently as death as they snuck up on the guards and took them out.

"And I'll come in leading the cavalry," Ethan said, just the faintest whiff of derision in his voice. But if he didn't like the idea of having to wait to come in with the police, he knew better than to say it. This was Danny's op, and he needed Ethan to go with Kaylee, not only to make sure the local police knew exactly what they were up against, but also to give Danny, Alex and Moreno enough time to get Caroline and the other girls out safely. Danny had a bad feeling that if the cops came blazing in, sirens blaring and lights flashing, it could turn into an ugly hostage situation in the blink of an eye.

He would get them out safely, Caroline included. He wouldn't acknowledge the possibility that Caroline could already be dead.

Danny heard the rumble of Ethan's engine fade in the distance as he and the other two men took off at a fast clip down the side of the road. Fortunately traffic was nonexistent, and they made it to the driveway before anyone could see them and wonder what the hell three heavily armed men were doing running down a rural highway in the central valley. When they turned down the driveway their pace slowed and they went on high alert, listening for any cars or other signs anyone was approaching.

They made it down the drive without incident and ducked into the brush, out of sight. Sure enough, Patrick Easterbrook's car was parked in the muddy drive in front of the rundown house. A sleek, black Jaguar was parked in front of it, and a black Mercedes SUV had pulled up behind.

A lone guard stood at the front door, a gun in his slack grip as he leaned against the wall looking half asleep.

Danny did a quick scan of the front of the house and saw no signs of security cameras or other surveillance. He nodded at Alex, who started thrashing around the bushes with enough force it sounded like a bear was trapped.

On cue, the guard straightened, yawned, and peered across the drive to the thick brush that flanked the drive. Alex let out a low, weird sound that could have been human or animal. Danny could feel the guard's curiosity pique. Shifting his grip on his pistol, the guy walked slowly to where they were hidden. Using his gun hand, he parted some branches for a closer look. Danny came around from behind and Tasered him right as he caught sight of Alex and Moreno. Danny quickly bound him with plastic flex ties, gagged him, dragged him into the bushes, and tucked the guard's gun into his own waistband.

They skirted around the house and took out two more

men guarding the back door. It would have been a hell of a lot easier shooting them than it was waiting to get close enough to take them out with Tasers, but he and his brothers had left enough dead bodies in their wake in the past several months. Danny didn't want to add to the pile.

But Danny didn't plan to be so merciful with everyone. When Danny found him, Patrick Easterbrook would meet the barrel of Danny's gun, or better yet the blade of his knife so Danny could experience Patrick's fear the moment before he died. He'd never felt like this, this blood lust, but he wanted Patrick to experience what his mother had felt the moment before Patrick killed her. Wanted him to understand the crippling fear that had been Caroline's constant companion.

Danny wanted him to pay with his life.

Focus on the mission. Do not let emotion take over, he warned himself. He couldn't give in to his rage, not yet. When that happened he got reckless and sloppy, and he had to keep his head in the game if he wanted to get Caroline out safely. She was the number one priority. Not his revenge, not even those poor girls trapped in that house.

They entered through the back door and moved silently down a dark hallway. Closed doors lined the hallway. Danny nodded and Moreno tried the first one. The door swung open to reveal a hospital bed along with some kind of electronic monitor. Danny moved in to take a closer look. A cabinet across from the bed held shelves full of glass vials, IV bags, gauze, and other medical supplies. On a corner table rested a tray of surgical instruments.

Birthing room. His skin prickled as he imagined the kind of pain and fear that permeated the walls. He suppressed a shudder and silently backed out. They continued down the hall, past what looked like an empty office, then a TV room. Low voices could be heard, and as they rounded the corner Danny saw two women working in a large kitchen. He nodded for Alex and Moreno to continue through the front entryway and up the stairs.

"Excuse me, ladies," Danny said, his tone conversational, the Glock he leveled at them all business, "can you tell me where I can find Patrick Easterbrook and somebody named Gates?"

The women looked up, freezing in horror as they caught sight of the gun. They both shot their hands up in the air, chattering shrilly in Spanish all the while. Danny repeated his question in Spanish.

They shook their heads, feigning ignorance. "I don't know anyone by those names," the first said. "We just help take care of the girls. Nothing else."

The second one nodded, but Danny saw her dark eyes flicker to a point just past his shoulder. Though his gaze didn't waver, he shifted his focus to the space behind him. Someone was coming up, doing his best to be silent, but the floorboards of the old house weren't entirely cooperative. He felt the air shift behind him as an arm raised and—

Danny turned, caught the guy's gun hand in his grip and broke his forearm with a sharp jab of his elbow. The guy screamed in agony, bringing two more people hurrying down the hall. More women, Mexican or Central American by the looks of them, all dressed in scrubs. They took one look at Danny and the fallen guard and went in reverse so fast they tripped over their own feet.

"Stop," Danny yelled in Spanish, and fired a shot out the kitchen window. Everyone froze. He heard scuffles and muffled screams coming from upstairs, but didn't take his focus off the injured guard. "How many more guards?"

"Three," the man groaned. "Upstairs with the girls." The thuds and yells coming from upstairs convinced Danny that Alex and Moreno were taking care of it.

"Where's Patrick Easterbrook? Where's Gates?" he said, feeling like a broken record.

Moreno came thudding down the stairs, a sheen of sweat on his face. "We took out three more guards, and found seventeen girls upstairs. No sign of Caroline."

CHAPTER 20

Caroline let out a choked cry as one of the goons came toward them and hauled Kate to her feet and grabbed Michael by the back of his hooded sweatshirt.

"No!" Caroline screamed, struggling against her bindings so fiercely she felt blood trickle over her wrist. "They haven't done anything! You have to let them go."

"Let them go? Are you kidding, that's the only thing this idiot has done right today." Gates turned his attention to Patrick. "Really. The girl's perfect, her looks and her coloring. And the kid," his smile was pure evil. "You'd be amazed what some sick fucks will pay to get their hands on a kid that age."

That was it. The bile surged in Caroline's throat and the meager contents of her stomach spilled on the dirt floor. The acidic odor mingled with the sickly sweet metallic odor of blood.

Gates didn't seem to notice.

"It's too bad you're not a little younger," he said, his reptilian gaze sending a shudder through her as it raked her body. "You're very beautiful, but a little on the old side to be truly useful."

One of the thugs gave her a lecherous look and murmured in Spanish, "She may be old for babies but she's still good enough to fuck."

Gates responded in Spanish as well. "Good point. No need to waste good pussy before we take her out."

She heaved again, this time nothing but bile, but didn't let on that she understood. "So what, you're going to kill me now?"

"No," Patrick protested. "I have to know what she knows, and who she told—"

"Too late, Easterbrook. Time to cut ties, pull up stakes and lay low for a while."

"But I can't leave Melody," Patrick protested. "I can't just let my wife think I left her."

"Don't worry. She won't think you left her. Not on purpose anyway." He and the thug exchanged nods.

This time Caroline knew what to expect. She squeezed her eyes shut just in time to miss the top of Patrick's skull exploding.

Danny froze at the sound of gunshots coming from the woods outside the house. Without a word he started sprinting for the door.

"Danny," Moreno yelled. "Don't go by yourself. Wait for us to secure things here."

Moreno's words met a brick wall as all logic and calm faded away. He couldn't wait. Caroline was out there somewhere, he could feel it, and every second he waited brought her one second closer to death. "You stay with the girls," he ordered. He burst through the front door of the house and sprinted across the drive, kicking up mud and gravel with his churning steps.

A trio emerged from the brush. Danny skidded to a stop and raised his gun to fire. "Freeze."

His own blood froze when he saw Kate Medford and her

little boy, Michael, being marched at gunpoint to the house. The goon grabbed up Michael and held him up as a shield, the barrel of his gun to the poor little guy's head.

"Drop it or I'll shoot the kid."

Danny drowned out Kate's screams as he dropped his gun to his side, slackened his muscles as though he was about to obey. The thug eased his hold slightly, letting Michael drop a couple of inches, easing the barrel from the boy's skull.

Enough for Danny to get a shot.

A single shot through the forehead. The thug dropped like a bag of rocks.

Kate looped her bound hands over the boy and pulled his small, shaking body to her.

Shit. There had to be a better way he could have done that. Now the poor kid was probably in shock and would be seriously scarred for the rest of his life. "I'm sorry," he said as he knelt next to Kate and cut first her ties, then Michael's. "He shouldn't have had to—"

"You have to get her," Kate interrupted, yanking Michael to his feet and casting a terror filled gaze behind her.

"Caroline? He has her?" Every cell went on high alert.

Kate nodded. "Patrick has her, and that other guy. They're going to kill her." Horror dawned across her face. "The gun. They might have—"

"Don't." He said it as much to himself as to her as he rolled to his feet. "Don't think it. Not until we know for sure."

Warm sticky droplets hit Caroline's face and she heard someone screaming, then harsh, male laughter. Her legs were jerked by rough hands and she felt the ties around her ankle tighten, then fall away.

She kicked and thrashed as hard as she could but couldn't

escape two pairs of rough male hands that pinned down her hips. Cold air hit her legs as her boots, pants and underwear were dragged from her body.

"Feisty little *puta*," one of them muttered in Spanish as he tugged at his fly. "She'll settle down once she gets the feel of my *verga* inside her."

"I doubt I'll even be able to feel it," she growled in Spanish and spat in his face. He drew back, momentarily stunned. Caroline seized the opportunity and slammed a bare knee into his groin. He howled and clutched at his crotch.

She struggled to her knees but was hit from behind by a sharp blow from the butt of Gates's gun. Her ears rang and her vision swam, but still she fought to get away.

Her breath left her in a rush as she was slammed onto her back. Rough hands shoved her thighs apart and a heavy weight settled between. She stared at a hole in the roof, gritting her teeth as she tried to pull herself out of her body, out of her mind, away from what was about to happen to her.

She heard a sharp popping sound and for a moment thought it was her own break with reality. The fumbling and probing between her legs stopped and she realized the pop was a gunshot outside.

Oh God, please don't let it be Kate or Michael.

The weight lifted and Gates dragged her by her hair to stand in front of him. The cold muzzle of his gun pressed against her cheekbone. He shoved her through the stall out into the barn, careful to keep Caroline in front of him. Old furniture and empty boxes were scattered across the floor. Several mattresses were piled haphazardly in the corner, the top one stained with rusty looking streaks.

Caroline didn't let herself contemplate where the bloodstains had come from.

Cold dirt and hay bit into her bare feet, and she tried not to dwell on the fact that she was half naked. She was still alive, and they hadn't raped her. She could endure a little nudity.

Gates ordered his henchman to take a look outside. The man obeyed, moving cautiously to the door. He slid it open a crack, letting in a streak of feeble gray winter light. Caroline watched, heart thudding against her ribcage as the man lifted his gun and craned around for a look. He shook his head, indicating he'd seen nothing. He took a tentative step outside, until only half of his body was visible. Caroline heard his footsteps crunching through dead leaves and gravel as Gates pushed her closer to the door.

Suddenly with a grunt the thug reappeared in the doorway. He opened his mouth to speak, but nothing came out but a choking sound. Caroline let out a horrified cry as a thick bubble of blood burst over the man's lips, soaking his chin like a macabre beard. As he fell to his knees, the man's eyes widened in horrified knowledge of his own death.

Gates cursed and dragged her back toward the stall. "Who's out there?"

"We took out your guards and the cops are on their way, Gates."

"Danny!" She couldn't keep herself from crying out in elated relief. "I'm back here."

Her exclamation earned her a punch to the head that made her ears ring.

"You two need to let her go," Danny said in his cold, hard, commander's voice.

Something bugged her, through her ringing, aching head. *Two*. He didn't know about Patrick.

"Patrick's dead," she yelled. "It's just Ga—" her call broke off in a shriek of pain as Gates dug his fingers into her breast and twisted hard.

"You hear that, Taggart?" Gates yelled. "You show yourself and drop your weapons or there'll be more than that before I finally kill her."

Danny hadn't even thought before he'd killed the other thug, he was so filled with the need to get to Caroline. He was nothing, a human obstacle standing between Danny and the woman he loved and the revenge he craved.

It was only when he heard Caroline call out to him that he could pull himself back. Relief flooded him, so strong it nearly sent him to his knees. She was alive. The shot he'd heard hadn't been for her.

But he was going to get her killed if he charged in like this. With Alex, Ben, and the police on their way, Gates was screwed, but he still had Caroline. Back up against the wall, he was as dangerous as any cornered animal. Danny needed to tread carefully if he wanted to get them both out of there alive.

Acid ate at his guts when she told him Patrick was already dead. Logically he knew it was better for them. Easier to take out one armed man than two. But his soul burned with the need for revenge, and the thought that it was beyond his reach left a bitter taste in his mouth.

None of that matters. Caroline is all that matters. She was still alive, and Danny was ready to face down the devil himself to make sure she stayed that way.

Danny appeared in the doorway of the stall, his empty hands raised. He was stripped down to a T-shirt, no weapons in sight. "Hear the sirens? They're on their way, Gates. We got Kaylee to the police, my guys have already released the girls at the main house. You might as well let her go."

Caroline drank in the sight of him. Huge. Radiating power. Utterly calm as he took in her state of undress and the sight of a gun pressed to her head and Marshall's dead body on the floor. His quicksilver gaze took in every detail, flickering only when it caught on Patrick Easterbrook's lifeless form.

His eyes narrowed and his nostrils flared, and Caroline sensed he was restraining himself from ripping the already dead body limb from limb.

"Lift up your pant legs," Gates said.

Caroline watched as Danny pulled up the legs of his pants one at a time, showing he had no weapons hidden.

"Come on," Danny said. "You're fucked already. How about you let her go and I'll give you a running start."

She could feel Gates tense behind her, felt the faint tremble of the hand holding the gun to her head. "Or how about this, asshole? How about I kill both of you for costing me millions of dollars and the loss of my operation?"

When Danny had first seen Caroline, he'd thought his head was going to explode. Bruises marred the creamy skin of her cheeks. She was naked from the waist down and he could see dark smudges on the tender skin of her thighs. Gates pressed the gun to her cheek so hard Danny could see the tip of the barrel leave an indentaton.

He watched Gates's finger flex against the trigger.

Everything stopped. The rage in his head quieted. The adrenaline pumping through his veins eased off, and everything came into razor sharp focus. He could pick out the individual beads of sweat on Gates's upper lip, see every single eyelash surrounding Caroline's scared, dark eyes.

As though in slow motion, he watched the muscles in Gates's arm and shoulder shift. He knew how Gates was going to move before his arm went into motion.

He was going to shoot Danny first.

Danny eased up on his toes and bunched the muscles in his legs. The second the gun started to pull away from Caroline's face he made his move.

He sprang, closing the distance in a split second, barely registering the sound of gunshots firing into the air. But he sure as hell registered the impact of one of the bullets slamming into his left side. He heard Caroline shriek as his body slammed into both of them.

He blocked out the pain screaming in his side as he spun himself away from Gates's gun hand and slipped behind Gates's body. Before the other man could react, Danny hooked his arm around Gates's neck and twisted his head sharply with his opposite hand.

A sickeningly loud crunch of bones and tendons rang through the barn and Danny felt Gates fall, deadweight, from his arms.

Danny took one step toward Caroline and faltered, his legs going weak under him. He thought it was relief until he heard her gasp, "Oh, my God," sounding like she was talking under water. His body felt chilled, the only warmth coming from the sticky liquid pouring down his side.

"Don't you die on me, Danny. You can't get me through all of this and die on me now," she sobbed. Pain lanced through him as she pressed her hands hard against his side.

Somehow through the pain and fog he noticed she was still pantsless. "Go get dressed, baby," he forced the words through rubbery lips. "I don't want the cops getting a look at what's mine."

Caroline let out a half laugh, half sob as she scrambled to put on her pants. "You have to be okay. You can't leave me."

"Won't leave you." His field of vision narrowed until all he could see was her face. "Love you too much." The bright halo of light surrounding her face grew smaller and smaller until she disappeared completely.

CHAPTER 21

Four days later

Caroline sipped a glass of wine and listened silently as the Taggart men spoke in low voices about the shocking discoveries they'd made in the last week and a half. Eighteen girls were rescued from Gates's rural hideout. Five were pregnant. In addition they found the remains of four bodies buried around the grounds. It was assumed they were the remains of girls who had died in complications from childbirth.

The information they discovered on James's flash drive told a chilling tale of a veritable baby factory, one of desperate couples willing to pay any price for a healthy baby who resembled them. In exchange, the adoptive families looked the other way, didn't ask any questions about a process that had to seem not quite kosher.

"I still don't understand why Mom felt she had to keep her volunteer work a secret from us," Ethan said. He was pacing around the kitchen, and hadn't sat still since Caroline had arrived.

"She thought we wouldn't care," Derek said. He was propped against an armchair occupied by his fiancée, Alyssa. Caroline still couldn't quite absorb the idea of serious, analytical Derek being engaged to a woman who up until six months ago had been one of the world's most notorious

party girls. Odd as it was, it worked. The connection between them was so strong it was palpable. "Seriously," he
continued, "that last year, how often did we see her? How
often did we talk to her? We were all fed up with the crying
and the drinking and who knew what else. Even you," he
said pointedly to Ethan.

Ethan ran an angry hand through his hair and halted his
pacing. Caroline remembered that Ethan was closer to
Anne than the other two. Or at least he'd tried to be. But
like Derek said, even Ethan had given up trying to have a
relationship with her when it seemed like all Anne wanted
to do was hide in her bedroom with a bottle of chardonnay.

"We'll never know her reasons," Joe said matter of factly.
He still looked tired and gaunt and old beyond his years.
But unlike the last time she'd seen him, the aura of utter de-
spair had dissipated. He didn't strike her as a man at peace,
but now that he knew the entire truth about his wife's fate,
he seemed to be on his way there. "The truth is, I failed her.
What happened to her was my fault for not listening to her
and giving her what she needed."

Caroline could feel Danny's arm tense behind her where
it was stretched across the back of the loveseat. She was still
trying to absorb the reality of being there, with Danny,
pressed against his side at a family gathering. His date. His
girlfriend.

At least she thought so. They hadn't talked much about
the status of their relationship after his barely audible con-
fession of love. But he'd certainly sounded eager to see her
when he told her to come over to his dad's place for dinner
and to pack a bag so she could stay at his place for a few
days.

God knew she was eager to see him.

It was his second day home from the hospital and the
first time she'd seen him in three days. Once he got to the

hospital and through surgery to stop the bleeding and re-move his spleen, she'd left him to recover.

Kate and Michael had been staying with her after their ordeal and Caroline had taken a couple of days to clear up her own legal issues. Once the truth about James, Patrick, Marshall, and Gates came out, the police realized they didn't have a case aganst her. Hector Ramirez, the inmate who had told police Caroline had tried to hire him to kill James, admitted he'd been paid to lie. Yesterday the DA had given a press conference and announced that Caroline Medford was no longer a suspect in her husband's murder and they would not be pursuing any further charges against her.

That huge victory had been tainted by what was happen-ing to Melody. The press was all over the story of Jennifer's illegal adoption, and Caroline didn't know how mother and daughter were ever going to recover.

She'd brightened considerably at the prospect of seeing Danny. Not only did she want to reassure herself that he was well and whole—she would have nightmares of him lying on the floor of that barn in a pool of his own blood for the rest of her life—but now they were finally free.

Free of the past. Free of the dark cloud of accusations hanging over her head. Free to move forward into the fu-ture together.

But as the conversation progressed and Danny became more and more withdrawn, a sick pit formed in her stom-ach and dug in its roots. She tried to shove it aside, but she couldn't shake the grim foreboding that maybe things weren't as different as she wanted them to be.

"Look, we can yammer about this as much as we want," Danny said tightly. "But the only unforgivable thing is that I didn't get there in time to kill Patrick Easterbrook myself."

"I think we all would have liked to have been in on that," Joe said grimly.

Caroline rubbed the bunched muscles of Danny's thigh reassuringly. It was eating at him, she knew, the fact that he wasn't the one to put the bullet in Patrick's head. He threaded his fingers through hers and absently raised her hand to his lips.

"I hate unfinished business," he'd said in the hospital, a little dopey from his meds. "Like to take care of things myself."

"I've got some unfinished business you can handle," she'd said, trying to lighten the mood, and had earned a sleepy, sexy, smile that curled her toes for her efforts.

Danny pushed himself up from the couch, a slight grimace the only evidence he had any pain from his wound. Caroline immediately stood to help him but he brushed her off. Still she followed him behind the granite topped island that separated the kitchen's sitting area and breakfast nook from the stove top and double ovens. The conversation about Anne Taggart, the choices she made and whose fault it was that no one had managed to discover the truth continued as Danny turned the roast he was searing in a large saute pan.

He flipped it quickly and it slapped down into the pan, spattering hot oil everywhere. Danny jumped back to avoid the spatter, wincing as the sudden movement was too much for his wound. Caroline put out one hand to steady him and reached for the tongs with the other. "Why don't you let me do that," she said, "and you sit down and take it easy."

"Stop coddling me," he snapped. "I don't need you hovering over me right now."

Pain speared through her at his unexpected outburst. "I'm not hovering, I just wanted to help," she said, then wanted to kick herself for feeling like she was the one who needed to defend herself. Boom. It had been less than a week, and already she was back in that old pattern, trying to smooth everything over when Danny got too impatient and frustrated with the world.

That pit of dread in her stomach had a growth spurt.

"What the hell is wrong with you?" Ethan asked the question that was on the tip of her tongue.

"Nothing is wrong with me," Danny said as he poured wine in the pan and threw in handfuls of carrots and onions to surround the roast. He picked up the pan and slid it into the oven, closing the door with a metallic clang. "I just wish we could stop talking about this shit. Every family dinner is like a goddamn *Oprah* show. It's over and done with, and trying to figure out what her problem was and trying to take the blame for what happened doesn't get us anywhere. We finally know what happened to her. It's over. Now let's stop wallowing around in all this emotional bullshit and move the fuck on."

Caroline stood frozen as Danny stormed out of the kitchen. As his heavy footsteps reverberated on the hardwood floors his words echoed in her head in an endless loop. *I can't deal with your emotional bullshit. Stop talking. Move the fuck on.*

Grief washed through her, as raw and devastating as the first time she'd broken up with him. No, this was worse, because she'd let herself hope that they really had a second chance. Just as they'd tried to push an intense high school romance well past its breaking point, Caroline had let herself believe that their brief, adrenaline fueled reunion of the past couple weeks could be the beginning of something new.

But even though everything had changed, nothing had changed. He was still the same Danny Taggart, and he would never let her in, and never tolerate her moments of neediness. And she was the same Caroline Palomares, and she'd never be satisfied with being shut out and shut down.

"I'll go talk to him," Derek said and started for the door.

Caroline held up her hand. "No, Danny and I have some things to discuss."

She set her wine glass on the counter and crossed the

hallway into the living room. Through the glass sliders at the other end of the room she could see Danny out in the yard. His muscles bulged under the long sleeves of his knit shirt and his face was grim as he stared off into the distance. She took a moment to study him, to drink in every nuance of his face and features, letting the memory of him as a thirty-five-year-old man overlay those she had of him as a twenty-three-year-old.

Different, yet gut wrenchingly familiar.

His silver eyes that could go from molten hot to icy cold in a heartbeat. His sharp cheekbones and hard jaw dusted with black stubble. His big, long fingered hands that could stroke her to ecstasy as easily as they could snap a man's neck.

She loved him so much it hurt, and she knew she always would. The realization that they could never make each other happy was so painful it nearly brought her to her knees.

He looked up as she stepped through the sliding glass door and raised an impatient hand. "Caroline, I really don't feel like talking right now."

She let out a half laugh, half sob as his words sent a stab of pain straight through her heart. She mustered every bit of strength she possessed to do what needed to be done. *Do it quick, like ripping off a bandaid. Let the blood flow.* "I think I know better than to ask that of you by now," she said. "So I'll do all the talking. I can't do this again."

His dark brows pulled together sharply. "Do what?"

"This. Us."

"What are you talking about?" His voice was sharp with irritation.

She folded her arms around herself as though that could stop her from breaking into a million tiny pieces. "I thought things would be different. I thought we could be different."

"It is different," he said looking bewildered. "Now I understand what happened and why you broke up with me—"

She could feel her herself weakening at his genuine confusion. "I didn't leave you because of the miscarriage, or even because you went out and got drunk when I needed to see you. I left you because you close yourself up and shut everyone out when you have to deal with anything painful."

"I just want to shut up and move on," he said. "What's wrong with that?"

"Because you don't move on. You think you do, but you don't. You just bottle everything up and let it fester until it destroys you from the inside out. And you don't let anyone else deal with their pain either. We're all just supposed to suck it up and move on like big, strong Danny Taggart. But not everyone operates that way."

"What, just because I won't spill my guts and cry like a girl, you're dumping me again? I love you!" It sounded almost like an accusation.

"And I love you too," she felt her heart crack in half as she said it. "I think I always will. But that doesn't mean we can make each other happy."

"This is ridiculous. Why are you going psycho on me again?"

The P word sent fury surging in her chest, hardening her against him like nothing else could. "I'm not going psycho," she snapped. "I can't believe I was stupid enough to think you could change or that anything could be different. You're doing the exact same thing you always do. Lashing out and pushing me away every time I try to get you to talk to me. Well I'm done. I'm ending it now, before I let you destroy me again."

His mouth twitched and she saw something flash in his eyes. That bleak, soul deep need she'd only seen from him twice before. A spark flickered inside her, igniting a feeble ray of hope as she acknowledged the ulterior motive she hadn't realized was there until that moment.

A tremor rippled through her body as she watched him, waiting for him to speak. For all her angry bravado, there was still part of her that wanted him to refuse to give up. *Fight for me. Fight for us.* Maybe this time when she backed him into a corner he wouldn't make the same mistake.

The vulnerable look disappeared as quickly as it had appeared, shut away behind his cold, gray stare, snuffing out the spark of hope.

His mouth took on a derisive twist. "Fine, if walking out on me is what you need to do, go ahead. I won't stop you."

Her eyes burned with tears and his features blurred. "I do love you Danny. And I hope you'll be happy someday."

He didn't come after her as she walked through the house and out the front door. She really didn't expect him to, but silly girl that she was, she hoped.

Three weeks later

All this fucking happiness was making him sick to his stomach.

Or maybe it was the scotch.

Nah, he thought as he sloshed more MacCallan into his glass. Had to be all the goddamned love in the air. Sickly sweet and radiating off everyone in the room, especially from Ethan and Toni who had announced a few minutes ago that they were engaged.

He took a healthy swig of the scotch and watched Alyssa give Toni a congratulatory hug. The lines of their bodies started to blur around the edges, letting Danny know the scotch was doing its work. He took another gulp to keep the magic going.

"It's gorgeous," Toni said, spreading her fingers and angling the platinum and ruby creation to catch the light. "It makes it even more special that you designed it personally."

"It was my pleasure," Alyssa said and gave Toni one final squeeze. "I'm just glad Ethan trusted me enough to run with it."

"I told her I wanted something as amazing and unique as you," Ethan said, embracing Toni from behind and pressing a kiss to her neck.

"Gag me," Danny muttered. Too loud, apparently because Toni, Ethan, Derek, Alyssa, even his father turned to glare at him. "I mean, congratulations, many happy returns, all that shit." He grabbed the bottle for another pour and wondered why the hell he'd even come tonight.

Oh yeah. Because after Danny hadn't shown up for work for the past three weeks and had avoided any attempts by his family to pin him down, Ethan had threatened to bring the weekly family dinner to Danny's place if he refused to come to them.

"Don't you think you've had enough?" Alyssa asked, her hip cocked as she looked pointedly at the bottle.

"Nope." As far as he could tell there wasn't enough booze in the world to get Caroline out of his head. But he was still hoping. *I do love you Danny. And I hope you'll be happy someday.* Her words echoed ceaselessly, until his days had taken on a dismal pattern. Wake up. Run long enough and hard enough to sweat out and puke out the toxins from the day before. Come home. Shower. Spend hours trying not to think of her, resisting the urge to call her. Reaching for a bottle of whatever was on hand to dull the edges of the memories. Hiding his phone from himself before he got too wasted so he wouldn't do something dumb like drunk dial her. Waking up the next morning to start the whole damn process over again.

Lather, rinse, repeat.

You swallow it up and let it fester until it destroys you from the inside.

Maybe she had something there. He took another swig of scotch to keep himself from thinking too hard about it.

"Yeah because drinking your face off is obviously the best way to deal with a breakup," Derek said.

"'Snot what's happening," Danny lied. "Y'know, you think jus' because you're getting married," liquor splashed his hand as he used his glass to gesture between the two engaged couples, "that everyone needs to be mashed—matched up. But who wants that? Who wants one pussy for the rest of his life? You think Ethan does?" he asked Toni, who hit him with a stony glare. "Honey, Ethan used to get more ass than a toilet seat. You think in a few more months he's not gonna go sniffin' 'round?"

"That's enough," the two Dereks said as they moved in to grab Danny's arm.

"Aw, come on, dude, like you have it so much better." Danny wrenched his arm out of Derek's grip, staggered, and spilled most of his drink down Derek's shirt. "Lemme tell you somethin' about Alyssa," he said in a stage whisper. "She's a little hellcat. You think she's going to be happy up here in the 'burbs making her little rings and necklaces when she could be partying on P. Diddy's yacht? She's wild. I saw the pictures—"

He almost felt relief when Derek's fist caught him square in the mouth and sent him to the floor.

Finally. Maybe someone would put him out of his fucking misery.

"Listen you asshole," Derek said as he grabbed Danny by the collar of his shirt and hauled him back to his feet. "You want to get shit faced and wallow in self-pity because you can't pull your head out of your ass enough to fix things with Caroline, that's your choice. But don't you fucking take it out on Alyssa and Toni." Derek released him and shoved him away. Danny hit the bar and sent a glass shattering to the floor before he steadied himself.

Through the boozy haze he could feel his jaw throb. "Din't mean to ruin the party," he said and took an uneven step toward the door. "I'll head out now."

A firm hand closed over his shoulder. "Let me drive you home, son."

Danny tried to shrug him off. "I'm fine."

Joe wheeled Danny around and gave him the steely gray stare that made Danny want to stand up straight and give a full salute even in his drunken state. "You're an idiot if you think I'll let you drive in this condition."

Danny clumsily fished for his keys and handed them to his father. When they got to his Jeep he climbed into the passenger seat, leaned back and closed his eyes. As the Jeep started to spin like a Tilt-a-whirl, he acknowledged that letting his dad drive was the right decision.

As they drove in silence he thought of Ethan and Toni and Derek and Alyssa and their bliss that burned him like acid. Why couldn't he have that? Why didn't she stay? He was shut out, excluded from their happy little club. Like a fat kid pressing his nose to the bakery glass. Flaunted in his face, just out of reach.

Danny woke up the next morning face down on the couch, head pounding, and his mouth tasting like he'd been eating shit sandwiches followed by a scotch chaser. Nothing unusual there. The only weird thing was that his jaw hurt and his father was sitting across from him, sipping a cup of coffee as he watched Danny drag himself out of his drunken sleep.

Danny eased himself into a sitting position, wincing as his brain ricocheted around his skull.

"So are you going to go after her or what?"

Danny rubbed his grit filled eyes and tried to focus. "Dad, it's a little early—"

Joe put his coffee mug down on the table with a thud that stabbed through Danny's eyes. "Son, you know I'm not one for giving advice. After what happened with your mother, I'm hardly one to tell you what to do with your love life. But you need to pull your head out of your ass, and soon, or you're going to destroy yourself over Caroline all over again."

It was way too fucking early and he was way too fucking hungover to have that conversation. "Dad, that's not going to happen. It's not like that with her. I'm not like..." He managed to cut himself off in time.

"Not like me? Is that what you were going to say?" Joe's mouth, so like Danny's own, pulled into a rueful half smile. "Danny, you're exactly like me. You're a stubborn, pig-headed know-it-all who doesn't know when to admit you're wrong. And when you love, you love so hard that when it ends you think its going to kill you."

Danny pushed off the couch and shuffled to the coffee pot, hoping the caffeine would help him stand up to his father's onslaught. "Don't you think that's a little melodramatic?" Sure, he walked around most days feeling like half of his guts had spilled out, but still . . . "And forgive me for pointing this out, but I wasn't the one who stopped my life and couldn't move on after Mom disappeared."

"You think you moved on from Caroline because you managed to sleep with a bunch of different women? Are you moving on now by shutting yourself off, ignoring your business and turning yourself into a drunk?"

Danny couldn't hold his father's piercing stare as the truth of his words sank in.

"I know you thought I was crazy, spending all those

years and all that money looking for your mother. But I would have given anything to have one more chance with her, to do it right. Any hope of that is gone now, and I have to live with that. Just as I have to live with the knowledge that she died, violently, and I didn't protect her. And she died not knowing how much I really loved her."

Danny swallowed around the painful lump in his throat. On some level he'd been aware his father felt all those things, but hearing the usually taciturn Joe say it out loud punched him in the gut.

"But what's really crazy is that Caroline is out there. She's alive, and she loves you. And you're sitting here in your cave drowning yourself in a keg of scotch. I can't believe I raised you to be such a quitter."

Danny's hackles rose at that. "It's not that simple, Dad. I can't make her happy. I can't be who she wants me to be."

"Bullshit. When did you even try?"

Danny was afraid he knew the answer to that. Any time Caroline had even hinted that she needed something more from him, that she was anything less than satisfied with what they had, he'd gotten defensive. He'd all but warned her outright not to ask him for something he didn't have to give.

"How do you know you can't make her happy unless you really try? I sure as shit never did with your mother. We loved each other, and I gave her a good life, and I thought that was enough. I'll regret that attitude till the day I die. Learn from my mistake. Talk to Caroline, figure out what she needs, and give it to her. That's how you make her happy."

Fifteen minutes later he was running through the woods, his father's words reverberating through his head as his feet ate up the miles.

What did Caroline need?

I kept hoping you would come after me. All that time, Caroline had been waiting, ready to give him another chance. And he'd let her go without a single protest.

Quitter his father had called him. Danny had always believed he was being strong, tough, not losing himself over a woman, not realizing all the while he was already gone. His father was right, he had quit on Caroline. And he'd let her quit on him.

She was alive. Caroline was alive out there, and she loved him, and Danny had admitted defeat before the war even began.

His dad was right. It was time for Danny to pull his head out of his ass and go after his woman.

CHAPTER 22

One week later

Mount Aspiring National Park, South Island, New Zealand

Caroline crested the ridge and paused to take off her Gore-Tex shell. Though the air at that elevation was cool, even in the middle of New Zealand's summer, she'd worked up a healthy sweat as she hiked the last pitch to get over the ridge. She stuffed the jacket into her pack and took several bracing gulps of water, half listening as the guide pointed out landmarks to Caroline and the other four hikers on the guided trek through some of the most gorgeous landscape Caroline had ever seen.

Jagged edged, snowcapped mountains strained for the sky, erupting out of the lush green valley. A shallow river wound its way through the valley floor. Caroline closed her eyes and imagined she could hear the frigid crystal water rippling over the rocky bottom.

Cool air whipped strands of hair loose from her braids. She drank in the scent of the wind, smelling of green grass and crisp snow. It was exactly what she needed. Kate had questioned her decision to travel halfway around the world alone to go on a multi-day trek with a bunch of strangers. But while Caroline had always wanted to travel to New Zealand, James had never wanted to go. Now she was free to do whatever she wanted, whenever she wanted, and if she wanted to go to New Zealand, by God she would.

Not to mention that going halfway around the world, across four time zones and an international date line made it somewhat easier to resist the temptation to call or e-mail or otherwise contact Danny.

But her thumbs itched every time her cell phone picked up service.

It was good, perfect. The clean air, physical activity, and stunning natural beauty distracted her from thinking so much about Danny. The landscape they covered between the lodges every day was wild and undeveloped, so different from her own world it was like she was visiting a different planet. The people were different too. The locals were friendly and laid back. No flinty eyed, emotionally stunted heart breakers in these parts. She could almost pretend she'd entered an alternate universe where Danny didn't exist.

Then she'd see something—an animal or a stunning vista—and she'd want to share it so badly with Danny it was like a physical ache. He would love it there. The craggy peaks and endless miles of running trails. In the past weeks at home and as she'd trekked the miles there she'd gone over their conversation a million times. Maybe she'd been too rash. Maybe she'd panicked. Maybe she should have stuck it out and given him another chance.

But she always came back to the same conclusion. If he'd wanted another chance, he could have asked for it. He knew damn well how to reach her. She couldn't spend the rest of her life, trying to beat down all his hard edges until she broke herself on them.

She opened her eyes and let her gaze drift over the other people in her group. The guide was an affable man in his late forties with a salt and pepper beard and a face burnished from years of exposure to the alpine sun. Of the five hikers, she was the only one not part of a pair. The other hikers were a married couple from Texas and two girl-friends from London who wondered gleefully how their husbands were managing alone with their young children. It was nice. If she wanted companionship at dinner, she had it. If she wanted to retire early and be anti-social, no one questioned it.

No one asked her too many questions. She never had to talk about her year of hell and how her run-in with an ex had caused her heart to implode for the second time in her life.

She took another breath and drank in the beauty. A break from her world and its ugly realities. She drank in every drop.

"Let's move on then," the guide said, satisfied everyone had had a sufficient water and view break.

Caroline slipped her pack on and was turning to follow when she saw a black dot moving swiftly up the ridge from the direction they'd come. Unlike the members of her group who leaned forward, trudging heavily up the steep slopes, this guy moved at a fast, steady jog, his pace never slacken-ing. He was nothing but a dot behind them as Caroline turned to follow her group.

A little more than ten minutes later—less than one third of the time it had taken Caroline to cover the same distance, she heard the crunch of gravel under jogging feet.

"Hey, I think this guy wants to pass us," she called up to the group. Everyone stepped off to the side to let Speedy Gonzales pass by.

"I think I'd rather join up with you all, if that's okay."

The slightly breathless voice froze the breath in Caro-line's chest and made her heart leap against her ribcage. She had to be hallucinating.

She turned around, lifting her gaze up, past the lean abs and broad chest covered in Capilene. Up the strong, tanned throat, jutting chin, and full, firm lips twisted into a tentative smile. To gray eyes full of warmth and hope and regret.

"Hi Carrie."

"What are you doing here?" she asked stupidly.

He moved closer and she could smell the scent of clean sweat clinging to his skin. "You told me you were waiting for me to come after you all those years ago. I was hoping that was still true."

It was all too surreal. She'd never heard of altitude sickness causing hallucinations but there was a first time for everything.

"Is there a problem here?" the guide asked.

"Nope," Danny answered. "I just needed to have a talk with Caroline."

"You followed me all the way to New Zealand?" she asked, still unable to process what was happening.

He reached out a hand and cupped her cheek. "It took me awhile to figure it out, big, dumb male that I am, but I finally realized that if I ever want a shot at being happy it meant chasing you down and begging you for another chance. So here I am. Coming after you. And I'm going to keep doing it until you say yes."

All of the reasons why that was a bad idea clamored in her head. He could make all the grand romantic gestures in the world but that wouldn't change anything. "Danny," she shook her head.

His thumb brushed across her cheekbone. "I know I have to get better. I know I have to learn to," he paused, "share," he said quickly as though the word tasted funny, "and not shut myself off from you. I can't promise I'll get it right away, but I'll try."

She leaned into his hand, absorbing his touch. "You came all the way to New Zealand," she said again, still not able to believe it. Still not sure she could let herself hope.

"I'll go anywhere for you Carrie. I love you." He cradled

her face in his hands and tipped her face up for his kiss. His touch washed through her like a balm, healing the cracks and fissures inside her until she couldn't imagine living another moment without him. "I love you so much," he whispered. "And I need you," he said, almost pleading. "I need to marry you and give you babies and be with you."

She threw her arms around his neck and kissed him back, tasting the salt of tears and the flavor of a man. A man who had come half way around the world to tell her he loved her. "I love you too. And I want everything."

He pulled her to him so tightly she lost her breath but she didn't care.

"You have to promise me something too," he said.

"Anything."

He pulled back to look at her, his gray eyes serious. "You have to promise to have faith in me, in us. You have to trust that even if I fuck up, I want to make you happy. No more keeping things to yourself until you convince yourself dumping me is the only solution."

"You'd come after me anyway," she said smugly.

"You're right," he said, his eyes turning molten. "But I'd exact my revenge." He kissed her again, hot and sweet as his tongue slid against hers.

Carrie opened her mouth to let him in and twisted her fingers in the damp hair at his nape. A loud throat clearing abruptly reminded her of their audience.

"This is quite romantic and all that, but we've got another five kilometers before we reach the lodge. And if I'm not missing my guess, I'd say you two definitely need a room."

Danny never wanted to hike with a boner again. The last five kilometers had been torture, not only because of his state of arousal, but because he knew he could complete the distance to the lodge in a little over fifteen minutes instead of the nearly fifty it took the straggling group. It took another twenty minutes to check in and get their room assignments. The lodge was bare bones, but thank God Caroline had a private room.

He stood next to Carrie, unable to keep his hands off her as she signed the registry. His fingers slipped along her long, silky braids. His hand stole up the hem of her shirt to touch the bare skin of her back. With her sun kissed, cosmetic free skin she looked young, carefree, and so beautiful it made his heart twist.

His. She was his and he wasn't going to fuck it up this time. And he couldn't wait to get her alone to start proving it to her.

She barely got through the door before he had her pressed up against the wall. Kissing her like a starving man, licking into her mouth and drinking in her taste. "Jesus, Carrie, I missed you so much." He slid his hand up her shirt to cover her breast and encountered the thick lycra fabric of her Jog bra. "Take off your clothes," he nipped at her neck. "I want you naked."

"Let me shower first. We're all sweaty."

"Good idea," he grinned and stripped off his shirt.

"Whoa boy. Showers are down the hall."

He followed her out of the room, grimacing when he saw the separate bathrooms clearly marked men and women.

Not exactly what I had in mind, he thought as he watched her disappear behind her own door. He beat her back to the room. He stripped down and lay on the bed, grinning as he caught sight of himself sticking straight up like a flag pole. Yeah, he was definitely excited to see her.

He licked his lips in anticipation as the doorknob rattled. Carrie wore a short white robe and a shy smile, her damp hair spilling in thick locks down her back. He could smell the fruity scent of her shampoo, the freshness of soap, and underneath it the warm musk that was all her own. His balls drew tight against his body and he felt like his cock grew another inch. "Come here, baby."

He caught her by the hand and pulled her down to the bed with him. He threaded his fingers in her wet hair and tilted her head back for his kiss as he rolled her under him. His cock brushed the silky skin of her thigh and he hissed in pleasure. "God I missed you," he whispered. The taste of her, the feel of her skin under his hands. All the sweeter because he never thought he'd have her again.

"Danny," she pushed against his shoulder. He pulled his mouth from hers and rolled to the side.

"What's wrong?" he asked.

"Nothing." She rolled to a sitting position and he propped himself on his elbows. "I was just hoping we could talk first."

Talk? He'd followed her halfway around the world and was sporting a dick so hard it could cut glass, and she wanted to talk? He shoved his frustration aside as he looked into her wide, expectant brown eyes. "Talk. Sure. I can talk. . . ." he trailed off, distracted by the curves of her breasts, revealed by the gaping neckline of her robe. *Focus. Ogling her tits is not the way to prove to her you can change.* He dragged his gaze back to her face. "What do you want to talk about?"

"Well," she said, twisting a strand of hair around her fingers. "I think it's important for us to talk about our feelings, how we're going to work through the hurt we've caused each other in the past, and recently."

Oh, shit. His mind drew a blank. Any hurt he'd felt would be obliterated by the first touch of her hand on his cock, but he didn't think she'd appreciate that. "Uh, I think as long as we listen to each other," what had his dad said again? "and try to uh, respect each other's needs we can work past it." He thought that sounded good. He nodded attentively and waited for her to take her turn.

Caroline opened her mouth but couldn't get a single word out before she started cracking up.

Realization dawned. She was messing with him.

"You should have seen your face," she said through gasps of laughter. "'Talk? Yeah, I can talk,'" she said in a low, dopey voice.

"Bitch," he chuckled as he flipped her to her back and pinned her. He untied her robe and pulled it open so he could look at her breasts.

"You love that side of me."

"I love every side of you."

Her laughter faded and her eyes got all misty. Suddenly it got so deep and real it was almost scary. He kissed her and felt something break open inside of him. Her robe seemed to melt away and she was all hot silk under his hands. His lips sucked and teased her breasts, his hand slid between her thighs to find her slippery wet and ready for him.

Part of him wanted to take his time, savor her, wring every bit of pleasure out of her. The other part wanted to claim her, get inside her, fuck her deep and hard, and feel her coming around his cock.

The primal part won out. He kneed her thighs apart and thumbed his cock into place, groaning at the feel of her pussy parting for him, taking him in. Sweet and hot and better than anything he'd ever felt.

He froze.

"What's wrong?" she panted.

"I forgot the condom." He started to pull away.

Long lean legs clamped round his waist. "It's okay. You don't need to wear one. As long as you're ready." Her dark eyes locked steadily on his. He knew exactly what she was asking.

"Everything. I'm ready for everything." He sank home, his eyes nearly rolling back in his head as he felt her closing around him, tight and hot with nothing in between them.

This time he was going to come inside her. The thought turned him on so much he almost came right then.

Every muscle flexed as he struggled for restraint. He kissed her, stroking in her mouth like he was stroking her with his cock. He'd never felt like this, not even before with Caroline, every part of him singing in pleasure as his heart burst inside his chest.

He could feel her tightening around him, hear her cries against his mouth. She came hard, shuddering and shaking around him while her body milked him. His orgasm burst through him like a wildfire, his cock twitching as he came, spurting hotly inside her.

He collapsed on top of her, so wrung out he could barely move. Caroline wrapped her arms around his back, hugging him close as she rained kisses on his neck and shoulders.

"Love you so much," he murmured. It got easier to say every time he said it, and felt better every time.

"We're going to do it right this time, aren't we?" she whispered.

He kissed her hard and felt a smile of pure happiness stretch across his face. "Damn right we are."

If you're HOLDING OUT FOR A HERO,
check out HelenKay Dimon's latest,
out now from Brava . . .

"You know something?" Josh cocked his head to the side as the corner of his mouth tugged upward. "I just figured out what it is about you that doesn't fit."

"Pardon me?"

He pointed at her forehead. "The way you talk. It's what throws off this whole picture."

A wave of confused dizziness hit her. "I have no idea—"

"There's emotion in your voice, well, sort of, but your body never moves." He nodded his head as if warming to the subject. "Makes me wonder if there's any feeling inside there anywhere. I'm betting no."

The shaking moving through her turned to fury. Ten more seconds of his garbage and he'd be feeling her hand smack across his face. "You don't need to worry about my body."

His eyebrows rose. "If you say so."

"I need your detective skills."

The lazy grin vanished as his back snapped straight again. "No way."

"What kind of response is that for a grown man?"

"The only one you're going to get."

"Could you at least try to be civil?"

"You killed that possibility a long time ago, lady."

Okay, she deserved that. He refused to understand her position, but she couldn't exactly blame him for the anger. "I'm not asking for me. I'm asking for Ryan."

"You pay a whole team of professionals to poke around in other people's private lives for you. Get some of them to do your work. You don't need me."

Lot of good all that money did so far. "I actually do."

"Well, that's a damn shame since I already have a job."

Time for a reality check. "Word is that might not be true soon."

"Visiting my office again, Ms. Armstrong?"

As she watched, he turned into a serious, uncompromising professional. He talked to her with a tone part soothing and part condescending. She sensed he would handle an interrogation the same way.

His disdain lapped against her. He didn't say the exact words, but he didn't have to. His actions spoke for him. He hated her.

Gone was the laid-back surfer-dude laziness that hovered around him making the business suit seem all the more out of place. Blond, blue-eyed with a scruff around his mouth and chin, he could play the lead role in any woman's bad boy fantasies. But behind those rough good looks lurked a man serious and in charge, tense and ready for battle.

Well, he wasn't the only one in the room fighting off a deep case of dislike. He needed to know she was not one of his frequent empty-headed bedmates. She could match his intellect and anger any time, anywhere.

"Most of the information I need about you and your current predicament is in the newspaper," she said.

"Most?"

She shrugged, letting him know he wasn't the only one who could tweak a temper.

"More snooping, Ms. Armstrong?"

"I call it investigating."

"Well, just so you know." His back came off the wall, slow and in command. "Sneaking around in my personnel file isn't the way to make me listen to you."

"Then let's try this." She reached into her purse and grabbed her checkbook. "I want to hire you."

"Don't."

She clicked the end of her pen. "Some money should get us started."

His hand shot out and grabbed her wrist before she could start writing. "Trying to buy me off isn't going to get you where you want to be."

When she dropped her hand, he let go as if touching her one more second repulsed him.

"That's not what I was doing." It was, but she figured pointing that out would only make him less receptive to her plan to help Ryan.

"Sure felt like it."

She skipped the crap and went right to her point. "Ryan didn't do it."

"Look, Ms. Armstrong. I get that this is a family issue."

She refused to blubber or beg. She'd cried enough for ten lifetimes since the whole mess started. "Call me Deana."

"We're not friends or colleagues, so Ms. Armstrong is fine." Josh took his pen out of his pocket and tapped it against his open palm. "And you may as well know I don't really care what happens to Ryan from here on."

She refused to believe Josh would be satisfied to let an innocent kid rot in prison. "You can't really mean that."

"I do. Trust me on this."

"You think it's okay to lock him away?"

"He had a trial."

"Well, I don't have the luxury of forgetting Ryan since I'm all he has at the moment."

"I'm sorry about your brother and his wife." Josh's voice softened along with his bright aqua eyes.

She could not let her mind go there. Not now. She had to keep her focus directly on Ryan. It was either that or lose her control, and that was the one thing she could not afford to do in front of Josh. "Then help me."

"I can't."

"You mean won't." Despite her attempts to stay calm her voice increased in volume as his decreased.

"We can use whichever word you prefer."

"Why not?"

"Simple."

"I have to tell you that I've found nothing simple in dealing with you so far."

"Then try this: I'm out of the rescuing business."

"That's ridiculous."

"It's a fact."

This was one brick wall she might not be able to work around. "I hardly believe you can turn it on and off like that."

"I didn't think so, either."

"And now?"

"I know I can."

"What is that supposed to mean?"

"Basically? Find another hero because I'm done playing the role."

Be on the lookout for
THE MANE SQUEEZE from Shelly Laurenston,
coming next month from Brava . . .

The salmon were everywhere, leaping from the water and right into the open maws of bears. But he ruled this piece of territory and those salmon were for him and him alone. He opened his mouth and a ten-pound one leaped right into it. Closing his jaws, he sighed in pleasure. Honey-covered. He loved honey-covered salmon!

This was his perfect world. A cold river, happy-to-die-for-his-survival salmon, and honey. Lots and lots of honey . . .

What could ever be better? What could ever live up to this? Nothing. Absolutely nothing.

A salmon swam up to him. He had no interest, he was still working on the honey-covered one. The salmon stared at him intently . . . almost glaring.

"Hey!" it called out. "Hey! Can you hear me?"

Why was this salmon ruining his meal? He should kill it and save it for later. Or toss it to one of the females with cubs. Anything to get this obviously Philadelphia salmon to shut the hell up!

"Answer me!" the salmon ordered loudly. "Open your eyes and answer me! *Now!*"

His eyes were open, weren't they?

Apparently not because someone pried his lids apart and stared into his face. And wow, wasn't she gorgeous?

"Can you hear me?" He didn't answer, he was too busy staring at her. So pretty!

"Come on, Paddington. Answer me."

He instinctively snarled at the nickname and she smiled in relief. "What's the matter?" she teased. "You don't like Paddington? Such a cute, cuddly, widdle bear."

"Nothing's wrong with cute pet names . . . Mr. Mittens."

She straightened, her hands on her hips and those long, expertly manicured nails drumming restlessly against those narrow hips.

"Mister?" she snapped.

"Paddington?" he shot back.

She gave a little snort. "Okay. Fair enough. But call me Gwen. I never did get a chance to tell you my name at the wedding."

Oh! He remembered her now. The feline he'd found himself day dreaming about on more than one occasion in the two months since Jess's wedding. And . . . wow. She was naked. She looked really good naked . . .

He blinked, knowing that he was staring at that beautiful, strong body. *Focus on something else! Anything else! You're going to creep her out!*

"You have tattoos," he blurted. Bracelet tatts surrounded both her biceps. A combination of black shamrocks and a dark-green Chinese symbol he didn't know the meaning of. And on her right hip she had a black Chinese dragon holding a Celtic cross in its mouth. It was beautiful work. Intricate. "Are they new?"

"Nah. I just covered up the ones on my arms with makeup, for the wedding. With my mother, I'd be noticed enough. Didn't want to add to that." She gestured at him with her hand. "Now we know I'm Gwen and I have tattoos . . . so do you have a name?"

"Yeah, sure. I'm . . ." He glanced off, racking his brain.

"You don't remember your name?" she asked, her eyes wide.

"I know it has something to do with security." He stared at her thoughtfully, then snapped his fingers. "Lock."

"Lock? Your name is Lock?"

"I think. Lock. Lock . . . Lachlan! MacRyrie!" He glanced off again. "I think."

"Christ."

"No need to get snippy. It's *my* name I can't remember." He nodded. "I'm pretty positive it's Lock . . . something."

"MacRyrie."

"Okay."

She gave a small, frustrated growl and placed the palms of her hands against her eyes. He stared at her painted nails. "Are those the team colors of the Philadelphia Flyers?"

"Don't start," she snapped.

"Again with the snippy? I was only asking."

Lock slowly pushed himself up a bit, noticing for the first time that they'd traveled to a much more shallow part of the river. The water barely came to his waist. She started to say something, but shook her head and looked away. He didn't mind. He didn't need conversation at the moment, he needed to figure out where he was.

A river, that's where he was. Unfortunately, not his dream river. The one with the honey-covered salmon that willingly leaped into his mouth. A disappointing realization—it always felt so real until he woke up—but he was still happy that he'd survived the fall.

Lock used his arms to push himself up all the way so he could sit.

"Be careful," she finally said. "We fell from up there."

He looked at where she pointed, ignoring how much pain the slight move caused, and flinched when he saw how far down they were.

"Although we were farther up river, I think."

"Damn," he muttered, rubbing the back of his neck.

"How bad is it?"

"It'll be fine." Closing his eyes, Lock bent his head to one side, then the other. The sound of cracking bones echoed and when he opened his eyes, he saw that pretty face cringing.

"See?" he said. "Better all ready."

"If you say so."

She took several awkward steps back so she could sit down on a large boulder.

"You're hurt," he informed her.

"Yeah. I am." She extended her leg, resting it on a smaller boulder in front of her and let out a breath, her eyes shutting. "I know it's healing, but, fuck, it hurts."

"Let me see." Lock got to his feet, ignoring the aches and pains he felt throughout his body. By the time he made it over to her, she opened her eyes and blinked wide, leaning back.

"Hey, hey! Get that thing out of my face!"

His cock was right *there*, now wasn't it? He knelt down on one knee in front of her and said, "This is the best I can manage at the moment. I don't exactly have the time to run off and kill an animal for its hide."

"Fine," she muttered. "Just watch where you're swinging that thing. You're liable to break my nose."

Focusing on her leg to keep from appearing way too proud at that statement, he grasped her foot and lifted, keeping his movements slow and his fingers gentle. He didn't allow himself to wince when he saw the damage. It was bad, and she was losing blood. Probably more blood than she realized. "I didn't do this, did I?"

"No. I got this from that She-bitch." She leaned over, trying to get a better look. "Do I have any calf muscle left?"

He wasn't going to answer that. At least not honestly. Instead he gave her his best "reassuring" expression and calmly said, "Let's get you to a hospital."

Her body jerked straight and those pretty eyes blinked rapidly. "No."

That wasn't the reponse he expected. Panic, perhaps. Or, "My God. Is it that bad?" But instead she said "no." And she said it with some serious finality. In the same way he imagined she would respond to the suggestion of cutting off her leg with a steak knife.

"It's not a big deal. But you don't want an infection. I'll take you up the embankment, get us some clothes—" if she didn't pass out from blood loss first "—and then get you to the Macon River Health Center. It's equipped for us."

"No."

"I've had to go there a couple of times. It's really clean, the staff is great, and the doctors are always the best."

"No."

She wasn't being difficult to simply be difficult, was she?

Resting his forearm on his knee, Lock stared at her. "You're not kidding, are you?"

"No."

"Is there a reason you don't want to go to the hospital?" And he really hoped it wasn't something ridiculous like she used to date one of the doctors and didn't want to see him, or something equally as lame.

"Of course there is. People go there to die."

Oh, boy. Ridiculous but hardly lame. "Or . . . people go there to get better."

"No."

"Look, Mr. Mittens—"

"Don't call me that."

"—I'm trying to help you here. So you can do this the easy way, or you can do this the hard way. Your choice."

She shrugged and brought her good foot down right on his nuts.